The Liaison

The Liaison

MARIA MATRAY & ANSWALD KRÜGER
translated by
RICHARD SHARP

William Morrow and Company, Inc.
New York   1976

Published in the United States in 1976.

English translation copyright © 1975 by
Cassel & Co., Ltd.

Published in Great Britain in 1975.

First published in German under the title
Die Liaison by Scherz Verlag, copyright
© 1973 by Scherz Verlag.

All rights reserved. No part of this book may be
reproduced or utilized in any form or by any means,
electronic or mechanical, including photocopying,
recording or by any information storage and retrieval
system, without permission in writing from
the Publisher. Inquiries should be addressed to
William Morrow and Company, Inc., 105 Madison Ave.,
New York, N.Y. 10016.

Printed in the United States of America.
1 2 3 4 5   80 79 78 77 76

Library of Congress Catalog Card Number 75-27203

ISBN 0-688-02987-6

Several summers ago a Western journalist visiting the World Hunting Exhibition in Budapest found two old, yellowing manuscripts in a little antique shop. One was in French, the other in Croatian. These were the diaries of Her Royal Highness Princess Louise of Coburg and her lover.

The journalist bought both books from the dealer, Janos Berlinger, for the equivalent of $200, smuggled them out of Hungary in his car, and had them translated. As best he could he sorted out the tangle of facts which, though meagre and not always reliable, seemed to have something relevant to say to this age of gradual decay. He put the two texts together, and amplified the highly personal notes of the two protagonists with contemporary press clippings and documents. To the completed work he gave the title of *The Liaison*.

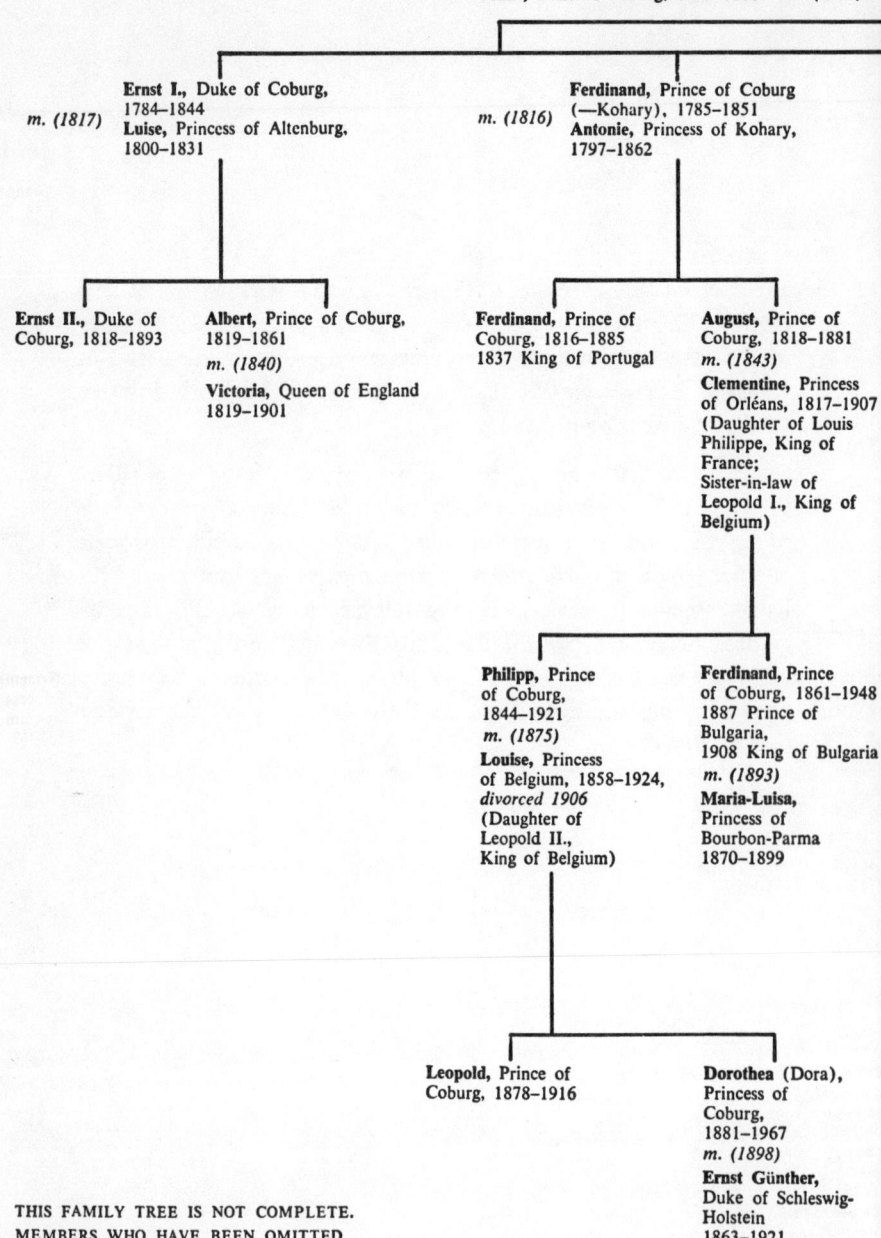

THIS FAMILY TREE IS NOT COMPLETE.
MEMBERS WHO HAVE BEEN OMITTED
ARE NOT MENTIONED IN THE TEXT.

MARIA MATRAY—ANSWALD KRÜGER

m. = married.

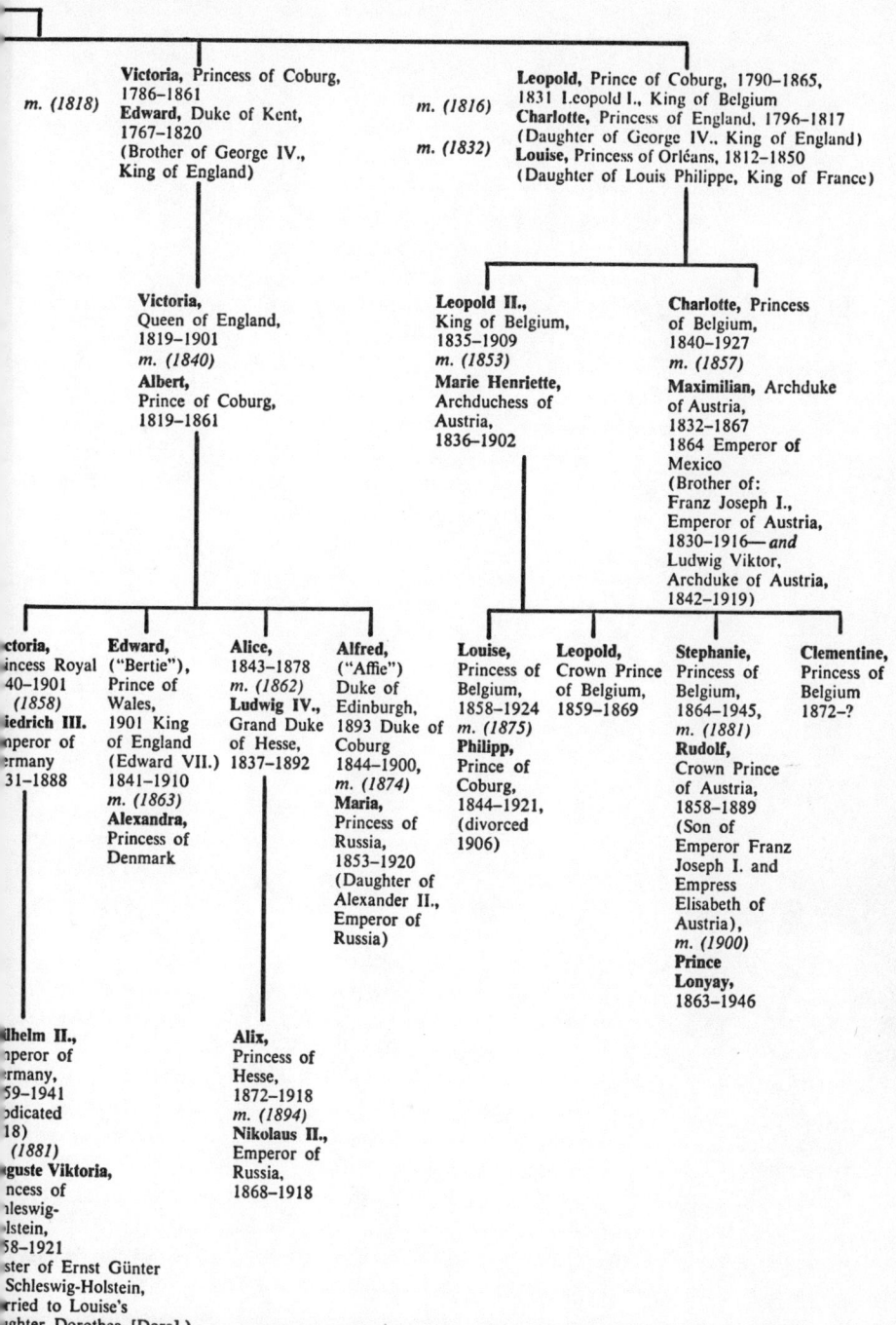

The Liaison

I

ℒ

Vienna, October 1895 Lunchtime passed, the usual deadly boredom. Philip, his mother and I sat round the table, which accommodates thirty people in comfort. This ensured that we were all separated from our neighbours by a chilly void which excellently summarizes our personal relations.

The footmen served with silent perfection. I gave a start each time that a silver dish materialized as if from nowhere at my left elbow.

I hate the dark splendour of this dining-room; hate the inquisitive, arrogant portraits of all the royal relatives with their long, sharp Coburg noses.

Nothing is ever said at the table. Old Princess Clementine is hard of hearing. To shout loudly enough for her to hear would be a breach of decorum, and a conversation between Philip and myself, excluding my mother-in-law, would be equally unsuitable. In any case, we have nothing to say to one another.

So I gazed silently at my own plate, as usual. At last the Princess rose from the table, and I kissed her hand and waited patiently until she had left the room. Then I left too, with the formal 'bon appétit' to Philip which is correct form in front of the servants, and went quickly to my room.

Antonia took off my dress and shoes, unlaced my stays and settled me on the couch.

For the hundred thousandth time I stared at the stucco-work of the ceiling, following its endless serpentine wanderings, until at last I fell asleep.

When I awoke I had a slight headache. For some reason or other I chose for the afternoon a green velvet dress that suits me particularly well, and with it the charming little felt hat with black ribbons that Philip says makes me look like a circus horse. Which only goes to show what wretched taste he has.

Countess Fugger asked whether we should be taking Dora and the governess with us. I said no.

Dora is very sweet and pretty, and I love her dearly, but she is dreadfully childish for her fourteen years. Her chatter often gets on my nerves terribly, and Mlle de Rouvignard's governessy pronouncements are even worse. Whenever the governess rebukes Dora I feel that her words are really meant for me. I shall get rid of her as soon as possible. Or better still, I shall ask the steward to dismiss her and see about a replacement. Perhaps he can find a governess who knows how to laugh sometimes. But even if he could, she would soon lose the ability once behind the walls of the Coburg Palace. If she's pretty, Philip will seduce her. Not that that would be of the slightest concern to me, but Philip's mother would know about it at once, although she's so deaf that she doesn't understand a word, and her eyes are so bad that she can't read any more. I don't know whether her disabilities have sharpened her instincts, or whether the old Princess has set up a private spy network among the staff. At any rate, nothing happens in this house but she knows all about it. And so that pretty, laughing governess that we haven't got would soon be replaced by a second Mlle de Rouvignard. So I might just as well keep the original. But I will *not* take her with me when I go driving in the Prater.

The coachman had harnessed up the dapple greys, the sun had come out from behind the clouds, and I leant back in the carriage, my headache forgotten.

Autumn is often sad, and I can't bear it. But this had become a lovely day, the leaves lying like a carpet on the carriageway.

We overtook the Archduchess Elisabeth Amalie. As the two carriages ran side by side for a few seconds, and we nodded to one another, the Archduchess glanced at my hat with its black ribbons and turned pale.

In Vienna one simply can't get these ribbons yet. I have my hats made in Paris, and so I'm naturally ahead of local fashion. That seemed to upset the poor thing terribly.

As we turned into the Hauptallee I noticed that several pedestrians were standing and gazing curiously over towards the riding track.

There, motionless, stood a horse, with a lieutenant of uhlans in the saddle. The horse was refusing to answer to his rider, and blocking the way to other horsemen.

The lieutenant put whip and spurs to the horse, which shied once or twice but then stubbornly dug its hooves into the sand and refused to budge. It seemed to be a young, spirited animal, not yet fully broken. Suddenly, it made up its mind on a surprise tactic, shied once more, bolted straight at the pedestrians, who scattered in panic, then galloped back onto the carriageway and made directly for our carriage.

The coachman, with considerable presence of mind, reined in the greys; Countess Fugger cried out in alarm; and I enjoyed the performance. A few yards away from us the lieutenant succeeded in bringing the horse under control.

I had a good look at this lieutenant. He was young, slim, his forehead beaded with sweat. As if he hoped to master the stubborn horse with his own stubbornness, his teeth were clamped together so hard that the skin over his cheekbones was paper-white. He glanced at me quickly, searchingly, and I thought: if I laugh at him now, he'll kill me. He could never forgive the humiliation of being laughed at.

Now my coachman whipped up the greys, and drove round the horse, which had once again become a motionless statue in the middle of the carriageway. After we had gone a hundred yards or so I gave the order to stop. I wanted to see how the contest between horse and rider would end.

The lieutenant eased his hold on the reins. Suddenly the horse seemed tired of its own antics. It turned obediently, and trotted back between the carriages, past us. On the lieutenant's face was a suppressed smile of triumph. He glanced briefly in my direction, then disappeared down the riding track.

For the next three weeks I went to the Prater every day, and every day I saw the unknown lieutenant. Sometimes I rode, sometimes I was driven, sometimes I drove myself. Sometimes I even took Dora and her governess with me. The Prater is a fairly big place, yet we always managed to meet. In the meantime the horse had made progress. It tried no more tricks, obeyed its rider and never again made him look a fool.

During the first week the lieutenant was content with brief, sidelong glances at me, which he seemed to think I shouldn't notice. Then he found that I smiled at him kindly, and took to saluting each time he rode by.

This evening we went to the opera—Philip, his mother, Leopold and I. Leopold is on a week's leave from the Academy. He looks arrogant, grown up. No one would think I could be the mother of such an adult son.

As a baby, he was my favourite, my little plaything. Although Philip found such behaviour quite unsuitable, I would spend hours in the nursery playing with him, to the annoyance of Nanny and his nurse. Three years later I was expecting again, Dora was born, and before I knew what was happening I had lost Leopold. His father had stolen him from me. Not that he took charge of the boy personally—Philip's interest wouldn't go that far; he was much too indolent. But he saw to it that the heir was brought up in a 'masculine' way and no longer exposed to my 'feminine influence'. Philip found him a tutor and concerned himself with the boy's place at the Academy and his future commission in the regiment.

At some time, early in Leopold's life, Philip succeeded in turning him against me. I don't know exactly when, or what he said, or what weapons he brought into the field against me. All that is certain is that Leopold deliberately and emphatically rejected me, and that Philip did nothing to prevent it.

Suddenly, I had acquired a little enemy in my own son. I made various attempts to break through the estrangement, but I always came up against a united front of father and son. I told myself that it was all Philip's doing, yet I couldn't help holding it against Leopold that he was so easily influenced.

Since that time, it has been difficult for me really to love my son. But then, he doesn't need me, or my love. His father and grandfather adore him. All his stupidity and insolence is forgiven, treated as charming 'naughtiness'. He has been placed on a pedestal, become a demigod—no, a god. With only one blemish—that I am his mother. Well, he will have to live with that.

Melba was making a guest appearance as Norma. Because Philip fancies himself to be musical, and also because it was said Franz Joseph would be coming to the Opera, we reserved a box.

Suddenly Philip whispered in my ear, 'Who's that fellow staring at you in that insolent way?' He pointed down into the stalls.

There sat my lieutenant: without sparing a glance for the divine Melba he was gazing fixedly up at me. But not with insolence; with admiration.

'I've no idea,' I said. 'I've never seen him before in my life.' I had to deny him, my horseman from the Prater, or we should have had another of Philip's unbearable scenes. And I wasn't in the mood for that. All the same, it was fun to see the little lieutenant again at the Opera.

After the performance we had supper at Sacher's. I had a lot of Champagne and was in a very good humour.

The Archduke Ludwig Victor came to our table—he is one of my admirers, and absolutely adores me. And in fact I quite like him. He is charming, witty, wicked in an amusing sort of fashion, and always knows the latest gossip.

This evening he paid court to me again in an extremely informal way. Philip was livid, but said nothing. He's far too much of a coward to try and silence the Emperor's brother.

The lieutenant has multiplied. He's not only in the Prater and the Opera, but all over Vienna. Standing in the Graben when I take Dora shopping at Braun's; trotting along the Kohlmarkt when I go with Countess Fugger to have an ice at Demel's; strolling on the Seilerstätte when I drive out from the Palace. He knows my routine better than I do myself.

Poor lieutenant, he's going to miss me soon. On Monday I'm going to visit my sister at Abbazia.*

January 1896, on the train   I wonder whether I really love Stephanie, or whether only the automatic ties of upbringing and family hold us together.

Superficially we're very much alike. Of course, Stephanie is six years younger, but she doesn't look it. But beyond that we are entirely different. She believes everything we've both been told about social position, honour, morals, etiquette. She has absolute faith where I have long had doubts. She takes seriously what I, now, can only laugh at. Sometimes this simplicity is touching, but often it can be maddening.

I am her confidante. From me she has no secrets—at least, that's what she tells me. I on the other hand have a thousand secrets, and confide none of them in her.

I have never confessed to her that there was a very close friendship between me and the Crown Prince Rudolf before he married her. Rudolf and I were both seventeen when we met and promptly fell in love.

I had already been married over a year by that time. Philip is fourteen years older than me. I loathed him from the first day—or rather from the first night; found him repulsive, lascivious and calculating where Rudolf was handsome, charming and lovable.

Rudolf thought the same way about me, for it was no

* Now Opatija, in Yugoslavia (Trans).

chance that he eventually married Stephanie. I had said to him one day, 'If you really want someone who will remind you of me, go to Brussels and look at my little sister!'

Naturally, I concealed from Stephanie the fact that the relationship between Rudolf and me was not really over.

I remember especially the time when the Crown Prince and Princess visited us in Hungary. The unsuspecting Stephanie couldn't go riding—her doctor had forbidden it. The rather less unsuspecting Philip had to play the perfect host and keep her company.

During that period Rudolf and I once or twice managed to shake off our tail of huntsmen and grooms and find refuge in a little barn. It was a long time since we had been in love, but we enjoyed ourselves—and enjoyed too the betrayal it meant. I had a genuine longing to wrong Philip, and Rudolf felt the same way about Stephanie.

Then I remember the weeks on Lokrum. Franz Joseph's brother Maximilian had fallen in love with the little island long before, and had had the half-ruined monastery of San Marco rebuilt for himself and Aunt Charlotte. If only Maximilian had not been consumed by ambition, he could still be living happily on Lokrum with his wife today, far enough from Vienna not to have to worry about his brother. But no, he had to be an Emperor. And of course he had to pick on the Mexican Indians, who didn't want him and promptly killed him. The adventure cost poor Aunt Charlotte her reason; she became insane. Rudolf loved and admired Uncle Maximilian, who was able to carry off his plans against Franz Joseph where Rudolf himself had failed. Years after Maximilian was shot dead in Queretaro, the Crown Prince bought the island. After Rudolf's suicide, Franz Joseph handed it back to the Dominicans, and the little castle became a monastery once more.

In Vienna there was 'concern over the health of the Crown Prince'. Whenever this excuse was produced it meant that there had been a row between the Emperor and his son. Either Rudolf had had one of his irresponsible articles published in a newspaper, or he'd embarked on another scandalous love affair. Then he was always packed off on his travels.

This time he and Stephanie boarded the yacht *Miramar* at Trieste and went cruising in the Adriatic. When they came ashore at Lokrum, Stephanie fell ill.

At the request of her personal physician a specialist was summoned from Vienna, and I, the dutiful sister, hastened to her bedside.

She had a high fever, and could only see visitors for short periods. So Rudolf and I were often alone together. But now we were both twenty-eight, not seventeen.

Perhaps we were oppressed by the romantic old walls of the monastery, or by the heavy scent of the almost tropical flowers. At any rate, we were often seized by a deep melancholy.

Rudolf cursed his wasted life, the wife he didn't love who could not even give him an heir, and his stubborn father, who showed every sign of intending to rule until Rudolf's own best years were over.

Infected by his sadness, I too complained of my life and my unhappy marriage. But Rudolf could spare no understanding for me. The years had made him more and more of an egoist. He thought only of himself, quarrelled with his own fate, and thought no one deserving of pity but himself.

Sometimes his mood suddenly changed, and the old gaiety was there, but with a strangely desperate undercurrent. At those times I really was afraid of him, and it was a relief to me when Stephanie's condition improved enough for me to return to Vienna.

What must Stephanie have felt when Rudolf killed himself and his levantine girlfriend Marie Vetsera at Mayerling? He took his last mistress with him to the grave, and so showed the world that my sister was nothing to him. It was deeply and bitterly wounding for her; I could almost believe that Rudolf had planned it for that reason.

I remember a big dinner party at home in the Coburg Palace not long before his death. Rudolf sat on my right, and Stephanie opposite me, fortunately half hidden by the table decorations.

Rudolf had stared at his wife for a few seconds, lost in his own thoughts. Suddenly he took a gold cigarette-case out of his pocket, opened it and held it out to me. In the lid I saw a photograph of Marie Vetsera.

'What do you think of her?' he asked, not even bothering to lower his voice. 'Beautiful, isn't she?'

It was the most tactless thing I had ever heard. I was appalled.

'Beautiful,' I said. 'It's a beautiful case.' And I looked quickly over at my sister, who was chatting casually with Philip.

That was the first time, and probably the only time, that I felt any sympathy for Stephanie.

* * *

G

29 January 1896 Went to Fanny's again, after a long time away. Not very inspiring. As I unlaced her cheap corset, I tried to picture to myself the Princess's expensive underclothes. But of course she won me round. She's all right in bed, the cow. Apart from that—more and more unbearable each time. When she opens her mouth I want to scream. Women like her ought to keep their mouths shut and never get out of bed.

Got dressed again straight away.

'Didn't you like it, dear? Wasn't I nice enough to you?'

I liked it all right. Because I had spent the whole time thinking of another woman. But I could hardly tell her that.

'Got another girl, have you?'

Wish I had! But I haven't made any progress at all. I greet her. She greets me back. That's all.

Wait, though! When you think about it, I *am* getting somewhere, or my name's not Geza. The way she returns the greeting: she's saying, 'Keep it up, Lieutenant! Don't ease off! Don't give up! Rome wasn't built in a day!'

God, what a woman!

She's the most exciting, most beautiful woman I've ever seen. The whole of Vienna is at her feet.

At least that meant it was no problem to find out who she was. You have to be from the back of beyond like me not to know her already. They say no one at the whole court spends so much on clothes as my goddess, and because she knows how to wear the clothes when she's bought them it seems the Princesses and the Archduchesses haven't got much to say for her. But as for the Princes and the Archdukes ...

And that brings me to the most important thing: I've heard from a reliable source that Her Royal Highness isn't one to let ceremony get in her way if she wants to enjoy herself. Good news! It seems that several of my young brother officers in the retinue of Imperial Field-Marshal Prince Philip of Coburg have had the pleasure of finding that out for themselves.

So now, of course, I'm getting really keen on her.

The daughter of Leopold II—a real Princess of the Blood Royal! That'd make a nice change from greedy whores and stupid servants' daughters! Never mind what they look like —a cart-horse is a cart-horse.

I must find out where she's gone to. She's been out of sight somewhere for a whole week. I've been riding up and down through the Prater like a damned fool in bitter cold, but my Princess has vanished.

30 January   Hard frost. Even so I hung around the Seilerstätte for three hours. But no luck.

Half frozen, I went into the coffee-house in the Johannesgasse. I picked up the *Presse* and flicked through it, and found it there by chance: 'Her Royal Highness Princess Louise of Coburg has left with her daughter for Abbazia, to visit Her Imperial Highness Princess Stephanie, who has been in Abbazia for some time.'

And in that moment I knew that I too would go to Abbazia.

Evening I must top up my war chest before I go, or I won't even get to Wiener Neustadt. My financial position is, yet again, extremely desperate.

2 February I've been chasing money for three days. It was never as difficult as this. Things are very tight everywhere. At least, that's what they say. The draper's wife gave me fifty crowns out of her husband's till, which was nice of her. That was a start anyway. I managed to touch Ferdl for another twenty-five. I told him I needed it for a girl who's had a bit of bad luck. He's a gentleman at heart. I got the rest from a Jew in the Rotensterngasse. Thanks once again to my father, may he rest in peace. I'll have to turn up in Abbazia without his ring and without a watch, but I'll have the best part of five hundred crowns in my pocket. Things don't look too bad.
Tomorrow I'm off. We'll see how much a Princess costs!

* * *

L

Abbazia, Wednesday I never used to be able to understand Stephanie's preference for Abbazia. I know it's fashionable, it's absolutely the done thing to be seen here. But why should I sit for hours in a train and then find myself looking at the same old faces that I see in Vienna and Budapest? Of course the country's very pretty, and I must admit that there are some really unbelievable walks by the sea, but taken by and large Abbazia is really dreadfully provincial, and can't be compared with Biarritz or Ostende.
Yet this time I'm happy enough to be here.
Stephanie has rented the Villa Amalia, which belongs to the Hotel Quarnero, and she asked me to come and stay there. But I only put Dora, her governess and the servants over in the

villa; for the Countess Fugger and myself I took suites in the hotel itself.

Stephanie has changed. She's less formal, more cheerful and she looks better than she has these past months. For this transformation there must be a reason, and I'm expecting her to tell me what it is at the first opportunity. Or I shall be very disappointed in her.

Thursday   Stephanie has fallen in love.

'Please, don't misunderstand me and above all don't think it wrong of me, if I tell you that I think I've found a new reason for living.' This was her complicated way of expressing something perfectly simple. 'I know the duty I owe to my rank, and I swear to you that I shall never commit an indiscretion, but it makes me happy to see true admiration in the eyes of a young man. Can you understand that, Louise?' And she looked at me imploringly.

After I had assured her that I did understand her, she went on, 'His name is Elemer Lonyay, and he's nothing. Absolutely nothing. Imagine—a Count! A Hungarian Count!' She might have been saying, 'A Bosnian roadmender.'

The 'Bosnian roadmender' came to tea. He is a well bred, aristocratic-looking young man, in whose eyes I could indeed see something like admiration for the widow of the Crown Prince of Austria.

Stephanie was dreadfully nervous. She was trembling with fear that I wouldn't like Count Lonyay.

Of course, we couldn't have tea alone, just the three of us; that would have been an unforgivable breach of etiquette. Our ladies-in-waiting were there, and our daughters— Stephanie's Erszi and my Dora—with their governesses. There were also a few officers, probably from the Count's regiment. And so it was a full-scale English tea-party, an institution that I absolutely detest.

I made my excuses early, and went over to the hotel.

I let my maid undress me, slipped into a negligée, and finally ordered a light supper, which I ate in the salon, where there is a balcony with a wonderful view of the sea.

Just as I was going to bed, Stephanie appeared.

'Why did you go so early? How did you like him? Hasn't he got lovely gentle eyes? Do you think I'm being a little bit silly?'

I'd seldom seen her so agitated. Her questions rained down on me, and I tried to answer them all.

'I do like him, he has got lovely gentle eyes. But it's true, you are being a little bit silly.'

Stephanie slid into an armchair.

'Yes,' she agreed, 'I am silly. Of course Count Lonyay doesn't really mean anything to me. I wouldn't want you to think that I was in love with him. Certainly not.' She raised two fingers of one hand, as if taking an oath. 'By everything I hold sacred. I went through such a terrible time with Rudolph. I was so deeply humiliated ... by him and by the whole Viennese court. So it's enough to make me happy if I find someone who really respects me.' And again she asked beseechingly, 'Can you understand that?'

Yes, I could understand that.

We went for some lime-blossom tea, and chatted on about nothing in particular.

Stephanie told me there's going to be a fancy-dress ball at the Casino the day after tomorrow, and we shall all be going in a big party. Then she rose, embraced and kissed me with a warmth I had never thought possible in her before, and left.

Now that I'm on my own I feel lonely. I am sad. But why? Nothing has changed in the last few hours. I was happy when I came here, I liked the place, the sun was shining, Abbazia was a pretty town. And suddenly everything has turned grey. What I should most like to do is leave. Go back to Vienna.

But how could I tell Stephanie that? What reason could I give her? None—there is none.

For the first time, I can realize that Stephanie is younger

than me. Oh, not that she looks it! It's her personality. She has a simplicity that I have never had. And then there's this incredibly pig-headed theory of hers about her social station. Can she really be so obsessed with her own value that she would let her Hungarian Count, her 'Bosnian roadmender', get away? That she can bask in his respect and adoration, yet for all other purposes consign him to his own proper place, somewhere impossibly far below her own?

The picture cheers me up. It's grotesque, yet I believe it is the truth. Just now I was ready to envy Stephanie her happiness, but now I know that she will fritter it away.

Really, I should be feeling sorry for her.

Friday In the morning I went for a walk with the children along the promenade.

The weather was stormy, the waves breaking with such violence on the rocks that the spray was drifting up to us. Conversation was impossible. We had originally planned to take the steamer over to Lovran, but there was no question of that with such a sea running.

At mid-day we met Stephanie at David's in the Kurpark, where we lunched excellently. Stephanie wanted to know what I was going to wear to the ball tomorrow. She herself meant to go as Marie Antoinette.

Only Stephanie could think that tragic queen a suitable subject for imitation at a fancy-dress ball. When I inquired whether she would appear with or without head she looked at me incomprehendingly, and Dora asked, her child's eyes large and round, 'How can Marie-Antoinette run around without a head?'

Mlle de Rouvignard has not told my daughter about the French Revolution. In her world, such things simply do not happen.

Ruthlessly, I informed Dora that the Queen of France had gone to the guillotine, a piece of information which utterly astonished her.

But now I had to give serious thought to the question of

what I would wear. I hadn't brought anything suitable with me from Vienna. Nothing had prepared me for the sort of sister who attends masked balls.

Friday evening   Diana, the goddess of hunting. I shall go as Diana!

Countess Fugger, assisted by the hotel's owner, Herr Lederer, had conjured up from Fiume a length of pale pink silk muslin that might have been specially created as the basis of a delightfully simple Greek costume. In fact the material really did come from the east somewhere. At this moment ten seamstresses whom Herr Lederer has drummed up from Abbazia and the outlying districts are sitting in a big room in the basement and stitching their fingers raw.

Herr Lederer has also found me a shoe-maker, a comic figure who hardly understands a word of German. Before tomorrow evening he's going to make me a pair of golden sandals with thongs that fasten up to the knee, and a golden quiver with arrows, and a bow. The energetic Lederer has also sent for the best hairdresser in Trieste, as my own dear Ilona would be out of her depth when it comes to the classical Greek style.

I'm full of enthusiasm for the idea. We thought of Diana by pure chance, after we had already toyed with Cleopatra, a Viennese washerwoman and Joan of Arc, and found them all wanting. Among the books that Mlle de Rouvignard had brought to Abbazia for Dora we found a beautiful illustrated edition of Schwab's *Tales from Classical Antiquity*. As soon as I saw the picture of Diana, my mind was made up. The costume and the shoes will certainly do very well. My only slight doubt is about jewellery.

Night   He is unbelievably beautiful, like a Greek god. He is both boy and man, slim-hipped, broad-shouldered, strong without being brutal.

I shall never forget his eyes as long as I live. They are grave, alert, watchful, nothing escapes them. And yet his glance is disarmingly direct, expecting everything but demanding nothing.

My knees feel weak when I think of him.

How did it begin? 'Your Royal Highness, permit me to introduce a brother officer from my regiment, Geza von Mattachich,' said little Sinzendorff. And there he stood before me, my lieutenant from the Prater, in a purple domino.

As he bent to kiss my hand, I said, 'We know each other.'

Sinzendorff was staggered. 'But this fellow's been practically begging me on his knees to present him to Your Royal Highness, and ...' he stammered.

Yes, it was stupid of me, that 'We know each other'. Now: 'We've met in the Prater,' I said mischievously.

Sinzendorff laughed, as if I had said something very funny.

'Her Royal Highness saw me breaking in a horse in the Prater,' said my lieutenant.

'It was a near thing whether it was the horse or me that was broken,' I said. 'The great thing was coming straight at me.' I said it mockingly, but it seemed not to annoy my lieutenant.

'That is why I couldn't miss the opportunity today of begging Your Royal Highness's pardon.'

'It shall be granted, if you will tell me your name again.'

'Mattachich,' he answered. 'Geza Mattachich.'

'Hungarian?' I asked.

'The title is Croatian,' said Sinzendorff, and now it was he who sounded malicious.

His tone annoyed me. 'I'm sure Croatia must be a beautiful country,' I said challengingly. 'Unfortunately I know it very little.'

'Beautiful. Unbelievably beautiful,' said the lieutenant, and he gazed at me with admiration.

I forgot that the masked ball in Abbazia was slightly ludicrous, the orchestra moderate, the costumes dusty. I warmed myself at the fire of the lieutenant's eyes, and waited for him to ask me to dance.

We danced, to the music of the Emperor Waltz.

My lieutenant led excellently; there was no danger that he would tread on my gold sandals. I could trust myself to him completely. I adore dancing when I have a good partner.

'What are you doing here in Abbazia?' I asked at last, simply in order to say something.

'I am here because you are here.'

'And how did you know that?'

'I know everything about you. I know when you go to the opera, or shopping at Rodeck's, or driving in the Prater ... and even when you go away to Abbazia.'

Herr von Mattachich was speaking to me as if to an equal; I'm not accustomed to that. 'Aren't you being a little disrespectful, Count?'

'I expect so, Your Royal Highness.'

It was some hours later when Antonia helped me into my negligée and Ilona took the gold arrow out of my hair and let it down. Then they both curtsied, wished me good night, and left me alone.

It had been an unexpectedly amusing evening. Stephanie and I had danced a lot, she rather too often with her Count Lonyay, I only twice with my lieutenant (who by the way is a *First* Lieutenant). One mazurka and one waltz.

The waltz and the Champagne must have gone to my head. I was still very hot. I pulled back the curtains and opened the door onto the balcony.

And there he stood! I didn't recognize him at once in the darkness, but I didn't cry out. Although as a rule I am easily frightened. He leant against the balcony and looked at me. He had taken off his silly mask.

'I have been waiting for this moment,' he said, quietly, and with a confidence that completely excluded any possibility of refusal. Then he came up to me, very impudently and very close. A strong smell of English tobacco came to my nostrils. With a gentle movement of his hand he pushed the negligée aside and kissed my breast.

But that was an unheard-of piece of insolence! For that he could have been flogged, even hanged. I had only to ring, to scream, to cry for help, and he would be arrested on the spot.

I did none of those things. I would be as sure, as impertinent as he was.

Without bothering to close the negligée again, I lay on the bed and put my arms behind my head. 'Get undressed,' I ordered him.

He smiled, and said, 'If Your Royal Highness pleases.' As if I had offered him a cup of tea.

Then he began to undress, without haste, as if he wanted me to enjoy the slow revelation of the beauty of his body.

Some time during the night I looked at us in the mirror. Myself very fair, very pale, and he, in the dim light of the lamp, as dark as a Sicilian. He has soft, golden-brown skin. My eyes strayed from the picture in the mirror to the man in my arms, who looked like a boy.

'How old are you?' I asked him.

'Twenty-nine.' He kissed me, drunk with sleep.

I was frightened. It's nine years since I was twenty-nine. The woman I saw in that mirror, kindly disguised by the silk lampshade, is thirty-eight years old and the mother of two children. When Leopold was born, this man was a child of eleven. When Dora was born, he was fourteen.

'What are you thinking about?' Geza asked; and when I didn't answer at once he became impatient. 'You must tell me what you're thinking about.'

'I'm counting.'

He sat up in bed and laughed out loud.

'What's so funny?'

'You're counting! I think that's marvellous. If a poor Croatian lieutenant wants to count, he counts. But Princess Louise of Coburg does her counting while she lies in bed with the poor lieutenant.'

Now I had to laugh too.

'What were you counting?' He put his arms round me, so that I gasped for breath. 'Tell me. At once.'

'You're crushing me ...'

'Yes. I weigh 69 kilogrammes. Can you change that into pounds and ounces...?'

* * *

G

Abbazia, Sunday morning   Everything venture, everything gain. The woman is worth risking your neck for.

And it could easily enough come to that!

I'm no beginner where women are concerned, and I would have thought it almost impossible that the old game could get me so excited. As if I'd just lost my virginity last night.

I stood on her balcony, not daring to show myself; that could have meant the end of everything before it had even begun. I stood there without moving, saying to myself over and over again, 'Go on! Open that door, my lovely Louise. If this night doesn't bring us together we shall have lost our chance for ever.' I was absolutely obsessed with the idea: she had to feel that I was near her. She *had* to.

Now it's six in the morning. I'm still as tense as if I'd just been with a woman for the first time. Well, Louise, you really are a Princess of the Blood. And now I know exactly what that means. In every possible way.

* * *

L

Sunday evening I was supposed to have lunch with Stephanie and the children, but I excused myself. I stayed in bed till twelve, feeling unspeakably happy. I thought about nothing, but just enjoyed my own comfort and well-being, and made an excellent breakfast.

Geza had made his way home at daybreak.

He had to climb over the balustrade to get round the partition that separated my balcony from Countess Fugger's next door, creep past her door, then repeat the process, which brought him to his own room.

I stayed out on the balcony a little while longer, and watched the sun rise. Certainly it had been more difficult for Leander to swim the Hellespont than for Geza to climb over the balcony, but the effect was the same: it was a risk taken for me, and it made me proud.

For the afternoon, Stephanie and I had agreed on a drive. We wanted to go past the lovely Vrutki Springs and over to Veprinac, where there is a beautiful old church on a high crag, and one can have tea in the village under the trees.

I had certainly expected that we would take the children and their governesses with us, but to my surprise Stephanie was alone in the landau when she came to fetch me. So she wanted to talk to me again.

When the last houses of Abbazia were behind us, and the driver had slowed for the steep ascent of the hills, she began.

'What is going to become of me, Louise? How is my life going to work out? I become terribly depressed whenever I think about it.'

I had little inclination to have my good humour dispelled by Stephanie's lamentations.

She bewailed her fate in being forced to live as the sorrowing widow of a man who had only despised and never loved her, and complained of the endless intrigues in Vienna, from which she was always having to run away.

I listened with only half an ear. 'Now let's talk about Count Lonyay,' I interrupted her at last, trying to sound as if I were making a joke of it. 'That's what you really want.'

She blushed. My little sister can still blush. How touching!

'Yes,' she admitted, 'I have been thinking about the Count. Perhaps I was not being quite honest when I said he meant nothing to me.'

'I didn't for a moment suppose you were.'

'Then you know what I'm going through?'

Stephanie is always thirsting after understanding. I became impatient. 'You aren't an innocent little girl any more! What are you waiting for? If your little Hungarian Count amuses you, why don't you go to bed with him?' I had never spoken to her so frankly before. The effect was dramatic. She stared at me as if I had asked her to run stark naked along the Kärntnerstrasse. She was too shocked to bring out another word. I had to laugh out loud.

'Oh, Louise, you are dreadful! I thought for a moment you really meant it,' she said with relief.

'Perhaps I did really mean it? Why not, anyway?' I teased her.

But now she was sure she knew where she was. 'No, no. You're just trying to shock me.'

There is no point in discussing such things with my sister.

As we sat in the garden of the inn at Veprinac, huddled in fur coats and drinking coffee, Stephanie was quiet and pensive.

'Have you ever thought of marrying the Count?' I asked her, and added laughingly, 'Holy Matrimony ought to clear your scruples out of the way.'

'I must confess that I have thought about it. Only the Emperor would never give his permission. And even if he did, our father would never, never allow it.'

I tried to dissuade her, but she couldn't be convinced.

'It's all the same to Papa whether I'm miserable or not. Do you know that he has forbidden me to return to Brussels? I implored him to let me come home. I begged Mama to use her influence on him. But it's useless. I shall have to stay in this horrible Vienna.'

'You should have gone to one of his mistresses, not to Mama. That was in ... let me see ... his Spanish period, wasn't it?'

Of all my father's escapades, his affair with the Spanish dancer Cléo de Mérode had given the worst public impression. Satirical papers all over the world got hold of the scandal, and the name 'Cléopold' is still with him today, although the dancer isn't.

It hurts Stephanie deeply when I speak of the King of the Belgians in this disrespectful way. She broke off the conversation, and delivered a lecture on the early history of Veprinac church, which she had presumably read in Baedeker before we left.

On the way back she suddenly leant over towards me and whispered, 'Perhaps, one day, I shall be able to be happy. I must just wait. Perhaps for a long time. But I am patient. Can you understand that, Louise?'

I could understand only that she had spoiled my good mood, and that many hours had still to pass before nightfall.

Wednesday evening A piano virtuoso, who takes pains to look like Franz Liszt but cannot play like Liszt, was performing in the music room of the Villa Amalia.

Stephanie had asked twenty or thirty people in for a musical evening. We all sat in reverent discomfort on little gold chairs that Herr Lederer had produced for the occasion.

The programme had been drawn up by Stephanie and the artist. After he had dragged himself and us painfully through works by Anton Rubinstein, Scarlatti and Berlioz he came to the *pièce de résistance* of his performance, the Hungarian Rhapsody by his great exemplar, Franz Liszt. I noticed Stephanie exchanging glances with Count Lonyay. The Hungarian Rhapsody had presumably been included as a mark of respect to him.

At that moment a number of officers appeared in the doorway, and among them I recognized Geza.

That was not part of our bargain! He had given me his word

that he would remain out of sight during the day. We could too easily become a subject of gossip, which, given Stephanie's ideas of rank and honour, could be very unpleasant for me.

I confess that I was happy to see him, but at the same time I was angry that he had ignored my request. Worse still: if he had to come, then why so late? If one is invited by the widow of the Crown Prince, one arrives punctually. Anything else is quite improper.

But to my amazement Stephanie smiled very agreeably at Count Thun, one of the new arrivals. I recognized too the riding instructors Zeileisen and Codelli. And the inevitable little Sinzendorff was also there.

The end of the Liszt Rhapsody was greeted with thunderous applause, particularly from the officers at the door. The virtuoso bowed, and gave us as an encore the Rakoczi March, which always makes any Hungarian heart beat faster.

I thought of my mother, who grew up in Hungary. She loved the country deeply. For her it means youth, freedom, happiness, all the things she has lost since she has been living in Brussels with a man whose notorious love affairs make him—and therefore her too—the laughing-stock of all Europe.

When the company rose to leave the room, the mystery of the late arrivals was explained.

Thun saluted. 'May it please Your Imperial Highness, the creatures have already laid down their lives for you,' he rasped.

At Stephanie's request these gentlemen had ridden to Fiume, and waited at the harbour for the arrival of the fishing fleet from Veglia, where, according to Herr Lederer, the best crayfish are to be found.

Thun presented Count Mattachich to my sister. 'Without Mattachich we could have done nothing, Your Imperial Highness. The men all speak nothing but Croatian, and amazingly enough Mattachich gibbered back at them!'

I was not pleased to see Stephanie thanking Geza profusely and all the other guests toasting him and the other officers when the cooks appeared later with a gigantic dish of red crayfish.

I want Geza to remain my own night-time secret.

Thursday I keep saying it to myself. 'You've embarked on an unimportant little affair with an unimportant little lieutenant of uhlans, which could only have happened in the special circumstances of Abbazia, and which will end as soon as you leave here.' I swear by all that is holy that I never had any other idea, and had never given any thought to the future.

But today, after ten days and ten nights, I know that there can be no ending now. I haven't got to that stage yet. I simply haven't finished with him.

Vienna is not Abbazia. The Coburg Palace has no balconies that one can climb over. Instead, it has a hundred watchful eyes and ears that follow me from morning till night.

What will happen now?

Friday Geza has found the answer. I must run a string of horses, and he can be my equerry. At present I have only five horses to ride in Vienna, ridiculously few. No more can be housed in the stables of the Coburg Palace, because the coach teams are there too. Philip doesn't like riding in town, and keeps his horses at Ebenthal Castle. The others are all on our Hungarian estates.

Geza thinks I need at least fifteen horses. He is quite right. So stabling will have to be found for them somewhere else. Preferably somewhere near the Prater. When we have found the accommodation Geza will buy the horses, engage the necessary staff, and give me riding lessons. He knows a great deal about equestrianism. Well, I myself saw how marvellously he broke in that headstrong horse.

There are no further problems. Geza is at present on sick leave as a result of a bout of marsh-fever which he caught on manoeuvres in Galicia last summer. He has had a bad time of it, but he's quite recovered now. As no one knows better than I do.

In two weeks he must report back to his regiment at Varazdin for examination by the army doctor. He may be passed fit for service.

Now I can't see why he must be examined in Varazdin. There are army doctors in Vienna too.

I must have a word with his divisional commander, Lieutenant-General Khevenhuller. A charming man, who was very flattering to me at the last Court Ball.

* * *

G

Vienna, 4 April I am the master of sixteen racehorses, which would stand comparison with the oldest and most famous stables in Vienna. I am master of five grooms and a female factotum of about two hundred pounds living weight who cooks, washes, irons and cleans for me. I have small but extremely pleasant living quarters, and another year's leave from the army. And I have a sweetheart who is one of the most sought-after women in the monarchy: beautiful, elegant, educated, of genuine royal blood and immensely rich. Not only immensely rich, but also immensely generous, which of course are two very different things. Two very important things too, be it noted.

And for all this the household of His Highness Prince Philip of Saxe-Coburg-Gotha pays me a respectable salary—so respectable, that I'm sure Louise herself must have arranged it. Tactful as she is, she naturally denies it. Not to be outdone, I assure her I believe her. That strengthens her self-confidence. (Though really, it should strengthen mine.)

The horses cost a fortune. But what is a fortune, where money has no meaning? And there was a nice little sum for me in the deal as well. As commission. And with a clear conscience, too, for it strikes me as both right and cheap. It isn't the Princess's money anyway, it's her husband's, and *he* strikes me as rubbish.

For the first time, I have something in the bank. A fine feeling. My father's ring and the watch have been redeemed; my

Jew won't be seeing me again for a while. Times have changed.

* * *

L

Vienna   Everything has worked out perfectly. The doctor has confirmed that Geza is by no means entirely recovered yet, although it's a long time since he last had an attack. Sometimes even doctors are capable of understanding things.

He has his stables, and sixteen wonderful horses. He gives me a lesson every day.

And yet I'm not happy. He lives in a little garret directly above the stables, and it always smells of horses, no matter how much perfume I splash around in it. I feel as if I'm sleeping with a stable-hand, and not with the handsome uhlan lieutenant Count Mattachich.

Geza suffers as much as I, but endures everything just to be near me. Here in Vienna any social contact between us is simply unthinkable. And so our evenings and nights must always be spent apart.

I think back with longing to the Hotel Quarnero.

Friday   Despite all our precautions, people are beginning to talk. Princess Levkova, who has a vicious tongue, has seen fit to remark on my sudden interest in riding in a most suggestive manner. As she is a close friend of my husband's—an exception, as he generally reserves his affections for women of the demi-monde—he must have heard something.

Tuesday   Yesterday we went to the Burgtheater, to see *Versprechen hinterm Herd* with Katharina Schratt in the leading role. An abominable production of an abominable play.

In that curious triangle Elisabeth–Franz Joseph–Schratt I

find the Empress Elisabeth by far the most impressive. She sought out Franz Joseph's mistress and brought her to him simply in order to be allowed to stay away undisturbed from his bed and from Vienna.

When his favourite is playing, His Majesty lives at the theatre. And where His Majesty is, Philip must be too.

In the interval he disappeared to pay his respects to the Emperor. Scarcely had he left the box when the Archduke Ludwig Victor entered it.

Not long ago the Princess Auersperg took me aside. I must be careful of the Emperor's brother, she warned me. I could expect nothing but harm from him in the future. He was a changed man.

I didn't want to believe her. But yesterday I could see for myself how right she was.

Without taking the slightest notice of Countess Fugger, he addressed himself to me. He had heard I had joined the Uhlans, he started off with his usual mischievous manner, and then asked me whether I was already having a uniform made.

I pulled myself together and pretended not to understand him.

'You're working very hard at your riding,' he went on impertinently. 'Strange, I would have thought you were so accomplished a horsewoman as to need no extra tuition. Well, you're not the only one in the family to be taking lessons.'

Now I really didn't know what he was talking about.

'Philip has retained the services of one of his old friends to instruct your son Leopold in the mysteries of love. Though whether she knows more about them than Leopold's own mother I take leave to doubt.'

I became aware of an irresistible desire to box his ears, and I don't know what might have happened had Philip not returned to the box at that moment.

The Archduke behaved as if nothing had happened. He wandered casually over to Philip. 'Louise says La Schratt is even worse than usual this evening. Is my noble brother of the same opinion?'

Philip adopted the face he reserves for occasions when he doesn't know what to say, and said nothing.

'Goodbye, Louise, and don't forget what I've told you,' said Ludwig Victor by way of farewell. He clapped Philip jovially on the back and said, 'Take care, *mon vieux*.'

With that he left.

'Can't you keep your mouth shut?' Philip said. 'He'll repeat what you said about Schratt to the Emperor straight away. You should know by now what a gossip he is.'

The good Countess came to my defence. 'His Imperial Highness was only joking. Her Royal Highness hasn't said a word against Mrs Schratt.'

No, he won't say anything to the Emperor about Katharina Schratt. But there are other tales he could tell. And I fear that they would find a ready audience in the Emperor.

Wednesday Great excitement in the Coburg Palace yesterday, and for once it was nothing to do with me.

Philip's sister-in-law, Princess Maria Luisa of Bulgaria, arrived unexpected and unannounced from Sofia. With her were her youngest son, little Kyrill, her steward, and an Italian nurse. Somewhere in the rear followed two maids, a pug-dog, a servant and twenty trunks.

Before a room had even been made ready for her she had a three-hour interview with our mutual mother-in-law. This appears to have been quite a violent occasion, or so I heard from Ilona, who heard it from a footman, who had served the ladies with port. But perhaps it was just that Maria Luisa had to shout to make Princess Clementine hear her.

Thursday Today Maria Luisa visited me in my apartments.

She looks like an old woman. I was alarmed—she is not yet twenty-six.

I'm sure it was intended as a mere courtesy call, but after ten minutes she started to cry and poured out her heart to me.

She has left Ferdinand, and will never return to him.

Now I understood our mother-in-law's agitation. It had been hard enough to find Ferdinand a bride of his own rank. He had toured up and down through the capitals of Europe, drawing a blank at every court. No one thought that he could hang on to that Bulgarian throne that he had acquired in such a single-handed and single-minded fashion. Eventually the Duke of Parma was persuaded to give Ferdinand his daughter. If María Luisa leaves him now it will go hard with this ambitious son of an ambitious mother.

I was expecting an exciting story—had she surprised Ferdinand taking part in some dreadful orgies, had she fallen so madly in love with another man that she was prepared to renounce for him her husband and her throne? Nothing of the kind.

Her actual reason was a disappointment to me. Ferdinand has recently informed his wife that he intends to have his two-year-old heir, Boris, baptised into the Greek Orthodox faith. Like everything else in Ferdinand's life, this is a matter of calculated policy. He is complying with a request from Czar Nicholas, and hopes in this way to gain Russia's friendship. Whether that will compensate for the enemies he's going to make at the same time only he can judge. The Pope has already threatened him with anathema if he proceeds with the idea. María Luisa, a Roman Catholic like all the rest of us, was so infuriated by the plan that she ordered her bags to be packed on the spot. She wanted to protect the heir to the throne from the fate that threatened him and spirit him away to Vienna. But Ferdinand must have suspected her; Boris had disappeared. So she took little Kyrill with her instead, and left Sofia. She assured me that she would never return.

Probably I'm not religious enough to be able to take María Luisa seriously, but I wonder: is she telling the truth, or is the whole story just a pretext to abandon Ferdinand and escape from life down there in the Balkans?

* * *

Evening I came back to the Palace from my riding lesson in high good spirits. The Steward, Freiherr von Kodolitsch, asked me to go at once to see Princess Clementine.

I found her in her boudoir. Philip was with her.

My mother-in-law can be really charming if she wants something from someone. She embraced and kissed me, admired my riding hat, and then asked me to undertake an unpleasant duty for the sake of the family.

I am helpless when people are so nice to me. I promised to do what she asked before I had even heard what it was. Then she came to the point.

Philip and I were to leave for Sofia, as soon as possible, preferably at once. Our mission was to prevent a scandal that threatened the Princess of Bulgaria and with her the whole family, by any means that we could. Philip would appeal to his brother's conscience, and my presence was essential to make the visit seem to the eyes of the world a normal private affair.

I had fallen into her trap. With her trembling senile courtesy she had caught me off guard. I could do nothing but make the best of a bad job.

As we left the boudoir Philip said, softly so that his mother shouldn't hear, 'I should be grateful if you would not bring your equerry on this journey.'

I am trying to be sensible. I tell myself that now, when everyone is talking about me, it's a very good time to leave Vienna. Even travelling with Philip has its advantages. But the truth is that I simply cannot imagine the prospect of living for weeks without Geza.

* * *

G

Louise has had to go with her husband to see the Prince of Bulgaria. Her brother-in-law. Something's up down there. His wife's upped and left him, and the whole dynasty seems to be tottering.

Which makes me a grass widower, for the first time since Abbazia. A sacrifice to Coburg family politics.

When you think about it, I suppose it's a compliment. It puts me in the same boat as the Emperor, Prince Bismarck, and the late Czar Alexander III. All three have found Louise's mother-in-law and her apparently unlimited ambition hard to take. None of the three great men enjoyed seeing Ferdinand so mad keen to grab the Bulgarian throne, and they all did all they could to thwart his dreams (which, as Louise says, were really his mother's dreams anyway). The Czar was determined not to have a Roman Catholic prince on the throne of Bulgaria, and especially not one of German descent. Bismarck showed plenty of sympathy for the loud noises from St Petersburg. As a favour to the Czar. He wanted a Russo-German understanding, and everything that stood in the way was repugnant to him. And Franz Joseph didn't want to annoy Bismarck at any price, which he inevitably would have done if he'd lent any support to Ferdinand and his ambitions. Even the Turks and the English were against it. But none of that could stop Louise's mother-in-law, with all her energy (and all her money!) from helping her favourite son in his chosen career. After the brother of her late husband had become King of Portugal, she was set on blessing the world with yet another ruler from the Austro-Hungarian branch of the Coburg family. Not only did she want it, she did it, in the face of all resistance. Even if the foundations of the new throne can still be made to shake easily enough. As we can now see yet again.

I can't help laughing when I think of the circles I move in now. Overnight—an appropriate phrase, overnight—I am as it were on intimate terms with the members of the club that rules Europe. 'Do you know, the Emperor's just told me that ... and Archduke Joseph said ... my father the King insists that my poor aunt, the Empress of Mexico ...' Good God, sometimes I have to pinch myself and ask myself whether it's all a dream. Perhaps I've dozed off again in the arms of one of the eight officers' whores back at Varazdin, and will wake any moment to find I have to rush like a madman to be back in barracks for morning stand to.

Monday   I miss Louise a lot. I've been alone for a week already. It's time she came back.

I went out drinking with Ferdl last night, the first time for a long time.

He wanted to know the whole story of the girl for whom he had lent me the twenty-five crowns back in February. At first I didn't know what he was talking about. Then I tried to get out of it—'A gentleman has his fun and keeps his mouth shut.' But I didn't get anywhere. He pestered me until I had to tell him the whole story. Eventually the cat was out of the bag: he wanted to know the doctor's name. Just in case, as he liked to put it. Maybe. But on the other hand maybe he was already in trouble. I told him I didn't know whether the girl had gone to a doctor or to some woman. She was so frightened she hadn't said a word to anyone, not even to me. Except that it would cost forty crowns. And that she would never make the same mistake again as long as she lived.

I got so carried away with the story that he was quite moved, and believed every word I told him.

In the end we picked up a couple of promising-looking girls. But they were washouts. The stupid bitches thought we seriously wanted to pay for their wine out of pure philanthropy, without thought of reward. But they'd come to the wrong address. We wished them an enjoyable evening and took our leave quickly.

Then I went home, and thought about Louise. One can enjoy oneself on one's own; there are worse things.

I can only hope she's faithful to me. On a journey like this one she'll meet all sorts of people; she could have who she liked. Although her appetite ought to be a bit blunted at the moment. At any rate she ought to know what I mean to her, and not only in bed.

She loves me. I know that. She's never loved anyone that way before. She's told me so often enough, my little king's daughter with her pearls and her diamonds. What must all that stuff be worth? Millions!

And it's different for me, too, this time. Now that she's away, for the first time for ages, I know how mad I am about her.

Ferdl's still at the Moulin Rouge. He was determined to go. Once nothing would have stopped me going with him; now I'm a good boy at home on my own.

If I told that to the others at the Casino they wouldn't believe it. It's ridiculous!

* * *

L

Sofia What's happened to me? How is it possible that I could change like this in such a short time?

Ferdinand offers me a life like a foretaste of heaven. I'm pampered, idolized, showered with gifts, feted. To no avail. I make efforts to be cheerful, to show nothing. But my thoughts are always in a wretched little garret in Vienna.

Ferdinand, the family pet and my youngest admirer in the House of Coburg, has become a potentate, a despot, a species now vanished from the civilized countries of Central Europe. His word is law. He can have people's heads cut off if he wants to.

Because he can't quite believe in his new royal state, he's grown a splendid full beard. Not only the beard has grown; his nose has too. It's very long. It reminds me of my father and grandfather. No coincidence this, because Ferdinand is not only my brother-in-law; he's my uncle, though he's younger than me. We're all related two, three, four times over.

He's just as mad as ever; unfortunately he's also just as mad as ever about me.

* * *

He looked unbelievably funny, waiting to welcome us at the station in Sofia. He was wearing white plus-fours, high boots, a brightly embroidered waistcoat over a wide-sleeved shirt, and on his head a comic little cap with a bunch of magnificent herons' feathers fastened in front by a large ruby pin. He reminded me of a conjuror.

As the special train drew in, the bodyguard presented arms. There was a general air of festivity, Ferdinand embraced and kissed us both, then led us to a state coach drawn by four grey horses. Geza would have liked them.

The coach must have been massively well built; it survived the drive to the castle despite deep pot-holes and missing paving-stones without apparent damage. The driver stopped for nothing, except a huge flock of sheep crossing the street in front of us in the middle of the city. The shambling creatures bleated loud and querulously when the shepherd tried to hurry them. I laughed, Philip tittered, and Ferdinand turned scarlet with embarrassment.

The castle looks from the outside like the country seat of a successful industrialist. It wouldn't stand comparison with the Coburg Palace in Vienna, or the other family palaces in Budapest and Paris. But inside it is really something to see, a mixture of east and west, of western luxury and the last word in Balkan primitiveness.

The master of the house assigned us rooms at opposite ends of the building. I was provided with a bodyguard, a giant in an extremely picturesque uniform who neither speaks nor understands any language with which I am familiar. At night this monster sleeps like a faithful dog outside my door. Should the idea occur to Philip of visiting my bedroom, I have no doubt that my giant would strangle him in cold blood. My only anxiety is that he might not refuse access to his lord and master.

My apartments include a luxurious bathroom with a tub made of Italian marble. But there is no running water and no geyser. In the morning a curtseying army of maids carrying buckets marches through my bedroom. Ilona and Antonia shake with laughter at this performance, and the Bulgarian peasant girls can't understand what my spoilt lady's maids find so funny.

There is no electricity. Arabian oil-lamps burn day and night in the corridors and the smaller rooms, giving off only a feeble twilight glimmer. Oriental candles flicker in filigree brass candlesticks, spreading a heavy, sweetish scent. Fantastic masks, brought home by my brother-in-law from his distant journeyings, glare at the visitor and fill him—or at least me— with terror.

The larger reception rooms on the other hand are as bright as day in the evenings. Hundreds of candles sparkle in flashing glass chandeliers from Murano.

Philip, always ready with some sarcastic exaggeration, maintains that the blinding light in the dining-room is intended to stop the cockroaches wandering in from the kitchens. For once, he could even be right.

Where his personal well-being is concerned, Ferdinand takes things very seriously. His chef was imported from Maxim's in Paris. The entire kitchen staff is French. The choice wines come from Germany and France. The servant girls are so beautiful that they seem to me a much better reason for Maria Luisa's flight from Sofia than the religious convictions of little Boris, a pretty child who was presented to us for inspection.

Every evening there are noisy celebrations. After dinner there is dancing. The Prince has seconded for special duties on my behalf all the most handsome officers and all the best dancers in the Bulgarian army. But none of them is Geza. Even so, I waltz tirelessly on into the early hours.

The officers are educated men who speak French and German, understand the art of conversation, and wear excellently tailored uniforms.

Philip whispered to me that all the uniforms of the Bulgarian officers' corps were a gift from his mother. She really had spared no expense where her favourite son was concerned. Coburg money is clearly in evidence all over the country, and ensures that Philip always behaves towards his brother with ill-concealed hostility.

When the two of them are talking together—that is, when Philip tries to discharge the duty which has brought us here—Countess Fugger and I take advantage of the opportunity to have a closer look at Sofia. The modern quarter, Ferdinand's pride and joy, is dreadfully tedious. On the other hand the old town is fascinating to me, especially the Mohammedan quarter.

It's as if one were suddenly set down in the depths of the East. The streets of the bazaar are narrow and shady; the pretty houses are open to the street, showing shoemakers, silversmiths, coppersmiths, saddlers and tailors at work in them. A world of men and children, filled with the scents of musk, cooking oil, mutton and freshly roasted coffee. Countess Fugger and I, in our bright summer dresses with straw hats and parasols, feel very out of place in this almost exclusively male environment.

The children stare at us with their coal-black eyes, torn between curiosity and fear. When curiosity gets the upper hand, and they venture too close to us, they are called to order by Ferdinand's secret police, who are always breathing down our necks.

Occasionally we meet a woman, slipping shyly past us with only her eyes visible in her veiled face. Even so she will look at us searchingly for a moment before dropping her eyes again.

Yesterday we ventured into the courtyard of the mosque. It was Friday, and it had never occurred to us that this was the Mohammedan Sunday. Before the door stood rows of boots, sandals and slippers, all tattered, all dirty. Just as I was about to cross the threshold our police shadows went into action. They barred the way, and spoke to Marie and me in their native tongue. We couldn't understand a word. Again and again they pointed to the rows of shoes. We wondered whether they meant that we too must take our shoes off if we wanted to visit the mosque. Then we noticed that all the shoes were men's. Were they trying to explain to us that women were not permitted to enter the holy place?

Soon we were surrounded by a curious crowd, whose attitude seemed not to be particularly friendly. We abandoned the idea.

Of course the secret policemen will report to Ferdinand, and he will complain to Philip. Philip will make a scene, and that will be the end of our expeditions to the old town.

Tuesday I've been trying to avoid any private conversation with Ferdinand. He has noticed this, and it irks him. Unfortunately rejection has always acted as a spur to him.

When I was younger I was sometimes really afraid of him. His eccentricities, his tendency towards mysticism made me uncomfortable. He believed in omens, and ceremoniously buried all his old cravats and gloves in the park, out of fear of the evil eye. I used to imagine that he was trying to put a spell on me. Late at night I had to play him the march from *Aida* on the grand piano while he held incomprehensible discussions with various evil spirits. The spirits usually ordered that I should do what Ferdinand wanted of me. But I never did. I played a sort of cat-and-mouse game with him, which amused me and tormented him. Or so he always told me.

Yesterday evening he danced with me, casually enough I thought, in a little room where we were alone together.

'Louise,' he said, 'stay here with me! I'll build you such a palace as you have never seen! I will lay the whole nation prostrate at your feet! I beg you, as I have never begged any woman in my life!'

My old fears were awakened. I was afraid of his hands, with their sharpened nails and the clusters of sparkling rings on their fingers. They were the hands of a magician, a gypsy—but not the hands of a Geza, in which one could trust.

I tried to make a joke of it. 'I don't know what Maria Luisa would have to say about that.'

He became angry. 'I'm rid of that old bigot! She's produced

an heir to the throne; that was all anyone asked of her.'

'Your mother is bound to convince her, persuade her to come back.'

'Don't worry! I've already told Philip that I won't see her again.' He tried to kiss me. 'I need you, Louise.'

'And what about Philip?' I asked.

'Would you like to see him out of the way? You only have to say the word. These things are easily arranged.' He laughed.

But I knew that I could easily have taken up his offer.

I asked Countess Fugger to spend the night in my room. After the maids had undressed me and left, I began to sob, without knowing why.

The Countess took me in her arms, and comforted me with a maternal tenderness that I never knew from my own mother.

'I know, darling,' she murmured; 'I know.'

I should have been lost without the Countess. She is my refuge—a true friend, and the only person on earth who I am absolutely certain loves me. Except Geza, of course. I bless the day she became my lady-in-waiting.

Her predecessor, an inquisitive, pernickety beanpole of a woman, was wished on me by my mother-in-law. To earn her thirty pieces of silver, she reported back to her employer an indiscriminate mixture of truth and falsehood. It took strenuous efforts on my part to get rid of her.

I'm not usually a good judge of character, but I can congratulate myself on my choice of Countess Fugger out of the many applicants for the position. Her kind face and her way of looking at me probably decided the issue. She is pretty, but in an unusual way, so that one only gradually becomes aware of it.

I didn't foresee then, though I should have done, that an attractive lady-in-waiting would engage Philip's interest. And he promptly tried to seduce her. She evaded him with tact and diplomacy, no mean feat, for he is persistent and brutal.

When he realized that he was not going to get what he

wanted, he tried to blacken her character in my eyes. This led to an interview between me and her in which I satisfied myself of her loyalty. Since then I have counted on her, and she has served me faithfully.

Philip calls her a procuress. A statement as disgraceful as everything else he says or does. If it's true that I can count on her discretion, and that she has sometimes helped me, the reason is her own conviction that I have a right to lead my own life.

For her own part, she makes no such demands on me. She comes from an impoverished branch of the ancient Fugger family, is unmarried, and—since she can expect no dowry—will doubtless remain so.

* * *

G

12 October   People are talking about us in Vienna. I'm not surprised. Well, if it doesn't embarrass Louise, I couldn't care less about it. I'm not married. And my father's no king. Just a little country squire, now alas no longer with us.

So far as my darling's lawful husband is concerned, I'm not sure what's going on. He's known for a long time what Louise and I have been up to. But he's playing ostriches.

He has his reasons, of course. If ever a man lived in a glass house, he does. His life is an endless sequence of love affairs. That's the way it's always been. When the unhappy Crown Prince was still alive, Philip was his confidant, drinking companion and strictly private master of ceremonies. And he was the star witness at Mayerling, along with Count Hoyos. That he survived the whole grisly performance without crossing swords with the Emperor is one of the many wonders of the House of Habsburg. Louise swears that Philip's place at the court was hanging by a thread.

And why didn't the thread snap?

Because Philip knew the secrets of Rudolf's private life better than the Chief of Police Krauss himself, though Krauss's spies kept permanent observation on the Crown Prince, on the Emperor's orders. That was why His Majesty opted for peace with Prince Philip of Coburg. Reasons of state, as it were.

He and his crony Hoyos know, too, exactly what happened at Mayerling. What *really* happened, I mean. And they've kept their mouths shut like gentlemen. From the first Imperial Communiqué saying that His Most Serene Highness the Crown Prince had breathed his noble last as a result of a heart attack, right up to the current version. Which is no more true than the original.

Officially, the position still is that the autopsy revealed an abnormal deterioration of the brain, complete proof that Rudolf took his life while the balance of his mind was disturbed. This golden bridge that the doctors built to the court (what must it have been worth to them?!) was the only way to ensure the Crown Prince a christian burial. And Marie Vetsera, who died with him, has to this day no official existence whatever!

The foreign newspapers saw to it that every rumour about the horror of Mayerling was given its due currency. So, of course, every one of them was promptly banned in Royal and Imperial Austria. But I wish I had a crown for every copy that managed to find its way over the frontiers all the same. One version was that Rudolf was having a little bit of fun with a forester's wife. The jealous forester caught them at it and castrated his rival on the spot with his hunting knife. Mad with pain, the heir to the Austrian throne grabbed his revolver to put an end to his suffering. Another story had it that he was challenged to an 'American duel' by the brother of the outstandingly beautiful Princess von Auersperg, after he had seduced her. The rules of an American duel require the two parties to draw from a hat containing one black ball and one white; whoever draws black must kill himself within a precisely stipulated time. The 30th of January, according to the French press, was the last day for Rudolf, who had drawn the black. There was also talk of a wild drinking orgy, at which Prince Philip of Coburg and

Count Hoyos, among others, had been present; in this version one of the noble guests smashed the Crown Prince's skull with a champagne bottle. At last the name of Marie Vetsera began to appear in the foreign press, and an important part of the tightly guarded secret was out.

The myrmidons of Krauss, the Chief of the Vienna Police, described her as a suicide, who had been found in the forest and buried at night in the cemetery of Heiligenkreuz monastery.

I can imagine all too clearly what plots were hatched in the Hofburg to explain away to the good citizens of Austria the shocking death of their beloved heir apparent. His sorrowing subjects had to swallow the story, but it's still sticking in their gullets today.

How astonished they would be, the beloved peoples of His Apostolic Majesty, to hear some of the spicy details that Philip of Coburg could have added to the picture. If they had learnt where their Crown Prince had spent the night before dispatching himself and his infatuated Baroness into the hereafter—in the bed of a notorious whore!

No, it was much better to come to terms. And so His Majesty suppressed his imperial wrath. That's what they call statesmanship. And the Prince retains the imperial favour. But, since Mayerling, he has become very prudent, taking pains to avoid any hint of scandal. He wouldn't risk subjecting Franz Joseph's good will to another test as searching as that.

I've given it a lot of thought. Louise could be right: perhaps that really is the reason the Prince leaves us alone. Well, I've no complaints.

* * *

L

Vienna   We have seen each other again, Geza and I. At last! At last! I could hardly wait, after the long weeks of separation; and it was the same for him.

The journey to Sofia has turned out in the end to have been completely futile. Philip's mission was a miserable failure. Ferdinand is much too self-centred and stubborn to let himself be deflected from any plan once he has formed it. The heir to the Bulgarian throne will be brought up in the Greek Orthodox faith, and that's that.

But the deaf old Princess Clementine, at home in Vienna, has brought off a great victory. She has managed to persuade Maria Luisa to return to her husband despite everything.

Yesterday the poor woman left with little Kyrill and her entourage for Sofia.

Friday 13 November   This is the darkest day of my life. A Friday the 13th in the traditional manner.

This morning, while I was breakfasting, the Steward came to my room and announced that His Majesty wished to see me at eleven o'clock in my sister's apartments at the Hofburg.

I had so little time to get up and dressed that I couldn't spare any to wonder what the Emperor could possibly want of me. But I never doubted for a moment that it would be something extremely unpleasant.

First I put on a violet dress with white silk sleeves. Then I thought that looked a trifle too frivolous, and sent for the black costume from Worth. That made me look like a widow. I finally settled for a silver-grey dress that suits me very well.

Every time I took off one dress and put on another my hair had to be done again, the selection of a hat was a matter for further lengthy consideration, and more time was lost over the question of jewellery. The problem was that I couldn't wear too little jewellery, which would have suggested an unbecoming humility. But, on the other hand, not too much, for it was still only morning.

All these problems had to be solved in the brief time at my disposal. As a result I arrived at the palace five minutes late, and His Apostolic Majesty was obliged to wait for me. In Franz Joseph's catalogue of criminal charges, lateness comes just above robbery and murder. Imprisonment, if not execution, seems to him a fit punishment for it.

Stephanie cast a horrified glance in my direction as I entered the drawing-room and dropped the customary curtsey.

The Emperor was gazing out of the window.

From behind, he looks extraordinarily young for his sixty-six years. He still has a very slender figure. Though that doesn't mean a great deal if one eats virtually nothing but beef. They say he can still wear the same uniforms he did as a young man.

'My sister is here, Your Majesty,' murmured Stephanie, almost inaudibly.

He turned at once, although he is so deaf that he could not have understood her. So he had known well enough that I was in the room, and had turned his back on me deliberately, as a reprimand.

The front view of him dispels the illusion of youth. But he looks more dusty than old. There is a wax likeness of him in Madame Tussaud's in Baker Street; it is a very good likeness, and I am always reminded of it when I look at him. I don't think I shall ever get this idea out of my head, because he moves like a robot, and his features are usually as stiff as those of the waxen face in London.

His Majesty extended his hand to me. He was looking at me, yet not seeing me; he seemed to be looking through me, as though someone else was standing behind.

I apologized for my late arrival, but he was not listening to me either.

He turned to Stephanie. 'Would you please explain to your sister why we are here?'

Stephanie was as pale as a corpse. 'It has come to His Majesty's ears that you were in a private room at Sacher's with a certain lieutenant of Uhlans,' she managed at last, with difficulty.

Now I knew where I stood.

It was my fault! Absolutely my fault and mine alone. Geza had warned me. 'You will be recognized,' he had said, again and again. But I could not be dissuaded from my plan. I had been looking forward to it too much—the idea of dining with him, just once, in all the elegance and decadence of a private room at Sacher's, as if he were an Archduke and I was his little sweetheart.

We entered Sacher's through a side door. I had turned up the collar of my fur coat, and was heavily veiled. In the corridor that leads to the private rooms we met Ludwig Victor. It *would* be Ludwig Victor. Since that dreadful evening at the Burgtheater I had not seen him again.

I walked past him, praying that he would not recognize me behind the veil.

As the waiter opened the door to the private room I turned my head briefly. Ludwig Victor was standing there as if turned to stone, gazing after us. He was obviously uncertain, but he suspected all right.

Geza had noticed none of this. He doesn't know the Archduke. Not wanting to spoil his good humour, I said not a word about the incident.

It's beyond my understanding now, but then I clung to the insane hope that Ludwig Victor would be too idle to chase round after a vague suspicion.

We drank a lot of Champagne, devoured a mountain of caviare and laughed about the discreet faces of the waiters, who kept their eyes fixed firmly on the plates and dishes while they served us, and always knocked and waited a few moments before entering the room.

Perhaps it was the Champagne, perhaps just the fact that Ludwig Victor was nowhere to be seen when we left Sacher's; anyway, I was more confident. And after days and days had passed without anything untoward occurring I really believed that everything had passed off all right.

An illusion which had now been utterly shattered.

'I ... dined at Sacher's?' I asked, plucking up the courage to sound angry. 'When is this supposed to have happened?'

'On Monday evening,' said Stephanie.

That was my salvation! We had been there on Sunday. Not on Monday. Now I could deny everything without having to lie.

'You were seen.'

'By whom? Who claims to have seen me?' I demanded.

The Emperor gestured to Stephanie not to answer this question, but she didn't notice.

'The Archduke Ludwig Victor,' she said.

I turned to face the Emperor. 'Your Majesty, I am the innocent victim of a slander. Ask my husband, ask anyone at the Coburg Palace. They will tell you that I never left the house on Monday evening. Philip would never shield me if there were any grounds for such an accusation as this.'

'Save your breath, madam. You will not convince me. I know everything.'

'I appeal to Your Majesty's well known sense of right and justice! I swear by everything I hold sacred that I did not go to Sacher's on Monday evening.'

'You yourself must be the judge of what you hold sacred, madam. But I earnestly advise you not to swear. Besides, it is not merely a question of the incident at Sacher's. I have said already: I know everything.' He sounded cold and distant.

So he was fully in the picture. 'Your Majesty, this is a matter of gossip—common, malicious gossip! How could you possibly believe that sort of talk?' Knowing very well, however, that Franz Joseph believes *any* sort of talk, and acts as the self-appointed moral judge of his court. Only the woman he sleeps with is sacrosanct. Katharina Schratt, his 'dear friend', is above gossip.

If he had been cold before, he was freezing now. 'Madam, you appear to forget who told me about this incident.'

'Your Majesty's brother. I had not forgotten. But even he can make a mistake. Certainly the Archduke Ludwig Victor has no right to bring accusations against me. Since you seem to be so well informed about everything, you will no doubt have heard of the difficulty I had in evading his advances.'

'The question is whether you wished to evade them, madam. But that is not under discussion here.'

I tried once more, although behind the Emperor's back I could see Stephanie with an imploring finger laid to her lips. 'I do not claim to be blameless, Your Majesty. But isn't it possible that the Archduke Ludwig Victor merely wants to revenge himself on me?'

'Do not trouble to defend yourself, I know everything,' he repeated monotonously. Then for the first time he looked me directly in the face. 'I regret that in the future you will not be permitted to appear at court.'

He left the room. Stephanie and I could do nothing but curtsey.

Scarcely had the door closed behind him when Stephanie began to cry. 'How could you do it?' she sobbed. 'How *could* you?'

'How could I do what?' I asked angrily.

'Go to Sacher's with that fellow Mattachich. He's ruined you. Can't you understand that?'

'So you believe what the Emperor says.'

'Are you trying to say that the Emperor is a liar?'

That was Stephanie, the Stephanie I have simply never been able to understand. God and the Emperor tell no lies. She still believes it, after everything Franz Joseph has done to her. But I didn't want to bring things to a head unnecessarily now.

'All right, then Ludwig Victor is the liar,' I said. 'I swear to you that I really was not at Sacher's on Monday evening.'

'Why did you ever get mixed up with him?' she moaned.

'With whom?' I inquired carefully.

'With either of them,' she answered helplessly, drying her eyes on her little lace handkerchief.

I explained to her that Count von Mattachich was my equerry and riding instructor and that was as far as his duties on my behalf went. Ludwig Victor was persecuting me with his lies because I had rejected him. I reminded her that the Empress Elisabeth had always refused to be left alone with Ludwig Victor, so that he could never claim afterwards that she had said anything she hadn't.

Stephanie looked at me, shaking her head. 'I really think you haven't realized yet what's happened. You are forbidden the court! Don't you understand what that means? How can you go on living in Vienna if the Emperor won't receive you? It's unthinkable! Everyone will point you out. You are branded! Outlawed! Soon no one will speak to you or want to know you any more! Just think what our parents will say!' She began to cry again.

Stephanie was right. I really hadn't understood, but now I was beginning to. This was no longer a matter of gossip and rumour. No, it was something more serious. Ludwig Victor has resolved to destroy me, and it looks as if he has succeeded. He can never get over the fact that a little Croatian lieutenant has taken the place he wanted for himself. And he will never forgive it.

Evening   I loathe it when Philip rages, when he threatens me, when he swears. But I loathe it most when he puts on a condescending, sarcastic manner. Then he is so revolting to me that I have to force myself to listen to him.

He was in that mood when he came to my room after I had excused myself from the lunch table. 'I assume your audience with His Majesty has taken away your appetite,' he began, settling himself comfortably in the fireside armchair.

I was lying on the chaise-longue. 'I have a terrible headache,' I said. 'I can't think now.'

'You can't think at all, headache or not,' he answered, in that tone that I hate so much. 'I have just come from the palace. The Emperor has told me everything. I regret that I must speak with you, despite your understandable headache.'

His calmness was infuriating me.

A great injustice had been done to me, I explained in injured tones. I could not possibly be blamed because the Archduke Ludwig Victor had gone running to his brother with this wild story that was pure fabrication from beginning to end.

'The Archduke Ludwig Victor is no liar,' said Philip, sounding like my sister.

I reminded him that we had had guests to dinner on Monday. Therefore I could hardly have left the palace. I pointed out that he himself could bear witness to that.

'Quite right,' Philip agreed. 'You can't have been at Sacher's on Monday.'

I felt a surge of triumph.

'But you *were* there on Sunday,' he went on. 'Ludwig Victor made a mistake in the day. I will put that right, of course. What is the next step? I should be glad to hear a word or two from you about all this. Have you any suggestions?'

I stood up. 'I expect you to challenge Ludwig Victor to a duel! That's the only way this matter can be disposed of.' I said it spontaneously, the first thing that came into my head.

Philip roared with laughter. 'Why should I fight him? Because he was wrong about the day, or because he has slept with you? I'd have to challenge half Vienna! And I'm not going to. One of your lovers might be a better shot than me.'

Tears of anger started into my eyes. It enraged me, that Philip, whose affairs were common knowledge all over the city, should dare to reproach me. I told him so in unambiguous terms. I complained too that his Princess Levkova had talked about me too freely—and too slanderously.

'Then I suggest you challenge the Princess to a duel,' he said, apparently still half-laughing. 'There is a delicious French piquancy about the idea of women duelling. As I remember it they wear hats, skirts and nothing else. They're naked above the waist. I can't quite remember whether they fight with pistols or knives. I don't take much notice of that aspect. But if you fight the Princess I'm prepared to be your second. The thought is getting me quite excited.'

I saw in his eyes a familiar flicker that warned me to be on my guard. It had too often happened that Philip, in the middle of a heated argument, would suddenly go on to make advances that bordered on rape. The thought of it made me feel physically sick.

I tried to distract him. 'You are simply too much of a coward to challenge the Emperor's brother.'

'More to the point, I'm simply too intelligent,' he said, almost affectionately.... 'You're still quite attractive for your age.'

'And you are disgusting,' I shouted. 'Don't touch me or I'll scream for help.'

He looked away from me, and became matter of fact. 'The suggestion that I should fight a duel on your behalf is simply absurd.'

'My father will insist on it.'

'Not when I have explained all the circumstances.'

There was no answer to that.

'The Emperor was very generous,' he went on. 'He assured me explicitly that the ban will only apply to you. I shall be welcome to see him as usual.'

'Congratulations. And what will happen to me?'

'You, my love, have made your bed and now you must lie in it. *I* haven't compromised myself with an equerry!'

Then Philip left me alone.

* * *

G

Saturday morning   Louise stood me up yesterday afternoon. The first time. She's always let me know when she wouldn't be able to come, but yesterday she didn't.

I must admit that I've let it worry me. Stupid! I've told myself again and again that there's no sinister reason for it. With all her commitments, something could crop up any time to make it impossible for her to get away. Yet I've been worried.

Originally I thought of going to the theatre. But I didn't.

My supper stood untouched on the table. I'd sent Theresa home long ago. The grooms too. I lay naked on the bed, smoking and staring moodily in front of me.

Around midnight I heard a coach draw up. Louise!

She had come in a cab; she asked the driver to wait. This nocturnal visit, and the hired transport, were something new. So my instincts didn't let me down, I thought. Something's gone wrong.

But she told me everything was perfectly all right. Her sister needed advice and help on a personal matter, she explained, and Louise had spent the whole day with her out at Laxenburg. She couldn't get word to me from there.

I was glad to see her with me, safe and sound, but her story had the ring of an excuse. I almost said so to her face, then decided not to. But I wanted to know what had really happened. An exchange of words, even one false note would have been enough to hurt her. Louise is quite absurdly sensitive about anyone doubting her word. So I kept quiet, and watched her carefully.

I really don't know what to think now. Some of the time she behaved quite innocently. Then I told myself that all was well. I was seeing things. Then before the thought was even out of my head she would suddenly start asking questions such as I've never heard on her lips before. And at once my doubts would begin all over again.

She told me, rather nervously but humorously enough, how she had slipped out of the palace. For the first time ever. Through one of the innumerable side doors. Countess Fugger had organized the whole thing.

The good Countess is worth her weight in gold. She never asks any questions, because she doesn't want to know any answers. She just wants to help the Princess in any way she can.

The secret expedition seemed to stimulate Louise. She drank three glasses of Champagne in rapid succession. There was a light in her eyes that at once began to have its effect on me. Already half reassured, I tried to kiss her. But she evaded my embrace with a determination which was quite new in her. At once my suspicions were reawakened.

Suddenly she wanted to know whether I had ever given any thought to our future.

'Our future?' I repeated stupidly.

'Yes,' she said. 'Why so surprised? How are we going to live from now on?' She looked at me, gravely and searchingly.

I didn't know what to say—an unusual experience for me. I admitted to myself that I had never given a thought to my own future. But I could hardly tell her that. I tried to explain that I was a soldier. Accustomed to letting the army take decisions for me. I could see in her face how little this answer satisfied her.

'We can't live like this for ever,' she said.

Her words rang an alarm bell in me, as if she had another surprise up her sleeve to be revealed at any moment. An unpleasant surprise that would affect us both.

Then she laughed again, quite casual once more, asked for another glass of Champagne, and laughed at the idea of Countess Fugger waiting outside in the cab. The Countess had got enormous pleasure from the adventure of the night expedition.

'It doesn't seem to be nearly so amusing for you,' I challenged her.

'Not at all,' she said.

'Then I don't know why you're beating about the bush. I've waited for you the whole evening. I had theatre tickets. But I stayed at home and waited.'

I stood up, lifted her from her seat, took her in my arms and began to unfasten the hooks of her dress. She loves me to undress her. It drives her mad. I've tried it often enough.

'We haven't been to bed together at night since Abbazia,' I whispered in her ear.

'But plenty of times in the daytime to make up for it,' she countered. 'Please let me go. I must get back. The cab is waiting. The Countess is waiting. I mustn't be late—I don't need to tell you why.'

I felt like ripping the clothes from her body. She must have guessed my thoughts.

'I appeal to your honour, Count Mattachich!' she said. It

should have sounded flirtatious, but it sounded serious instead. As if she had meant it.

I let her go.

She tidied her hair, put on her hat, and drew the thick veil over her face. Then I helped her on with her cloak.

Gazing after her as she drove away into the night, I was again assailed by all manner of doubts. I have still not managed to get rid of them.

Louise was different. Quite different from usual.

What was behind that strange visit? Why did she come to me in the night if not to sleep with me? What reason could there be? Did she want to tell me something and then find she couldn't do it?

I ransacked my mind for the answer.

Has she got another man? Or has there been a reconciliation in the House of Coburg?

For the first time since we met, I have the feeling that she's keeping something back from me. No—I'm *sure* she is!

I really ought to start thinking about the future. On the off-chance that it's still not too late.

* * *

ℒ

Saturday   I wanted to talk to Geza. Tell him everything, ask his advice. I went to him in the middle of the night. But I couldn't say a word.

What could I say? 'You were right. We should never have gone to Sacher's. Now it's happened, and I don't know what's going to become of us.'

In bed at last, I couldn't go to sleep. I rang for Antonia and asked her to bring me a glass of sugared water. That always helped me when I was little. But I seem to have outgrown it—it did nothing for me. I lay awake for hours.

Eventually I did go to sleep, and had a horrible dream. I was dressed up as an odalisk, with a gorgeous oriental robe and a veil over my face. I was driving in an open carriage to a state ball at the Hofburg. The coach stopped, I got out, and I walked up the steps to the door between two rows of torch-bearers. Suddenly two giant footmen barred the way. I tried to slip past them but they seized me and tried to force me back. I shouted and struggled. At last I succeeded in breaking free. My costume had been torn to shreds. Naked I ran up the great staircase between two more rows of torch-bearers, and reached the ballroom ahead of my pursuers. The celebrations were in full swing. Franz Joseph and Katharina Schratt were leading the polonaise. I ran to him but he danced away from me. The two footmen ran up behind me. I dodged between the couples, pleading for help. They neither saw nor heard me. They danced past me—no, *through* me, as if I were a ghost. The pursuers caught up with me, seized me, dragged me away. Then I woke up.

It was broad daylight, and my room was friendly and warm; slowly I calmed down.

Antonia brought my breakfast. As I sat in bed, drinking chocolate, the horror of the dream faded. Even the events of yesterday took on a less forbidding aspect. Things can't be as bad as they seem, I thought; everything will sort itself out.

Countess Fugger was announced. Her serious face dampened my optimistic morning mood, and the note she handed me wiped it away altogether. It was from Stephanie.

DEAR LOUISE, *it ran*. Erszi has a terrible cough. Dr Widerhofer says she must be taken south at once. I've been packing as fast as I could, and when you read these lines we shall be already on our way. I don't yet know where to—I've been thinking of Merano or Bolzano if it's warm enough there now. In great haste, your devoted sister, ST.

I pushed the tray away and got out of bed.

As soon as I was dressed I went in to Philip.

As he knew, I said, the Emperor had decided to make my life in Vienna intolerable. I would therefore have to face the consequences.

'What consequences?' he asked, pretending to be only mildly interested.

'Divorce.'

Philip looked at me as if I had suggested that we should step down into the gutter.

'Divorce is against my principles of honour and decency, as well as being against my religion. Divorce is totally immoral. A Prince of the House of Coburg does not get divorced.'

'If a daughter of the King of the Belgians is prepared to do so, a Prince of the House of Coburg need have no scruples!'

That shaft struck home. He knew that my father had originally hoped for a better marriage for me.

I should have married into a ruling house. On my mother's insistence the King had finally given way, and so sealed my fate.

'I have nothing to add to what I have said,' said Philip angrily.

'Your paean to morals, honour and decency is very touching. You must forgive me if it doesn't entirely convince me, coming from you.'

Philip kept his temper with difficulty. 'I admit without qualification that our marriage was a mistake. But it cannot be undone now. We have lived our separate lives—I admit that too. But up to now we have always succeeded in avoiding any scandal. It is not my fault that your criminal stupidity has at last led you to overstep the bounds of decency. Unfortunately, there is no longer anything to be done about that, either. Not even by means of a divorce.'

Now I had to struggle to remain calm. 'Since I have so criminally overstepped the bounds of decency, as you put it, the world will have no trouble understanding it if you divorce me.'

'There is nothing to be said on that subject.' His tone was crisp and final. 'The sacrament of marriage is holy to me.'

Now I was finished with self-control. I told him to his face why he refused a divorce. Not out of piety. Not out of any considerations of morals or decency. But simply because my father is the richest man in Europe, probably in the world. Because on my father's death my sisters and I will inherit the vast territory of the Belgian Congo, with all the colossal wealth of rubber and copper which that territory holds, and which are my father's alone. Philip would never relinquish such an inheritance, though he himself is master of the countless millions that his grandfather acquired in Hungary when he married Antonia von Kohary. (Yes, that family knows how to marry!)

Philip let the accusations flow over him without turning a hair. It didn't matter to him what I thought. Divorce was out of the question.

'Very well,' I said. 'So you will not agree to a divorce. What do you want of me? Am I to sit here in my room while you amuse yourself at court?'

Philip told me that I was free to withdraw to our estates in Hungary. That in fact would suit him very well.

'I shall certainly leave Vienna,' I assured him. 'But I'm not going to Hungary. I shall become a traveller, like the Empress Elisabeth. I shall live on the Riviera, if I feel like it, or in our palace in Paris; or I shall tour the spas of Europe. I shall take Countess Fugger, my physician, a secretary and a complete retinue. As a royal princess should.'

'Don't forget your equerry,' said Philip sarcastically.

'Oh, no. I shan't forget him. Who else could I entrust with my horses? Dora and her governess will also travel with me. That will stop evil tongues wagging.'

Philip's nerves were not as steady as he wanted me to think. He would never let me take Dora with me, he shouted now.

The more noise he made, the more confident I felt.

'Well, if that's your last word, then I know what I shall have to do. I shall stay in Vienna and dine every evening with my equerry at Sacher's. The food is excellent; we've both been very satisfied there. If we feel too bored in a private room we'll simply sit in the restaurant. One can always count on meeting old friends there. And now I'll leave it to you to decide what will suit you best.'

* * *

G

Sunday We're striking camp in Vienna. I know hardly any details as yet. Only that Louise and the Prince have agreed to run separate households until further notice. Louise just put her head round the door to let me know the news. She had to dash off again at once.

The Coburgs have a palace in Paris. (Is there anywhere they haven't got one?) That will be our first stop.

We shall be travelling in great state. All the horses are coming with us. I'm very glad about that, of course. They are just coming into peak condition. It would be a crime to hand them over to strangers in such wonderful shape. All my work would go down the drain.

Louise thrust ten thousand guilders into my hand. I've never seen so much money all at once. When I asked her what I was supposed to do with it, she laughed and said, 'Pack the horses.' My jaw must have dropped a bit. 'Buy yourself a brand new wardrobe with the rest. And please don't be mean about it. Paris is the most elegant city in the world. Soon you will be appearing in public there with the daughter of the King of the Belgians on your arm. Don't forget that, my little Croatian lieutenant.'

She knows how the words 'Croatian lieutenant' annoy me.

'Now don't be cross,' she went on happily. 'I'll never say it again. I'll appoint you my secretary. Will that satisfy you?'

I stuffed the money casually into my pocket and said, 'I will consider Your Royal Highness's proposal.'

'Do so, Count, and let me know your decision tomorrow afternoon. I shall be here as usual.' She hesitated a moment. 'For a lesson. In Paris things will be more comfortable. I promise you that.' And she gave me her hand to kiss.

So I shall get to know Paris at last. I'm looking forward to that enormously. And I'm glad that Louise and I will be more comfortable there. In fact I'm *very* glad. But it won't stop me making a close study of the beauties of the city.

What shall I do with all this money in my pocket? I think I'll start by visiting a tailor and a shoemaker.

If I understand the situation correctly, there are going to be some rather decisive changes in my personal position. I think that in the circumstances we shall soon need a new equerry.

Ozegovich could be the right man for the job. It would really be a laugh if he came with us to Paris. I might as well write to him anyway and see if he's interested.

28 November 1896 Now I know at last why I attended the Academy. Without the knowledge of logistics they taught me there I should really be out of my depth now.

For three weeks I have been occupied from morning till night getting ready for our departure for Paris. I hadn't the slightest idea how great an effect it was going to have on me. Not that I have anything to complain of. God forbid! It's only that I've had to adjust rather suddenly to some dramatic changes in my life.

Until now, going on a journey has simply meant wandering into a station and buying a ticket to somewhere. That's all changed. Totally. In the exalted society in which I now move one travels by special train. No, I tell a lie. We travel in *two* special trains.

In the first train are Louise and her lady-in-waiting. Then

there's Princess Dora, Mlle Rouvignard, Louise's physician Dr Schnee, my humble self, and a hand-picked cross-section of the servants, all provided with sleeping accommodation appropriate to their status. All this involves two coaches and a dining-car. This train has precedence over all others en route, which cuts four hours off the express schedule from Vienna to Paris. The second train will bring the rest of the servants, the bulk (and I do mean bulk) of the luggage, the horses (with fodder), two coaches and everything else we're dragging along with us (from Louise's bed to Dora's grand piano).

At first Philip's steward was supposed to be arranging everything. But as it became increasingly clear that it was all beyond him, I arranged through Louise for the whole performance to be left to me. Since then all the problems have finally been solved. I've had to sweat over some of them. Every decision on what should and should not be taken, every new 'definite' date of departure has had to be changed x times over. The extra costs we've incurred just by these constant revisions don't bear thinking about. But money is obviously the only thing which is of no interest at all. I shall have to revise my attitude to it in future if I don't want to make a bad impression.

2 December Now everything is really perfect: Artur von Ozegovich is coming with us. His telegram has just arrived; I'm fetching him from the Ostbahnhof in a few hours' time.

II

G

Paris, 16. 1. 1897. Grand Hotel. Suite 21-4   I, Geza Count Mattachich, am living like a god, in Paris!

I live in an unbelievably elegant suite on the top floor of the best hotel in Paris. I have my own manservant—Mirko, a countryman of mine. I've given up eating—I dine instead, at Maxim's or the Ritz or Prunier's or anywhere else where the price is high enough.

I have to keep reminding myself how hard up I was such a short time ago, and how often my lamented father's ring and watch found their way to the pawnbroker; i helps me view my present circumstances with proper amazement.

When Louise pressed those ten thousand guilders into my hand, I reckoned I was near enough the richest man in Vienna. Today I handle very different sums. My Louise is the soul of extravagance. She makes me look a real miser. But I'm an apt pupil; I improve from day to day. There's no easier habit to catch than throwing money about.

The horses have so far simply been enjoying a Parisian holiday. (For that matter, so have I!) In all these weeks we have been riding in the Bois just once. Ozegovich has had to employ four stable-boys to give the nags a bit of exercise. He has taken over from me as equerry, while I have progressed to the office of secretary.

Since being invested with this new dignity, I've discovered some very sophisticated tastes I never knew I had. I'm a member of the Jockey Club, where I play the obligatory roulette and baccarat and lose like a gentleman. If it still hurts me a little to chuck away that lovely money in this way, no one notices.

I have also become something of a dandy, and dress in the

very latest English fashion. Viennese tailors, I discover, are light-years behind the times.

My new life-style even includes Culture. Every première sees us in our box at the Opera. We make regular visits to the Comédie Française, where I have to make equally regular efforts to stay awake. I've even been dragged round the Louvre more than once. Very exhausting.

On evenings when Louise is otherwise engaged at official receptions, I take myself off with Artur Ozegovich to the Folies Bergère. We never take seats, but stroll round the *promenoir*. A couple of weeks ago I wouldn't have known what a *promenoir* was, but now Artur and I saunter about like true Parisians in the horseshoe-shaped space behind the seats, watching: watching the girls who come here looking for custom, the students who can't afford the girls and have to make do with the optical illusions on the stage, the provincials with their mouths drooping open in astonishment, and the usually pretty spectacular antics of the singers, dancers and so on and so on.

I'm really glad, though perhaps it's rather cheap of me, that Artur had that little bit of bother and had to resign his commission. We still get on damned well together. Without him it would sometimes be pretty tedious here. I think I'll have to relieve him of his duties with the horses soon—they take up too much of his time. I'll hire a new equerry, and promote Artur to courier. Then he won't be so tied down, which will be an advantage for both of us.

My own duties as secretary consist mainly in paying bills, which Louise conjures up for me with unflagging energy. If she sees a style of hat she likes, she promptly orders ten in different colours. If a shoe suits her she has a dozen pairs made. Then after a week or two she finds the first pair has gone out of fashion, so the others are all thrown away, or given away. Of her dresses, I won't say a word: each costs a fortune, and most of them she only wears once.

So far I've been drawing on an account that Philip opened for her at the Crédit Lyonnais. On top of that she has an income of 72,000 guilders a year from Vienna, and an allowance from her father of 30,000 Belgian francs. It all adds up to quite a tidy sum. But one doesn't have to be a genius to see that it can't last long if we go on at this rate.

She really is insanely generous, my Louise. With herself and with me. It could almost be embarrassing sometimes if she wasn't so tactful about it. She never hints that she wants anything from me in return for her open-handedness. I belong with her, and should live just as she does.

Well, if she insists, I'm happy to oblige.

III

Karlsbader Bote, 25 May 1897

Our city has for some days now been privileged to welcome a noble guest, Princess Louise, daughter of King Leopold II of the Belgians and wife of Imperial Field Marshal Prince Philip of Coburg. The Princess is travelling with her daughter, Princess Dorothea.

Mr Artur Ozegovich, Her Royal Highness's Courier, arrived here as an advance guard in early May and rented the villa Sonnenblick for the noble lady and her retinue. Sonnenblick is one of the finest properties Karlsbad has to offer. The palatial house is richly furnished, and surrounded by a vast park containing the stables and greenhouses.

Her Royal Highness's secretary, Count Geza von Mattachich, has taken a suite at the Grand Hotel Pupp. His Excellency informs us that the Princess intends to take the waters here for at least four months. In the autumn Her Royal Highness will leave for Merano, and then winter on the Riviera.

Princess Louise is renowned for her beauty and elegance. She is considered the brightest star of the Courts of Vienna and Budapest. Her son, Prince Leopold, is a pupil at the Austro-Hungarian Cavalry Academy; her husband, Prince Philip of Saxe-Coburg-Gotha, manages the colossal family fortune and the estates in Hungary and Bohemia.

Yesterday the Mayor, Dr Stefan Durek, called to pay his respects to the Princess and bid her welcome to the town. He found Her Royal Highness in excellent form. She invited Dr Durek to a soirée she will be giving at the villa tomorrow evening. The young Russian pianist Serge Rachmaninov will be playing, and the orchestra for the dance has been brought in from Vienna itself. It promises to be a dazzling party. Among

the guests will be the Duke of Schleswig-Holstein, Ernst
Günther, brother of Her Majesty the Empress of Germany.

L'Ami du Peuple, Marseilles, 12 November 1897
   Princess Louise of Coburg has arrived in Merano, Austria,
with her retinue. According to a reliable source, this consists
of one lady-in-waiting, one secretary, one courier, one personal
physician, one governess for her daughter, six chambermaids,
five footmen, two cooks, four kitchen maids, one cellarer and
four gardeners. The Princess never travels without her stable
of sixteen thoroughbreds, as well as her coaches and teams.
The animals are entrusted to the care of an equerry, two
stableboys and six grooms.
   Her Royal Highness's luggage consists of nearly a hundred
enormous trunks. A figure of 125 parasols has been mentioned
(Princesses apparently have no need of umbrellas!), 75 pairs
of satin shoes, 110 pairs of boots, countless expensive gowns
for every hour of the day and night, dozens of hats, cloaks,
furs, gloves, mountains of lingerie and—last but not least—
a jewel case that would be the envy of the Czarina of Russia,
who is famed for her jewels.
   Princess Louise is not, of course, the only member of a
European royal house to live and travel in such style. Her
expenditure, though considerable, is nothing out of the ordinary.
   Why bother with all these details then, especially when they
concern so charming a lady as the Princess Louise?
   Because it is sad that such luxury can go on in Merano when
not far away, in Milan, things are very different. There, people
are starving; desperate women are attacking the bakers' shops;
ugly incidents occur every day between the police and the
military on one side and the wretched populace, driven to
desperate measures, on the other. The roots of the problem are
rising prices and unemployment.
   So, one might ask, why worry about Princess Louise, who
provides work and employment for an astonishing number of
people? Is is not both the right and the duty of the aristocracy

to share their wealth with the people? To provide a livelihood for as many people as possible? A miser is every bit as anti-social as a profligate, it might be argued.

But unfortunately, in this case the books don't balance. For our source informs us that our spendthrift princess is living far beyond her means. Yes, even the very best people can do that!

Tailors, shoe-makers, furriers, milliners and jewellers, never mind the ordinary tradesmen who provide the noble household with food, have to wait too long, and often in vain, for their accounts to be settled.

If certain rumours can be believed, it seems that there are even promissory notes in circulation bearing this noble lady's signature. So far they appear to have been settled by her husband, Prince Philip of Coburg.

What can be said here is that the Princess, in the circumstances, is swindling honest working men out of their hard-earned payment, to which they are entitled, and so seems to be demonstrating the ugly *reductio ad absurdum* of that rule that says it is the duty of the aristocracy to release their funds into public circulation.

It is to be hoped that the noble lady will settle all her obligations before she leaves Merano, so that her leave-taking from that lovely town will not be clouded with hostile feelings.

Gazette de Nice, 10 January 1898

Her Royal Highness Princess Louise of Coburg has rented the villa Le Paradis, one of the finest properties on the Riviera.

The Princess will be arriving in Nice some time next week.

We understand that a suite has been reserved at the Hotel de France for her secretary, Count Geza von Mattachich.

IV

L

I am very glad that we have decided on Nice, though I thought at first that perhaps Cannes would be just a little more *en vogue*. Cannes is now the favourite place for the English, because a golf course has been opened there. The first on the whole Riviera, I understand. But now that we have been here a few days I realize that Nice has more charm, more originality. And our villa, Le Paradis, promises to live up to its name.

Vienna seems really provincial in contrast to the Riviera. The society here is cosmopolitan and very, very elegant. I saw at once that my wardrobe would need a comprehensive overhaul. Hats, for instance, are noticeably larger here, and already, in February, adorned with the most beautiful artificial flowers, blossom and veils. Probably we shall all be wearing fur hats by August. Leg-of-mutton sleeves are *passé*. Long gowns are worn all day, not just in the evenings. The best fashion house in Paris now is Doucet's, which has quite overshadowed Worth and Paquin. I have sent for M. Doucet to come here and advise me.

The Côte d'Azur owes its rise to fame not only to its warm winter climate but above all to the Casino at Monte-Carlo. Like a giant magnet, the tables attract people from all over Europe and America. Above all the Russians, whose passion for gambling seems to be unequalled anywhere.

In the summer, of course, it's far too hot here. No one could endure it, and one has to go elsewhere. But if Le Paradis turns out to be all it promises I shall buy it, and make it our permanent winter quarters.

Dear Countess Fugger complains that Nice is dusty and terribly overcrowded. She also goes in fear of her life from all the motor cars here. She claims that people are run over at the rate of almost one a week. Well, crowds and motor cars don't trouble me. On the contrary I love living here, and am in excellent form.

One can go for delightful walks to La Bastide and the Paillon valley. Yesterday we visited a zoological garden owned by the Countess de la Grange. They say that she made the money to start this business by plying another, perhaps even more lucrative trade. Having seen her, I can well believe it.

I stroll for hours through the streets, letting myself be led into temptation by the magnificent window displays in all those elegant shops. My walks almost always end at the flower market—I have never seen anything to rival it for colour.

Vienna now will be in the grip of ice and snow. I hope all my old friends are freezing and catching their deaths of cold.

* * *

G

Nice, 10 February 1898 About an hour ago there appeared in my hotel a Minister of the Austrian Crown in full working order, and a real live Field Marshal. My meteoric rise to the highest circles of Viennese society really takes my breath away. These two gentlemen were appearing as seconds for His Highness Prince Philip of Saxe-Coburg-Gotha. Despite the ritual gravity with which they discharged their duties, I had difficulty in keeping a straight face.

The Prince wants to fight with pistols. If after the second exchange of shots honour has not been satisfied, the affair is to be concluded on the spot with heavy sabres, until one of us is incapable of continuing.

As is correct in such exalted circles, their Excellencies—Honved Minister Baron Fejeryary and Field Marshal Count Wurmbrand—conducted the affair so courteously and dispassionately they might have been inviting me to a pheasant shoot. I replied promptly in the same vein: it would be my pleasure to give the Prince satisfaction and to accept his conditions. I also accepted without demur the proposed site of the duel, the arena of the Military Riding School in Vienna. At my opponent's request we agreed on 8.30 on the morning of 18 February. I undertook to name my seconds well in advance, and to appear punctually at the rendezvous.

With that, the formalities were over.

I then offered the gentlemen a glass of sherry, which was gratefully accepted. Over the sherry we exchanged a few significant words about the weather, and speculated whether Spain and the United States would go to war over Cuba—a war which Wurmbrand declared the heathen American Republic would certainly lose.

Then I saw my guests out of the hotel and into their coach. I wished them a pleasant journey, and looked forward to seeing them again in Vienna.

And so I am to fight a duel with the Prince. That's no surprise. What does surprise me is that he's waited so long.

Why now? But I needn't worry about that. My problem is to nominate my seconds. Before I say anything to Louise, I must wire Ferdl. He will arrange all the necessary details straight away. Fortunately he's absolutely reliable. It'll be the devil of a rush for him.

* * *

L

Geza has just left. I don't know how I shall endure the hours, days, nights, until I know the truth.

The blackguard! The dishonourable, disgraceful coward! He wouldn't challenge Ludwig Victor. He required no 'satisfaction' from the Emperor's brother. But he demands it of Geza.

He has known for two years what was going on between

Geza and me. Has known every detail, as if he had been with us day and night. And now he suddenly feels himself wounded in his non-existent honour? All of a sudden? Why? I've racked my brains but can think of no explanation. The thought of Geza being exposed to this monster's vengeance makes me shudder.

I begged him to take me with him to Vienna. I wanted to abase myself before Philip, to grovel at his feet and beg him to spare Geza. Geza just laughed at me. Duels are matters for men, he told me, and women shouldn't interfere. I think these men with their idiotic ideas about honour regard a duel as a sort of divine judgement. God loves best him who shoots straightest.

Years ago, when we were hunting in the Carpathians, Philip brought down a stag with a single shot. At long range. On a misty day. In the Riding School it will be broad daylight, and there will be barely twenty-five yards between the two of them.

I know that he desires Geza's death. He wants to take from me that which I love. He will aim at Geza ... but it is me he will hit.

If he kills Geza I'll murder him.

And if Philip is to die? What then? Could I still love a man who has shot my husband dead? If I am to be quite honest, and I will be, the answer has to be yes. I could. It may sound callous, but it is the truth. I can't forgive that fat, scented, rich skinflint for chaining me to him simply in order to get his hands on my father's money.

But whatever I may secretly wish, I cannot hope for it. For if Geza kills Philip he will be arrested on the spot. I am convinced of that. Other duellists are allowed to cross the frontiers before the report of the fatal outcome is officially known to the police. But on 18 February the myrmidons of the law will be waiting outside the barracks, and they will lock Geza up the moment Philip is dead.

How perverse of my husband to insist on 18 February for the duel. My birthday. My fortieth birthday!

Geza is thirty-one. He looks older. No one could possibly

think he was only thirty-one. Countess Fugger herself told me so only a few days ago. And of course no one would think to look at me that here is a woman who is going to be forty in two days' time. When Ernst Günther arrived in Nice yesterday and came to pay his respects, he looked at Dora and me, compared us carefully, and said, 'How are the two lovely sisters?'

But I shouldn't lose sight of the fact that the Duke of Schleswig-Holstein was probably hoping to further his own plans with this flattering compliment. Specifically, he would like to marry Dora. But I refuse to start making decisions now about the future of my sixteen-year-old daughter.

It's nine o'clock. Dora has just been in to say good night. Dear Marie Fugger has just had a little supper sent up to me. But I haven't touched it.

The train taking Geza to Vienna must be somewhere in Italy now, approaching Milan.

I am lonely. Lonely as I have never been since that blessed day when I took Geza with me into exile. What seemed a catastrophe, and would have been if Franz Joseph and Philip had had their way, was luck, pure luck. I can think of no other man; only of Geza. His embraces, his tendernesses, mean more to me than all the embraces I ever received before I met him. And time cannot hurt us. Yesterday night was as exciting as the first, in Abbazia. No, *more* exciting. I must not think of it, or the time of waiting will be unendurable.

*   *   *

G

18-19 February 1898   Ferdl has performed wonders. He is a real friend, a man one can always rely on in any situation. He's had damned little time to do everything.

The gentlemen had no trouble agreeing on a referee and an attending doctor. They stayed together until two mounted troopers, who had been standing by on Wurmbrand's orders, brought back the agreement of the two people chosen to do what was asked of them.

Meanwhile the details of the proposed passage of arms were meticulously settled. As I had instructed them, Ferdl and Skarda agreed with every suggestion of the challenger's, without protest.

For the duel with pistols, the conditions are as follows: weapons to have rifled barrels, distance twenty-five paces with no moving forward, fire to be exchanged twice, twenty seconds allowed for each shot between the commands 'Ready: Fire!' and 'Stop!' In case the combat had to be continued with swords, the conditions were: heavy cavalry sabres with sharpened points, stabbing permitted, to last until one of the combatants becomes incapable of continuing. Such incapability to be confirmed by the doctor.

On the day before the duel the referee, Colonel Count Karolyi, called a further meeting of the seconds. At this meeting he exposed his opinion that the conditions for the swordplay were too savage. He proposed that the points of the sabres should not be sharpened, and that stabbing should be prohibited.

Honved Minister Fejeryary, acting on instructions, refused this amendment, and was supported by Count Wurmbrand. The Field Marshal even offered the opinion that stabbing should never be outlawed in a sabre duel. In his experience, stabbing—whether permitted or not—was all too common in the heat of the fight. Accordingly in every case either the principals or their seconds should be disqualified, but in his experience this never occurred in practice. In any duel in which he was involved, said Wurmbrand, he would like to see this state of affairs precluded from the start, as it was both morally and honourably quite unacceptable.

My own seconds offered no comment, as they had been instructed. Nevertheless, Count Karolyi insisted on a relaxing of the conditions. Otherwise he threatened to resign his function. Eventually it was agreed that, if recourse to swords became necessary, protective bandages would be worn on throat, wrists and all arteries.

I myself arrived in Vienna during 17 Feb. and installed myself at Sacher's.

Towards evening Ferdl and Skarda appeared at the hotel and brought me up to date on everything I needed to know. I thanked them for their help and friendship, and asked them to dinner.

It was as excellent as ever. Sacher's will always be Sacher's. Even if one has been living it up at Maxim's in the meantime. We drank a bottle of Champagne a head, and said not a word about the next day.

After dinner I asked my friends to excuse me, told the porter to see I was called promptly at 6 a.m., and went to bed.

From early childhood I have mastered one supremely practical habit, and mastered it so well that many people have envied it. In unpleasant, threatening situations, where inconvenience or even serious trouble seem to be brewing for me, I can lie on a bed, pull the covers over my head, and fall fast asleep in seconds.

But this time it didn't work. Again and again I found myself picturing in my mind the events of the coming day. I couldn't help myself. But whatever form the pictures took, they were always awash with blood. Sometimes my opponent's; often my own. I tossed and turned, and began to get terribly cold. Though the room was well heated, and I had a thick duvet on the bed.

I knew from what Louise had told me that Philip of Coburg was a useful man with a gun. In her first moments of horror about the duel she had told me of some really miraculous triumphs of his at the hunt. To reassure her, I explained that a man might be handy with a rifle and yet no use at all with a pistol. But she assured me, trembling, that he was equally at home with pistol shooting. Years ago, she said, he and Crown Prince Rudolf had been in the habit of settling their innumerable idiotic wagers with pistol-shooting contests. Philip often came off best, althought Rudolf was acknowledged to be an outstanding shot.

In Nice I didn't take Louise's warnings any too seriously, comforting myself with the thought that almost ten years had passed since Rudolf's death, and that in the meantime my opponent had reached a time of life where the eyes start to weaken, and the hand is not quite as steady as it was.

But now, in the silence of the night, a few hours before I was to step out to face my challenger, with my knack of dropping off to sleep having for the first time deserted me when I most needed it, things looked much more menacing. Again and again I heard Louise's troubled voice describing my opponent's unusual skill with a pistol.

I don't know when it was that I at last managed to go to sleep. When one of the hotel staff knocked at my door and told me it was six o'clock I sat up in bed with a start. I climbed out of bed with leaden limbs. I felt as if I hadn't slept for a moment.

During the night the frost had etched thick spirals and patterns on the window panes. Outside in the street the lamps were still lit.

It was a long time since I had worn uniform. As I put it on now I realized that I had gained weight considerably. I resolved to keep an eye on my figure in the future ...

... The future!

I couldn't help laughing. For how could I be sure, on this cold winter morning, that I had any future at all?

Sharp at eight I was told that the coach was waiting outside.

As I stepped out of the hotel the cold struck me like a blow in the face. The driver told me that the thermometer had dropped during the night to its lowest point of the year.

We drove across the Schwarzenberg-Platz and down the Heumarkt. In the Stadtpark the bare winter trees were covered in a thick sheath of hoarfrost.

In the Ungarnstrasse the driver asked me whether I should be long at the Riding School. If it wouldn't be too long, he said, he could wait. I agreed; then superstition won after all. I sent him away.

My two seconds had arrived before me. Unlike yesterday evening, they were now in uniform. We had scarcely had time to exchange a couple of words before Colonel Count Karolyi and Dr Poindl appeared.

Skarda and Ferdl had already met the Colonel. Skarda introduced me, and Karolyi then introduced us all to the doctor, a rather preoccupied, reserved-looking middle-aged man.

Count Karolyi wore the white uniform of the Hussars, and a resplendent blue dolman tied at the throat with golden cords. He was about fifty, a dazzling apparition who behaved towards me with immaculate, sophisticated courtesy.

Now two luxury carriages drove into the arena. From one emerged Prince Philip; from the other Honved Minister Fejeryary and Count Wurmbrand. The coaches disappeared again immediately the way they had come, and the gates of the arena were closed.

Philip of Coburg and his seconds were all wearing the uniforms of their field rank.

Ferdl was quick to make a joke of this. 'You've got nothing to worry about here,' he said. 'With all these generals about they're bound to use blanks.'

The ensuing formalities were tense and ceremonious. The seconds shook hands briefly, then acknowledged (but without shaking hands) the opposing principals. Then I saluted Philip as his rank of Field Marshal required, but received no acknowledgement but a hostile glare.

Referee and seconds paced out the firing distance, checked the weapons and drew lots for them. They carried out their duties with studied gravity, and spoke only in lowered voices, as if they were on a theatre stage behind the lowered curtain and taking care to let the public learn nothing of the spectacle that was about to unroll before them.

In the broad brick quadrangle of the inner courtyard the principal actors stood, each a good fifty yards distant from his neighbour. Two of them, Philip and myself, had our predetermined roles to play. The doctor's part was not yet written.

The setting had been chosen with professional care. Although we were in the open air, we were screened from observation by uninvited visitors. The arena was separated by its windowless rear wall from the four long single-storeyed buildings where the stables and offices of the Riding School were. The only entrance, the massive wooden gate, was shut. Hardly a whisper of sound from the world outside could reach our ears. We were in a desolate, walled-in desert in the heart of Vienna.

At last the preparations were over. After Count Karolyi had warned us to observe the regulations laid down to the letter, and to fight fairly, we were off: Philip and I faced each other, twenty-five paces apart, the safety-catches of our pistols already off.

He looks older than he really is. But I had no time to concern myself with his appearance—Karolyi, his watch in his hand, was already giving the order: 'Ready ... fire!' As he spoke each word I saw his breath clouding in front of his serious face.

It was my shot first.

Twenty seconds are not long. I raised my pistol. My opponent stood motionless. His eyes were fixed on the muzzle of my pistol as it slowly moved upwards. Two hands' breadths below the line of his belt, my hand stopped. I couldn't resist taking aim, just for a moment, at the target where the German revolutionary Lassalle had been hit during his disastrous duel in Geneva. I registered the look of horror on my opponent's face, and have to confess to a sneaking satisfaction in it. I would have liked Louise to share that moment. I was counting softly. About five seconds left. Now I snapped my arm up and fired in the air.

For me, the joke had been worth it. The little Croatian lieutenant had had his moment.

Now it was the gallant General's turn.

If there was one way to give further offence to Philip of Coburg, it was that shot in the air. I watched, as injured vanity and rising anger darkened the red flush that the cold had already put in his fat face. Whether this last provocation had been necessary I can't say; but there was no doubt that I now faced a man resolved to see it through to the end.

As he now took aim at my heart I had a good look at him. He was, I thought, smaller than Louise. He made up for it with an enormous head with protruding eyes and a massive nose. His mouth was thin, almost non-existent.

There's nothing to be particularly proud of in having supplanted this decaying roué in the affections of the beautiful Louise. Yet there was something undeniably aristocratic about him. In the worst possible sense, of course. He gave an impression of imperiousness, contempt, arrogance, cunning.

Because he wanted to make so absolutely sure, he aimed for a moment too long. A mistake that a really fine shot should never make. Only two or three seconds were left. Then time was up. At the last possible moment the shot whistled past my left ear. I felt its breath on my cheek before I heard the report.

The game continued. I fired in the air again, and again the Prince missed his target. Although he was taking the most elaborate pains to be sure of hitting me. So much was perfectly clear to everyone present.

For my own behaviour I can think of no explanation. There were a host of good reasons for it ... and as many against. Including some very cogent ones. My decision was not the result of prolonged heart-searching, nor even of serious reflection. It was intuitive. Both times. Even as my first shot went into the air, I had no idea what I would do with the second.

If there was going to be a second. Which was by no means certain.

The seconds collected up the pistols. With exception of my opponent, everyone was satisfied with the proceedings so far.

Count Karolyi summoned the seconds to him. They spoke quietly together. Then the referee turned to the Prince.

'These gentlemen and I have agreed to ask Your Royal Highness whether he perhaps considers that honour has now been sufficiently satisfied, and whether reconciliation between the parties may now be possible.'

A curt 'No' was the answer to this eminently honourable proposal.

Now the swords were issued. Despite the bitter cold we removed our tunics. The protective bandages were put on.

Karolyi, with no mask or protection of any kind, came and stood very close to us. In this way he hoped to prevent the fight turning into indiscriminate butchery.

After the first exchange I knew that the Prince had little chance of settling things in his own favour. Although this must have been equally apparent to him, he attacked grimly and rather recklessly. He neglected his defence criminally, while I was able to parry his attacks without effort.

As he attempted a lunging tierce, arm outstretched, I was only just able to turn my blade aside at the last moment; otherwise in his blind rage he would have impaled himself with all his weight. It would probably have killed him. So I simply nicked him on the right forearm, just by the bandage. The blood flowed freely, and the contest was immediately stopped.

The doctor confirmed a deep stab wound, its effect partly blocked by the bandage. He put a temporary dressing on it. Then he consulted with the seconds and Count Karolyi.

These gentlemen were unanimous that the injury to his right arm had rendered my adversary unfit to continue. The duel was over.

Unlike Philip of Coburg, who climbed into his coach with

Dr Poindl and drove away without a glance in my direction, their Excellencies Fejeryary and Wurmbrand were at pains to express their appreciation of my conduct during the duel.

The events of that morning were soon being talked about in the city. Of course the wildest rumours were circulating. Sometimes the Prince was dead; sometimes I was.

That evening the Coburg Palace decided to issue a communiqué, since with things as they were it was senseless to try and hush the affair up any longer.

It appeared in the *Freie Presse* on 19 Feb. and announced that the Prince's condition was satisfactory. He was up and about, but was obliged to wear his arm in a sling and was confined to the palace for the moment for fear of complications.

In an editorial comment, the same paper announced: 'The Lieutenant fired both his shots in the air, whereas the Prince aimed and missed twice.' This information must have pleased Philip greatly. It did me.

I bought a dozen copies of that edition. Louise and our friends in Nice should have their entertainment too.

Ferdl and Skarda saw me to the station, although we had spent almost the entire night celebrating.

Skarda had brought another sensational item of news. His cousin, who works at the Cabinet Office, told him this morning that the duel had been arranged at the insistence of the generals. The Emperor's adjutant, Field Marshal von Bolfras, had been asked to convey to His Majesty the deep disquiet felt by the general staff at the spectacle of an Imperial Field Marshal sitting quietly by, year in year out, while his wife carried on an immoral relationship with another man. The Emperor, despite his known religious objection to duelling amongst his officers, eventually had to admit that his supreme commanders were becoming increasingly restless. He himself had requested the Prince to send his representatives to me. And Philip, to make the best of things and not appear as a coward, had spread word around that he had only recently become aware of the liaison. Under the piercing gaze of his colleagues on the general staff he then had to risk everything and try to fight in such a way that every taint of cowardice would be removed from him.

My intention originally was to return to Nice yesterday evening. But it was worth staying on another night to be able to tell Louise that piece of news.

As the train pulled out, I gave each of my seconds a gold cigarette-case. I had had the things made at Rodeck's and the date, 18.2.1898, engraved on them. Not a particularly cheap gift. But I think Louise will quite understand.

* * *

ℒ

18 February 1898   He is alive! Alive! Alive! Nothing else matters. As soon as I received his message I wired to him: 'This is the most wonderful birthday of my life.'

Out of pure fear—and, I must admit, superstition too—I hadn't dared to arrange any celebrations. As soon as I heard the good news, out went the invitations, with apologies for the short notice.

The ballroom at the Negresco was quickly hired, a lavish supper ordered, an orchestra engaged. Ozegovich had his hands full arranging everything, but he copes superbly with such matters. He spares no effort and no expense: everything is perfect and there is plenty of it, just the way I like it to be.

I had the team harnessed up and drove round to M. Hartog. He is the best jeweller on the Riviera, a real artist. He can stand comparison with Cartier and all the competition from the rue de la Paix.

In his shop I found exactly what I wanted: a simply beautiful necklace of diamonds and large sapphires with matching earrings. Naturally it wouldn't have done to ask the price, but I hope it will be very, very expensive, because I have had the bill sent to His Royal Highness Prince Philip of Coburg in Vienna. I asked M. Hartog to put a little card in with the bill. On it I wrote: 'This is your thank-offering to Count Mattachich for his magnanimous gesture in sparing your life. I hope you will be able to sign the bill all right with your injured right arm.'

It amuses me enormously to be able to force Philip to give me such a lovely birthday present.

19 February, morning   It was a lovely party, except that Geza wasn't there. I thought about him all the time.

In Vienna it would be simply unthinkable to send out invitations at midday for that same evening. But here people live much less formal lives.

No one took offence; everyone came. They understood that of course I couldn't make any arrangements before I knew the outcome of the duel.

Many of the guests who honoured me with their presence yesterday are people I have known for years. Philip and I have often stayed with the Duke and Duchess of Chartres in Normandy. The Prince of Joinville has been hunting with us in Hungary. And with his brother, the Duke of Montpellier, I've danced many a Parisian night away.

They all know, of course, that there's been a scandal about me in Vienna. But it doesn't trouble them. The French aristocracy is much freer from convention and prejudice. Perhaps it's because they live in a republic. They have no court, no Franz Joseph, not even a Napoleon III now, though he was just a nobody like the rest of his family and generally ignored by true royalists. In a certain respect my local friends are in a rather similar situation to my own. We are all homeless. That makes for a bond.

The supper was so outstanding that I was almost tempted to

engage the Negresco's chef myself, but that would have been ungrateful. So I asked the good Artur Ozegovich to convey him my thanks in the form of a thousand-franc note.

Dora looked pretty and very grown up. I let her stay up till midnight. Ernst Günther is very keen to become engaged to her, but I can't bring myself to give my permission. At thirty-five he is far too old for her.

None of my partners could waltz like Geza. My Croatian lieutenant and his Belgian Louise, as he sometimes calls me, can out-waltz anyone, even in Vienna, where they think they have a patent on waltzing.

About midnight we drove into Monte Carlo, to the Casino.

I lost a fortune, but I couldn't care less. Lucky at cards, unlucky in love, and vice versa. Unlike Geza I have no passion for gambling. Even so, I enjoy the private rooms. It fascinates me to watch the activity. The hush when the croupier says *'Rien ne va plus'* and the ivory ball rolls is simply breathtaking. One can hear nothing except the humming of the gas lights and the merry clicking of the little ball jumping from slot to slot. Then it settles, and such a noise breaks loose you'd think that a room full of mutes had suddenly been given the gift of speech.

Most players are incapable of concealing their feelings, though they all do their best. There's one old lady I nearly always see there who is the exception. They say she is a Russian Grand Duchess. That could even be true, as she is literally festooned with jewellery. The lobes of her ears have been so stretched by the weight of her great pendant ear-rings that they'll soon be brushing her shoulders. Her face is a mask. Not a trace of a frown to tell when she loses; not a hint of a smile if she wins. When the ball starts rolling her left hand moves automatically to the great golden crucifix she wears round her neck as if she were the Pope, while her right clutches at a mascot that always sits on the green baize in front of her, a silly little tin soldier. That's her only reaction. At two o'clock on the dot she puts away the tin soldier, rakes in her *plaques*, gives the croupiers a really princely tip, and goes, without a glance for anything else around her.

At dawn we drove back over the Corniche, teeth chattering. Little Gramont suggested we drive down to the harbour at Villefranche for some *Soupe à l'oignon*.

The first fishing-boats had already come in and had just unloaded when we reached the Bistro. I was amazed to see so many people up so late.

It was a splendid moment, when we—the ladies in their rich gowns and jewellery, the men in full evening dress—sat down peacefully together with workmen, fishermen and sailors. It was all very democratic, and we all laughed a lot. After the onion soup and a few glasses of dubious Cognac I was a little tipsy and very tired.

When I was in my bedroom at last, and Antonia and Ilona had undressed me and let down my hair, my eyes couldn't stay open another minute.

My bed was empty; still, it had been a lovely night. I had painlessly crossed the threshold into my forties, and Geza was alive.

I went happily to sleep.

V

𝒢

Nice, 2 March   A message from Vienna today. From Barber. He will be here the day after tomorrow.

What can he want? It must be something to do with that promissory note that falls due in the next few days.

Barber could have saved himself the journey. There isn't the slightest chance that we can honour the bill. Our financial situation is extremely precarious at the moment.

I sent a telegram back at once, telling him to get the money from the Coburg Palace. Not in as many words, of course, but clear enough. After the row over the duel, the Prince will never allow a bill with his wife's signature on it to be dishonoured. From what Skarda's cousin told us, he can't possibly afford that.

3 March   Ozegovich just turned up with the latest edition of the *Gazette de Nice*.

On the second page, where no one can miss it, is an announcement from Prince Philip of Coburg informing tradesmen and private citizens alike that he will no longer take responsibility for his wife's debts.

That's his revenge for the necklace and ear-rings that Louise forced him to 'give' her for her birthday!

Another thing: all the European newspapers have given heavy coverage to the duel. None of them shows him as much of a hero. Now it looks as though he's decided to stop paying to hush up an affair that the whole world knows about already.

Artur was still here when a page brought a second telegram from Barber. He's had no luck in the Seilerstätte, and will be in Nice tomorrow.

So far as I remember, this is a little matter of 450,000 guilders. Our exchequer now holds barely twenty thousand.

After today's announcement in the *Gazette*, we shan't be able to raise another franc of credit on the whole of the Riviera. I'll wager that the hotel slaps a big fat bill in front of me tomorrow. And not just the hotel, either.

That's the position.

I have no idea what will happen now. The only certainty is that there are hard times ahead.

We'll have to think of something or the whole affair will blow up. With a hell of a big bang.

Maybe the best thing would be to get out. While we can.

5 March   Barber is here. We had a preliminary talk as soon as he arrived yesterday evening. I started by being uncooperative, saying the Princess was very annoyed. 'Why do I bother to employ one of the best and most expensive lawyers in Vienna if he can't prevent my being pestered with this sort of trivial nonsense?' And: 'Perhaps I had better look for someone who will take better care of my interests.' That was the sort of thing I told him she'd been saying.

But this line didn't fool the old fox for a minute. Far from it: he was prepared to sever his connections with Louise on the spot. That was all we needed. Nothing at all would be achieved by letting Barber go.

So I swiftly tried another tack. I put all the blame on Louise. She was irritable and nervous, because she didn't really understand these things. And I assured him that I myself had complete confidence in him, now and always.

When we at last had the conversation on a reasonable footing, it turned out that we had Philip's announcement to thank for all the row. He hadn't just put it in the *Gazette*, as we thought; it was in every more or less serious newspaper in Europe. The Havas agency had been brought in to make sure the announcement had maximum circulation. From Budapest to London, from Naples to St Petersburg, the whole world could see that

Philip of Coburg had strangled the goose that laid his wife's golden eggs.

On the same day that the announcement appeared in the Vienna *Freie Presse*, the bankers Reicher and Spitzer had stuck two worried faces round Barber's office door. In their safe sat a promissory note for 450,000 guilders, signed by Louise. They wanted to know whether Prince Philip would be prepared, in spite of his public statement, to honour this bill in his normal way. Or whether these new circumstances meant that the paper (it fell due on 20 March) must be presented to the Princess herself.

Barber had then paid two visits to the Coburg Palace, one before he wired me, one after. No good: Philip was not at home. However, his Steward, Kodolitsch, informed Barber in very plain terms that His Royal Highness had no intention of meeting the bill. He had made his attitude to this and all similar questions perfectly clear in his announcement. And that was that. Good afternoon.

When the lawyer had made his report, he looked at me long and hard. Then he said: 'You will recall, Count, that I was responsible for arranging this loan. Let's face it, you were desperate for the money, at any price. I must ask you to remember that you expressly told me so yourself. It would be more than embarrassing for me if the bankers who helped you on my recommendation were now to suffer as a result.'

His hangdog face goaded me into a pretty sharp answer. 'But haven't you missed the point there, Doctor?' I said. 'These bankers of yours are common usurers. For a modest bridging loan, just for six months, they take fifty per cent interest. It seems to me that these delightful people are in our debt, rather than the reverse.'

'I must admit, Count Mattachich, that you have a point there. But of course no judgement can possibly be given at this stage.'

'What do you mean?' I asked coldly.

'Very simple. First, the bill must be paid.'

We were back to the beginning.

There was no point in beating about the bush any more. I admitted that we were currently in no position to meet the bill, and asked Barber to do his best to obtain an extension.

He had expected this, and had already made inquiries. In the circumstances, he said, Reicher and Spitzer were prepared to be reasonable.

I saw a gleam of hope. 'On what terms?' I asked.

'You must ask his Royal Highness Prince Philip of Coburg to guarantee the bill,' said the lawyer.

I had to laugh. 'If I had the Prince as a guarantor, I could raise the cash now from the Crédit Lyonnais or the Bank of England. At *three* per cent!'

Barber shrugged his shoulders.

'No, my dear chap,' I went on, 'the gentlemen must forget all this business about a guarantee. After all that has happened it is completely out of the question.'

'In which case I can see no hope of avoiding disaster,' said Barber. 'There is not much time left. So far as I am concerned, I have done what I can.'

He was anxious to go straight back to Vienna. But I finally managed to persuade him to stay a little longer, under the pretext that I had to discuss things fully with the Princess.

* * *

L

Geza keeps talking about the 'grave situation' we are in. We must find some way out, he says. And quickly. His endless chorus is: 'We have no more money. Can you understand what that *means*?'

Well, I have never touched any money in my life, so it doesn't mean very much. A Princess of the Blood Royal is not allowed to handle money. Her bills are paid by her secretary or her lady in waiting. Geza does this chore for me now, and I'm very grateful to him, of course.

He finds it childish of me not to be able to understand

financial matters. But I really don't think anything very dreadful can happen to us! No one is going to refuse credit to the wife of a multi-millionaire and daughter of an even more multi-billionaire. (Not that I am really quite sure what 'credit' is.) And Philip can publish as many announcements as he likes— so long as we're married he has to take care of me. Probably he's trying to make me go back to him with all these tiresome pinpricks. But I never will! And when he finally agrees to a divorce, he will have to provide me with a settlement appropriate to my rank. That is only logical; my sense of justice tells me so.

Countess Fugger sat next to me in the coach. I noticed that she was looking at me out of the corner of her eye. She wanted to say something, try and advise me. But I was so overwrought at the prospect of seeing him again after all these years that I was in no state to listen to her. Though of course I know that she means well.

The frightened respect that I had always felt for him as a child was still there. It threatened to hinder me today just as it had then. There was a memory that I couldn't get out of my head. A stupid memory, perhaps, but one that was indissolubly linked with my recollections of my father.

In the garden at Laeken grow the best fruit-trees in Europe. We children were strictly forbidden to pick anything from them. One evening I was walking in the garden by myself. It was nearly dark. I was strolling along the gravel path. Suddenly I saw, half hidden under the leaves, a wonderful ripe peach.

I made certain no one was looking. Then I quickly snatched the peach and ran into a grove of trees where I could hide. I ate the peach so quickly that I didn't even taste it. Then I washed my sticky hands in the fish-pond and walked back to the castle.

Next morning I was summoned to see my father. He said to my face that I had been stealing fruit. I was so surprised I admitted it at once. The punishment was harsh: two hours between the double doors.

My mother was there while the court was in session. She knew just how much I feared this punishment: the nurse always found me in floods of tears when, as had happened after my previous convictions, she came to release me from my dark prison after I had served my sentence. Yet my mother said not a word in my defence.

For two full hours I stood imprisoned between the double doors leading to the schoolroom, reproaching myself bitterly. I had been a thief, never reflecting that my father (whom I equated with God) would notice it at once. My father saw everything, knew everything, from him there were no secrets.

Later our old gardener told me that the King always counted the ripe fruit. He said it quite casually, with no idea of what his words meant to me. So my father was not after all gifted with divine omniscience: he always knew when a peach was missing because he counted them himself.

Even then, I tried to use this discovery to fight the respect which my father commanded in me. But if I did manage to make his pedestal a little lower, at the same time I felt a growing fear of him, this king that counted his fruit like a miser and took terrible revenge for every loss.

As our carriage now turned through the gate into the park of Les Cèdres, I caught myself watching for peach-trees.

The Steward was waiting outside the villa (which in fact was more like a castle). He showed us into a salon and promised to inform His Majesty of our arrival.

So this was the house my father had built on Cap Ferrat; the house to which my mother was never allowed to go.

I knew from the Brussels papers that the King very rarely appeared in his capital now, as the Congo took up all his time. What this villa on the Riviera had to do with the far-off Congo was never entirely explained.

We were on time for the hour he had set for the audience: he had arrived in Cap Ferrat five days previously, and I had written to him at once.

He kept us waiting.

Every minute that passed made me more nervous. The

Countess tried to make conversation, but my answers were so monosyllabic that she soon gave up.

Suddenly the connecting door to the next room, which had only been pushed to, swung open. I expected to see my father, but instead a tiny dog appeared in the doorway.

I had to laugh out loud.

'The King has always had a taste for little dogs,' I told the Countess, happy at the childhood recollection. 'He once had a terrier he called Squib. He used to play with the dog on Sundays instead of going to Mass. My mother would give him pious lectures about it. The King ought to set a good example at Court. Although my mother's admonitions usually had no effect at all on him, he always went to Mass after that. But he took the terrier with him, striding dignified and serious into the chapel with the tiny dog under his arm. While my father sat with his eyes shut, either asleep or day-dreaming, the animal listened carefully to everything. Stephanie and I used to find it so funny, we had a terrible struggle not to giggle.'

And I started to laugh again, though it was entirely out of nerves. The Countess joined in my laughter.

Then I heard the well known voice. 'You seem to have a great deal to laugh at.' My father stood in the doorway.

Countess Fugger curtseyed, I kissed my father's hand and followed him into his study.

My God, I thought, he's shrunk! I was still looking at him with a child's eyes and forgetting that I had grown in the meantime.

He sat down at his desk and indicated vaguely with his hand that I should sit opposite him.

I had last seen him thirteen years before, in Brussels, on his fiftieth birthday. Now his beard was even whiter, his hair even thinner, his nose longer and his eyes harder. There was no hint in his face of any pleasure at this reunion, not even that chilly half-smile of politeness with which one acknowledges an enemy.

He looked at me, frowning, and then said impatiently, 'Well?'

I felt defiance rising in me. I would not make it that easy for him. 'How is Mama?' I inquired.

'Ill,' he growled. 'As disgusted with your scandalous behaviour as I am.'

We had come to the point already. So I told him why I had come. I asked for his permission for a divorce, explaining that Philip could certainly be persuaded to take this step if the King of the Belgians sanctioned it. I explained to him in detail how and why it was impossible for me to live with Philip. He, my father, had had misgivings about this marriage, years ago. And he had been right, I told him, for today Philip and I were both unhappy. The marriage had been a mistake, but one that could still be put right by a divorce. And no doubt a sensible financial agreement could be reached.

While I spoke he fiddled absent-mindedly with some papers. When I had done, he said, 'Is that all?'

I nodded.

'My dear girl,' he said, and I had never heard an endearment so coldly spoken; 'you are lucky. You have an umbrella: your husband. What you do under your umbrella is nobody's affair but your own. The only important thing is that you should keep it. So you must go back to Vienna and carry on your married life as you did before. In public, that is.'

When he said it, the monstrous significance of the words didn't immediately dawn on me. I realized only that he was refusing to help me.

Now I had to confess that Philip was no longer paying for my day-to-day expenses. I told my father of the newspaper announcement with which Philip had delivered himself into the hands of the satirists and me into those of my creditors.

For the first time something like a smile distorted my father's face. 'Absolutely right! That was clever of him,' he said.

I described my desperate financial position, and said that I didn't know what would become of me now. And, at last, I asked him for money.

'Giving money to you would be like pouring wine into a bottomless jug,' he explained calmly.

'Then at least pay my urgent creditors,' I begged him.

'Supposing I were to part with a single franc to your creditors. Your credit, which Philip has so wisely undermined, would immediately be good again. The dressmakers would start hanging clothes on you again; the milliners would come and shower you with hats, and the jewellers with jewellery. In a word, your debts would get bigger and bigger. You will get only one thing from me.'

I watched him, tensely.

'A single ticket to Vienna, and, for my own sake, a special train. But nothing else.'

After a few empty courtesies, I was dismissed.

The Steward saw Countess Fugger and myself to our carriage, and we set off back to Nice.

I sat as if stunned.

When I saw Geza's expectant face, I burst into tears. I told him to put his arms round me, and clung to him tightly. It was as if I had stepped out of an icy cave into a warm, welcoming room. And although that was a comforting feeling, my tears would not stop.

Geza was as kind as ever. No need to explain that I had failed; it was written all over my face. Yet I had to tell him everything, in detail.

I told him, word for word, what I had said and what the King had said, but of my father's terrible indifference I said nothing. The King simply did not accept me as a person of flesh and blood. I meant nothing to him. The little dog that had come running into the room was closer to his heart than his own daughter.

He had never been any different. What in fact had I expected? Why should he have changed? Why should I fare any better than my mother had done? He has never made any attempt to conceal his complete indifference towards her. He never talks to her, never even acknowledges her presence. If she suddenly ceased to be there, he would not even notice.

My little brother, the Crown Prince of the Belgians, died at the age of ten. From that day onwards, my mother's life became increasingly wretched and futile. My father forced her to go to bed with him again, though it must have cost her an appalling effort of will. She promptly became pregnant again, and the atmosphere at Laeken improved for a while. I was fourteen then, and though I didn't really understand things I could draw my own conclusions.

When my mother gave birth to another girl, my father flew into such a rage that he had to be forcibly removed from the room where she was confined. For days my mother's loyal servants watched at her door in case he should attempt to harm her.

At last my father resigned himself to fate and gave up hoping for an heir. The Queen had failed in what he considered to be her only purpose in life. We—Stephanie and I and our new little sister—were the miserable evidence of her failure, and were held jointly guilty with our mother. We existed, and there was nothing to be done about that. Our father's feelings for us stopped at that point.

Knowing all that, as I did, how could I have expected anything from today's interview? It was my own fault that I was so bitterly disappointed. But this realization did nothing to make me feel better.

It was while I was repeating to Geza what the King had said that I first understood what he had really meant when he spoke of my 'umbrella'. He cares nothing about the change in my life—nothing at all! Except that I have *admitted* being in love with another man. That is a breach of etiquette, a far more serious matter than any consideration of morals or honesty. 'No one cares what you do so long as you do it under your umbrella.'

'He's as bad as Philip,' I sobbed. 'Every bit as bad. Can't you see how degenerate he is, to give me advice like that? How hypocritical and dirty he is?'

'What I can see,' said Geza, 'is that he isn't going to part with any cash. And I will admit that worries me more than his moral failings.'

*   *   *

G

7 March   Louise was expecting some miracle out of her reunion with her father, though God knows I warned her not to place too high hopes on him.

And so the whole venture was a complete fiasco.

I've never seen her so crushed and helpless before. She was crying with rage and despair by turns. It seemed as if she would never calm down again. In the end I could only think of one thing to do: I tucked her up in bed and tucked myself in with her. That did it. No problem is ever insoluble.

When I suggested later we should call off our supper date with Duke Ernst Günther for that evening, she wouldn't hear of it. She was completely herself again, and said she would be delighted to accept His Grace's invitation.

In the hotel, while I was dressing for dinner, I found a note from Barber. He asked for an appointment, urgently. I had been carefully avoiding him until I had heard the results of Louise's interview with her father.

An hour later I was walking down the grand staircase to the foyer and thinking that I would have to tell Barber tomorrow just how desperate our position was, and is, when I saw him come in through the revolving doors and go over to the porter.

I've rarely moved so fast.

On the first floor I stopped to think. There was no point in going back to my room: any minute a page would be knocking at the door to announce Barber.

'The servants' door!' I thought suddenly. I walked, or rather ran, along the corridor, dived behind a curtain at the far end, and found myself on the back stairs. In full evening dress, top hat in hand, there I was a few moments later slinking out undetected through the back door of the hotel.

At supper I was rather silent. But not Louise. She sparkled with jewels and good humour. She was transformed. While I still found myself pondering what I could say to Barber.

Then I had a last desperate idea.

Waiting for a suitable moment, when Louise was being welcomed by a crowd of friends, I asked Duke Ernst Günther to grant me a private audience on the following morning. It was, I hinted cryptically, in connection with his proposed engagement with Princess Dora. We agreed on half-past ten.

8 March I sent a message to Barber asking him to join me for a late breakfast around noon, left the hotel (through the front door this time) and walked up to the west end of the town.

It was a particularly fine morning. I welcomed the blue sky and the even bluer sea beneath it as a favourable omen for the outcome of this meeting. Though Ernst Günther of Schleswig-Holstein is certainly not my type, and I would only too gladly have avoided the encounter altogether. But needs must when the Devil drives. Pity poor little Dora, marrying that fellow.

Ernst Günther is a cold, humourless Prussian. He fancies himself and his boring little duchy like nobody's business—*and* that doesn't stop him bragging all the time about the Emperor being his brother-in-law. Anyone who has the privilege of speaking with His Grace for three minutes knows all about that relationship.

His sister, the Empress of Germany, was nowhere near the front of the queue when they gave out good looks. But compared to her brother, she came out of it pretty well.

It seems, anyway, that things are not too good at the moment between Ernst Günther and his imperial sister. And between him and Wilhelm II they're even worse. The Comte de Pignard told me the story—he claims to have got it from the French Ambassador in Berlin.

The Court at Berlin had been working itself into a state of nervous hysteria over scurrilous anonymous letters addressed to various members of the Imperial Family. Not even His Majesty was spared. It was a matter of malicious mud-slinging which showed not only perverse imagination, but an intimate personal knowledge of the private lives of the addressees. The consequence was an outbreak of sterile mutual suspicion at Court which led to an assortment of duels and criminal cases, and eventually forced Wilhelm to intervene in person to avoid the scandal becoming even more public.

Officially, the culprit was never detected. Among the inner circle, it was whispered that the letters suddenly stopped two years ago when Ernst Günther—immediately after a visit by Chief of Police von Richthofen to the Emperor—had a stormy interview with his brother-in-law and rushed away from Berlin to the solitude of his Silesian estates at Primkenau. At any rate the Duke, addicted though he was to the fleshpots of the German capital, has never been seen in Berlin again.

The whole thing may just be a rumour, though Pignard swears it's true. But rumour or not, whenever I look at this Duke I think myself lucky I'm not in Dora's shoes.

Note that I was a perfect gentleman, and said nothing of all this to Louise. In fact I'm very glad that Dora will be going to the altar at last. Better for Louise and me that we should be rid of her.

'May I say at the outset,' was my rather formal opening to the interview, 'that I have ventured to arrange this meeting without the knowledge or permission of Her Royal Highness.'

'She will not hear of it. No one will hear anything unless I have your express authorization to divulge it. You have the word of the Crown Prince of Schleswig-Holstein,' he said pompously, sitting attentively upright in his chair. 'Fire away, Count. All ears.' He sounded revoltingly Prussian.

'Your Highness and Her Royal Highness will soon be joined by close family ties,' I began.

The Duke interrupted jovially. 'Can't be sure of that. My dear future mother-in-law—as I hope I can confidently call her —is still keeping me dangling. Seems to enjoy it. Can't think of any other good reason, anyway.'

'Yes and no,' I said. 'There are reasons. But not personal ones—I can assure Your Highness of that.'

'Glad to hear it, glad to hear it. And now, my dear Count, please stop keeping me in suspense!'

'Well, you are aware that your future in-laws' marriage is not going too well.' I looked at the Duke. His face showed not the slightest reaction. 'Now Philip of Coburg has thought up another way to ... how shall I put it? ... make a spectacle of Her Royal Highness.'

'Something to do with that sinister announcement?' inquired Ernst Günther.

'Quite right, Your Highness, the announcement is all part and parcel of the same incredible game. The latest is, though, that the Prince refuses to pay his wife the income due to her.'

This was no less than the truth. Philip has so far not parted with a single crown of the joint revenues.

'It's quite understandable,' I went on, 'that she should have the odd bill or two sent to her husband. But she doesn't do it for fun! Quite the reverse. Her Royal Highness is seriously embarrassed. Particularly because this has all led to an increasing ... er ...' I tried to give the impression that I couldn't finish the sentence.

'An increasing ... er ...' repeated the Duke, his face impassive. Then, impatiently: 'Well?'

'What should I call it ... an increasing financial crisis in the Princess's own affairs,' I said, almost shamefacedly.

The Duke shook his head. Silent. Uncomprehending.

Anonymous letters do get written, even in these circles. But to have no money—that's something one doesn't mention. I realized that I must reassure him and get him interested again if anything was to come of this venture.

'All this is merely the result of an unfortunate combination of circumstances,' I went on hastily. 'That's obvious to anyone who knows that Her Royal Highness is one of the richest heiresses in the world. And who in all Europe *doesn't* know? These difficulties will be over in no time. That's not in doubt.'

The Duke was still shaking his head.

I let the cat out of the bag. 'But you can see that the atmosphere is not suitable for her to consent to her only daughter's wedding, and to celebrate the betrothal in proper style.'

Ernst Günther of Schleswig-Holstein stood up. He lit a cigar, slowly and deliberately, blew a couple of clouds of smoke into the middle distance, paced up and down a bit, and at last asked gratingly: 'And what, Mattachich, do you think I should be doing to put Her Royal Highness into the right humour to decide in my favour?'

'Her Royal Highness needs a small short-term loan to tide her over her present difficulties—a loan that would be punctually repaid.'

The Duke stood still, listening.

I explained patiently that the most urgent need was for funds to settle outstanding bills. 'A helping hand from Your Highness, as a member of the family,' I went on, 'would certainly pay dividends.'

'Mattachich, stop beating about the bush!' he growled. 'Short and sharp, if you please!'

As the fellow stood there before me, his face red with rage at a question that had not yet even been asked, I knew that there was not the slightest chance of finding sympathy, let alone help, from this quarter. But now I was angry too and determined to shake this pompous windbag out of the last of his composure.

'For this loan, Her Royal Highness needs a guarantor whose status is above all question,' I said pointedly.

'What form must the guarantee take?' asked the Duke.

'A signature on the bill in question,' I said. And added tranquilly: 'The signature of a personage such as yourself, Your Highness. The Princess must sign first, then you as her guarantor.'

That struck home.

'Bills! Guarantees! Credit status!' he exploded. 'Am I dealing with the Rothschilds?'

Unfortunately not, I thought.

'Know what I mean by Rothschilds? Jewish usurers!' He began to pace up and down again. 'Bad business, damned bad business, what you tell me about the Princess's money. Can't understand that husband of hers!' He stopped and looked at me. 'You understand him? Man's a monster!' He set off again. 'Incredible! Appalling! Hadn't the slightest idea!' He stopped yet again. 'And this proposal of yours, my dear man. Absurd! That sort of thing may be done in Croatia, but, forgive my saying so, a German Duke—especially one closely related to the Imperial Family itself—does *not* sign bills!'

At last he'd found a chance to drag in his Imperial sister.

'To be frank, I can hardly imagine the daughter of a King of the Belgians doing something like that either!'

If only you knew how many other bills have got that signature on them, I thought.

'She'd better damned well go to her father. He's got more money than all the Rothschilds put together. And,' said the Duke by way of conclusion, 'you and I had best forget this conversation.'

I stood up.

'But you can leave me out of this once and for all,' he said. 'Then let's forget it, that's what I say. Right?'

Barber had known nothing of my attempt to persuade the Duke to stand as guarantor for the bill. I wanted to see how the idea turned out before I told anyone. As things stood, there was no need for me to mention it at all. But what would happen now I could not begin to see. I faced the prospect of lunch with the lawyer in an extremely pessimistic frame of mind.

I had been expecting to find Barber in an ill humour, and was surprised to find him expansive and amiable. In fact I hardly knew him like this. He's normally a wretchedly dry fellow—a classic pettifogger.

The reason for his good humour was, simply, Nice. He was in love with the town, and had almost made up his mind to bring his wife there for a couple of weeks next winter.

'In my profession you have to derive some benefit even in the worst cases. Otherwise you're finished,' he philosophized. And then he told me, beaming: 'I walked up to the castle. Up that wretched staircase, the Montée Lesage. Then past the ruins of the old castle up to the very top of the hill. Do you know those stairs? They start on the rue Ponchette.'

'I know them. But only from the bottom,' I said truthfully.

'Oh, what a pity! The view from up there is indescribable. You can see right down the coast to Antibes. It's worth two of our Kahlenberg in Vienna. The sea here! The sky! The sun! And at this time of year, I ask you! It's only March! When I think how cold it is in Vienna now, I shudder. And do you know when I was up there?'

I shook my head.

'First thing this morning. I was on my way by eight. So you can't wonder that I've brought back a good appetite.'

Lunch had been served in the meantime, and Barber fell on it with enthusiasm. The Chablis too, which I'd ordered with the ham, he pronounced excellent.

As I was topping up his glass yet again, he said: 'I've been talking a lot, but I've been watching you too, my dear Count.'

I looked at him inquiringly.

'You don't look to me,' he went on, smiling, 'as if you're going to be able to put forward any valuable new suggestions.'

I had no choice but to confess I had made no further progress. Of course, I didn't put it as bluntly as that. I said that I still had various irons in the fire, and we must be patient for a few more days.

'No amount of patience and energy will stop the clock,' he answered. 'In a couple of days now that bill must be met. Bills are like the Last Judgement; when it's time, it's time.' He laid down his knife and fork. 'But I should be a poor sort of lawyer, and unworthy of my hire, if I'd relied on you.'

I learnt that he had been in touch with the bankers in Vienna, by telegram. He had managed to make them understand that there was no question in the circumstances of obtaining Philip's guarantee. They had promptly agreed to accept as a substitute guarantor the Princess Stephanie.

I realized at once that this was now our only chance of meeting at least our most urgent difficulties. The rest would then be in the hands of fate. Something else came into my head: with Stephanie's surety we might even succeed in getting our hands on a little pocket money. We're as good as cleaned out.

I took the bull by the horns, and promised to get Princess Stephanie's signature, provided the new bill could be increased by a modest amount in Louise's favour.

When we parted two hours later, we had agreed on terms: Louise would sign a new bill at once, payable within three months (that is, on 20 June this year) for a total of 750,000 guilders. Of this sum, 450,000 guilders would go to pay the first bill (which fell due on 20 March), 150,000 would be given to us to meet other commitments, and the rest Reicher and Spitzer would keep against fees and expenses.

Barber hopes to conclude the deal by telegram today. He wrote the message in my presence, and encoded it; only the initiated can tell what sort of transaction is going on.

Now it's a question of waiting patiently for a few hours. Perhaps despite that unattractive Prussian the day still holds what its blue sky promises.

* * *

ℒ

8 March   I am alone. Geza and Ozegovich are in Monte Carlo. Dora, Mlle Rouvignard and Countess Fugger have gone for an evening walk.

Geza and I have been within a hair's breadth of our first serious argument. But I kept my temper and said nothing. I am very proud of that. If it had been Philip instead of Geza there really would have been an almighty explosion. But my feelings for Geza are so warm and loving that I was able to behave sensibly. Above all I know that, whatever Geza says or does, he is acting in my interests.

It's all to do with this stupid bill. It falls due soon, Geza says, and for some reason or other we need another one. For that he wants my signature—and Stephanie's.

I asked him what on earth the bill had to do with Stephanie. He said that without my sister's signature it was worthless, and I *must* write to her at once asking her to sign her name on the paper and send it back to me by return of post. Even if I send the letter off today the answer won't be here for six days, and that is absolutely the last moment.

As soon as I made the feeblest little protest he became terribly excited. I knew that if I told him how reluctant I was to ask any favour of Stephanie we should have a very unpleasant scene. So I calmed him down and packed him off to Monte Carlo. He has an absolute passion for gambling. Perhaps he'll win a fortune at the Casino. I should be so pleased for him.

What can I write?

'Dear Stephanie, Philip is behaving like the lout he is. He has been telling the newspapers that he will not be responsible for his wife's debts. He won't catch me like that! That won't make me go back to him. But I do rather need a few hundred thousand guilders, just until someone makes him realize that he can't let me starve. Be a darling and sign your name under mine on the enclosed bill, otherwise the lawyer from Vienna won't let us have any money ...'

Impossible! Completely and utterly impossible! If I was in Vienna, I could perhaps explain things to her (or Geza could). But in a letter? I'm sure Stephanie has never heard the word *bill* in her life. I hadn't myself until a month or two ago. So she will never understand what's going on, and she'll ask her Steward or one of her minions. So all Vienna will know: Louise of Coburg is ruined!

I shall not give my enemies that satisfaction!

Besides, Stephanie has been behaving really disastrously since I left Vienna. I asked her to come and see me at Karlsbad. She refused, with the silliest excuse she could find. According to her narrow-minded code I have 'compromised myself'. And now she's afraid that if she keeps in touch with me she'll be compromised too.

Under the circumstances, how could I ask a favour of her? It can't be done. It really cannot be done.

But how can I make Geza understand that? He's sure to keep on at me again about the 'seriousness of the situation'. So I have promised to sit down and write the letter straight away.

I must make a decision. That much I do know. But which?

About midnight, Geza came back from Monte Carlo. I don't think he won.

He asked me at once whether I had written to Stephanie.

I said, 'Your stupid bill is already on its way to Vienna.'

* * *

G

16 March 1898   The bill came back from Vienna this morning. Punctual to the day. And with Stephanie's signature. Louise says her sister didn't enclose a note. Not a single word. But that can't hurt us. We've got the signature, and that's the main thing.

I took the paper straight to Barber, who's been sitting nervously around on top of his bulging suitcases for days already. He has no more eyes for the charms of Nice. He is very relieved at the way things have eventually turned out. Two hours after I delivered the bill into his hands he was sitting in the Vienna express.

So now the old bill will be met punctually on the twentieth, and Barber can get hold of 150,000 guilders cash for us. We owe him about 12,000 crowns. He'll keep that back, and send us a cheque for the rest at once.

And so at last we can breathe. Considering the mess we were in just a few days ago, that's real progress.

VI

Wednesday This morning I had a very friendly letter from Ernst Günther's mother. She writes that she would like to meet Dora personally, and invites her to pay a visit to Primkenau Castle in Silesia. The Duchess Adelheid sees this betrothal as a foregone conclusion. In a couple of carefully worded sentences she hints that Philip is in favour of Dora's visit provided that I have nothing against it. Philip's behaviour is always immaculate when it costs him nothing.

Can I prevent this journey? I should like to, but can I?

Since we left Vienna, Dora has improved enormously. The friendly atmosphere in which we have lived since escaping from Philip and the cold palace on the Seilerstätte has suited her well. As it has me. She accepts Geza ... but as what, I wonder. As a servant? Counsellor? Friend? Or something more? I have no idea.

Dora is nothing like so childish as she was only a few weeks ago. That too may owe something to the change in our surroundings. Even the old sourpuss Rouvignard has mellowed. How happy we could all be if Philip was a little less mean ... and if Dora would stay with me.

Why do I feel so determined inside not to let her make this trip to Silesia? In the first place, probably, because letting her go would mean I had agreed to her engagement. Besides, I'm a little afraid of the influences she would be exposed to there. With what eyes will she see me when she comes back?

While I was thinking, Ernst Günther was announced. This precise timing of his visit increased my unease, although the Duke made himself very agreeable.

He too has had a letter from his mother today, in which she expresses the hope that I will agree to Dora's visit. The child should be accompanied by her governess and a maid, he said, as if it only remained to arrange the technicalities.

While he was speaking, I watched him carefully. I didn't like what I saw. I told myself there was no good reason for this sudden revulsion. But the thought that this man, four years older than Geza, could sleep with my little girl was simply horrifying to me.

I asked how long the visit was to last.

That would be up to me to decide, he replied politely. His mother had expressed a wish to present Dora to his sister, the German Empress Augusta Victoria. And so she was planning an additional little excursion to Berlin.

Suddenly Ernst Günther became formal. 'I am aware, madame,' he said, 'of the difficulties with which you have to contend. I should like you to know that you may count on my support.'

I had made it a firm rule never to discuss my private problems with anyone but Geza. To involve a third person would have struck me as extremely indiscreet. So, since I was not sure what he was getting at, I asked him: 'What do you mean?'

'Please do not take my words as interference; they were meant only as an expression of my respect and friendship. Prince Philip's behaviour towards you is beyond words. Unforgivable. And I am certainly not alone in thinking so. My Imperial brother-in-law'—he meant the Emperor Wilhelm II—'has nothing good to say of Philip of Coburg.'

Ernst Günther took my hand in his.

'I shall be sure to tell the Emperor of the latest developments when I see him. His Majesty will be furious! You have good friends at the Court of Berlin, madame. Friends on whom you can always rely. I too can bring my influence to bear if necessary. I am, after all, a member of the Prussian ruling house ...'

And so he went on in his official-sounding way, which I had always found rather funny, while I was torn between my original misgivings and gratitude for his offer.

'May I telegraph to my mother saying that you have agreed to the visit?' he asked at last.

I told him to come back tomorrow.

Night When I went to Dora's room she was sitting at her mirror in her nightgown, while Minette brushed her hair. I sat down and waited until Minette had finished her task.

Dora is becoming more and more like me to look at. That is exactly how I must have looked at her age. But I was already married then, and had behind me what still lies ahead of her. The thought depressed me very much.

What will become of her if she really does marry this Prussian Duke? There is a difference of eighteen years between their ages, even greater than the difference between Philip and myself. What do I know about Ernst Günther? They *all* have pleasant manners and behave respectably—that means nothing. The time comes very soon when a man's real character emerges. And what is Ernst Günther's real character? I've heard something about a long-standing attachment to some Frenchwoman. That irritates me, but I can hardly hold it against him. Oh, why is it so hard really to know anybody?

When Minette had left, Dora turned to me.

'Did you want to talk to me, Mama?'

Yes, I wanted to. But now I found it difficult. 'I'm sure you know that Duke Ernst Günther has asked for your hand?'

Dora looked at me with her clear, blue child's eyes. 'I suspected it,' she said calmly.

'Papa has agreed. He thinks it would be a good and desirable marriage for you. I on the other hand have not yet given my consent.'

Dora continued to look at me, in silence.

'Before I make up my mind, I should like to hear from you what you think of Ernst Günther.'

'What *I* think?' She sounded astonished.

'Yes! It's you that would be marrying him—no one else.'

A little vaguely, Dora said now, 'I don't really know what

you expect me to say, Mama.' And then: 'The Duke is always very polite and pleasant.'

'That isn't enough if you have to spend your life with him.'

'Of course not, Mama. But I'm sure you know more about him than I do.'

This degree of submission was too much for me. 'Dora, please try to understand what I'm saying. I am aware that in our circles it is not customary to ask young girls whether or whom they wish to marry. But I am making it a condition of my consent that you want to marry Ernst Günther. If you can't stand him, if he is repugnant to you, then——'

'He isn't repugnant to me,' Dora said, sounding as if I had asked her whether she liked mayonnaise.

I became more and more nervous, and started saying things I had never meant to say. 'Your grandmother had to agree to marry the Crown Prince of the distant Belgians though she had never met him. She was a year older than you are today, and lived happily with her parents in Hungary. She defended herself as well as she could, but it was useless. In Vienna she was betrothed by proxy, to the Emperor's brother. Which made her already the official consort of a man she had never seen. And this man, your grandfather, my father, nineteen years old, didn't want to marry her any more than she wanted him.'

'Why are you telling me all this?' Dora still looked quite bemused.

I didn't want to be interrupted; I had something I must say, and I wanted to have done with it. 'They both spent miserable lives together. Today she is a bitter, disappointed woman and he ... does as he wishes.' I started a new tack. 'I myself only knew your father casually when we were betrothed. I didn't resist the engagement. And that didn't help me either. But I had no idea what lay ahead of me. And that's why I must be honest with you,' I went on determinedly. 'We have never been happy together. It doesn't matter whose fault that is. But you only have one life. And when you do everything wrong at the outset ...' I felt tears come to my eyes.

When I confessed to Dora that my marriage had been a

disaster, it was as if a heavy curtain had fallen between us. She withdrew into her shell. I had said things that she would rather not have heard.

'I don't understand why I need to hear all this,' she said, fixing her eyes on the silver brush that lay on the dressing-table in front of her.

'You are better off than my mother or me. No one asked us what we wanted. You don't need to grope your way blindly into an unknown future. You have a mother who asks you what you want. If you don't want Ernst Günther, you have no need to marry him. I promise you that, never mind what your father says.'

'Papa thinks I should marry the Duke?'

'So it seems.'

'I'm sure he wants what's best for me.'

Dora is a horribly well-bred young woman. Mlle de Rouvignard has done her work well.

I was not yet ready to abandon the struggle. But I told her of the invitation to Silesia. And that the Duchess Adelheid intended to take her to Berlin and present her to the Empress of Germany.

Dora seemed pleased. 'I have always wanted to see Berlin and Potsdam,' she said.

'So you would like to go?'

'It isn't up to me to decide, of course.'

'But you would enjoy it?'

'Yes, I think so.'

I forced myself to a decision. 'Very well, if you would like to go, you shall go. Mlle de Rouvignard and Minette will go with you.'

Dora's eyes shone. 'When can we start?'

'Soon, very soon, I think. But this does not mean I give my consent to the engagement. I shall decide about that when you come back and we have been able to talk again.'

'Just as you say, Mama.'

I stood up. Dora stood too. I put my arms around her and kissed her.

'You really don't need to worry about anything on my account, Mama,' she said, smiling at me kindly.
'Of course not, darling. Good night.'

Wednesday   I didn't go to sleep until nearly morning. When I woke, it was eleven o'clock. As I was drinking my chocolate the Duke was announced.

I kept him waiting until I was dressed and my hair was done. I was in no hurry. On the contrary—every minute that I could postpone this conversation was precious to me.

The clock was striking one as I came into the salon.

Well, let's get it over with quickly, I said to myself; and I forced myself to be pleasant. I asked him to convey my warmest thanks to the Duchess for the invitation, and to assure her that Dora was looking forward eagerly to the trip.

'Then I may say that all is well?' asked Ernst Günther, beaming all over his face.

'I will give her three weeks. Not a day longer! In three weeks at the very latest she must be back here again.'

'Of course, madame, if you wish.'

'I do wish,' I said firmly, and looked Ernst Günther straight in the eye. 'Will you please ensure that my child is back in three weeks from now? Can I rely on you?'

'You have my word, madame.' He sounded genuine enough. 'Have you decided on a date for her to leave here?' he asked then.

'The sooner Dora leaves, the sooner she'll be back here again. How about Monday?'

'Excellent!' he said enthusiastically. He clicked his heels and kissed my hand. 'I shall see to all the necessary arrangements at once.'

And so it was settled. On Monday Dora leaves for Silesia—and I shudder already when I wonder whether she will be the same when she returns.

VII

G

Tuesday   The long-awaited cheque from Barber came yesterday.

I cashed it straight away, and settled only the most urgent debts. Above all our staff's back pay. Then outstanding hotel and restaurant bills, stabling fees and forage bills. That used up half the money pretty quickly. Now at last we're solvent again, at least for a while. So long as nothing unexpected crops up, of course.

Even so, I can't get these wretched money problems out of my mind. It makes me laugh, though. Here I am involved with one of the richest women in the world, and worrying over my accounts like some cobbler. The sums are bigger certainly. But the answer is always the same: bankruptcy.

This afternoon Artur and I tried to get some sort of idea of our liabilities. (Or rather, of Louise's liabilities—when you think of it, this is all nothing to do with me.)

The job was so depressing that we soon gave it up and drove off to Monte Carlo instead. We only meant to have dinner there. But then we dropped in at the Casino for a few minutes. A damned expensive few minutes.

I had a premonition that this time everything would work out well at last. I've certainly been waiting for it long enough. But no luck again. One should ignore premonitions.

On the subject of premonitions ... After we got back I looked in on Louise for a bit. Nothing doing though. Dr Schnee was with her—she had a migraine and was worrying about Dora. She really has got a bee in her bonnet there. Hope we'll hear something soon.

*   *   *

L

Thursday   I was sitting in bed drinking my chocolate when Countess Fugger brought me a telegram.

From Ernst Günther, I thought, terrified. Dora is ill! Something dreadful has happened!

I have heard nothing from her but a single postcard saying she had arrived safely at Primkenau. The card was over a week old now, so naturally I was very anxious.

Normally I would have asked the Countess to read me the telegram, but some strong feeling prevented me. I asked her to put it on the dressing-table, where it lay undisturbed until I was bathed and dressed.

Then I took it, and went into the salon.

My heart was in my mouth as I opened the envelope. I had to read it several times before I understood the sense of it. It was not from Silesia at all, but from Vienna. From that lawyer, Dr Barber. I heaved a sigh of relief.

But slowly the thought occurred to me that the contents could perhaps have unpleasant enough significance. REQUEST YOUR ROYAL HIGHNESS TO WIRE VIENNA PUBLIC PROSECUTOR RITTER VON KLEEBORN CONFIRMING THAT BILL IS GENUINE AND IN ORDER. DR BARBER

Geza will have to handle this, I thought. He understands this sort of thing better than I do. But Geza wasn't there. I read the telegram again.

They want me to confirm that the bill is genuine and in order? Well, of course it *must* be! Otherwise Dr Barber could not have sent us the money. It was beyond my understanding why I should confirm it now—and why to the Public Prosecutor, of all people.

After I had spent some time in extremely complicated reflections, I said to myself: Don't try and deceive yourself, Louise.

You know very well what this is about! Someone in Vienna has realized that Stephanie's signature is not genuine. That's what this telegram means. That, and nothing else.

What should I do now? Admit that I had signed instead of my sister? How can I tell the Public Prosecutor that for reasons which are none of his business I was very reluctant to ask a favour of my sister? A small favour which would normally be taken for granted between close relatives?

I rang the bell and had my carriage brought to the door.

In a few minutes I was driving into the town with Countess Fugger, ostensibly to go shopping. I ordered some lingerie from Mme de Saligny; not even very nice lingerie, but I remembered that her establishment was not far from the post office.

As we drove past the post office, I told the driver to stop, and said quite casually to the Countess, 'I must just go in there for a moment. I won't be a minute.'

The Countess looked astonished, and made ready to come with me.

'No, Marie, I'm going by myself. I have secrets even from you.' It was meant to sound flippant, but it probably didn't, for Marie looked at me anxiously.

I had never been in a post office before in my life, and I expect I behaved rather gauchely. Everyone stared at me. A clerk sitting behind a counter gave me a telegram form on which I was supposed to write my answer to Barber. I pondered over it, kept making mistakes, and had to ask for several new forms, which the clerk appeared to begrudge me.

At last the message was ready, and I gave it to the clerk. It ran: TO PUBLIC PROSECUTOR RITTER VON KLEEBORN, VIENNA. AM EXTREMELY ANNOYED AT MESSAGE RECEIVED FROM DR BARBER. BILL NATURALLY GENUINE AND IN ORDER. LOUISE PRINCESS OF SAXE-COBURG AND GOTHA.

The clerk was indiscreet enough to read the message, and demanded four francs fifty centimes. I told him to send the bill to Le Paradis, but he refused. Eventually I had to run out to Countess Fugger and ask her for twenty francs.

She looked at me in complete bewilderment, but handed me

a note without asking anything.

I went back into the post office, gave the clerk the money and said, 'You may keep the change.'

I was very relieved to have this unpleasant incident behind me. We drove on to my shoemaker and ordered some delightful little boots, which are all the rage just now.

Then we went back to Le Paradis.

* * *

G

Friday   I read in the Vienna *Presse*'s Court Circular that Princess Stephanie is seriously ill. A lung infection with high fever. The paper says there is grave danger unless her soaring temperature can be checked within the next twenty-four hours. I wonder whether I should tell Louise. But she would set off for Vienna on the spot.

Never mind Stephanie's illness, I can't think my Louise would find a rapturous welcome from the Viennese Court. On top of that she'd be surrounded by people lecturing her about me and telling her God knows what. Much better not to let it come to that. She's nervous enough already about Dora.

Perhaps Stephanie's condition will improve and the problem will solve itself.

Monday   A letter came from Barber this morning.

MY DEAR COUNT

It is my unpleasant duty to acquaint you with various extremely embarrassing developments which have taken place here during the last few days.

As Your Excellency knows, as soon as I returned from Nice I took the necessary steps to settle the matter in question as quickly as possible, to the satisfaction of all concerned.

As the tangible proof of my efforts on your behalf, a new cheque in favour of Her Royal Highness for the agreed sum was forwarded to Your Excellency. I must assume that it reached you there safely. At that point, so far as I was concerned, all outstanding commitments had been scrupulously met.

So I was the more shocked, as you may imagine, when I learnt of further developments. Originally I thought it unnecessary—unfortunately, I must now add—to inform Your Excellency that when issuing the latest bill our Viennese bankers did hesitate for a moment because Her Imperial Highness Princess Stephanie had signed herself *Crown Princess*, a title which of course she can no longer use. I regarded this as an oversight, nothing more than a purely theoretical breach of protocol and tradition. I was therefore able without too much difficulty—and in all good faith, of course—to reassure the gentlemen that in all the circumstances no one could entertain any reasonable doubts about the authenticity of the signature.

With hindsight, I can only reproach myself most bitterly for my carelessness, as a result of which the reputation of my practice has, as things have turned out—unless a miracle occurs—suffered such a blow as has never occurred before in more than thirty years of irreproachable professional conduct, during which I have enjoyed the patronage of the highest circles in the land.

You will no doubt have heard of the illness which has overtaken Her Imperial Highness the Princess Stephanie during the last few days. Medical bulletins have repeatedly stated that the noble patient is in serious danger of her life. Messrs Reicher and Spitzer had to face the possibility that they might lose their guarantor of the bill, and considered it their duty to have the Princess's signature authenticated while this was still possible. As it turned out, despite my assurances there were still certain doubts attaching to the matter of the authenticity of the Princess's signature. The bankers therefore addressed themselves to Her Imperial

Highness's Steward, Count Choloniewsky, and asked for confirmation that the Princess would, as it were, officially take responsibility for the bill signed by Princess Louise of Coburg.

The answer came by return of post, and was a great shock. Count Choloniewsky asserted in a short and formal note that Her Imperial Highness knows nothing of any bill, let alone one endorsed by herself. If such a signature existed, therefore, it must necessarily be a forgery. To clear up this mysterious affair, the Count's letter ended, his office had applied to the Public Prosecutor and asked him to spare no efforts to unravel the affair.

That, my dear Count, is how things stand at present, to the best of my knowledge. I am only a lawyer, and thus have not the art of concealing my feelings with words. It looks as though our Imperial Family, ten years after Mayerling, stands on the brink of another scandal—and the thought that I myself am implicated in it appals me.

I am writing to you because it seems to me appropriate that you should be informed of the way in which matters have developed here. Regretfully, I must excuse myself from proceding any further in the matter on your behalf. I am not prepared to take responsibility—or even joint responsibility—for what is to say the least a highly irregular affair, which was originally absolutely nothing to do with me. That I have nothwithstanding almost certainly become implicated in it is bad enough.

Believe me, Your most obedient servant,

    DR BARBER
    Solicitor and Barrister-at-Law

* * *

L

If I didn't know that Geza has my interests at heart, I would have to be cross with him. I am, a little, even so. He has never spoken to me before as he did today. Nothing but reproaches and more reproaches. Philip himself couldn't have behaved worse. (No, forgive me, Geza! Philip would have behaved *much* worse.)

It was all to do with this bill, of course. Geza lost his temper completely when he learnt that Stephanie's signature isn't genuine. I admitted straight away that I had signed it for her. Then he stared at me incredulously, as if he couldn't believe his ears.

With wide, frightened eyes he told me the story of a brother officer of his who was apparently sentenced to three years' imprisonment just for writing his uncle's signature on a bill.

Of course, it was bad luck that Stephanie had to go and fall ill just now. No one could have foreseen that. But even if she is ill, all this would never have happened if I hadn't stupidly written 'Crown Princess' instead of just 'Princess'. I don't know how I could make such a mistake. I must simply have been absent-minded. Usually I am particularly careful about matters of rank and title. This *faux pas* is quite unlike me. Yet it happened. Voilà! I can do nothing about it now.

* * *

G

Monday evening   Louise forged Stephanie's signature! She says it in the same tone as she might say, 'I borrowed one of her hats.'

For a moment I completely lost control of myself, but I might as well have saved myself the trouble. It was like talking to a brick wall. A Ruthenian recruit who had never seen a knife and fork would have understood more of what I said. I had to ask myself whether it was an act, or whether she really believes all she says. At last I knew that she *does* believe it. *Sancta simplicitas!*

Perhaps I'm making a fool of myself. Perhaps forgery is accepted in royal circles.

'Geza, they can't try *me*!' she kept crying, her eyes wide with innocent honesty and as angry as an angel. 'Can you quote me an instance, a single instance, where the daughter of a reigning King was brought before a court along with petty thieves and drunks and ... and whatever other criminals there are?'

And of course I couldn't quote her an instance. It may even be that she's right. Let's hope so. Because I freely confess that this affair scares me stiff.

Look at it objectively, and I'm in the same position as Barber. I didn't have anything at all to do with what happened. But I shall be lucky to get out of it with a whole skin.

I've just been to see her again. In the meantime she's acquired a little common sense. I've made it clear to her that a scandal is as good as certain unless we take the initiative at once.

After much toing and froing we've agreed that only Stephanie herself can help. For a moment we considered whether Louise should set out to see her straight away, but rejected the idea almost at once. Louise would never be given a chance to speak to her sister alone. But only that would justify the trip at all.

Louise was visibly relieved when we dropped this plan. The thought of a confrontation with Stephanie under these circumstances was obviously hateful to her. And so she was the more eager to agree with my suggestion that she should telegraph to Stephanie at once, appealing to her sisterly loyalty and help. Louise gave me carte blanche to send any message I liked in her name.

So I wrote out a wire and had it sent immediately.

AM VERY PERTURBED AT YOUR ILLNESS AND SINCERELY WISH YOU SPEEDY RECOVERY. PLEASE DON'T LEAVE ME IN THE LURCH IN THE AFFAIR YOU KNOW OF. WE ALWAYS STOOD BY ONE ANOTHER AS CHILDREN. DESPITE EVERYTHING THAT'S HOW IT SHOULD BE BETWEEN US NOW. PLEASE WIRE AT ONCE SAYING ALL IS WELL. WITH LOVE, YOUR AFFECTIONATE SISTER, LOUISE.

* * *

Tuesday evening   No word from Vienna.

Wednesday   Still no answer from Stephanie. I have the feeling that something's brewing.

Could be that Stephanie won't answer, because she's completely in the power of this damned Count Choloniewsky and the rest of the Court clique. Or maybe she was never shown the telegram at all. Thinking about it now, it was pretty naïve to hope to achieve anything with a telegram.

Today it's rained all day. The weather suits my mood down to the ground. I'm sitting here staring out at the grey wetness beyond the window and wondering how we're going to drag ourselves out of this mess. I haven't found the magic words yet. Even so, one thing has become clear to me. The signature is and remains a fake. There's nothing we can do to change that. If we could, Stephanie could say she was delirious with fever and talking nonsense; now that she's better she remembers that out of sisterly affection she did agree to guarantee the bill, etc.

These are pipe-dreams. For practical purposes there's only one way out: pay the damned bill as soon as possible! Today rather than tomorrow. If we can do that, no harm will have been done. Besides, we'll get the paper back in our hands. Without the body there can't be an inquest.

In one thing at least my Louise was right. It isn't so easy to lay charges against her. The more I think about it, the more improbable I think it is that we'll come to that.

On the other hand even a Princess can't be allowed to forge signatures whenever she feels like it.

So perhaps it would be the best thing for everybody if we paid up quickly and the bill disappeared from the picture. I don't suppose Louise would get the Order of Franz Joseph, but maybe they'd be glad enough in Vienna to have the affair quietly liquidated like that.

750,000 guilders is an awful lot of money. Now Louise will have to prove that Royal Princesses can achieve more than mere mortals. This is the crisis. That money must be found—and fast!

* * *

L

Geza's making things very hard for me. He says I must raise some money. I! If all my noble relations aren't prepared to let me come before a court of justice like anyone else, then it's going to cost them something—that's what he keeps saying.

He made this point so vehemently that I had to laugh. 'All right then,' I said. 'Who shall we bleed?'

'Let's start at the top, with the Emperor,' he decided. 'What relation are you to Wilhelm II?'

'Willy is my second cousin,' I said. 'He is Queen Victoria's nephew. His mother, the Empress Frederick, is my father's niece.'

'That's good enough! He's our man.'

I protested. With Dora likely to be presented to the Imperial couple in Berlin any day, it's out of the question to trouble Willy with something like this.

Geza seemed to understand this. 'Are you related to the Tsar?'

'Queen Victoria is Alix's grandmother.'

'I'm sorry, but who is Alix?'

'The Tsarina. She is my niece.' Hastily, I added: 'Though of course she's almost the same age as me.'

Geza thought a moment, then decided. 'Russia's too far away. The journey would be too expensive.' He thought again. 'Franz Joseph is a non-starter, unfortunately. What about Queen Victoria? If she's your niece's grandmother, that makes her one of the family too.'

'Of course. Her mother and my grandfather were brother and sister. That made my grandfather Victoria's uncle. But he was her cousin, too, because of his first marriage to her cousin Charlotte.'

'Charlotte?' He looked at me helplessly.

'Charlotte was the only child of George IV. She would have become Queen of England, but she died while her father was still alive. So Victoria inherited the throne. And my grandfather accepted the Belgian crown when it was offered to him. Victoria and he were close friends anyway, and he arranged her marriage with his nephew Albert. So he became her uncle twice over.'

Geza shook his head. 'It's a complicated family, yours,' he said. 'I don't know how you remember it all.'

'It's just about the only thing they taught us when we were children.'

'Could we have a moment's revision: I still haven't understood what your relationship to Queen Victoria is.'

'I thought I'd made it perfectly clear,' I said, laughing. 'She's my aunt.'

'Do you get on with her all right?'

'I often used to stay with her. With my parents when I was young, and then later with Philip. At Windsor and at Balmoral.'

Those visits to Balmoral were among the horrors of childhood. That gigantic grey building, isolated in the middle of the Highlands, used to fill me with fear. I was convinced that there were ghosts in the castle. When the muslin curtains flapped in the wind I saw all manner of ghosts. At night I used to think I could hear the rattle of iron chains, and I drove the nurse mad with my fantasies until she was every bit as afraid as I was.

'Queen Victoria is tiny and fat,' I explained to Geza. 'Although she looks a bit ridiculous, everyone has great respect for her. When I was little I was absolutely convinced that she had castors instead of feet. She moves like one of those toys children drag along behind them. I always wanted to lift up her dress and look at her castors, but of course I never dared. Imagine, the poor woman brought nine children into the world. All nine are still alive, all nine are married, and they all have huge numbers of children of their own.'

'An English prince for every throne in Europe,' mocked Geza.

'No—a Coburg for every throne,' I corrected him. 'Victoria herself is half Coburg, and her husband Albert was *all* Coburg. Bismarck once put it well: "The Coburgs are the stud farm of Europe."'

Geza thought that was priceless. Had my governess told me that as well? he wanted to know.

'No. That was the German Ambassador in Vienna at a reception at the Hofburg,' I told him. 'And Victoria was always very grateful to my grandfather for bringing her her darling Albert.'

'Then we'll take this opportunity of paying off a little of what she owes—to her niece,' Geza decided.

The picture of myself appearing as a supplicant before my Aunt Victoria filled me with real panic. I tried to protest, but then Geza said something that stifled rebellion at birth: 'Are you going to let Philip bring you to heel, then?'

No—never that. Reluctantly, I said I was prepared to write to London.

But Geza was against the idea of announcing our visit in advance. 'That'll give her the chance to make excuses,' he said. 'You'll have to take her by surprise, so that she can't refuse to see us.'

* * *

G

2 *April 1898* After we'd been through her entire illustrious family, we settled on Queen Victoria. I think the old lady might be the easiest to persuade to help her niece out of the mire. So it's decided: we shall go to England.

Louise has been slow to understand the stakes we're playing for, but I think she's eventually grasped it the better for that.

We mustn't waste a single day, and I've insisted that we

must leave for England tomorrow. Louise hates doing things at such short notice, but I refused to bargain with her. She only wanted to have a dozen or so dresses and hats made for the journey. I'm glad I was able to stop this. God knows we've got dresses and hats enough already.

It's important to keep our destination a secret. That's why we shall take the ordinary train to Turin, which proves nothing about where one is really going: the way to Munich or Vienna goes through Turin too. Once there, we shall take a Pullman—no question of a special train this time, of course. *Not* a good way of covering one's tracks. Louise already feels as if she's travelling 4th class, like a peasant-woman going to market.

We shall be quite a small party. Only the two of us and Countess Fugger. And the servants. Three maids for the ladies, a manservant for me. Louise wanted to take Dr Schnee, but I was able to talk her out of it. Every person we can leave behind represents a little more weight in the war chest. Anyway, England is supposed to be full of excellent doctors, whereas I regard dear old Schnee as a wretched disgrace to his profession. He is a nice fellow and a comfort for Louise—sometimes a bit of a father confessor too—loyal and devoted. But so far as his medical qualifications are concerned, I think he'd be better placed as a garrison M.O. in Czernowitz* than personal physician to a Princess.

Artur has already gone off to Turin as advance guard, to arrange everything about the Pullman. He'll meet us there tomorrow evening and then come straight back to Nice.

I've made it clear to him that he must look after our little flock here until we are back again. Not that that will be much of a problem; they are loyal and reliable people. All he'll really have to do is make sure that the horses are exercised and looked after. And that not too much money is spent. Though I've left plenty: no one need starve while we're away.

Creditors he must put off until Louise's return. Our exchequer can't stand any unnecessary little expenses nowadays. Officially we are in Vienna. That's what he is to tell anyone

---

* Now Chernovtsy, in the Ukraine (Trans).

who asks for us. And for the benefit of any especially stubborn creditors, we are in Vienna to raise money.

Artur, bless him, would have liked to come to London with us. And I would have been delighted to have him there. But he is an old soldier, and understands that there are important things at stake here.

'Don't worry,' he said, just as we were saying our goodbyes, 'Artur Ozegovich will hold the fortress of Nice to the last franc! Then you'll have to relieve it.'

He is beyond price. There should be more people like Artur in the world.

VIII

L

On the train Our journey in this Pullman coach is the height of discomfort. One feels hemmed in, unable either to move or to sleep.

Tomorrow morning we shall be in Boulogne; tomorrow evening in London; and the day after will come the interview I dread so much. Every turn of the wheels brings it nearer.

I last saw Aunt Victoria four years ago. It was a big family celebration at Coburg. Duke Ernst II had died in 1893—he was the head of the House of Coburg, but he died without having managed to produce anything that could pass for a heir. Victoria—who sets at least as much store by her ancestral house as she does by England, India and all her overseas possessions put together—managed to arrange it that her son Affie, the Duke of Edinburgh, became the new head of the family, which incidentally was worth a handsome income of seven million crowns a year to him. So Affie and his Russian wife Maria, the daughter of Tsar Alexander II, came over to Coburg. Both were completely at sea with the German language, but no one cared. A year later we were celebrating the marriage of Affie's daughter Melitta with Grand Duke Ernst Ludwig of Hesse.

Victoria's personal appearance was the high point of the Coburg family gathering. To greet her, Willy had her own regiment of Prussian dragoons drawn up on the station platform. The special steamed in, the regimental band played 'God Save the Queen', everyone stood to attention, presented arms, saluted, waved or just stared.

At the door of her car there appeared that fat little figure that has remained imprinted on my memory. Since the death of her husband, whom she always referred to as 'my dearest Albert' she still wore mourning.

She embraced her son, Affie, the new-laid regent of Saxe-Coburg, and her nephew, Willy, the Emperor of Germany. Then she was carefully lifted into a litter and carried the few paces from the platform to the coach. Aunt Victoria's 'castors' were no more: at seventy-five she could scarcely move under her own power.

In the coach she perched on a high cushion next to Willy, for she hated it if anyone sitting beside her was able to look down at her.

Meanwhile a colourful retinue of Indians, Scots and similar exotica had emerged from the coach, to be gaped at by the citizens of Coburg like strange animals in a zoo.

I was first presented to Aunt Victoria at a soirée in the great hall of Ehrenburg Castle. It was the eve of the wedding, and should have been a merry celebration; instead, it was a solemn tribute to mass widowhood.

The assembled company stood in ranks as the Queen, leaning on a stick, entered the hall. Behind her came her eldest daughter Vicky, the widowed Empress Frederick of Germany; and the Duchess Alexandrine, widow of the late head of the House of Coburg.

I must admit that the three figures of permanent mourning in their black silk dresses struck me as ridiculous. Victoria's 'dearest Albert' had already been dead thirty-three years, the Emperor Frederick six, and Duke Ernst over a year.

But Victoria is a really enthusiastic widow. She finds it despicable and immoral for widows to remarry. I heard of a lady-in-waiting of hers whose husband died and whom she dismissed on the spot when the widow announced her intention of remarrying.

It's a positive miracle that Victoria hasn't introduced widow-burning into England. Her favourite and much-envied Indian servant Abdul Karim, the 'Munshi', could easily have persuaded her to do it had he wanted to. He is supposed to have enormous influence over her, as her legendary Scottish servant John Brown did before him.

Why do all these grotesque memories come to my mind when

I am running to her to beg her for help? To allay my fears of this coming meeting?

I don't know whether this woman really rules England. I can't be the judge of that. I only know that she rules her own family. With an iron hand. But—and this is my only hope—with love also. I could feel that even as a child, and I was jealous. At Windsor there was none of that cold insensitivity that pervaded Laeken. Victoria's family life had been exemplary, quite unlike my own parents'. Both marriages had once been arranged by my grandfather. How sad that he had not had the same lucky touch with my own father and mother.

* * *

G

In England   The journey across France went off according to plan, and pleasantly enough. At Lyons and again at Paris we were moved to other trains, but never needed to leave our coach. In that respect it was as good as having a special.

We were very well looked after too. Artur had prudently arranged by telegram with all the major stations along the route to tend to our personal needs, and the best hotels and restaurants in each place had been engaged. At Paris we were even waited on by Maxim's.

As it turned out, the only real privation was the water—more precisely, there was no hot water for washing (or, in my case, shaving). The designers of these otherwise excellently appointed coaches had strangely made no sort of provision for this at all. But in the end the problem was solved. Our coach was left standing for quite a while in a siding at the Gare de Lyon in Paris before being hauled round the *ceinture* to the Gare St-Lazare, whence it set off again later. My servant Mirko made use of this time, with the aid of a railway worker, to bring over a dozen kettles full of hot water from the kitchen of the station restaurant, so that we could all at least freshen ourselves up.

At Boulogne we left the train for the ship. The crossing of the Channel, in calm conditions, went off without incident.

But a great surprise awaited us in Folkestone. A huge crowd, I would guess at least a thousand men, women and children all in highest spirits, packed the quayside between the harbour and the station. The expectant crowds with English colours on their coat lapels and their cloaks, the children waving coloured paper flags, blocked the way from the wharf to the platform.

Louise was so dazzled by the spectacle of all these celebrating Britons that for a moment she seriously believed that they had come to welcome her, and became quite annoyed when I laughed at her.

But a moment later my spirits too had plummeted. When I inquired what all the fuss was about, I learnt that it was in honour of none other than the Queen herself, who—unbelievably!—was on her way to the Riviera. I was told that she had rented a villa on the outskirts of Nice, at Cimiez. Her special was expected at Folkstone any minute, and she would then cross the Channel on board the royal yacht *Victoria and Albert*.

It would be the Riviera! Louise, still rather irritated by my earlier behaviour, immediately began to put the blame on me. She had *told* me we should announce our visit in advance. Then this disaster could never have happened. But of course I had expressly forbidden it. She would thank me to remember that. And now we were paying the price.

We were indeed. The Queen's train had by now arrived at the platform, which was sealed off by soldiers. We couldn't see this for ourselves, but we could hear the musical battle between the crowd bawling 'God Save the Queen' and a military band playing marches. The noise was shattering, and the whole performance had little in common with my own preconceptions of the well bred, reserved British temperament.

Hemmed in by the rejoicing crowd, we could at least see from where we stood the quay—also sealed off—where the royal yacht was tied up. Outside in the roadstead two torpedo boats waited with steam up to escort the *Victoria and Albert* across to France. A naval band which had taken up position by the covered gangway leading on board the yacht now began to play as well, and the general noise and uproar became even worse, if that were possible.

Although it was only a few yards from the train to the ship, the Queen covered the distance in a carriage which had presumably been brought there for the purpose. On the box sat the driver, a Highlander in a kilt. Next to him, with a horn on his knees, was some kind of postilion. Behind the coach on the step stood two footmen. In front and behind the coach rode three officers of different regiments in full dress uniform, and on each side rode a groom in livery, complete with top hat. All on magnificent Arab horses.

We could only see the performance for a few seconds; and we could only just make out the figure of the Queen in her closed carriage. Then it stopped at the covered gangway, and was out of our sight.

'Now Aunt Victoria is being lifted out of the coach into her wheelchair and pushed up the gangway,' said Louise bitterly. 'A fine mess we've made of this.'

An hour later we were in the train, bound for London. After the first shock of the unexpected events at Folkestone we had seriously considered for a moment whether we should abandon our journey on the spot and go back to Nice, and perhaps speak to the Queen there. Perhaps the relaxed southern atmosphere would be a more favourable climate. But then we decided to continue to London, for two reasons. One was purely practical: our luggage, which despite all our economies was still very considerable, could only be reclaimed when we got to London, as Artur had sent it straight there from Turin. There was no chance of doing anything about it in Folkestone. The second reason helped us bear the momentary annoyance of the first.

Louise, who had been on the verge of tears a few minutes earlier, suddenly became cheerful again. She had decided to regard the departure of the Queen of England as a good omen for the success of our mission. Now she was firmly resolved to extract the money from her cousin Edward, the Prince of Wales, from whom she could expect a much more sympathetic hearing than she would have received from her pious aunt. As she explained to me, she would never have been able to visit the Prince in England without first paying her respects to the Queen. That would have been an unforgivable breach of Court etiquette. But now she could turn directly to Edward. She was obviously thrilled at the idea of being able to sort out the whole unpleasant matter with him instead of the Queen.

I find her idea entirely acceptable, and am convinced that now, with a little luck, our journey will not have been in vain. Prince Edward (amazingly referred to by his family as 'Bertie') is well known to be no enthusiast for mourning. That information has reached the darkest corners of the Austro-Hungarian Empire. It is said that he and Crown Prince Rudolf used to enjoy some very merry celebrations together in London. Apparently they even shared the favours of the already legendary English beauty Lily Langtry, who was then energetically pursued by the scions of every rich and noble family in the island.

However things turn out, I said to myself, we've certainly made a good exchange.

* * *

L

We really are travelling under an unlucky star. I slept badly, although my suite at Claridge's is very comfortable, and woke with a severe headache. And this was how I was to go to meet the Prince of Wales? I trembled to think of it. I hadn't even got Dr Schnee to give me a soothing powder. Geza really is treating me very meanly.

Marie Fugger hardly allowed me time to breakfast. She literally hounded me out of bed, because she had promised Geza that I would be ready to leave by eleven. I cannot bear having to rush.

I had been worrying half the night about what to wear. Of course I know how much store Bertie sets by external appearances, and how susceptible he is to feminine charms. Eventually I had decided on a creation from Maison Doucée, a delightful mauve dress with a stand-up collar and slightly crimped sleeves. Now it suddenly transpired that this dress had been left behind in Nice. Everyone blamed everyone else and my temper began to fray; I became really quite ungracious.

There was nothing else for it: I should have to choose another dress. And that took time, of course. I decided on one from Armand, exactly the colour of my hair, with a pink crêpe-de-chine bodice and two pleated flounces on the skirt.

By an absolute miracle the matching hat and the right parasol had been remembered.

I flung a Russian sable stole over my shoulders, looked at myself in the mirror, and found the result satisfactory.

Geza, who is living at the Savoy, had already been at Claridge's for over an hour and was sitting impatiently in the lounge. When I finally made my entrance he stood up and gazed at me with such unconcealed admiration that it made me feel warm and very happy. I would have preferred to linger there, but Geza was very military: duty before pleasure!

Countess Fugger, who doesn't know London, asked the driver to point out the sights for her, while I tried to concentrate on the problem before me. But it was no use. My head was completely empty. All the words that I had so carefully rehearsed during the night, the words which would paint Bertie such an irresistible picture of our problems, were forgotten. Completely forgotten! I was in despair.

Too soon, the coach was drawing up outside Marlborough House.

Footmen helped us down, and we stepped into the great hallway.

There we were welcomed by the Prince's steward, some Scottish lord. Mac-something. In the excitement I forgot his name.

His Royal Highness would be most upset at having missed

me, the Scot explained. He had left the previous day for Sandringham, and so had unfortunately not received the note announcing my arrival. From Sandringham he was going on to Scotland for the shooting, without returning to London first. In fact, it was uncertain when he would be returning to the capital.

When I inquired after the Princess, I was told that she was staying in Copenhagen, visiting her father, the King of Denmark.

So a plague on both their houses!

All the same, I felt an enormous sense of relief. Not that I would admit as much to Geza, of course. The dreaded begging session had been spared me.

I expressed my regrets to the Steward. As I should only be in London for a few days, it would unfortunately be impossible for me to wait for the Prince or the Princess to return.

The Scotsman showed us to our coach, and behaved in every way impeccably.

Marlborough House had been my grandfather's while he was married to the English Princess Charlotte. After her death he had lived on there for many years. I suddenly remembered that, as the coach began to move, and I turned round.

Above the roof the flag was flying!

I could not help myself: I wept with rage, so bitterly hurt and humiliated did I feel. Marie put her arm comfortingly round my shoulders, but I couldn't stop crying.

When we reached the hotel I drew my veil over my face and hurried through the foyer as fast as I could.

Geza was sitting in the lounge flicking through a fashion magazine. 'Back already?' he asked in astonishment.

Marie Fugger said, 'His Royal Highness is not in London. He is staying at Sandringham and then going on to shoot in Scotland.' Dear Marie was trying to spare my feelings.

'His Royal Highness certainly is in London,' I cut in sharply, 'but he has managed to avoid me with some wretched excuses.'

Then I sent Geza away and went to bed.

* * *

G

One may lose a battle yet win a war. Every officer cadet learns that on his first day.

Louise's noble cousin would not receive her.

Her pride is bitterly hurt, and though mine wouldn't be affected in the least by such a thing, I can't say that I'm exactly in high spirits.

This so-called hospitable island doesn't seem to like us. I can see us having to leave very soon. Louise will have to put all her energy into chasing the Queen herself now. As we originally intended. At least she can't evade us in Nice. If we camp day and night outside her villa.

There was no point in trying to discuss new plans with Louise. She was almost inarticulate, and locked herself in her bedroom.

It was the end of the lunch hour. In the streets there was an astonishing coming and going, at least for me, as I was unused to it. Thousands of people, most of them probably office staff and assistants from the shops in Bond Street, Oxford Street and Regent Street, with a few civil servants from the near-by Government offices in Whitehall, were streaming back to work. As well as these, cosmopolitan London naturally has a mass of foreigners of every conceivable colour staying here on holiday. Not forgetting the blasé but obviously wealthy representatives of the native upper crust. Between them they give the street a colour and splendour that one would probably find nowhere else on earth.

I became more and more interested in the spectacle, until my ill humour began to fade. Especially I was fascinated by the crowd of pickpockets, beggars and whores—these last already well represented in Lower Regent Street and the Haymarket, even at this early hour. I've never seen anything like it before. Not even in Paris.

* * *

L

I was lying on my bed in my negligée, staring at the ceiling. Some time or other I must have fallen asleep, because suddenly I found myself waking to hear the Countess whispering in my ear, 'The Prince of Wales!'

I jumped out of bed. But before I could even glance in the mirror he was standing in the doorway.

I didn't understand what she was saying.

'His Royal Highness the Prince of Wales,' she repeated urgently. 'He's next door in the salon.'

My hair hadn't been done, I wasn't even dressed, and I had no idea how I looked. It all annoyed me so much that I just gaped at him stupidly, unable to say a word.

He came over to me, kissed me on both cheeks, then held me at arm's length and looked at me searchingly. 'My God, but you're beautiful,' he said. 'You look like a little girl.'

He had put on a great deal of weight since I had last seen him. His hair was thinner, his beard greying.

'I thought you were at Sandringham,' I managed eventually.

'No, my dear, I'm not at Sandringham. That was a diplomatic excuse.'

'Why?'

'Because it would be most unsuitable for me to receive you, you silly girl!'

'Why?' I asked again.

'I'll explain later. You will have supper with me this evening.' And before I could answer, he went on, 'I'll pick you up at the hotel in an hour.'

* * *

I had never had to get dressed in such a hurry; but things had never gone so well. Ilona did my hair better than ever before, my glorious new evening dress from Worth was out ready in seconds, and I wore the notorious jewellery that Philip had involuntarily given me for my fortieth birthday (and not yet paid for, as M. Hartog in Nice never ceased to remind us).

Punctual to the minute, I found myself sitting with Bertie in his closed carriage, the complete adventuress.

I had decided to get things clear from the start. 'Next time you pretend to be at Sandringham, tell your Steward to lower the flag first.'

'Mac is an imbecile.'

'I thought it was very, very nasty of you.'

'I am overwhelmed with remorse,' he said, beaming all over his face. 'But for this damned coach and these tight trousers I should kneel down on the spot and beg humbly for forgiveness.' So saying he took my hand and kissed it. 'Can you forgive me?'

'Only if you tell me honestly what that pantomime at Marlborough House was all about.'

'Your husband has been most ungentlemanly. He sent the Queen a most detailed letter, complaining bitterly of your behaviour. He told her all sorts of fascinating tit-bits about your disgraceful new life, and asked her most urgently to refuse you any assistance if you should come to her. I received suitably firm instructions myself.'

'Philip is such ... such a dreadful, disgusting ...' I was speechless with rage.

Edward laughed.

'How Philip, of all people, can call *me* degenerate ...'

'He does though,' confirmed Bertie enthusiastically. 'And to me, my dear cousin, it makes you twice as attractive.'

We drove to Kettner's, a French restaurant in Soho. M. Kettner had once been head chef to Napoleon III. He had settled in London before the collapse of the French Empire, and opened a restaurant here.

A private dining-room had been reserved for us, very much

like a Viennese *separée*. That amused me greatly. Because I know I can speak freely with Bertie, I told him the whole story of the private room at Sacher's, and what followed.

Bertie was vastly amused and laughed at my imitation of Franz Joseph conducting that fateful interview in Stephanie's apartments.

'And the root of the trouble—what does he look like?'

'Wonderful,' I said fervently. 'He has the loveliest soft brown eyes, the body of an Adonis, he rides like a god—and he adores me.'

'I must say, I find it extraordinarily depressing to sit with a desirable woman in a private room and have to hear her singing the praises of her lover!'

'I was only answering your question,' I apologized.

Bertie sent for M. Kettner, and after consultation they agreed on a menu that turned out to be exquisite.

Bertie would have been quite happy to chatter, joke and flirt a little all evening but I could never allow that. As soon as it was at all possible, I led the conversation round to my own situation. I explained my straitened circumstances, though of course without reference to the sinister bill. I confessed that I had come to London to ask his mother to help, and had unfortunately missed her.

Bertie drew happily on his cigar. 'The notion of asking my mother to help finance your ... adventures is an exceptionally original one, but alas somewhat lacking in realism. You should know what a prude she is. After Philip's letter, you would never have been allowed to see her.'

Now I plucked up all my courage and asked him for money.

That seemed to alarm him. 'What sort of sum are we discussing?' he inquired.

'Seventy-five thousand pounds,' I said. (Geza had worked it out for me.)

'I'm afraid you've come to the wrong address. I'm flattered to think you expect me to be able to let you have seventy-five thousand. That is exactly half the income that my thrifty mama allows me for an entire year. Out of that I have to support a number of ladies of my acquaintance, and then of course I have an excellent wife to keep as well. Not to mention all my other expenses. The money is never enough, of course. I am as deeply in debt as you! But then I don't worry my head over it, and I should advise you to do the same.'

'You must have more sympathetic creditors than I have.'

'Very possibly,' he conceded.

'Probably they regard it as an honour to be permitted to lend money to the future King of England.'

'Very possibly,' said Bertie, now all smiles again. 'Fortunately they don't realize that my mother is immortal, while my own liver is nearly sixty years old and due to retire. Your health!' And he raised a glass of Champagne and drank to me.

When the waiter had cleared away the last plates, opened another bottle of Champagne, and discreetly withdrawn, Bertie lit another cigar, blew a few clouds of smoke, and asked with evident casualness, 'Did you enjoy the dinner?'

'It was superb. Really quite exceptional,' I assured him, truthfully enough.

'I'm glad to hear it,' he went on. 'Because now you will be able to stand it better if I tell you the absolute truth.'

'I could stand it well enough however hungry I was. Because I am sure that you mean only the best for me.'

'Quite right, my dear, quite right,' he said, refilling the glasses. 'It would be madness for me, of all people, to criticize your morals. That would never occur to me—and even your husband would hardly dare to do it.'

'Of that I am less sure.'

'Well, that's neither here nor there,' he went on. 'I'm only concerned with you—I'm very fond of you, Louise. You're a very silly girl, stubborn as a mule, and if you go on like this you will get into very deep trouble indeed.'

I didn't at all care for this sort of scolding. 'What are you talking about?' I asked; it sounded a little peevish, but that seemed not to worry him.

'This: you're breaking the rules of the game. Your father cannot overlook it, my mother would never overlook it, and even Philip can't condone it. Look at me—God knows I'm no faithful spouse. But I follow the rules.'

'What are the rules?' I demanded stubbornly. 'I don't know them.'

'Don't talk nonsense. Of course you know them. We all knew them before we could add two and two. It's all a matter of appearances. Of what people seem to be. Do what you like, but do it discreetly, so that other people hear and see nothing.'

There it was again: my father's 'umbrella'. Everyone had the same answer.

'It's your misfortune to be a woman,' he went on. 'The rules favour men marvellously.'

'There's nothing I can do to change that.'

'I should hope not, indeed.' Bertie's sermon was for ever spiced with these little compliments. 'Many ladies of whom I am very fond have had the same trouble as you. Married women, daughters of the greatest houses in the land, and so on and so forth. But they all managed to avoid scandal.'

I could not possibly let that pass. 'Now, please wait a moment,' I cried. 'If I were to try and count all the scandals in which you and your ladies have been involved, I should need several more hands. Why do you think a gaggle of pious matrons assembles every week to thunder against the immorality of Marlborough House, and kneel down with the Bishop to pray for the moral salvation of England's future king?'

'Newspaper rumour. Nothing more,' he contested. 'Anyway, we weren't discussing me. Let's assume that you manage by some incredible stroke of luck to get together seventy-five thousand pounds. So you pay your most urgent debts, and no doubt there would be a little left over. What happens when that has gone? How will you manage then? Tell me that.'

I had asked myself the same question a hundred times, but never found an answer.

'Of course, it's easier for me to criticize than to be helpful. I think you should go to Philip—'

'Never!'

'Let me finish. There is no other way. There must be a

reconciliation between you. For appearances' sake, that's all. You'll have to send your Adonis packing, at least for a little while, until this blows over. If you are very tactful and very careful, things will sort themselves out. Even Franz Joseph will relent in the end.'

'It's no good. I *can't*,' I said passionately, feeling myself near to tears. 'I can't explain it, but I have such an overwhelming physical aversion to Philip that I couldn't bear even to touch his hand, to be in the same room with him and least of all ... well, I needn't go any further.'

He shrugged. 'You must lead your own life, Louise. I can only say what I should do in your place. If a reconciliation is really out of the question, then for God's sake think out a touching story and try your luck with the Queen. Miracles can happen.'

'What sort of touching story?' I didn't understand what he meant.

'I'll give you an example. A charming, lively young Countess, whose name I shall not mention, was amusing herself with one of her good-looking footmen. Everyone knew that she had simply seduced him. Well, there were complications, and she had a child. Her family were completely outraged, and would have nothing more to do with her. Whereupon the Countess went to the Queen and confided in her. She managed to arouse the Queen's deepest sympathy. The poor girl, as my mother put it later, had been first chloroformed and then raped by the unscrupulous lackey, and the heartless family were punishing the innocent victim, instead of bringing the real culprit to justice. Well, if you can think of something like that to convince the Queen of your innocence, you'll have her eating out of your hand.'

'That won't be easy,' I said, sighing.

'One more word of advice: don't bring me into it. She has the worst possible opinion of me. She considers me lacking in ability, disapproves of my way of life, complains about my debts, and already weeps for her Empire when she thinks of my accession to the throne.'

'I must confess,' I said in a whisper, 'that I'm afraid of her.'

'So am I.'

It sounded so sincere that I couldn't keep a straight face, though a few seconds before I hadn't felt in the least like laughing.

'Don't laugh,' he said, laughing himself. 'I have been afraid of her all my life. But you and I are not the only ones. Your father is afraid of her too. Even though she likes him, and is even prepared to overlook his indiscretions. But when he meets her he trembles with fright, like a schoolboy with a strict teacher.'

The thought of my dreadful father quaking before the little old lady cheered me up. 'He has a lot to answer for,' I said.

'Who hasn't, Louise? Let us be forgiving. So, go to Nice and try your luck with my mother. And be warned: she is pious, bigoted and prudish. Scandal is an abomination to her; divorce is a sin. She is autocratic and extraordinarily stubborn. But she has a kind heart. Very kind, if one knows how to appeal to it. That is your chance. Your only chance!'

As we drove back, he put his arm round me in the darkness of the carriage. It was not at all a cousinly gesture.

'Why don't you send your Adonis back where he came from and stay on in London?' he whispered in my ear. 'I think we two would get along together very well.'

I tried to laugh it off. 'There's too much competition here.'

'Nothing for you to worry about.'

'It isn't as simple as that, anyway,' I said evasively.

'Where there's a will there's a way,' he answered, and he already sounded possessive. 'Tomorrow morning I leave for Sandringham.'

'Am I supposed to believe that?'

'From now on you are supposed to believe everything I say! Every afternoon a special train leaves St Pancras to bring my guests to Sandringham. You need only ask for the Prince of

Wales's special. I shall be waiting for you, my dear little cousin. Remember that.'

At that moment, fortunately, the carriage pulled up outside the Savoy.

Our farewells, under the eyes of the liveried pageboys who opened the door, were very formal and decorous. Bertie had to make do with kissing my hand. I thanked him, answered his significant 'Au revoir' with nothing more than a smile, and disappeared inside the hotel.

Upstairs Geza was waiting. He had been sitting in my salon for three hours. He took me in his arms, grumbling about the smell of cigar-smoke in my hair, and kissed me.

IX

G

Paris, 9 April 1898 We arrived here yesterday evening. This time, of course, Louise is not living in the Palais Coburg, as she had done in previous years, but in a hotel—the Westminster. I am in the Grand Hotel again, in my old rooms.

The surprise that greeted us on our arrival in Paris was no less than we had met in Folkestone a week before, though here the agent was not a Queen but a humble letter. From Artur Ozegovich. I had cabled him that we should be staying in Paris a few days before our return to Nice. Now it begins to look to me as though Nice will not be seeing us again after all!

Artur's letter ran as follows.

DEAR GEZA

Fortune has been kind to keep Her Royal Highness away from Nice during these recent days. And you too can thank your lucky stars that you weren't here. You haven't missed much.

I can scarcely describe what has been going on since we parted in Turin—and still is going on. I can only hope that your journey met with the expected success, and that you are on your way home with a sack of gold (although you said nothing of such matters in your telegram), for otherwise I must advise you to give Nice as wide a berth as possible. But first things first.

I had hardly got back from Turin when Dr Schnee told me that M. Hartog, the jeweller, had called personally at the Villa Paradis, and demanded in very impolite fashion to be received by Her Royal Highness. When the Doctor assured him that she had left, this normally well mannered gentleman lost control of himself and began to utter all manner of slanders and threats against the Princess. He grew so noisy about it that the footmen and maids came running in, thinking Dr Schnee was in need of assistance. The little bauble merchant can think himself lucky he didn't have me to reckon with—I'd have given him a lesson in how to behave in other people's houses, and especially a house tenanted by a Princess of the Blood. It seems to me that our French friends have forgotten their famous good manners since their country had the misfortune to become a republic. But this upheaval was no more than a gentle hint of what was to come.

Next day the same little man turned up again, waving an official payment order. To be on the safe side, he'd brought the bailiff along too. Fortunately I could truthfully assure them that there was no money in the house (the cash float that you left with me was safe in my hotel) and that the Princess had taken all her jewellery with her. I told them, as we had agreed, that she was in Vienna to discuss business matters with her Steward. I had heard from you, I said, that you would be receiving a large sum of money there on the Princess's behalf, and I was expecting you both back in Nice any day.

There was no reasoning with Hartog; he wanted his money and he wanted it now. The good bailiff, conscious of the fact that this was no ordinary defaulter but the authentic daughter of the King of the Belgians and a lady hitherto well thought of on the Riviera, found the whole matter distasteful. Finally, with great reluctance, he officially sealed the cupboard containing Her Royal Highness's wardrobe, swearing long and solemnly that he would remove the seal again the moment the owner returned, as he had no doubt that the whole thing was a mistake, and M. Hartog's claims would be settled in full.

I was glad when the two of them left us in peace. As yet I had no idea what still lay ahead of us.

The jeweller or the bailiff must have talked. Perhaps it was even one of our own people that couldn't keep his mouth shut. The fact is that the story of the distraint of Her Royal Highness's goods spread like wildfire the length and breadth of Nice. Next morning, very early, Schnee sent a footman to me at the hotel with the urgent request that I should come at once to the Villa Paradis, where a mob of creditors was already running amok.

I leapt into my clothes and rushed to the doctor's aid.

Outside the locked gates of the estate I saw a good dozen people gathered. They were shouting at poor Schnee, who was standing with a footman inside the locked gates and trying to calm them. One man was wrenching with both hands at the bars of the gate and trying to force the lock. Others, probably not directly involved, were watching the spectacle with obvious interest.

I sent the lad who had come to fetch me round to the stable, to alert the grooms. They were on the spot within minutes. Between us we commanded sufficient respect to control the situation for the moment. The doctor, much alarmed, managed to open the gate briefly, and we entered the grounds without any of the crowd daring to hinder us or try to force their way in after us. Schnee and I went on into the house, while the servants, on my instructions, took up their positions outside.

It had all started, I now learnt, when as a result of the events of yesterday some fool of a tailor had turned up with a bill at seven in the morning and demanded immediate payment. While Schnee, who had been alerted by one of the footmen, was still dealing with the fellow the butcher Vernon arrived; Vernon's steak, as we all know, is superb but his manners seem to leave something to be desired. Nevertheless Schnee managed to calm them both, by promising them payment of their accounts in full the very next day. But in the street outside the house they met Maillot who had somehow or other met up with the proprietress of the milliner's shop on the Quai St-Jean-Baptiste (a pretty, rather cuddly blonde, as I'm sure you'll remember, but also a very tough one). By a stroke of luck, Schnee had had the garden door closed again after the first two creditors had left. So now all four were standing outside and pouring out their hearts to each other. Suddenly they all started clamouring to see Her Royal Highness's secretary. The doctor sent word to them that you were away.

Within a very short time there were more than a dozen people gathered outside and demanding entry. There were even two women from the flower market there. The normally quiet street became crowded; passers-by stopped to join the crowd. A general chatter and argument began to start.

This was the position when Schnee, who had no idea what to do next, finally sent for me. The footman who came for me had to leave secretly, climbing the fence behind the house, to avoid being detected by the crowd.

And so, a few hours later, there occurred a scene which certainly did little credit to the name of the villa and has since been the talk of all Nice. The details of what happened outside the house I cannot tell you. At any rate, by late afternoon over a hundred people had congregated there. Bakers, tailors, coal- and timber-merchants, drivers, waiters, flower-girls, laundresses, seamstresses, and the devil knows what else besides. To say nothing of pickpockets and riffraff from the docks. And of course the innumerable gawping bystanders.

Shortly before eleven one of the grooms came and told me that the mob was making ready to smash down the garden gate. I immediately went out to the courtyard but the gate was already down. I saw our own people trying heroically to keep back the tide. They were overwhelmed. I quickly slammed the heavy oak door, at the very moment that the first infuriated fists began to beat against it. Then someone shouted, 'Round the back! We can do it at the back!'. The noise at the front door subsided, and I ran into the salon. The leaders had already smashed in the glass doors and were standing right inside the room. When they saw me they seemed to come to their senses for an instant, but the others —thirty or forty of them—were pushing from behind, and the scum of the gutters poured through the whole house.

This is exactly—*exactly*—what the French Revolution must have been like. Ignoring the bailiff's official seal, they tore open cupboards and drawers and looted whatever they could get their hands on and carry away. Dresses, coats, shoes, parasols, hats—even underclothes. When the police arrived the whole brawl was already over. The villa looked—and still looks—like a battlefield.

I will spare you—and myself—the full details of the endless police inquiries and interrogations we have had since then. The Mayor of Nice personally sent in his card and apologized for the disgraceful behaviour of his citizens. The local press has written of nothing else ever since. At first they were all against the thugs who had dragged the good name of the town in the dirt; but then they became spiteful, as journalists will, and indulged themselves in long outpourings about the allegedly enormous debts of the Princess, and her private life, with many mentions of your own name. Today, according to the *Gazette*, His Majesty King Leopold II found himself unable to escape his daughter's creditors, who, since the full story of events here has become known, have been arriving from San Remo, Merano and even Vienna. The King (according to the papers) has engaged a special bodyguard to defend him against these importunities, and has announced publicly that he will bear absolutely no responsibility for the Princess's debts.

Yesterday Dr Schnee, acting on his own initiative, sold the horses, which enabled him to settle some of the most urgent bills. I know, my dear fellow, how deeply this particular disaster will affect you, but with things as they were I didn't see that there was anything I could do to oppose the sale, particularly since there are signs of discontent now among our own servants, and these signs are growing from day to day. At any rate, I shall make sure that we keep back enough of the money to pay their back wages and also, if it should be necessary, their transport back to Vienna or their homes.

And so, as things have turned out, I can see no further

prospect of an enjoyable stay here for any of us, including Her Royal Highness. I ask you therefore to send me further instructions as quickly as possible, preferably by telegram, as to what I am to do now. Instructions should be sent to Poste Restante, Nice.

I am sincerely sorry to have to give you such wretched news, but—I say again—I am only glad that you and especially Her Royal Highness have not had to endure with me the complete breakdown of normal human standards which has taken place here.

This is the longest letter I have ever written. I wish it had never been necessary.

Please let me hear from you very soon.

Your loyal friend

ARTUR

* * *

L

Scandal is an abomination to the Queen, Bertie had warned me. A finer example of a scandal than the one now unrolling under her very eyes in Nice would be beyond the wildest imagination. Any attempt to go to her for help has become entirely pointless.

This morning a Prince Oscar of Hohenlohe was announced at the hotel.

Marie Fugger and I gazed at one another in consternation. How does anyone know that we are in Paris? We have visited no restaurants, taken all our meals in our rooms and scarcely ventured out of doors—all to keep our presence here a secret.

The Countess eventually suggested that, despite my express wishes to the contrary, the hotel must have published my name in its list of guests.

We debated whether we should receive the Prince or not,

and concluded that the devil you know is better than the devil you don't. I had him asked up.

Prince Hohenlohe, who is quite a young man, gave a very Prussian performance, trying to conceal his obvious distaste for the task that brought him here behind a veneer of insolence.

He had been to Nice, he informed us. When he told Ozegovich that he had urgent business with me on behalf of Duke Ernst Günther of Schleswig-Holstein, Ozegovich gave him my Paris address.

I was immediately concerned, afraid that something had happened to Dora.

'Have no fear, Your Royal Highness, the Princess is in excellent health,' Hohenlohe assured me. 'She asks me to give you her fondest regards.'

'What is the matter, then? Why have you been sent to me?' I asked impatiently.

'It has been suggested that under the circumstances Your Royal Highness would prefer Princess Dora not to return for the present,' he mumbled.

'To what circumstances do you refer?'

'It seems that certain ... complications ... have arisen in Nice.'

'I know nothing of that,' I said coldly.

'Duke Ernst Günther thinks it would certainly be your wish to spare Princess Dora the excitements consequent on these ... complications,' he went on undeterred. 'He has therefore sent me to ask Your Royal Highness's permission for Princess Dora to remain a little longer at Primkenau.'

'That is against our agreement!' I exploded. 'The Duke promised me solemnly that my daughter would be brought back on the agreed date, without fail. I demand that Dora comes here to Paris. At once! In the next few days! Tell them that —no, send a telegram. And do it this minute!'

'Forgive me, Your Royal Highness, but that would be pointless.'

'What ever can you mean?'

'I regret to inform you that under the present circumstances there can be no question of the Princess's return here.'

'What are you talking about? In that case I shall telegraph Primkenau myself.'

'That will serve no purpose,' he countered. 'His Majesty King Leopold has been observing events in Nice at first hand, and has promptly informed your husband of everything that has happened there.'

Now I heard the truth of it at last: Philip had given orders that Dora was not to be allowed to return to me. For the present she should stay with Ernst Günther's mother, then travel straight to Vienna.

I felt as if this young coxcomb had slapped my face. My consternation was such that I couldn't utter a word.

'I think it would be better for you to leave now,' said the Countess Fugger, and showed him abruptly out of the room.

I locked myself in my bedroom. After ten minutes, or it may have been two hours, someone knocked. Geza.

I opened the door.

He took me in his arms and looked down at me searchingly. 'Was it very bad?' he asked.

The Countess seemed to have told him everything.

I nodded.

'Don't take it so hard. It's a blessing that Dora isn't coming back,' he tried to console me. 'She doesn't worry about you, and you needn't worry about her. She would only be in the way while we do what has to be done.'

'They deceived me! The invitation from Ernst Günther's mother was just a pretext to take Dora away from me.' I fought back my tears. 'Can't you see how cunningly they planned it all? My father telegraphs to Philip, Philip notifies Ernst Günther, Ernst Günther keeps Dora. Stephanie doesn't answer the telegram; my mother hasn't written to me for two years. They're all in league against me.'

Geza shrugged his shoulders. 'It's about time that penny dropped.'

He was too preoccupied with his own thoughts to spare any time for my grief.

'We've pretty well come to the end,' he said. 'Or have you still got some father, grandfather, uncle or cousin who can give us the money for the bill?'

The bill! I had completely forgotten it. 'No,' I said. 'There is obviously not a soul in the world who will advance me so much as a guilder.'

Geza began to pace up and down the room.

He stopped by the window and stared out into the street. After a while, he said: 'If I disappear, Philip will take you back. He will forgive you and pay the bill; your life will go on as it did before. Or not so very differently.'

'And you?'

'I shall go to Varazdin, tell the regiment that I'm recovered from the malaria, and report fit for duty.'

'Is that what you want?'

'I can bear it. Will you go back to Philip?'

'Is that what *you* want?'

'No!'

I was vastly relieved.

'We'll crawl out of this somehow,' said Geza. 'But I must have time to think.'

'Why don't we just stay in Paris?'

'Hohenlohe will already have wired Philip to tell him your address. Every moment makes it more likely that the police will turn up here—the Vienna authorities will send them,' Geza answered. He looked at me for a moment. 'If you're quite sure you don't want to creep off home——'

'Never!'

'... then I know what to do. We'll go to my mother.'

'To your mother!' He had scarcely ever mentioned her before.

'She is a country châtelaine,' he said. 'She lives in a little castle—at least, that what she calls it. In fact it's just an above-average farmhouse. But it's tucked away in the Croatian mountains, not very far from Zagreb. They won't find it so easy to trace us there.'

'And what would that achieve?'

'We should have time to think, without being hounded by creditors. The bill falls due on 20 June. I don't think anything much can happen to us before then. I hope not, anyway. At Lobor——'

'Lobor?'

'That's the name of the place. At Lobor we shall at last have some peace. Also, our family lawyer lives there, old Dr Tonkovich. I can ask his advice. He was my late father's best friend; he's clever, skilful, and patronized by all the best Croatian families.'

The thought that Geza's simple friends might be able to save me where my own all-powerful family had failed was simply grotesque. Yet to me it was like a bright ray of sunshine on a dark horizon. 'Do you think your mother will accept me?'

'She will count it an honour to receive you.'

'But suppose we get her into trouble too?'

'That wouldn't stop her helping us. She will love and protect you as if you were her own daughter.'

X

G

12 April, en route for Croatia Across France in a Pullman again, but this time in the opposite direction.

In a few days our situation has taken a marked turn for the worse. Not that it was good when we set out for England. But now our whole future is one great question mark.

This morning Artur boarded the train at Turin. I had sent him express instructions by telegram.

He reported again, in detail, everything that had happened in Nice. I can only say that I am sincerely glad to have been spared this pantomime. So our ill-fated journey to England achieved one thing at least.

Dr Schnee will wind up Louise's household in Nice. (So far as there is anything left at Le Paradis *to* wind up.) Artur has already released a number of our servants. All received their wages in full and the price of a ticket home.

Artur told Schnee he would meet us in Paris and send him further news from there. But for that news Schnee will have to wait. The whole story was a red herring to set a false trail for the large number of creditors still gathered in Nice. For it is vital that no one should know where we are really going. Not the creditors, and especially not Kleeborn, the Viennese Public Prosecutor.

As far as he could, Artur provided Schnee with money. I hope Schnee doesn't delay until everything is gone, but takes himself off to Austria in good time with the remnants of our faithful staff.

Milan lies behind us. The plain of Lombardy is full of the

smell of spring. In Croatia it must already be fine and warm.

I am happy to be coming home again, even if the reason is not a particularly pleasant one.

I have agreed with Artur that we shall start by installing ourselves with him at Brežice.* From there I shall go on alone to Lobor, to make everything ready for Louise's arrival. And to have a preliminary word with Mama. I should like Louise to feel at home in Lobor the moment she crosses its threshold.

On the Adriatic   By Venice we had already been travelling nearly 48 hours. Louise would like to take two days to recover from the tiring rail journey. But I insisted on pushing on. For us to book in at a hotel in Venice could never have passed off unnoticed. And that is one risk that we simply dare not take.

So we hardly paused at all in the City of the Lagoon. Artur had the good fortune to find a ship that was not only sailing almost immediately, but was making for Fiume without putting in at Trieste. This direct route cuts the sea time by half. In any case, Trieste is crawling with the Austrian Navy. Louise could easily be recognized by one of the officers. In Fiume there is much less danger. And once we put the city behind us we shall be in deepest Croatia, with not a soul to care a damn about us.

In Croatia   No one asked to see our papers when we landed in Fiume. At last something has gone as I had hoped. A good omen for our stay here.

I leant over the rail as the ship entered the Gulf of Kvarner. Off Lovran, the ship held a course close to the shoreline. I recognized every house, every tree.

Even before Abbazia hove in sight, Louise was on deck. We stood side by side in silence.

* Small town 30 miles north-west of Zagreb (Trans).

From behind a spit of land appeared the hotel in which we had spent those first mad nights together over two years ago. Louise raised a hand and pointed over to the shore. She stood like that until the hotel had vanished from sight again.

Without looking at me, she said, 'You are not going to send me back to Philip—is that clear?'

'Precisely what I intended to do, Your Royal Highness,' I teased her.

'I'm serious, you know,' she said. And tears ran down her cheeks as she said it.

North of Zagreb From special train—those were the days —via Pullman, then the more or less comfortable first-class compartment (Fiume–Zagreb) and now a prehistoric narrow-gauge railway. But I absolutely refuse to read any symbolic significance into this steady decline. Especially when I look out of the window. Then I see a familiar countryside; just to look at it makes me feel better, and nearer home.

It seemed wise to keep our stay in Zagreb on as tight a rein as possible. I would have liked to play guide and show Louise the lovely old town, but we could not disregard the risk of meeting one of my old comrades from the garrison at Varazdin, only fifty miles away. Zagreb is the headquarters of XIII Corps, to which my own 13th Uhlans belong. Any officer of the regiment can come to Corps HQ at any time—and with our usual luck we should have walked straight into his arms. We must avoid that at all costs.

I'm pleased to see Louise watching the country and the people with obvious interest. And that even the funny little railway line affords her a certain amusement, even though we've been travelling three full days from Paris now, and sometimes she can hardly keep her eyes open.

In an hour we shall be at Konjscina. There we shall be met by Artur's people, and at Brežice Louise will at last be able to get some proper sleep.

* * *

151

L

Brežice, Thursday   BREŽICE. I have never before in my life even heard of this place with its unpronounceable name. No railway leads here; no railway leads anywhere from here. But now I am in Brežice. The last station joined to civilization by a railway line is a good hour from here. It begins with a K. Although Geza and Ozegovich too have told me the name a hundred times I simply can't remember it. In any case, I have no great desire to immortalize it in my mind. It was nothing particularly attractive.

The journey from K. here was accomplished in a rig that must date from the days of Maria Theresa. Or possibly even from those of Suleiman the Great, when the Turks still ruled here.

Like Geza's mother, Ozegovich refers to his family home as a 'château'. This is obviously a common form of exaggeration in Croatia. In fact it's a simple, sprawling building, looking rather like the servants' quarters on a smallish country estate.

Ozegovich's parents and his sister are nice people who speak quite good German. Almost everyone else in the house speaks Croatian, and nothing else. And I don't understand a word. The servants chatter, babble and cannot appreciate that my own servants don't understand them any better however loudly they shout.

The 'château' is very well kept. The floors are of unvarnished, white scrubbed wood; the furniture antiquated but solid. They seem not to have heard of wallpaper here, and the walls are simply painted white.

Ulrike Ozegovich, the sister, handed me a lovely little bouquet when I arrived and made an unsuccessful attempt at a formal court curtsey. Artur's mother kissed my hand; his father compromised with a deep bow.

The parents have given up their own bedroom for me, while I remain here. I suspect it's the only usable one in the house. So Marie Fugger and I will spend our nights in the Ozegoviches' double bed.

My maids look very sulky, so I haven't asked them what sort of accommodation they have been offered.

In the evening I found that the Ozegoviches had asked all the dignitaries of Brežice and the outlying villages to dinner. This was a breach of the agreement that our presence should be kept as secret as possible. But apparently they couldn't resist the temptation to show us off a little.

A long table had been laid: it almost collapsed under the weight of this giant banquet. There was wild boar, venison, hare, pheasant, partridge, veal—all in quantity enough to feed a regiment. Everything was served with no particular subtlety, but tasted excellent. The wine, produced locally, is heavy and aromatic.

The guests behaved rather gauchely. Perhaps they felt constrained by my presence. The art of conversation is one not familiar to them, and respect for me apparently deprived most of them of speech altogether. The ladies' dresses had a rather home-made look, while the evening dress of their partners could obviously look back on a long and useful life. I did my best to be polite and friendly, but the meal passed tediously and formally.

Every now and then I caught Geza's eye. He has long outgrown this society—if indeed he ever belonged to it, which I can hardly believe. He seemed to be embarrassed by them, yet at the same time to be afraid that I would hurt their feelings by some careless word—which of course I could never possibly have done. When he saw that I was talking to them kindly and without any condescension, he smiled at me gratefully.

After I had endured it all bravely for some hours, I expressed my thanks to my hosts, and Countess Fugger and I went up to our room.

There everything had been made as comfortable as possible.

We sank deep into huge, soft mattresses, while the monstrous duvets nearly stifled us.

Our disappearance had given the guests their tongues back. Far into the night laughter and loud voices came echoing up to us. At last we heard the coachmen at their work; with a cracking of whips and the clatter of hooves the coaches pulled away.

There followed a silence that was almost overwhelming.

'Good night, Your Royal Highness,' came Marie Fugger's voice softly from the mountain of feathers at my side.

For a moment I was shocked: had there been a hint of irony in her voice? But then I thrust the suspicion from me.

'Good night, Marie,' I said, equally softly.

The hospitable Ozegovich household could not accept that my morning meal never consists of anything more than a cup of chocolate. On the tray that Antonia brought up to my room were heaped butter, honey, eggs, jam and every possible kind of bread. Antonia explained that she had done her best to resist when this giant breakfast was thrust upon her, but her protests had been greeted with incomprehension. She had failed to make any impression on the Croatian babel in the kitchen.

Entirely against my usual custom, I fell to with enthusiasm. Everything tasted of the country, excellent and fresh. The sun was shining outside, and I felt really well.

When I was dressed, Geza was announced. In this house he is a stickler for correct etiquette, which pleases me.

He had come to say goodbye, he told me. He was about to leave for Lobor to tell his mother of our impending visit. He promised to be back in Brežice by evening.

Ozegovich appeared a little later to ask whether I should like his father to show me round the estate. Since with the best will in the world there is absolutely nothing else to do in Brežice, I agreed.

Old Mr Ozegovich, so reticent only yesterday, became a mine of information as he showed us round the outbuildings.

With old-world charm and respectful courtesy he led Marie and myself across a yard and past a steaming dunghill to the byres, pigsties and stables.

He has an almost personal relationship with his animals. In that he reminds me of Geza talking about his horses. Probably it is a Croatian characteristic to set brute beasts almost on a par with human beings.

The old man told us the name and age of every sow and knew exactly how many litters she had thrown in her lifetime.

When we came to the horses, he fished a couple of carrots out of his jacket pocket, and gave them to me to feed to a dear little gangling foal. It was fun to feel the animal's soft, warm lips against my hand.

The byre was spotlessly clean, but the cows alas were not at home, the proprietor explained; they were out at pasture. In a separate, solidly built compartment we could admire Dragomir, the stud bull. He looks very impressive and fearsome. He has sired hundreds of offspring: all the cattle in Brežnice and district are his sons and daughters, old Ozegovich told us proudly.

Then we made a tour of inspection through the fields. I sat beside the owner on the box and was allowed to drive. I've driven often in the Prater, of course, and on our estates in Hungary, but rarely have I derived so much pleasure from it.

The countryside is delightful—wooded hills and cultivated fields jumbled up together. The people are friendly, and their peasant costume very becoming.

On our return we sat down to a splendid family lunch. Frau von Ozegovich and Ulrike were more forthcoming than on the previous day, though one could hold a proper conversation only with the master of the house, whom I found myself liking more and more every minute.

After lunch Marie and I crawled back into our feather fortress. I was quite exhausted with the fresh air, the exercise, the good meal and the heavy wine.

Paris, London, Nice, Vienna—they are on another planet.

I look forward to the future with renewed hope. In this simple land one can live one's own life. Perhaps Geza and I really will find a breathing-space in Lobor. Perhaps he will manage to solve these stupid financial problems; perhaps everything will turn out all right. Perhaps.

* * *

G

The reception I got from Fiedler should have put me on my guard. None of the pleasure and enthusiasm that one expects at a meeting of old friends. But I was already too involved with the prespect of seeing my mother to take much notice of the behaviour of our old steward.

Mama received me in the salon.

It was not only my own unusual situation that made me go to meet her with an emotion I had never felt before. For the first time, I think, I was worried by her appearance. Before, one would always have thought her younger than she really was. Now I found her aged beyond her years, and it frightened me. Though I didn't show what I felt, of course.

I had never doubted that this interview would turn out as I hoped. So the turn that the conversation immediately took was a complete surprise to me.

Mama knew already where I had spent the previous night. And she knew who with.

For that we must thank old Ozegovich's idiotic brainwave of asking half the district to dinner in our honour!

My mother told me without preamble that she disapproved as strongly as possible of my relationship with Louise. I should not think for a moment of introducing her to the Princess. She could only hope, she said, that our unorthodox visit to the Ozegovich house implied a last bastion of decency which I myself had erected in a moment of lucidity, realizing how

156

impossible it was to bring my extraordinary *ménage* under the same roof with my own mother.

'My reputation and honour have been blameless all my life. So long as I am alive and mistress of Lobor, nothing will change that,' declared Mama with unshakable resolution. 'If you think you can go on living in sin with this Princess, who has abandoned her husband and her children like a common slut; if you think you can hold our honoured family name to be the laughing-stock of the cheap press, then you must find some other base for your dishonourable life—not your parents' house! Alone, you will always be welcome here. So whether you stay, and if so for how long, is entirely in your own hands.'

I could not conceal my disappointment—and my shame. My mother had made a decision whose consequences must have been perfectly clear to her. Without even having discussed it with me first! Without knowing Louise! On the basis of nothing but common newspaper scandal and God knows what dirty rumours. My consternation was transformed into violent anger.

'What are you talking about?' I shouted at my mother. 'You give credence to gutter scandal before you even try to hear my side of the story. You sit in judgement on matters of which you know and understand nothing, and on people you have never met!'

I was using my parade-ground voice. I realized that, given our respective temperaments, this sort of dispute would lead to nothing less than catastrophe. A catastrophe which for deeply personal reasons I wished to avoid above all things. But I could not help myself.

There had never been any scene between my mother and myself remotely comparable to this. Yet she was not in the least impressed by my demonstration. On the contrary: she seemed even to have expected it, or something very like it. That was the only explanation I could find for the calmness with which she met the onslaught. Her iron self-control, her cold composure and her show of imperturbability as she clung to her resolve drove me to distraction.

'The Princess is one of the most honourable women who has ever lived!' I raged, as if I had already decided that only sheer volume could carry conviction. 'She will come to this house tomorrow, and she will find shelter here from a world of liars and hypocrites! I have given her my word. I expect everyone—and that means you in particular, Mama—to receive her with respect and friendship. I shall watch you all carefully, and God help *anyone*—without exception—who does not observe the rules of hospitality. It would be as well for you to make that clear to Baron Fiedler. And he can pass the message on to the others, down to the junior herd-boy! We shall arrive in the early afternoon. It will be the first time that a King's daughter has set foot in Lobor. You, Mama, will do everything you can to ensure that her reception is worthy of the occasion.'

Without waiting for an answer I stormed out of the room.

In the courtyard I met Fiedler. I told him that my mother wished to speak to him and was waiting for him in the salon.

Then I swung into the saddle, clapped spurs to my horse, and galloped away.

* * *

L

Geza is back. I was as happy to see him as if he had been away for days.

His mother sends me her warmest respects and says she is looking forward greatly to my arrival.

Tomorrow we shall go to Lobor.

Countess Mattachich did *not* send me her warmest respects. I was not welcome in her house. She was not prepared to spend a single night under the same roof with me.

Geza had to confess that he had lied to me. He thought he had brought her to her senses, but when we arrived we found the doors locked against us.

Geza battered with both fists on the gate. Eventually a grating opened and the frightened little face of a maid appeared. She informed us that the Countess had left post-haste very early that morning and had ordered that the house should be locked and barred. With that, the girl made as if to vanish again.

Geza gave way to a storm of rage of which I should never have believed him capable.

This produced immediate results.

Within seconds Baron Fiedler, the Countess's Steward, was on the scene. Geza told him curtly and pointedly that he, as the son of the late Count, was now master here, and that the staff would in future take their orders from him, not from his mother.

Gates and doors were thrown open, the staff gathered to bid us a rather uncertain welcome, and followed by our scanty household we crossed the threshold of Lobor.

I was completely flabbergasted. Never in my life had I been so received—and this from the mother of the man who meant everything to me. I fought back tears of humiliation; I should certainly have given way entirely to my disappointment and shame were it not for Geza.

He looked so pale that I was afraid he would faint any moment. If he had had his sword I have no doubt that he would have murdered someone. The atrocious behaviour of his mother had made him so furious he would have been capable of anything.

The servants must have sensed this, for once we had forced our way into the house we found ourselves surrounded by cringing, servile people.

In no time at all the shutters were thrown back, the dust-sheets pulled off the furniture, our luggage carried upstairs. Geza insisted that his mother's own room should be prepared for me. The gardener arrived, almost invisible behind a huge bunch of flowers; a maid brought a basket of fruit; elaborate industry replaced the hostile defensiveness that had first greeted us.

Amid this turmoil, I moved like a puppet, without saying anything or indeed having the will even to think. The completely unexpected insult had stunned me. Marie Fugger was no less astounded. Even our maids were at a loss for words, as they silently unpacked our cases.

Geza issued orders, instructions, and in a very short time the house had taken on a friendly, welcoming air.

He led me into the salon. We were alone.

He stood there before me, still deathly pale. 'My mother has done us an unforgivable injury.' His voice sounded strange. 'I shall never forget or forgive it. I don't know how I can bear to look you in the face.'

This morning I had seen a new side to Geza. I would have thought it impossible to see someone every day for two years and then not know them! He had become a general, a leader of men! A man who demands and compels obedience. Who knows what he wants and gets it. There was nothing here of that nonchalance, that attractively casual air that I had always associated with him. I admired him. And this admiration shook me out of my trance.

'I love you, not your mother,' I said.

Geza took me in his arms and kissed me with a new, almost desperate violence; I surrendered on the spot.

* * *

G

Artur is back from Vienna.

It was agreed that he would make no attempt to communicate with me on the way. You can never be sure what may be going on. Better safe than sorry. But by the time he was over a week overdue I was becoming a little nervous. And so I was the more delighted to see him. He apologized for his long absence, which he said was unavoidable. As compensation, he brought good news. And something more too: money.

Louise had decided (not without some prompting from me) to part company with that wretched jewellery, recently the property of the unattractive M. Hartog of Nice. There had been so much about it in the papers that the souvenir value of the original joke had been ruined for us. That made Louise's parting with the baubles that much easier. Artur had sold them in Vienna for 15,000 guilders—a very fair price for that sort of transaction. It certainly does something for M. Hartog's standing, in my eyes, which should be some consolation to him. Though hardly enough, I imagine.

But the news that Artur brought was worth far more than 15,000 guilders.

After our arrival at Lobor I was anxious to find out, as quickly as possible, the exact present position in the affair of the bill. Our whole future is after all very largely dependent on it. If information was to be had at all, it would be in Vienna. Neither Louise nor I could appear there ourselves. So the role of agent fell to Artur. It meant I had to tell him the whole story. But that I could do with a clear conscience: he is an absolutely trustworthy friend, and as mum as the grave.

The plan of operations he and I devised ran as follows: Artur would go to see Dr Barber and let him know that because of financial problems he had parted company with us. On bad terms of course. Artur would explain that he still had a very substantial claim on us, and so wanted to consult Barber. In this way, we hoped, Artur would gain the lawyer's confidence and worm out of him how things stood from our point of view. No one could be better informed than Barber. Quite apart from the fact that there was no reasonable alternative way for Artur to gain a more credible—and promising—entrée into the affair.

Artur Ozegovich's tactics in the execution of this plan deserve the highest praise. I can think of no one who could have carried off a difficult task more efficiently.

Barber still has nothing good to say of us. (I can hardly hold that against him.) Nevertheless his initial pessimism has vanished. And he is manifestly no fool. His change of heart must be based on hard facts. And that can only be good news for us.

The last we had heard was that Princess Stephanie's household had taken the story to the Public Prosecutor's office, where Dr Kleeborn was to solve the mystery of the forging of Stephanie's signature. Kleeborn, so Artur now discovered from Barber, suspected that there might be more to the affair than met the eye. Rather than take a hammer to this delicate situation, Barber tiptoed into the lion's den: he went to see Prince Montenuovo. Montenuovo is not only His Majesty's Court Marshal, but also a diplomat. As is no more than his duty and responsibility. Still, it should be expressly recorded in his favour. The Prince didn't try to dodge the issue, as his colleague Choloniewsky had in Stephanie's case, but did the sensible and obvious thing: he opened discussions with Philip of Coburg. After their first meeting word was passed to the Public Prosecutor from the Hofburg that the affair should be handled (in Barber's words) 'with discretion and delicacy'. Dr Kleeborn took the hint. On the threshold of the twentieth century even the almighty Court of Vienna Justice can no longer *order* something to be done or left undone. It must simply ask: in this case for discreet and delicate action. Even so, people know where their duty lies, and so did Kleeborn. He dismissed the complaint on the spot. And Dr Joseph Wach, the Examining Magistrate investigating the charges, prudently ceased his activities. (The charges had tactfully been brought 'against a person or persons unknown'.)

Barber gave Artur to understand that, in his opinion, the scandal had been suppressed on the intervention of no less a person than the Emperor himself. If this theory is right—and the close relationship between Montenuovo and his master supports it—then Barber is effectively saying that Philip will meet the bill. Not at all as a favour to Louise—God forbid!

But simply under massive pressure from above.

Barber spoke about these developments with obvious relief, Artur finished. The lawyer could now see a real hope that all his fears for his good reputation, which he had thought irretrievably doomed by his unfortunate involvement, might after all turn out to be groundless.

Artur of course recognized at once the consequences of all this for us, and had great difficulty in concealing his joy from Barber.

I had even more reason for joy, and less reason to hide it. I embraced Artur, kissed him on both cheeks, and hauled him off immediately to the wine cellar.

There (as a subsequent check revealed) we drank five bottles of Champagne and one and a half of Slivovitz.

When I came to my senses late in the evening I was stretched out on the drawing-room sofa with a truly memorable hangover. Baron Fiedler announced that the Princess had already dined and retired to bed. Before doing so she had given orders that the semi-conscious Herr Ozegovich be loaded into a carriage and packed off to his relatives at Brežice. To make this procedure as unobtrusive as possible, the horse on which he had arrived at Lobor in the afternoon has been stabled here.

* * *

L

Geza need no longer get up at night to go back to his hotel. Nor does he have to scramble over balconies, as he once did at Abbazia—he simply stays with me. We sleep together until broad daylight in his mother's bed, and don't give a damn what Marie Fugger, the servants, Baron Fiedler or anyone else may think of us.

When we are tired of lovemaking, I lie buried in his arms. When I turn over in my sleep I no longer find an empty space, but his warm skin under my hand. At dawn, I often sit up in bed and look at the face next to mine. I admire the curve of his eyelashes, run my finger gently over the stubble of his twelve-hour beard, and can hardly wait for him to open his eyes and smile at me. I had forgotten how beautiful simple things can be, and how I have missed them during the last two years.

The château ... I must have gone native, to call it a 'château'. Well, the château stands on a wooded hill overlooking the village of Lobor. We gaze down from a flat hilltop like the robber barons of the Middle Ages. A single steep path joins us to the world below. We are surrounded by other, higher mountains, but separated from them by uncrossable ravines.

We have no dining-room. Our château is too small for that. We eat in the hall, before the giant fireplace, where whole treetrunks burn every evening, though it isn't really at all cold. Gipsy musicians play to us, four insolent-looking young men whom Geza rounded up from somewhere. Their leader is called Zoltan: everything about him is black: his eyes, his hair, his twirled moustache, and his fingernails. But he plays like a god. His violin can exult, weep, dance, wail. The eyes of the other three never leave Zoltan's fiddle: cymbals, viola, bass follow like faithful dogs wherever the leader's fantasy takes them. If we are ever driven from this new paradise, we shall take the gipsies with us!

Not a word is ever said of the troubles that threatened to strangle us in Nice, London and Paris. I can let myself think they have dissolved into mist. Lobor is a kingdom of dreams.

I can dream of buying all the surrounding mountains, throwing up a high wall round this giant estate, and living here with my lover for the rest of our lives. With the heady wine, the crackling fire, the music of the gipsies and the long wild nights.

Geza had asked the lawyer Dr Tonkovich to come and visit

us. This is his father's old friend, the man who was to solve all our problems.

The new lady of the manor looked her most beautiful, to receive him as he deserved. But he never came. The woman in whose bed Geza and I are sleeping must have poisoned him against me.

To be honest, it didn't matter a great deal to me, but Geza was deeply hurt by it. And because his hurt rebounded on me, he tried to make up for it with such infinite tenderness that I was glad in the end that the lawyer never came.

About half an hour from Lobor by coach is Zlatar, about ten houses bigger than Lobor itself. This village boasts a very primitive inn, and there yesterday a visitor arrived from Vienna. A gentleman, who drove in a coach from the station at K. to Zlatar.

Geza's spies have described the man: he wears a light summer coat and a white panama hat, carries a cane with a silver knob, and has a pince-nez hanging round his neck on a black cord. The luggage he has with him suggests he will be staying for several days.

Geza is worried because the visitor's elegant appearance has little in common with the inn, which he thinks is suspicious.

I am worried too, but for a different reason: that pince-nez strikes a chord in my memory. Such a pince-nez adorned the neck of a lawyer who often visited the Coburg Palace, to discuss with Philip behind locked doors matters not intended for my ears. My informants told me that it was usually a question of getting rid of some mistress of whom Philip had tired.

* * *

G

I don't at all like this business of the strange man from Vienna who has arrived at the inn in Zlatar.

Louise thinks she has identified him from the comic glasses they say he wears. That seems to be a rash assumption. Even so, there's something fishy about him.

The thought that our presence here may already be known to our enemies in Vienna is rather a depressing one.

We must be careful.

* * *

ℒ

The same pince-nez; the same man! Name Bachrach, Christian name Adolf, occupation lawyer. Dr Adolf Bachrach, privy councillor.

He drove over from Zlatar to Lobor in an old landau. The horses were as old as the rig they pulled, and after one failure refused to have anything more to do with the steep ascent to the château. So the doctor had to climb the hill on foot, and arrived twenty minutes later, bathed in sweat and breathless, to pull the bell at the front door.

Geza was out with Baron Fiedler on a tour of inspection; there's a tract of woodland he wants to clear. So I had to receive the lawyer alone with my lady-in-waiting.

After a servile greeting, the privy councillor looked at me, shaking his head with an expression of the deepest sympathy. He could find no words, he said, to express his embarrassment at having to meet me, Princess Louise of Coburg, in such spartan surroundings, and so on, finding in fact enough words to make himself tediously clear.

'I don't know what you're talking about,' I countered cheerfully. 'I'm very happy here. I feel better than I have felt for years. The country is beautiful, we are well served and equally well housed. What more could one ask?'

The sadness did not leave his face. 'I had no idea that Your Royal Highness was being forced to live in such primitive conditions,' he wailed.

'There is no question of force,' I said coldly. 'Now, Doctor, what brings you to Lobor?'

Without answering my question he went on, in the whining tone that was getting on my nerves, 'I thank God that I have at last succeeded in finding Your Royal Highness.'

'You have been looking for me?'

'Indeed I have. And the noble lord on whose behalf I have been acting will be enormously relieved when——'

Knowing the answer already, I asked him who his employer was.

'Your Royal Highness's husband!' His face was radiant, as if he had mentioned the Archangel Gabriel in person.

I was icy. 'Prince Philip should have spared himself the expense of sending you.'

'I am happy that you should be so concerned to spare your husband unnecessary expense,' he answered, with audible mockery in his voice now. Then he tried to tell me that not only Philip but also my children had been deeply concerned for my welfare since they had lost track of me in Paris. 'The Prince's most ardent wish is for Your Royal Highness to return to him at last in Vienna,' he finished.

'You must have your little joke,' I said, putting every ounce of sarcasm I could muster into the gibe.

'He is ready to forget and forgive everything that has happened.'

'I am sure he is. But I am not.'

'Dear lady,' he implored me, 'do not reject the outstretched hand of forgiveness. The unfortunate incident that caused Your Royal Highness's departure from Vienna is a painful memory to Prince Philip. I am to tell you that he still holds out some hope that the Emperor may once again allow you to appear at court. I am to tell you expressly that he will do everything in his power to bring this about.'

I gazed at the man and tried to work out what was going on behind those pince-nez. Did he really believe all this rubbish?

'In a word,' he continued, 'if Your Royal Highness should

decide to return to the Coburg Palace, everything will go on just as before. Prince Philip promises that.'

'And for once I believe his promise!' I could not suppress my bitterness. 'I'm sure things will indeed go on just as they did before. Just as unbearable as ever. And that is why no power on earth will make me return to Vienna. Tell Prince Philip that from me.'

As Bachrach, unperturbed, launched into another oily speech, I cut him short. 'Please don't trouble, my dear Doctor. My decision is final.'

'Am I really to say that?'

'If you please. You have done all you could; congratulations. But for Philip and me divorce is the only possibility. Nothing else. If you can make that clear to him I shall be greatly in your debt.'

'Impossible, madam. Please put this thought out of your head. He will never agree. Never.' Suddenly Bachrach was speaking plainly, the mask cast aside.

'Dr Bachrach, I am only too aware that you already know—through your professional experience—the reasons why our marriage could never succeed. Please remember that!' I glanced at Countess Fugger; she said nothing, but I knew she agreed. 'I am not trying to make myself out to be innocent, but my husband and I have nothing with which to reproach each other. What sort of sense does it make to try and hold together by force something which ceased to exist long ago?'

Bachrach looked at me in annoyance. 'You are forgetting the ethical side, Your Royal Highness. Prince Philip is not only an exceedingly moral person——'

'My dear man,' I said impatiently, 'you are drivelling.'

'... but also deeply religious,' he pursued, ignoring my intervention. 'He is a good Catholic. Therefore divorce is impossible.'

'The law of Austria allows for judicial separation. You as a lawyer should be aware of that.'

'I am aware of it, madam. The law of Austria, yes; the law

of Rome, no! Divorce is irreconcilable with my client's principles.'

Now I understood.

Although the Countess threw me a warning look, I was not prepared to hear any more of this twaddle about Philip's sacred principles. Without any attempt to mince words, I said crisply and plainly that I knew exactly why Philip refused me a divorce and insisted on my return: he will not give up his hopes of the inheritance that falls to me on my father's death. He cares nothing about me, he never has cared about me, but money is different. And only money! Although he is a rich man, his avarice knows no limits.

I must have been speaking more loudly than I knew, for now the door was flung open and Geza entered. 'What's going on here?' he demanded anxiously.

I was mistress of myself again. 'My secretary will show you out,' I said, and turned to Geza. 'Dr Bachrach would like to leave now.'

Then I left the room and went upstairs to my bedroom.

* * *

G

The insolence of this lawyer, Bachrach, and the thick-skinned way he flaunts it so carelessly, are beyond words. Creatures like him take an almost perverse pleasure in pursuing any kind of business, the dirtier the better. Philip could not have chosen a better man. 'Better' meaning more evil, repellent, cunning and insensitive. Besides, the man is dangerous. Very dangerous. Even in that, he is worthy of his master. It would be infantile to have any illusions about that.

I found Louise, accompanied by Marie Fugger, in a violent argument with Dr Bachrach, and I at once recognized the character who had been described to me recently—the new guest at the inn in Zlatar.

Before the two ladies left the room in anger, immediately after my appearance, Louise introduced us. So the chips were down. We each knew whom we had to deal with. So we could cut out the formalities and get down to business.

I must admit that Bachrach was the quicker, and immediately snatched the initiative. With staggering insolence he took the bull by the horns and offered me a bribe—a little matter of 100,000 guilders. To earn it, I had merely to give my word as an officer, in writing, that I would leave the Princess at once and never attempt to approach her again. That was all. He had the authority and the means to give me the money on the spot, if I should feel able to meet the conditions.

I considered for a moment whether I should shoot the fellow down—no, rather beat him to death like a mad dog with a log from the fireplace.

He must have read in my face what was going through my mind, for he hastened to add, 'Please regard me as the mere mouthpiece of His Royal Highness! The ... proposition, shall we call it? ... is his. I have only to pass it on. That is my profession.'

Looking at him, I thought I detected a hint of mockery in his features. But then a thought occurred to me: let him mock if he wishes, but to kill him and so deliver myself to the hangman would be the summit of idiocy. I could give his principal no greater pleasure. This realization enabled me to regain immediate control of my feelings. 'Please tell His Highness,' I said calmly, enunciating every word with careful clarity, 'that I cannot accept his offer. As a reward for sparing his life in a duel, as everyone knows I did, the price is rather too high. He isn't worth 100,000 guilders, or anything like it. For his wife, on the other hand, the offer is too low. Much too low. Insultingly low. That would cost him more than he will ever have. Ever! Tell him that. And now please get out of my house and stay out, before I set the dogs on you. They are bloodhounds. I feel I ought to warn you that I'm almost sure the dogs won't like you very much.'

A few minutes later Louise and I watched from the balcony

of our room as Bachrach walked slowly down the path to the village, where no doubt his ancient landau was waiting.

*   *   *

ℒ

Wednesday evening   How dare Dr Bachrach make Geza such a degrading offer? What does he take him for? The man is a wretchedly poor psychologist if he thought for a moment he would get his way by that stratagem. His only excuse is that he is acting on Philip's behalf. Philip thinks any man has his price, and assumes the worst of everyone.

Thursday   We must be on our guard with this lawyer. He has not returned to Vienna to pass on my message to Philip, but is still staying in the inn at Zlatar. What are his plans? Why hasn't he left?

Geza is afraid that Bachrach intends to have me abducted. In Vienna I would have laughed at him; even in Nice I should have thought it impossible, far too fanciful; but perhaps here, in this fanciful country, nothing is impossible.

Geza has armed the servants with hunting rifles and whips. He himself now carries a pistol everywhere he goes. An armed guard has been posted at the foot of the hill leading up to the château. No suspicious-looking person will be allowed through.

And so here we are on our hilltop; our own prisoners.

Friday   The guards are on the road day and night. We never go riding now, the gate is locked and barred, we hardly even venture into the garden.

Everything has been calm so far, but maybe this is the calm before the storm.

Yesterday I woke in the middle of the night to hear one of

the hounds baying horribly down in the outer courtyard. Immediately the whole pack joined in.

I woke Geza out of a deep sleep. He grabbed the pistol from under his pillow.

Meanwhile the dogs were baying wild and furious.

Geza jumped out of bed, threw on some clothes, and made to go downstairs. I begged him to be careful and not to expose himself to danger, but he took no notice and opened the bedroom door. At that moment the barking stopped. Everything was silent as the grave, except my heart, which was beating so wildly I felt sure Geza must hear it.

'What was that?' I asked, my throat dry.

He shrugged his shoulders. A fox, perhaps, he suggested, trying to get into the chicken coop and being frightened off by the dogs.

Ten minutes later he was fast asleep again.

I envied him. I was much too worked up to close my eyes. Even the silence now seemed to me menacing. I was almost sure that something would happen, though when and what I didn't know.

I went to sleep at last at cockcrow. I must have had a terrible dream for Geza woke me saying I was whimpering and crying in my sleep.

The memory of the dream was gone; but the fear remained.

Tuesday He has gone!

The lawyer has left. Geza's informant, a goatherd from Lobor who was taking his cheese to market in Zlatar, saw it with his own eyes. Yesterday a travelling trunk was loaded onto the old landau in which Bachrach had made his vain assault on our fortress. A few moments later Bachrach himself emerged, in elegant summer coat and panama and accompanied by the innkeeper. He said his goodbyes, climbed aboard, and left.

A massive weight has been lifted from my mind.

Geza is relieved too, though he won't admit as much. He

tells me solemnly that there is no reason to be less careful or relax our defences. Bachrach is still dangerous, in Vienna or here in Zlatar.

Thursday morning I felt as though the sun had come out again after a long rainstorm. I was full of such a spirit of adventure that I knew something was bound to happen.

I decided to give a party. Considering the circumstances, alas, it could only be a very small party. I consulted with Baron Fiedler, left all the details to him, and sent a messenger to fetch Artur Ozegovich from Brežice. I would have liked to invite his family too, in return for all their hospitality to me, but Geza has taken umbrage at old Ozegovich's failure to keep our visit secret. Geza thinks that we have this indiscretion to thank for our unwelcome visitor from Vienna.

So there were just the four of us: Geza, Marie Fugger, Artur and myself.

I took a long time getting myself ready, made life miserable for Ilona and the maids just as I did in the old days, and finished up looking as though I were going to a first night at the Paris Opéra. I wore the Worth dress that I had on when I supped with the Prince of Wales in London. But none of the Nice jewellery, alas; I wore my pearls instead.

The gipsies gaped at me in astonishment and the servants looked on wide eyed when I eventually swept down into the hall. They had never seen me like this before.

Geza and Artur were in evening dress; Marie Fugger was wearing one of my old gowns, a gift that suits her very well.

In the candlelight the simple rustic room was transformed. Countess Mattachich's best china and finest glasses adorned the table. Baron Fiedler had arranged things excellently. I almost regretted not having asked him to dine with us, but despite the good service he has rendered us I think that at bottom he remains the Countess's man, and my enemy.

The cook had so far been no more than mediocre, but today

he surprised us all with an expert display. The food was very good and the wine first class.

I felt excited and happy. Even Geza, who had at first been rather subdued, found my good humour infectious. By the end of the second bottle of Champagne he was the merriest of us all.

Jumping to his feet he cried, 'Zoltan! Give us a csardas.'

With a touch of his forelock and a servile 'As my lord wishes' Zoltan began to play, so passionately and irresistibly that none of us could sit still. Geza danced on his own the length of the hall and back, then he pulled me from my chair, and we danced together as if we had been at a village csardas somewhere in the Hungarian countryside. The music grew wilder and wilder; we couldn't stop. Even the tranquil Marie Fugger was infected, and found herself dancing with Ozegovich.

At last, out of breath, I collapsed in a chair and drank two quick glasses of Champagne. I began to feel it going to my head, but I didn't care; we were all in the same state.

Try as I will, I can't remember today what happened after that, or at least not coherently. Only details stick in my memory.

I know for a fact that at some point Geza sent down to the cellars for two bottles of old brandy, left over from his father's day. We helped ourselves freely to the magnificent spirit, and persuaded the gipsies to join us.

Then, I remember, Zoltan played haunting Hungarian tunes very softly in my ear, while I sat at the table with my head in my hands and the tears pouring down my cheeks. And I was very happy.

I remember too how Geza tried to stick one banknote after another to the gipsy's damp forehead, and one after another they fell to the floor, without Zoltan ever interrupting his music to try and pick them up. We laughed like madmen at this.

Some time during the night Geza ordered that the huntsman should be fetched from his bed. The old man appeared and in a quavering voice sang us the most beautiful Croatian love songs. Geza held me in his arms and translated word for word.

As day broke, we were all drunk.

Zoltan threw Geza's banknotes in his face, and made me wild declarations of love in Magyar. I was glad Geza didn't understand. Even so he must have suspected something, for suddenly he dragged his pistol out of his pocket.

I let out a cry; the others went very silent.

Without a word, Geza slipped the safety catch and, very quickly, one after another he shot out six candles. After each shot he gave Zoltan a look that must have brought the gipsy rapidly to his senses. Then Geza drained a great glass of brandy and flung it against the wall. I know that much, at least.

But how I reached the bedroom I cannot remember. When I woke, my clothes were strewn all over the room.

Antonia complained a little later that she and Ilona had sat up for me half the night and then, when I did come, the Count wouldn't even let them undress me.

* * *

G

Saturday This morning an official messenger came from Zlatar with a sealed note to be delivered only to me personally, and against a receipt. It comes from the headquarters of XIII Army Corps in Zagreb, and orders Geza Count Mattachich, Lieutenant, 13th Uhlans, to present himself at 8 a.m. sharp on 29 May (that is, two days from now) before the Senior Medical Officer at the Prince Eugen barracks in Zagreb for an official report on his medical condition. Failure to comply with the order, it goes on, will be regarded as absence without leave and refusal to obey a superior officer, and punished accordingly. The paper was signed by a Major Adriano, a name I don't know; but, more significantly, he signs 'on behalf of His

Excellency General Anton Freiherr von Bechtolsheim, Commander, XIII Corps, and Officer Commanding, Zagreb.

This 'on behalf of' business is very irregular. Even more irregular is the thought that a Corps Commander and Officer Commanding a military area should concern himself with the health of a lieutenant. And officially, what's more.

Thanks to Louise's influence my leave had been extended by one year in January 1896; in March '97 it had been extended again, this time for two years, to 30 April 1899. So this summons to a medical inspection comes as a complete surprise.

In any case, how on earth does anyone at Zagreb know I'm here at Lobor? I've asked myself that again and again. Yet at Corps H.Q. they're so sure of themselves that they give me only forty-eight hours' notice to report.

It's ten days now since Philip's lawyer called here. He left last Monday, and could have been in the Seilerstätte in Vienna a day later. The Prince, who of course happens also to be a Field Marshal of the Imperial Army, would thus have had time to get in touch with his colleague General von Bechtolsheim. And who would refuse a favour to a man so highly placed in the Vienna hierarchy as Prince Philip of Coburg?

Yes, that's the simple explanation of the puzzle. The thing is clear. Too clear by half. Louise's husband has stretched out his long arm to Lobor. After the failure of Bachrach's mission he's going to try another tack.

I sent at once to Artur, asking him to come as soon as possible. Then the three of us examined the question from every conceivable angle. Louise was—and still is—extremely disturbed at the summons from Zagreb. Her view of the new situation is a completely subjective and touchingly naïve one; but then no one knows Philip better than she, so her contribution was often very informative. Eventually we reached a unanimous verdict: after the affair of the bill was suppressed on the highest authority, so that there was no hold to be obtained over us that way to affect Louise or her life with me, Philip came up with something else. I am still a soldier—there are possibilities in that! The day after tomorrow I shall probably be passed fit for duty. It wouldn't surprise me if I find myself packed off at once to some godforsaken garrison in Poland or Transylvania. Once I'm back in military service and subject to the direct weight of military discipline, there are ways and means a-plenty of preventing me living with the wife of a Field Marshal! And nowhere would be more suitable for that strategy than the bleak garrison towns of the eastern marches, where there are often more soldiers than civilians. There I could do nothing without its being immediately common knowledge. And Louise, of course, would be even worse off.

If the glorious Royal and Imperial Army is really prepared to stoop to play Prince Philip of Coburg's little games for him, I shan't hesitate to face the consequences and say my goodbyes, however hard that may be. What will be, will be. Artur accepted that too in the end. But for the moment there is nothing to do but wait, and keep cool and calm. In thirty-six hours I shall know more.

I shall leave for Zagreb tomorrow afternoon and spend the night there in a hotel. I shall need to get a good night's sleep and be at my best to face whatever awaits me.

* * *

L

There can be no peace for us!

No sooner do we think we have gained a little breathing-space than the next danger looms on the horizon. And this time the horizon is very close: the day after tomorrow Geza must report in Zagreb.

My head is swimming from all the theories we discussed. And at the end, we know exactly what we knew before: that Philip of Coburg is the root of all evil.

What is the remotest, darkest corner of the great Austro-Hungarian Empire? Olmutz? Tarnopol?* Sarajevo? Wherever

* Now respectively Olomouc (Poland) and Tarnova (Rumania) (Trans).

they send Geza, I shall follow. Though there is one place, one single place in the world, where I cannot follow—or only with the greatest reluctance: Vienna. But Philip won't think of that. He is not clever enough. Fortunately.

So what will our future life be like?

Could I live in ... let's say Olmutz—could I rent a villa in Olmutz and set myself up there, known all over the town as the mistress of a lieutenant? It sounds absolutely impossible. Preposterous! Until now I've travelled with the sort of household befitting my rank, which naturally includes a secretary. There was no breach of etiquette involved. And the secretary happened to be Count Mattachich. But what would happen now would be really scandalous. Philip must feel sure that I would shrink from that.

But he is wrong! I shrink from nothing now—nothing!

In Zagreb   The church clock has just struck. It is two in the morning. I am sitting at a rickety table covered with a dusty red plush cloth, and writing by the miserable little light of a miserable little oil lamp.

Geza is asleep. His nerves are stronger than mine. But his brow is furrowed, he grinds his teeth convulsively in his sleep, and tosses and turns so violently that there is no room in the bed for me.

Originally he didn't want me to come to Zagreb with him, but I refused to stay in Lobor. I couldn't have endured it, waiting there alone to hear what the result of the examination would be.

'Are you sure the journey won't be too exhausting for you?' he asked with concern. When I said no, he looked at me with gratitude.

We decided to travel as light as possible. Geza managed without his manservant, Mirko, and I took only Antonia and Ilona—after all, one must do one's hair and wear something. Marie Fugger is here too, of course.

We chose the Prukner, a quiet hotel described as 'moderate'.

Which means even the first-class hotels in Zagreb can scarcely be fit for human habitation.

Arriving late in the evening, we went straight upstairs and ordered a little supper to be brought to our room. Geza ate heartily, while I couldn't touch a bite, and concentrated on dulling my senses with the heavy local wine.

In bed, we lay for a long time in each other's arms. That was all. We didn't even kiss. I was dead tired and soon fell asleep. But soon I woke again, and stayed awake.

I have a secret plan, of which Geza knows nothing. If things go badly tomorrow (my God, are they going well today?)— I mean if they pass him fit—I shall go to see his commanding officer, this General Freiherr von Bechtolsheim. After all, I've contrived to get Geza excused duties twice already—with a little luck, why shouldn't I do it again? Though my luck has not been exactly reliable lately.

I know Bechtolsheim. I'm sure I know him. But try as I may, I cannot remember now where it was we met. Yet I can see him clearly in my mind's eye: tall, thin, grey moustache, bulging eyes, slightly stooped. But where can it have been? Hunting with the Esterhazys? At a reception at the Hofburg? Something to do with Rudolf? Or was he even a guest at the Coburg Palace? That would explain a lot. And it would also mean that my visit was doomed to failure.

But I will not let myself be discouraged, despite this comfortless room. I ordered Antonia to pack the delightful blue dress from Paquin, that I've never worn; in that I should be able to make an impression on the C.O., Zagreb, even if he is a friend of Philip's, as seems more and more probable.

XI

G

4 June 1898   Under garrison arrest, Zagreb. It's not easy to describe what's happened in the last few days. In fact it's damned difficult. Memories come crowding in on me, and I want to write everything down at once. But of course that can't be done. So, at the risk of making myself dizzy, I must tame this waterfall of thoughts, slow it down, tidy it up, and then carefully write each thought down, one after another. That's what I must do! Whether I *can* do it, God knows. But I'll try.

Until recently I kept a diary just for fun. I started it when I first met Louise in Vienna (though we'd already known each other by sight for a long time). I don't remember why. Maybe just because it was the fashion. And then I found I couldn't stop the damned thing.

Now things are very different. Now my own neck may be at risk, and I must try to make every entry as clear and accurate as I can. Two things can happen now. They may let me out of here soon, telling me it's all been a mistake. A regrettable misunderstanding. In this case I'd like to have it all down in black and white, how an officer with a clean record was treated by the army he has served faithfully for eleven years. So that I can bring those responsible to justice—and I will, as sure as my name's Mattachich. On the other hand, this idiotic farce may turn nasty. Which I must confess I haven't allowed myself to imagine. In that case I shall need exact, reliable records of everything, if I'm to save my honour and my skin. I must be able to recall in detail every interview, every conversation. Day and night. At will. Because if not I shall be on my own, forsaken by God and man. The man who can't defend himself with his own resources is doomed beyond hope. So is the man who can, often enough.

At 8 a.m. sharp on 29 May I presented myself (properly dressed, of course) in the offices of the Medical Section at the Prince Eugen barracks.

The duty officer at once announced me to his superior, Major Rosenthal, who didn't keep me waiting for a moment, which I much appreciated.

We had never met before, so the interview began with introductions. I learnt that Rosenthal had only just been promoted and posted to Zagreb; previously he'd been a battalion M.O. at Lvov.

As it turned out he knew nothing whatever about me, which he seemed to regret and apologized for. The fault, he assured me, was not his. He had only been briefed yesterday afternoon that this interview was arranged for this morning. By dint of some hasty investigations he had discovered that I belonged to the 13th Uhlans. But of course there hadn't been time to have my case history sent from Varazdin.

And so it was from me that Major Rosenthal first learnt that I had for years been unfit for service, thanks to an extremely acute and persistent dose of malaria I'd caught on manoeuvres; and that my sick leave officially didn't expire till next spring.

The honest medical officer was as much in the dark as I was. He could make neither head nor tail of the whole story. We were discussing our joint amazement at this unexpected and apparently futile proceeding when, without the formality of a knock, the door was flung open and a Major, a stranger to me, burst into the room, followed by four soldiers armed with pistols.

The Major stepped up to me and asked, 'Lieutenant Count Mattachich?'

Caught completely off my guard, I answered automatically, 'Yes, sir.'

'Don't move. Not a muscle!' He turned to the doctor. 'Sorry

about this, Rosenthal. Official business, you understand.' Turning back to me, he introduced himself 'Major Franz, Town Major, Zagreb.' Then: 'Lieutenant, in the name of his Excellency the General Officer Commanding, I have to inform you that you are under arrest.'

I find that I'm much more excited writing about the scene today than I was when it actually took place a couple of days ago. The calm I showed in the face of the amazing appearance of this officer and his armed guard seems quite inexplicable to me now. I remember that my first reaction was to glance at the M.O.—I wanted to know whether he had been in the plot. Not that it mattered in the least. But Rosenthal was as shaken as I was. No doubt about that. In some strange way it comforted me. I was glad he at least was no conspirator.

'Are you armed?' inquired the Major.

I shook my head.

'I should prefer not to have to search you here. I should be grateful if you would give me your word as an officer that you are not carrying a firearm.'

'I have already said as much, Major, and that will have to suffice,' I answered. With a hint of a smile, I added: 'But if you insist, I can give you my word as an officer as well. I had no idea what I was walking into here. Otherwise I should certainly have come armed. I received a summons to a medical inspection. I didn't know that the Austro-Hungarian Army had taken to playing with marked cards!'

'I didn't hear that, Lieutenant. I'm doing my duty, that's all,' said the Town Major, and it was easy to see that he wasn't enjoying it. 'Please follow me quietly.'

'Where to, Major, if I may ask?'

'To the cell block.'

I put on my cap and turned once more to Rosenthal. 'So our business is explained, and finished. I must thank you for your friendly treatment of a brother officer. It was a pleasure to meet you. Goodbye.' I saluted.

I went to the door, with two soldiers in front of me, two behind. At the door I hesitated and asked perfectly calmly,

'May I know why I have been arrested, Major?'

'I don't know. I can't say,' he answered, and gestured at me to carry on.

We left the room. Behind me the doctor called, 'Good luck, Lieutenant.'

Our odd little group attracted suitable attention as we marched across the vast parade ground to the cell block. Soldiers and officers alike stood and stared after us.

When we finally halted outside the great iron door leading to the cells, and were waiting for it to be opened, the Major said unexpectedly, 'I really don't know what this is all about, but from what I've heard it'll soon be cleared up to everyone's satisfaction.'

I looked at him in surprise. He nodded his head encouragingly. Then I realized that this optimistic announcement was supposed to give me a little courage in the face of that grim iron door. I supposed that the impulse came from a sudden surge of fellow feeling, and had little to do with the facts of the case. Grateful though I was to the Major for his good intentions, I felt violent resentment and bitter pessimism. I could see how the land lay. No half-measures for the great Philip of Coburg—that would be absolutely out of character. He will throw in the full weight of his influence, his connections and his money to bring me down.

In the cell block I was handed over to the Provost Marshal, Captain Sekulic, and his Sergeant, Senft.

Sekulic was a countryman of mine—he even came from the same neighbourhood. I sensed at once that despite his exalted position he was a decent sort of fellow, one you could talk to. A solitary gleam of light on a dark morning!

We started with a painstakingly thorough medical check: I was required to strip stark naked there in my cell. Sekulic apologized for this formality, which he explained was a strict regulation that could never be waived. All my pockets, and even the lining of my tunic, were rigorously checked. It turned out I had nothing on me that could cause any offence against the regulations covering officers under close arrest.

Previous experience had prepared me for a long session with the doctor, with much toing and froing: I intended to use the interminable delays to bring my diary up to date. And so, that morning I had remembered to conceal about me a pencil and a little black notebook. Even these were now handed back to me.

In fact, as I say, I was allowed to keep everything, even a considerable sum of money I had on me. But on a sudden impulse I gave Captain Sekulic my watch and chain, and my ring, and asked him to take them to Louise at the Hotel Prukner and give the two heirlooms into her safe keeping. My real motive in this was simply to let Louise know as soon as possible what had happened and where I was. Once she knew what had happened I knew she would move heaven and earth to have me released, or at least to establish contact with me and do what she could to improve my living conditions.

With barely concealed delight I realized that the trick was going to work. My compatriot Sekulic was obviously enthralled at the prospect of meeting, and perhaps even speaking to, Her Royal (and by now notorious) Highness Princess Louise of Saxe-Coburg-Gotha. He promised me that he would go straight to the Hotel Prukner and hand the valuables over to the Princess. Then he left me in the charge of Sergeant Senft and hurried away.

Senft—a South Tirolese, as I discovered—waited patiently until I was dressed again. He then explained to me that, as an officer, I could pass my time more or less as I liked; there were for example no set times for me to get up or go to bed. The regulations even allowed an officer to 'eat out', which did *not* mean that I was free to leave the barracks at meal-times, but simply that I could have meals sent in to me from any restaurant I chose in the town. At my own expense, of course. I at once announced my intention of taking advantage of this, and handed him 100 crowns by way of a cash float. We agreed that my meals should come from the Budweiser Restaurant in

Ilica Passage, Senft having assured me that the Budweiser was still by far the best place in Zagreb, and that all the Generals dined there as a matter of course.

This, it seemed, was the most important thing out of the way. Sergeant Senft saluted impeccably (I am after all still a Lieutenant, and his superior officer), about turned and quick marched.

I was alone in my cell. I heard two heavy bolts being shot, and the key turning in the lock. The sergeant's footsteps faded. It was quiet. It stayed quiet.

And I had time to see how I was housed.

The cell is four paces long by two broad. But enormously high in proportion: at least fifteen feet, I reckon. One of the short sides is taken up by the heavy, iron-bound door with its massive lock. There is a peephole at eye-level so that they can look in from the corridor and see what's going on inside; when it isn't being used this is covered by a flap on the outside. Opposite the door, but so high that only a thin strip of sky is visible, is a narrow, barred window. It would be a bold dreamer indeed who could dream his way out of this place.

The furniture is probably standard for an officer's cell: one narrow cot with two coarse woollen blankets; one small cupboard; one simple table; two stools; one wash basin, probably blue-painted once upon a time; one jug, ditto; one tin mug; one bucket and one cloth to cover it. Lighting doesn't seem to have caught on here yet—no oil-lamp or candle to be seen. (And no electricity, of course.)

The only luxury is an iron knocker on the inside of the door: with this the tenant of this rather old-fashioned apartment can attract a little attention if he has something to tell the outside world.

I had been left to my own devices for perhaps a quarter of an hour when I heard footsteps. They stopped at my door, it opened, and Captain Sekulic came in.

Sekulic reported that he had gone straight to the Hotel Prukner. Despite every effort, however, he had unfortunately not been able to see the Princess herself.

'So you gave my things to Countess Fugger, I suppose,' I said.

'No, there was no Countess Fugger there. Not as far as I could find out.'

'Well?' I was beginning to smell a rat.

'Things are all a bit confused at the Hotel Prukner,' Sekulic went on. 'There was no one who could, or would, tell me anything when I asked for Her Royal Highness. In the end I spoke to a gentleman from Vienna.'

'A gentleman from Vienna?' I was thoroughly alarmed now, though I could make no sense of all this. 'What do you mean, sir? Please, don't keep me in suspense: what happened?'

'The gentleman from Vienna came down straight away to see me. A Privy Councillor, Dr Bachrach—he said he was Prince Philip of Coburg's lawyer and representative.'

I was stunned.

The Captain noticed my shock. 'He didn't make at all a bad impression on me, actually; he had very good manners, and behaved with perfect propriety, if I'm any judge. I told him who I was and what I was doing there. Then it turned out that he already knew all about this afternoon—what happened to you, I mean. That was a bit of luck—saved me going into any details of the business.'

Slowly I found I could speak again. 'Bachrach ... Bachrach here in Zagreb! And he knows what's going on!' I hammered my clenched fist against my forehead in impotent fury, until my head sang. 'I see it all now!' I groaned. 'I never thought it could be so easy. So ridiculously easy!'

'Please, Lieutenant, calm down,' said the Captain. I noticed that he was taken aback by my violent reaction.

I pulled myself together, as well as I could. 'If you please, sir, did you find out anything about the Princess? Where was she? Where *is* she? What has Bachrach done with her?'

Sekulic shook his head. 'I think you're wrong about that fellow, Mattachich. But I'm not going into that now. You're in no state to discuss anything.'

'I'm quite all right again now, sir,' I hastened to assure

him. 'Please excuse my behaviour just now. I should very much like to hear anything you know about Her Royal Highness.'

'I'm afraid I don't know anything. Anything at all. After all, I could hardly ask Dr Bachrach—I had no authority to do that. I just told him why I was there; he was very agreeable about it, and told me I could just hand over the watch and ring to him. He would pass them on to the Princess, in accordance with the owner's wishes.'

'And so you gave Bachrach the stuff?'

'Yes,' the Captain admitted. 'I felt sure that was what you would want me to do. But looking at you now, Lieutenant, I wish I'd never got involved in this business at all.'

'No, sir; you must forgive me. We are at cross purposes here. I'm really most grateful for what you've done. Very grateful. It didn't go the way I planned, the way I expected. But that has nothing to do with it, believe me. The only thing that bothers me is that fellow Bachrach.'

'What have you got against him?'

'If he is here in Zagreb—and in the Hotel Prukner, of all places—it means no good for the Princess. That worries me. It worries me more than the mess I'm in myself, in fact. Much more!'

Captain Sekulic looked at me doubtfully. 'I don't really know any of the details of all this, Mattachich—and I can't discuss them with you, and don't want to—but obviously I can guess at a few things. If I can offer you a word of advice: there are things you should try and forget. Push them out of your head. You'll need all your wits and nerves about you here. More than anything else you'll need them; and for yourself, alone. Or you'll find yourself caught up in a machine that will swallow you whole. If you can't concentrate coldly and grimly on that —and *only* on that—you're done. It'll be over quickly, and over for good. No one's acting for you here. No lawyer, no family, no friends, no superior officer. You're absolutely on your own. The man who can't drag himself out of the shit by his own hair is dead. It's a difficult trick, and you'd do well to concentrate on it. And on nothing else.'

We looked at each other for a few moments. And I knew that, whatever else happened, Captain Sekulic was on my side.

'I dare say this is all Greek to you, Lieutenant Mattachich. After a couple of sessions with the Interrogating Officer you'll see what I mean well enough though. I understand you're going to see him in the morning. And now, excuse me.'

He sketched a salute, and left me alone.

I heard the bolts shot and the lock turned; already the noise was almost familiar.

The Captain had succeeded in giving me a hint of what I could expect in the situation where I now found myself; I understood him better than he seemed to realize, in fact. After all, I am a serving officer, and I know a little about the Austrian system of military justice. But nevertheless my thoughts were always and exclusively of Louise.

Why couldn't Sekulic see her? I wondered. And what lay behind his story that no one at the hotel could tell him anything about her? That could only mean one thing: instructions, pressure, in fact strict orders—from a third party. When I left the hotel early this morning there was nothing to suggest that anything out of the way was going to happen.

So what *has* happened?

Bachrach of course holds the key to everything. He knows why I have been arrested. He knew how and when it would happen. He timed his move perfectly. The moment I was out of the hotel, he struck. They must have been shadowing us from the moment we arrived in Zagreb. Yes, of course they must ...

Yes, but what the hell *happened*?

Are they in all seriousness going to charge the Princess with forgery? The thought seems preposterous. Preposterous, but not to be disregarded. Philip of Coburg is no normal man, to be measured by normal standards. He is a monster. When he comes up against a brick wall he puts his head down and butts his way through it. I turned down his insulting 100,000-guilder bribe. Did I sentence Louise when I did that?

What do they do with a royal princess charged with obtaining money by false pretences? Detain her for questioning? I can hardly see that happening. And anyway, what has Bachrach to do with this?—I ask myself that over and over again. He is not a policeman, not even a criminal prosecutor.

How can Bachrach accept something on Louise's behalf? She hates the fellow like poison. Of her own free will she wouldn't let him pick up a glove she dropped. So is she no longer a free agent? Like me?

I'm going mad; everything goes round in circles: Louise, Bachrach, Philip ... Philip, Louise, Bachrach ...

And where the hell is Marie Fugger? It seems she was as hard to reach as the Princess. And instead one gets: Bachrach! That's a laugh! That's ...

I don't know how long I worried away at the problem, looking for the shaft of light that would make everything clear; all I know is that no light came. I was in a maze, and if there was a way out I couldn't find it. Time and again I ran into a solid wall, or found myself standing where I had already been.

I was brought to my senses by the sound of the cell door opening. Sergeant Senft stood in the doorway. He clicked his heels and announced: 'Sergeant Senft and Gunner Trmcik, sir. With your lunch, sir.'

And there it was: a great pile of dishes, giving an impression of almost fairytale luxury in these surroundings: property of the Budweiser Restaurant in Ilica Passage and containing a complete lunch for one. Gunner Trmcik was carrying a basket with crockery, a napkin and assorted cutlery. But no knife: Sergeant Senft apologized for that. The meat had already been cut into individual mouthfuls by the kitchen staff at the restaurant. By the chef's own hand, Senft emphasized. This way of serving meat could unfortunately not be avoided. No knife can be given to any soldier under arrest, no matter what his rank.

The Sergeant asked me to knock when I had finished, and then they left me alone. The door was closed again.

I ate three spoonfuls of soup. Do as I would, I could manage no more.

It must have been a good hour later when I heard the sergeant coming along the corridor. I knew his tread by now. He stopped outside my cell. I noticed a brief gleam of light at the spyhole, then darkness again. I knew that Senft was looking in at me.

'What is it, Sergeant?' I asked.

Now he opened the door.

'Just wondering if it was all right to clear away, sir.'

'Yes, take the stuff away,' I said.

He picked up the dishes disapprovingly and peered inside.

'Gawd, sir, that wasn't much of a lunch!' he burst out. 'They won't take this lot back, you know. It'll all have to be paid for, to the last heller.'

'Can't be helped, Senft. I'm not hungry.'

The Sergeant looked at me and thought for a moment. 'Well, if it's got to be paid for I might as well take it myself,' he said eventually. 'If it's all right with you, that is, sir.'

'Of course it's all right with me,' I said, laughing for the first time that day.

'Oh, it's not for me, sir. God forbid! There's this mate of mine, Sergeant Nagy from Stuhlweissenburg.* In charge of the horses, he is, but I reckon he eats more than what they do. I've never seen a chap put it away like he does. I feel sorry for his parents, I can tell you. The army would have to pack up if we all ate like that! His Majesty the Almighty Emperor himself could never afford it.'

'My compliments to Sergeant Nagy, and tell him to do himself really proud.'

'Thank *you*, sir—he'll do that all right.'

Senft piled up the dishes.

'He's a very religious bloke too, Sergeant Nagy,' the Sergeant saw fit to confide before he locked me in again. 'Prays every night, he does, and runs off to church every Sunday. He'll remember you in his prayers all right, sir.'

* Now Székesfehérvár, in Central Hungary (Trans).

'That won't do me any harm,' I said.

And then I was left alone again to whatever fate awaited me.

My cell is on the third floor of this massive four-storey building. The walls and floors must be immensely thick; I can't hear a thing, above, below or next door. Every now and then I hear someone shouting an order down in the yard, but it sounds very far away. The only sounds I can really make out are what I hear in the corridor, through the door. That's how I know that both the next-door cells, right and left, are occupied too: I hear the doors being opened and closed, and sometimes the Sergeant and his men announcing themselves before they go in. That means there are officers in those cells too. I'd be interested to know if they know why they're there. Or whether they've been treated as disgracefully as I have.

For supper I had sausage, cheese, bread and tea. All on the bill. Gunner Trmcik brought it to me.

After that I did what I could to spruce myself up. What that involves here I prefer not to write about.

It was still daylight outside when I lay down on my cot. I was amazed to find how exhausted and tired I suddenly felt.

Soon after that I must have dropped off.

The Interrogating Officer, Captain von Karapancsa, isn't my type. We shall give each other a bad time. Or rather, he'll give me one. Because our respective positions are just about as different as it's possible to be. He calls the tune, and he can make me dance just as he likes. When I think of the importance and the power which this man—this man alone—will have, if my arrest eventually leads to a court martial, I might just as well be buried already.

As soon as the usual formalities were out of the way, we crossed swords.

The Captain started the interrogation proper with: 'You

know, of course, why you have been arrested, Lieutenant. Have you anything to say?'

'I know absolutely nothing! I have absolutely no idea, sir. I find the entire proceedings against me completely outrageous,' I answered passionately and full of righteous indignation.

'I have your record here.' He waved a piece of paper. 'So don't play the innocent country boy with me, Mattachich,' he snapped back icily. 'A man of your type can't play that part. And, above all, kindly moderate your behaviour. Otherwise I fear we shall get on very badly.' There was no mistaking the cynicism in his tone.

And so our interview had begun as it was to continue.

It really began in the morning after my first day in prison, when Captain Sekulic informed me that I was to appear before the Interrogating Officer in the afternoon. I was very pleased at this information: a meeting with the responsible officer of the garrison court would, I hoped, produce not merely information as to why I had been arrested but also an explanation that it had all been an oversight, a regrettable error. I had by no means rejected the possibility that this first conversation would result in my immediate release.

The thought filled me with enthusiasm, so that the morning passed quickly, and I enjoyed my lunch.

Sergeant Senft had put on his best uniform when he came to fetch me, just before two in the afternoon. He led me down to the guardroom, where a Sergeant of the Guard and a soldier were waiting with fixed bayonets to take charge of me.

'Sergeant Weidlinger and Lance-Corporal Sedlacek,' the Sergeant introduced them as they both came to attention. 'Come to take you to Captain von Karapancsa, sir, in the courtroom. If you'd be kind enough to follow me, sir.'

And so once again I must have looked a strange sight, marching across the parade ground in step with the sergeant, while the lance-corporal followed three paces behind with his bayonet still fixed.

The thought of having to cross the town like this was not a pleasant one: the gaze of gaping civilians would be even harder to bear than the curious glances of soldiers. But it turned out that the court building lay within the barrack area, though at the far end from the prison. And so the triple-act was performing for a military audience only.

The garrison court was a new, two-storey brick building, which looked friendly enough from outside in comparison with the grim old walls around it.

My escort led me straight into the official interrogator's anteroom. A clerk vanished for a moment into the inner room, then opened the door wide. We went in.

Three officers were sitting at a long table: a Captain in the middle and a Lieutenant on either side of him.

The table was covered with papers and documents. On the wall behind the Captain hung a crucifix; next to it, a portrait of Franz Joseph dwarfed the figure of Christ crucified.

The Lieutenants had risen to their feet when I came in; the Captain remained seated.

My two escorts stood to attention. I followed their example.

'Sergeant Weidlinger and Lance-Corporal Sedlacek with prisoner, sir,' announced the sergeant. 'Lieutenant Count von Mattachich, sir.'

The Captain thanked them, whereupon my escort saluted again, then marched out of the room. Apart from myself, all the participants in the ritual had performed with practised fluency.

'Please be seated, Lieutenant Mattachich,' said the Captain. He indicated a chair facing the long table.

I thanked him and sat down. The Lieutenants sat too.

'You are now in the presence of the Garrison Court, Zagreb,' the Captain began. 'I am in charge of your case. I am Captain von Karapancsa.' He glanced now at the man on his left. 'Lieutenant Anzi, my aide.'

Anzi nodded to me.

The Captain turned to his right.

'Lieutenant Joost,' he said, 'Court Recorder.'

Joost too nodded curtly.

Karapancsa is a tall, thin man: the elegant, dashing type,

sure of himself, clever and eloquent too. From his voice and his appearance he could be of Hungarian descent, I thought. The name suggests Turkish blood, perhaps from some settler in Hungary a few hundred years back. Relations between His Majesty's Hungarian and Croatian subjects never have been the best. That's not to say that my countrymen don't often get on excellently with individual Hungarians, but in general there's always a latent hostility between us. And I became suddenly aware of it, as I sat there facing the Interrogating Officer. He (like his aide, Lieutenant Anzi) wore the uniform of the military judiciary. I put Karapancsa in his middle thirties; which means he must have a dazzling career behind him to have made it to Captain and Interrogating Officer by that age. In the army you have to keep an eye on the careerists, whatever their specialities!

Both lieutenants are about twenty-five. Anzi, a short, wiry lad with black curly hair, must be an Italian. Joost, the Recorder, is a hussar, and so not a lawyer; probably just temporarily seconded from his unit for this job. He makes the most favourable impression of the three. A typical cavalry officer. Where he comes from I couldn't say as he hasn't yet opened his mouth (nor has Anzi).

After our first brief passage of arms, both Karapancsa and I tried to be more or less polite, at first with some success.

'If you persist in the story that you don't know why you have been arrested'—Karapancsa was picking up the threads again, once he had satisfied himself that our first exchange had been duly recorded by Joost—'of course I shall be glad to explain the charges against you.'

'I should be most grateful, sir.'

'According to an inquiry now pending in the Vienna Provincial Court, you are strongly suspected of having forged a bill of exchange.'

'*I* am suspected?' I exploded.

'I believe I expressed myself clearly, Lieutenant,' answered Karapancsa. 'The forgery is alleged to concern the signatures of Her Imperial Highness Princess Stephanie and her sister, Her

Royal Highness Princess Louise of Saxe-Coburg. The latter of course you know very well. Isn't that so?'

'So I forged the bill,' I said. At that moment I realized what a conspiracy my enemies had put together. *I* had forged Stephanie's signature. And Louise's as well! That is a diabolical master-stroke, a unique work of art! But I was snatched away at once from the flood tide of thoughts bursting in on me.

'From what you say, I must assume that you at least know which is the bill in question, Lieutenant.' Karapancsa looked at me for a moment. Then he said: 'Would you like to admit straight away that you did forge those signatures?'

'I admit nothing, sir!' Suddenly I had become aggressive again. Quickly I added in a more moderate tone, 'Because I have absolutely nothing to admit.'

'"So I forged the bill." I believe that's what you just said?'
'Correct.'
'*The* bill. So you do know which bill we're talking about.'
'I can guess,' I said carefully.

'Very good.' When Lieutenant Joost raised his head from his writing, Karapancsa went on: 'Now, will you please tell us who in your opinion was responsible for those signatures.'

There was no time to reflect. Nor did I need any. Without hesitation I said:

'Princess Louise and Princess Stephanie, of course. No one else. Any other story is pure fantasy.'

The Captain stared at me sceptically. It was not difficult to see that he didn't believe a word I said. 'Fantasy,' he repeated. 'Do you really believe that, Mattachich?'

'No, probably fantasy is the wrong word,' I corrected.
'Aha.'

'Probably it is a simple matter of a criminal conspiracy against me that lies behind all this. May I inquire, sir, whether the Provincial Court in Vienna has any evidence whatever to substantiate this charge?'

For the first time the Interrogating Officer seemed less sure of his ground. I noticed that he hesitated a moment and glanced quickly at his aide, Anzi, before the answer came. 'I have had no direct contact with Vienna about this case,' he said.

There was another pause. Longer than the first. In the total silence of the room you could have heard a pin drop.

'I wonder if I might know, sir, on what grounds I have been arrested, if not on an official request from Vienna?' I inquired.

'Certainly you may,' said Karapancsa, a shade too loudly. 'Dr Bachrach, a Privy Councillor, a lawyer, and the representative of His Highness Prince Philip of Coburg, filed the charge. He has given credible assurances to this court that we can expect a warrant for your arrest at any time, from the Public Prosecutor's office in Vienna. The investigations—in which the Court Marshal's office is also very closely concerned—are almost complete.'

'Says Dr Bachrach!' Despite the deadly seriousness of my position, I couldn't help laughing aloud.

'The Zagreb Garrison Court has no reason to doubt the Privy Councillor's information. But before the court acted it took the precaution of seeking the opinion of its ultimate authority, General von Bechtolsheim, the G.O.C. Zagreb. He has expressly authorized the proceedings against you.'

'Well, if the General has expressly authorized it, then of course that's all right,' I said, making no attempt to conceal my sarcasm. I was no longer in any state to control my emotions. 'I'm not talking now about the substance of the charge against me, sir. There *is* no substance to it, anyway. I am talking about this Dr Bachrach. Personally. To my knowledge he is neither a public prosecutor nor a policeman. And certainly not an examining magistrate. He is the representative of my sworn enemy, and that's all. How can this court—an imperial military court—act on nothing more than the wish of a prejudiced civilian? Without this man needing to produce any evidence, or even any really solid grounds for suspicion?'

'You'll have to leave that to us,' Captain Karapancsa said harshly.

'Captain'—my voice had risen again—'we aren't talking about crime and punishment here, are we? We're talking about Geza von Mattachich, and how to get rid of him!'

Karapancsa rose from his chair. The Lieutenants and I followed suit at once.

'You've been away from active service too long, Mattachich,' he said, almost softly. 'I'm going to leave you to yourself for a few days. I hope that you'll come to your senses, and that when we next meet you'll know how to behave properly.' Then he shouted for the guard.

The anteroom door opened and Sergeant Weidlinger appeared. 'Sir?'

'Take Lieutenant Mattachich back to his cell.'

'Sir!' Weidlinger moved over to my side. 'Follow me, sir, if you please.'

I didn't move.

The Sergeant looked at me in amazement. Then he turned to the Interrogating Officer for help.

'With your permission, sir,' I said firmly, 'I'd like to put one more question.'

'Whatever good will that do?' asked Karapancsa, amazed.

I took this as agreement, though it was probably not so intended. 'I should very much like to know, sir, what has become of Her Royal Highness Princess Louise of Coburg, who was travelling with me when I arrived in Zagreb two days ago.'

Karapancsa thought it over a moment or so. Then he calmly lit a cigarette, took a couple of puffs, and smiled at me kindly. He held all the trumps. He knew it, and he played them ruthlessly. 'Her Royal Highness left by special train for Vienna at noon yesterday. Her lady-in-waiting went with her. And, you may be interested to learn, so did your friend Dr Bachrach.'

I don't know how I got back to this cell. I must have moved completely automatically, like a robot, a mindless thing. Incapable of taking in any more of what was going on around me.

How long I lay here on my cot I don't know either. As my awareness of the actual situation gradually returned, I was in darkness.

I looked out of the cell window. It was night. I was frozen.

Just as I was, still wearing tunic and boots, I crawled under the blanket. I began to feel warmer, and forced myself to bring some sort of order into my whirling thoughts.

So Louise had gone back, to Vienna and the Coburg Palace. And in the obligatory special train, too. A point which the Interrogating Officer had not failed to stress. And here I sit in prison, awaiting trial on a charge of forgery. A forgery I did not commit! When you think that my case concerns the signature of two members of the omnipotent Viennese court, they'll give me a good two years more than that Lieutenant Jubelsky I told Louise about in Nice.

My Louise!

So it's happened; the thing she said could never happen: she has given in to her husband, upped and left her darling Geza. While he is in prison on her behalf.

No, that's wrong. Not *while* but *because* he is in prison. This act of force against me was a necessary preliminary to enable them to part her from me. Before Bachrach could get his hands on his 'noble' client's wife, and take her back to him, he had to get rid of me.

This is the end then. It was foolish to imagine it could end any other way. Back under the power of her husband, in the bosom of her family, without contact with me, or even news of my whereabouts, Louise will give up.

To deceive oneself is pointless: it is the end, the irrevocable end.

I started flicking through my diary.

A melancholy pastime. I found the entry describing our first night: how with the waltz rhythms of the ball still ringing in my ears I climbed over the balcony and into her bed.

Yes, here it is. 'Everything venture, everything gain. The woman is worth risking your neck for.'

Today I added to it:

'Everything venture, and a broken neck.'

* * *

L

June 1898 There is no mirror in my room. But if I open the window, I can see my reflection in the glass. My eyes are swollen with weeping. The sight is unbearable, even though the window-pane is kinder to me than a mirror would be.

The only comforting thing around me is the green trees outside the window. But the view is soiled by the iron grating that separates me from them.

Every morning an old man passes below my window, leaning on a stick. He shakes his head, all the time. I wonder whether it's some affliction, or whether he is simply saying, 'No, no, no,' rejecting everything in and around him. I wish I could. I wish I could scream aloud: 'No, no, no!'

But I don't scream. I just behave normally. Very, very normally.

I wonder if Geza got the letter I wrote him in Zagreb. Or did it vanish for ever in the pockets of that devil incarnate, Dr Bachrach.

What would have happened if I had shot him down with the pistol under the pillow, the one that Geza hadn't wanted to take with him when he went for his medical? Or perhaps it's myself that I should have shot? No, no, no! That would have made it too easy for them.

I can't sleep any more. As soon as it's dark, images of that last morning in Zagreb come crowding into my memory.

I see the door closing behind Geza, and myself left alone, in a dreadful bed in an ugly room in a small hotel. But loneliness was a blessing compared with what followed.

I lay there, crying into my pillow, and the door was opened. Simply opened. Three men came into the room, and one of them I knew: Bachrach.

I sat up and shouted, 'Marie! Help, Marie!'

As Bachrach was shouting, 'Stop that noise! Be quiet!' Marie came rushing in.

'What is going on here?' she demanded of the intruders—and I should never have believed her capable of such aggression.

'We have come to take the Princess,' Bachrach answered. 'Her Royal Highness will be travelling to Vienna with us today.'

I felt at an incredible disadvantage and quite ridiculous, sitting there in bed with the blankets up round my neck, but I cried out, 'Where is Count Mattachich?' and ordered the Countess to send for him at once.

'It is no use, Your Royal Highness,' said Bachrach. 'The Count has been arrested.'

Marie Fugger looked at me in terror.

With all the energy I could muster, I demanded who had dared to arrest my secretary, and why. What charges had been laid against him?

'There is no need for Your Royal Highness to worry about that. You can safely leave that to the military authorities. They know what they're doing.'

When I refused to drop the subject, and went on demanding to be told the reasons for the arrest, Bachrach said it was a question of alleged forgery of a bill.

I was in no way prepared for that. It came like a thunderbolt. Geza and I had both been certain that the affair had been forgotten. I gazed speechless in front of me.

The lawyer said, 'Please get up, madam. Your train is waiting.'

I shook my head. Just like that old man down in the garden. I was trying to cope with two mental images at once: Geza under arrest, and myself dragged off to Vienna with the terrible Bachrach. But the pictures became blurred in my mind, so that I understood nothing.

'Please hurry, madam.'

I asked, more for something to say than any other reason, why I was wanted in Vienna. What was Bachrach going to do to me?

'You will be returning to your husband's protection.'

If there is one thing of which I was certain, unalterably

certain, it was that never again would I enter the Coburg Palace. I informed Dr Bachrach of this in no uncertain terms.

Dr Bachrach glanced meaningly at one of his two companions. 'In that case, I propose that Your Royal Highness should first visit a sanatorium.'

'As long as Count Mattachich is under arrest, I shall not leave Zagreb,' I said firmly.

Bachrach didn't take that up. Instead he apologized, with unmistakable sarcasm in his voice, for forgetting to introduce his companions. One—the one with whom he had exchanged that glance—was Dr Hinterstoisser, the medical officer of the Viennese law courts (the *law courts?*); the other was the Zagreb police chief. His name was given as well, but I didn't catch it; I was already busy with speculating why a doctor and a policeman should be here at all.

'The Chief of Police has reinforcements standing by,' Bachrach warned me. 'If you refuse, I deeply regret that we shall have to take you to the station in a rather undignified manner.'

Now the Countess Fugger went into action. She pointed out that it was out of the question for me to discuss things with three men while lying in bed. She asked them to leave the room so that I could get up.

The doctor and the policeman turned to the door, but Bachrach stopped them. He regretted that I must get dressed in the presence of my visitors, as it was thought that I might try to escape, or even to kill myself. Although I gave him my word that I should do no such thing he stuck to his demand, and the Countess's scathing comments would not deter him.

I asked the Countess to call my maids.

When Ilona and Antonia appeared I explained to them that I must get dressed, but that the three gentlemen were refusing to leave the room. This, I said, showed a marked lack of both decency and respect. I therefore had no alternative but to ignore their presence altogether. I asked the maids to do the same. Then I threw back the bedclothes.

At least Bachrach now felt he could safely turn his back, and the others followed his example.

To this day, I don't know where I found the spirit to act as I did. I was obsessed with the idea of gaining time. As if time could help me now!

When I was dressed, and my hair had been done, I asked Marie, 'Have you breakfasted yet, Countess?'

Marie said no.

I instructed Antonia to order breakfast for the Countess and for myself.

As soon as the maids had left the room Bachrach turned to me angrily. 'What is the meaning of this foolishness, Your Royal Highness? It is late. We must hurry.'

Pretending not to have heard him, I calmly sat at the table, and gestured the Countess to her chair also.

While I sat there, trying to set my thoughts in order, I watched the Privy Councillor opening doors and cupboards and rummaging in the bed; eventually he found Geza's pistol, under the pillow. He seized it triumphantly, saying to the others, 'There—you see how right I was not to leave the Princess alone?'

Now I had at last realized what I should have said at the very beginning. But before I could even open my mouth two waiters entered, laid the table carefully, and brought bread, butter, jam and coffee; then they vanished again. The Countess poured the coffee for me.

I pushed the cup calmly away, and turned to the Zagreb police chief. 'I wish to make a statement,' I said firmly. '*I signed that bill.*'

'You don't even know which bill we're talking about,' said Bachrach angrily.

'I forged the signature of my sister, the Princess Stephanie.'

Countess Fugger stared at me aghast.

'Release Count Mattachich at once,' I said. 'I am ready to repeat what I have just said before any court.'

Geza knew better after all, I thought to myself. A king's daughter can indeed be brought to trial. Just like that brother officer of his who forged his uncle's signature. I was almost pleased at the thought that Geza had been right all the time.

My visitors said nothing.

I stood up, and went over to the Chief of Police. 'Come along,' I said.

The man remained motionless.

Dr Bachrach cleared his throat. 'Exactly as I told you,' he said to the doctor. 'I would have bet you that the Princess would try to take the blame on herself. She is completely under the influence of this fellow Mattachich.'

Now my self-control deserted me. Only briefly; but every night when I remember it I curse myself for it. I told Bachrach furiously that I would not stand for his disrespectful manner and demanded that he should observe normal etiquette; I beat upon the table with my fists; and I repeated over and over again that Geza was innocent, and that I should be arrested in his place.

When I looked into the coldly watchful eyes of the three men, I saw that it was all in vain. I felt tears rush to my eyes. Because I would not for the world have wept in front of them, I said no more. I sat down again at the table and tried to drink a mouthful of coffee.

The Countess laid her hand comfortingly on mine. I read so much compassion in her face that I felt better at once.

'What am I to do, Marie?' I asked her softly.

But not softly enough. 'Be sensible, Your Royal Highness,' Bachrach answered. 'Come with us, and don't make a scene. You don't want to create a scandal in this place.'

The Countess nodded her agreement. 'There is nothing else we can do.'

I was not ready to give in so easily. Never! I must achieve something before I surrendered.

'I insist on two conditions,' I said sharply to Bachrach. 'One: you will promise me by everything you hold sacred' (as if there was anything!) 'that I shall neither have to set foot in the palace on the Seilerstätte nor have to see the Prince of Coburg. I desire never to see him again!'

'Yes, Your Royal Highness, on my word of honour. But now it really is time to go.'

'The second condition, Doctor. I should like to write a few lines to Count Mattachich and I should like them handed to him today without fail.' I stopped and turned quickly to the Chief of Police. 'Perhaps it is you I should ask to see to that.'

But Bachrach was already swearing that he would personally guarantee my wishes were carried out. 'But please consider a moment, Your Royal Highness,' he added, 'whether it is really fitting for a person of your rank to correspond with this man. You might compromise yourself by writing to him. Remember, Mattachich is under arrest.'

'I need no advice from you on how to behave, Doctor,' I said coldly, and asked the Countess to bring me pen and paper.

This is my confession, I wrote. *I hereby solemnly affirm that it was I who signed the bill in question and appended the signature of my sister, Princess Stephanie.* I signed it with my full name and title, and added a postscript: *Make use of these lines, my dear Count. I should be deeply dismayed to think that you would suffer any embarrassments on my account. Your friend*, L. VON C.

I sealed the envelope and handed it to the Chief of Police. But before he could put out his hand to take it, Bachrach intercepted him and took the note himself.

It is time to put it down at last in black and white: I am in Professor Obersteiner's private clinic in Vienna. In Döbling. It seems to be a 'closed clinic', an expression I have never heard before in my life. What they used to call a madhouse. But 'they' were wrong, because here I am, and I am not mad.

In my excited state at Zagreb, I had accepted the word 'sanatorium' without question. If I had envisaged anything at all, I suppose it would have been something like the Kurhaus at Baden bei Wien.

The first inkling I had of what lay ahead of me came when I boarded the waiting private train at Zagreb to be greeted by a wardress and three warders in white coats. Bachrach explained, with unparalleled impertinence, that the men had been engaged by the doctor in case I should have a fit! I informed him that I had never had a fit in my life, and had no intention of doing so in the future.

Yet I wished that I had the strength to go mad there and then, to rush out onto the platform screaming for help. But I was afraid of the warders; I thought they would put me in a straitjacket. Without a word of complaint I allowed things to happen as they would.

Besides, everything seemed very unimportant compared to the fact that Geza was in prison.

The wardress is still with me today: Berta Schnelzer, a big, strong woman who could have coped alone with the emergency for which her three colleagues were engaged.

The have taken away Ilona and Antonia. They were sent back to Lobor, under escort from some Croatian policemen, to pack my clothes and personal belongings and send them on here. Bachrach promised to pay them their wages, and their fare to Vienna. But I know how much value to set by his promises: even my luggage has not yet come. The two girls sobbed bitterly when we said our goodbyes, and so did I.

The chambermaid they've given me here is called Olga; she comes from Bohemia. I don't trust her an inch. In fact there is only one person near me now whom I can trust: Marie Fugger.

The doors here have eyes and ears, though no handles. Marie and I have found a place in my room, in the corner just by the door, where we are out of sight of the unseen eyes. We sit there and whisper together.

Marie tells me steadfastly to keep my courage, not let myself go, not cry, and answer all questions simply and truthfully. Dear Marie still believes in the truth, despite everything. So she doesn't know Philip yet.

I tell her all my sorrows: Geza must think I'm not lifting a finger to help him! How could he know that I've been dragged off to this place?

Marie is waiting for permission to make a few urgent purchases for me in the city. Then she will wire Ozegovich, telling him to come to Vienna at once. When he is here she can tell him everything, and he will try to establish contact with Geza. But we don't know yet how he and Marie can meet, or where.

Professor Obersteiner is said to be a very brilliant man. On my arrival he greeted me respectfully, and asked whether he could do anything to make my stay more pleasant.

I told him he could start by removing the bars from my window.

He gave a rather forced laugh, and said that unfortunately that was impossible. But if I would like any diversions or amusements, he could certainly be of assistance.

I asked for a piano.

It stands there now, against the wall. I have hardly touched it. It seems perfectly absurd to play the piano in these grim surroundings.

'How long must I stay here, Professor?' I asked him.

'That is entirely up to you, Your Royal Highness,' he said.

'Oh no,' I contradicted him heatedly. 'Not me! It is up to the man who has had me locked in here—my husband.'

'There Your Royal Highness is in error,' he tried to persuade me. I had, he said, been brought to the clinic entirely at the request of the Imperial Court Marshal's Office, which of course was responsible for all members of the court.

'Then that office is merely acting on the orders of the Prince of Coburg. Or, if you prefer, at his request.'

When he tried to make excuses I informed him that I knew the background of the story far better than he, and he would not change my mind.

It enrages me beyond measure to think of this great scientist lending his name to such an injustice. I think he guessed my thought. At any rate, he took his leave of me rather hastily, after promising to visit me every day.

But he never comes.

Instead he sends his senior doctor, Hartl. A man of about forty-five—polite, cold and suspicious, as I gather from the fact that he is always setting traps for me. We chat about unimportant things, then he will suddenly catch me off guard with a totally unexpected question, quite unrelated to what has gone before. One was: 'When was Princess Dora born?'

He won't catch me like that. 'On 30 April 1881.' I know the date.

'In which regiment is your son serving?' He sounds like a schoolmaster.

'None,' I answer. 'He is at the Academy.'

Wrong! Leopold has long left the Academy, Dr Hartl informs me. He is serving as a lieutenant in the 9th Hussars.

I didn't know that. I had no idea. I have to explain to Dr Hartl that I have no contact with Leopold, and we don't even write.

'Doesn't that sadden you, Your Royal Highness?' he asks, watching me closely.

'No,' I say coldly.

Not telling him that during the first few months of my new life I wrote to Leopold several times, but all my letters came back unopened.

* * *

G

Captain Karapancsa told me he would leave me to myself and my fate for the time being, and since he is clearly intending to do so (I have already been sitting in my cell for ten days and nothing has happened), I have decided to put the time to some use. As well as I can in these limited circumstances. I asked Captain Sekulic to get me something to read: books on military law. What little I learned about the subject on training courses was for amusement only; this is life and death. Literally. Meanwhile I've become convinced that my wrongful arrest was only the first in a long chain of well planned miscarriages of justice. If I'm still to have any chance of escaping from the infernal machine, I'll at least have to know how it works.

My request was forwarded by Sekulic to the Interrogating Officer. That is the rule. To my amazement, Karapancsa made no objection. Now I sit all day brooding over a thick volume, nearly as old as the law it discusses.

My studies have brought one thing home with shocking clarity: everything set down in this book, and presumably followed in practice, is a crying disgrace to a country that counts itself a part of the civilized world. This brand of justice has always been done in strict secrecy behind high walls, and that is the only possible reason why the medieval punishments meted out here haven't aroused an outcry.

One could almost envy the French for their Dreyfus Case. Although I'm by no means convinced of the innocence of the French Captain, his countrymen at least learnt a lot about the bizarre habits of their military courts. I'm sure that there will soon be some changes in this field on this side of the Rhine.

The legal basis for military justice in Austria-Hungary, here on the threshold of the twentieth century, is the 'Theresian Criminal Statute ... of 31 December 1768'! But in spirit its roots are in the Middle Ages. The High Middle Ages. Make no mistake about that.

The Court Martial itself, which sits behind closed doors, consists of the Interrogating Officer and seven other officers. The president, who is the senior officer present, has two votes; the others, except the Interrogating Officer, have one each. Only the I.O. is a trained lawyer. The other seven are all specially seconded for the case from active service units. They are laymen, ordered to perform a legal duty of which they have in practice absolutely no understanding.

The person on whom all depends is the Interrogating Officer. The 'criminal statute' of the late Maria Theresa invests him with an authority (still valid today) which is as near Divine as makes no difference. He is examining magistrate, public prosecutor, counsel for the defence and judge, all in one.

Then there is no hearing in the normal sense. The accused only appears once before the judges: to hear the transcript of his remarks to the Interrogator during his preliminary examination. He has to sign, confirming that this document in fact does represent a true record of what he said. Once this is done, he is taken back down, and only appears before the court again to hear his sentence read.

The seven officers form their verdict exclusively on the strength of the Interrogator's written report on his inquiries, the so-called 'votum informativum'. By the terms of paragraph 231 of the Statute, the Interrogator must 'produce from the assembled data and arguments a coherent whole; discuss the facts of the case comprehensibly and exhaustively; explain his opinions as to the accuracy and adequacy of the said arguments' and finally 'propose his legal verdict clearly and definitely'.

The seven laymen on the panel of judges are, by the terms of this literally criminal Statute, in no position to form their own opinions should they wish to. The case is seen by them only at second hand, through the Interrogator's glasses. They may not even hear or question the accused, nor a single witness, material or expert.

Yet the Interrogator is not the supreme authority. He is subordinate to the Corps legal expert. And he in turn is acting under the instructions of *his* superior, the Corps Commander. In my case, the instructions of General von Bechtolsheim. This arrangement ensures that the Corps Commander can have things exactly as he wants them. At least in a case where he wishes to influence the result.

For over two thousand years prosecutors, defence counsel and judges have striven to bring the truth to light; they have scrutinized every ground for suspicion, every extenuating circumstance; their efforts have complemented and balanced each other. This fundamental principle of justice, hallowed for centuries among all civilizations, has been expressly forbidden in royal and imperial Austria by this savage law of 1768.

My reading was very informative. Unfortunately, it did nothing for my confidence. Quite the reverse!

What I can expect from Captain von Karapancsa I already know from our first meeting. I know, too, how much protection the law affords me: none whatever. And when I remember that Prince Philip and General von Bechtolsheim are personal friends (as Louise was sure she remembered they were), then I need cherish no illusions about my future; I can sit back confidently and expect the worst. Well, *bon appétit*!

* * *

L

There is a coffee-house on the Schottenring where ladies can go without chaperones. That's where Marie will meet Ozegovich.

Tomorrow she will be going into the city to buy me some linen (they treat me very meanly), as my luggage hasn't yet arrived. And so tomorrow, at last, she will be able to go to the post office and send a telegram to Brežice.

Marie thinks the message will reach Ozegovich in forty-eight hours, but I'm very doubtful. As I remember Brežice, it seems impossible that a telegram could ever arrive there at all.

Marie will try and arrange a meeting for next Thursday.

This morning a nurse came to see me. She asked me to come over to the main building, to be examined by a Professor Sommer.

We set off, accompanied by Marie Fugger, Olga and Berta Schnelzer. For the first time I was able to get some idea of this place—when I arrived I was far too perturbed to take anything in properly.

My door (with its missing handle) leads into another little room—the lair of Cerberus, Berta Schnelzer. Beyond that there is a hall, and a flight of steps leading down. Marie and Olga's rooms are on the ground floor. We four are the only people in this block. The meals are obviously sent across from the main building.

We walked across the park—the garden, as it really is. A few patients were walking there, men and women, some in white coats and some in their own clothing.

Whenever we passed one of these walkers, I was aware of an inquisitive glance. I returned it with equal curiosity. This man ... that woman ... are they mad? Is that what mad people look like? Exactly like Marie Fugger, Berta Schnelzer, Olga? Exactly like *me*? What sickness keeps these normal-looking people here? Or is it just that they, like me, were in somebody's way?

We entered the main building, climbed a flight of stairs. We were shown into the surgery.

Professor Sommer is a man in his late sixties, I should imagine. He has kindly blue eyes, a grey goatee beard, and a friendly nose propping up a pair of gold-framed glasses. His nose and cheeks are crisscrossed with tiny blue blood-vessels, which show that the Professor is fond of his red wine. Later in our conversation he freely admitted as much, and I laughed again for the first time since leaving Lobor. It did me an amazing amount of good.

'Your Royal Highness,' he told me, 'your mind is no concern of mine. I know nothing whatever about it. I am much more interested in your physical well-being.'

Olga had to half undress me; then I was measured, weighed, my pulse and blood-pressure taken. Then came a whole series of peculiar tests with a needle, a little toothed wheel and a fine hairpin. To test the sensitivity of my nerves, he explained. After that he checked my reflexes. And throughout the whole interview he kept making little jokes, making me laugh.

When the examination was over, I asked him, 'What is your diagnosis, Professor?'

He looked at me, kindly.

'Normal. Completely normal.'

I cannot describe what these words meant to me. I wasn't even sure exactly what he meant by them, but they gave my spirits a tremendous boost. So much of a boost that I ventured to ask, 'What exactly do you mean by "normal", Professor?'

He looked at me cheerfully, winked, put his head on one side, and said, 'The patient shows no sign of degeneration, no nervous disorders; she has a fine, normal physical development and appears healthy. That is what my report will say.'

I could have thrown my arms round him. I realized for the first time how much the 'asylum' atmosphere had oppressed me and sapped my self-confidence.

'Your pulse is a little quick; almost 100 beats per minute. But it's strong, healthy and rhythmical. No need to worry any more about that,' he added.

I walked back across the park between my companions, my head high. People passed me as they had on the way over, and still stared, but I no longer had anything in common with them.

This afternoon I had a visit from Bachrach. He brought with him another man, whom he introduced as Dr Karl Ritter von Feistmantel, president of the Lower Austrian law society, from Vienna.

In honeyed tones, and as gently as if he feared to wake me from some deep sleep, Bachrach inquired after my condition.

'Thank you Doctor,' I replied in a normal voice (which seemed to alarm him). 'I am in the best of health. In every respect. Physical and mental.'

Whatever I said during the afternoon, Bachrach would glance towards his companion: a glance that said, You see how mad the poor thing is? What did I tell you?

And each time Dr Feistmantel would nod his head in grave agreement.

I became impatient. I told Bachrach that I couldn't believe he had come merely to inquire after me, and suggested that he should come to the point.

He did. He told me that his companion, Dr Karl Ritter von Feistmantel, had been appointed by the Court Marshal's office to be my temporary supervisor.

I turned to Feistmantel. 'Could you explain to me what a supervisor is?'

Feistmantel looked at me, smiling benignly. They had obviously told him that I had the mental abilities of a six-year-old child, and that was how he addressed me. 'Well, Your Royal Highness, it's like this. Say a young girl's father dies; the law appoints a guardian to take care of her instead of her father.'

'Dr von Feistmantel, I am not a little girl, and my father is very much alive. So what exactly will your duties be?'

'The Court Marshal's office thinks——'

'You mean my husband thinks,' I interrupted.

'With all due respect, Your Royal Highness, I am speaking about the Court Marshal's office—or, if you prefer, the Marshal himself, Prince Montenuovo. Well, their opinion is ... their entirely *impartial* opinion is that Your Royal Highness's ...' he hesitated ... 'health at present does not permit you to safeguard your own interests. So I have been instructed——'

'When you speak of my health, Doctor, I imagine you mean my mental health.'

'Since you insist, yes,' he admitted.

Bachrach was watching us closely, frowning.

'Then as I understand it,' I went on, taking pains to be clear and precise, 'the Court Marshal's office—completely uninfluenced by outside pressures from, for example, my husband —has suddenly suspected me of mental incompetence. And this although up to my present, entirely involuntary visit I have not been in Vienna for more than two years. So no one could even see me, much less check on my mental health!'

'I must venture to contradict Your Royal Highness there,' said Feistmantel heatedly. 'A check-up did take place. That was why my colleague, Dr Bachrach, visited you in Croatia. I must admit that it is entirely due to his appraisal of the situation that you are here, and in safety.'

I turned to Bachrach. 'You must have truly supernatural powers! Did you really have this sudden inspiration sitting in your office in Vienna, that said I was mentally ill and you must rush to Lobor to see me? I assume that is the journey we are talking about?'

Bachrach was delighted to get into the argument. 'I must ask

Your Royal Highness to remember that I always have acted, still am acting and not doubt shall continue to act only as the representative of the Prince of Coburg. It was at his bidding that I made the journey to Lobor.'

'So I was wrong in saying you have supernatural powers—it is in fact Prince Coburg who has them?' I asked sarcastically.

'The Prince could worry about your health without needing to visit you. Even from Vienna he could recognize that you were exposed to very dangerous influences you were powerless to fight, influences which made intervention absolutely vital. I need name no names.'

'Are you referring to my secretary?'

'To Mattachich, yes.' He sounded insolent.

'You mean *Count* Mattachich,' I corrected him.

'By all means. If your husband had not acted, you would have fallen irretrievably into the power of this man. He would have been able to make ruthless use of you, to compromise you even further. Only the Prince's timely intervention——'

'My dear Doctor.' I stemmed the tide of words. 'In Zagreb you gave me your word of honour that you would take steps to have my letter delivered to Count Mattachich. Did you do so?'

'But of course, Your Royal Highness! I promised it solemnly.'

So Geza has my confession, I thought jubilantly.

'As was my duty,' Bachrach went on, 'I passed your letter to the Public Prosecutor's office in Vienna. It goes without saying that any letter addressed to a prisoner under examination must first pass the censor. To my utter astonishment your letter was opened and returned marked "not to be forwarded". So, against my will, I was obliged to read it. I was deeply affected by what I read. There could be no stronger argument than that letter for your presence in ... in a place such as this.'

My courage, and my self-confidence, were shattered.

I asked the two men to leave me alone.

Bachrach resumed his greasy, conspiratorial manner, while

Feistmantel assured me of his sympathy and his willingness to help me if he could.

The one is as disgustingly deceitful as the other.

Professor Obersteiner avoids visiting me. He has a guilty conscience. With reason.

Today he sent the Matron to see me, to inquire why I never play the piano. The Professor, she said, had hoped that the instrument would help to pass the time, and now he had heard that I never touched it.

Why don't I play? I tried to give the Matron a convincing reason. I explained that music was something happy, joyful, utterly unsuited to my present mood.

But, she said, surely there were compositions that were anything but cheerful?

That I had to concede, but explained that melancholy music would make me even sadder, and so would certainly be no distraction for me.

The truth I could not tell her. I play the piano very badly, and get no pleasure at all from it; I had a music teacher when I was little who made my life a misery.

Then she asked me, again on behalf of the invisible Professor, whether there was anything else I would like.

I asked her to make some suggestions.

She asked whether I enjoyed reading, embroidery, or drawing.

I read little, detest sewing, and draw almost as badly as I play the piano. Even so, it seemed somehow deficient in me to have no interests at all. So I asked for an easel, palette, canvases and oils—although my artistic achievements have never extended beyond pencil sketches.

She counted it a triumph to have wrung this out of me. When I saw her happy face I decided to humour her, and asked for reading matter as well.

After she had gone I spent a long time wondering what she had thought of me. Once I should have been entirely indifferent; but here I am for ever thinking of the impression I make on the people and things around me. I cherish the childish hope that they will let me go if I can convince everyone of my sanity. If I am too friendly and forthcoming, they'll say, Ah, she's adjusting to her new life much too quickly. On the other hand if I am sarcastic and arrogant, surely that will be put down as an abnormality? If I tell them openly and honestly of the role Philip has played in my committal here, they'll probably put that down as paranoia. However I behave, it will rebound on me.

I am becoming noticeably less certain of myself.

In the afternoon the easel arrived, with three canvases, a box of oils, a bottle of turpentine, a number of paintbrushes, palette, pencils, charcoal and a sketching block.

I was also handed thirteen books and several illustrated magazines.

My room looks like an artist's studio.

'What illnesses did you have as a girl?' Dr Hartl asked me. He is supposed to call me 'Your Royal Highness', but he rarely seems to remember.

I pondered. Wasn't there ever anything wrong with me? Yes, of course—measles. 'I've had measles,' I said, with relief.

'When was that?'

'When I was a girl.' He glared at me. It must have been the wrong answer.

'Any after-effects?'

'Not that I know of.'

He made a note. Then: 'What other illnesses did you suffer as a child?'

I suffered a great deal as a child; but not illnesses.

Whatever can I tell him? I thought hard. Suddenly I remembered something. Mama took Stephanie and me on a journey to Luxembourg. It was summer, and very hot. That was when

I fainted for the first time in my life. It was a big day—Stephanie was jealous, Mama was anxious, the doctor put it down to pubescence. 'I fainted once,' I said.

That was what he wanted to hear. He looked at me with interest. 'Can Your Royal Highness remember at what age this happened?' He was even using my title now.

'I was nearly fifteen.'

'Oh, you were still just a girl.' That seemed to quench his interest. 'What about later illnesses?'

I shrugged my shoulders.

'Any contagious or infectious diseases?'

'Typhus,' I admitted.

'When was that?'

'It was winter.'

He looked astonished.

A silly answer. 'It was winter,' I repeated. 'In Spain. I can't remember the exact year.'

'Can you perhaps remember how old you were?'

Well, how old *was* I that year in Spain? It must have been about a year after my marriage. But when was that? I hope he doesn't ask me that, I thought. I remember having my seventeenth birthday soon after the wedding. 'I was seventeen or eighteen,' I told him.

Dr Hartl said, 'Quite right.'

He was playing the schoolmaster again.

'This typhus, was it a bad attack?'

A very bad attack, I told him. I lost a great deal of weight and felt wretched; it was a long time before I was more or less myself again. I couldn't stand any sort of exertion, but felt an urgent need for fresh air; the castle in the Pyrenees where we were staying was heated with an inferior, smelly kind of coal, so that I often felt sick. If I tried to go for a walk I soon became exhausted. Philip had no patience with me; because of me our stay in Spain had to be prolonged, which didn't suit him at all.

While I faithfully reported all this, Dr Hartl nodded agreement now and again. When I had finished he leafed through his papers, found what he was looking for, and said: 'Your husband puts it like this: "Her Royal Highness Princess Louise was often delirious during her convalescence, and her behaviour was irritable and obstinate in the extreme."'

'Delirious? My temperature was alarmingly high! Perhaps I was delirious at the crisis of the fever. But when I was convalescent I was very definitely *not* delirious. And what good would it have done being stubborn with an autocratic husband fourteen years older than me?'

Only after I had spoken did it occur to me that he had just quoted a statement from Philip himself. Those papers, lying in that black folder in front of him, are the evidence Philip has carefully collected to cast suspicion on my mental health. Who will the Doctor believe if I deny Philip's pronouncements? Me? Can he believe me? Dare he? Or would he too then be thrown to the Court Marshal?

'What about accidents?' Hartl asked now, leafing through the papers again. 'Has Your Royal Highness ever had an accident?'

I could not control my anger. 'Why don't you read all about it yourself? I know you've got it all down in there.'

Dr Hartl smiled patiently. 'I'd rather hear it from you.'

'I can't remember any accidents,' I said stubbornly, though I knew well enough what he was after.

'I'll give you a clue,' said Hartl. 'Styria.'

'Yes, that's right, I did have an accident there,' I admitted. 'We had a hunting lodge at Admont, in Styria. But of course you know that already. While my husband was out hunting one day I went for a walk alone. In fact it wasn't a walk so much as a climb. What was more, the ground was damp and slippery. I lost my footing and rolled down a steep slope. I collected some lovely blue marks in the process, too. Fortunately I managed to get hold of a tree in the end, or it could well have gone very badly with me. I just sat there for a while, to get over the fright.'

'Were you conscious?'

'Very much so.'

'And how did you climb back up?'

'The same way as I went down. But considerably more slowly.'

'With no outside help?'

'Obviously. I told you, I was alone.'

'And did you have any after-effects from the fall?'

'Yes. As usual, when I wasn't feeling myself and needed a little sympathy, my dear husband made a scene instead because I had gone out without a lady-in-waiting. And because I'd collected a few grazes on my face. And because my absence had caused a lot of worry.'

'Is that all?'

'As far as I recall. But no doubt you have a much more exciting account of what happened. May I hear it?'

Dr Hartl smiled. 'According to my notes, you fell about a hundred feet over a cliff and were found unconscious four hours later.'

I laughed loudly. Too loudly, perhaps.

'For four or five days you were only intermittently conscious, couldn't recognize your surroundings, couldn't speak clearly, complained of pains in the back of your head, and had heavy contusions all over your body.'

'Contusions?'

'Bruises. Blue marks,' he explained, still smiling.

'That was at least ten years ago ...'

'Sixteen,' he corrected me. 'It was in August 1882. You were twenty-four.'

'And yet Prince Philip remembers all these significant details so clearly. How very uncharacteristic.'

'The details come not from His Highness but from a ...' he looked at his notes, 'Professor Braun.'

Philip's personal physician. A man who would swear I had fractured my skull if Philip told him to.

'After this fall the doctor recorded an increasing irritability, a change in feelings and attitudes, in his noble patient, which he says became ever more striking.' Even the sombre Dr Hartl now had a note of irony in his voice.

And what does that note of irony mean? Is he trying to tell me that he knows the whole thing is a fairy-tale? Or is he making fun of the doctor's rather pompous style? But by now he was serious once again.

'The Prince recalls another event, which seems to be more significant,' he said, producing another piece of paper from his folder. 'Your Royal Highness suffered a miscarriage. Is that correct?'

I nodded.

'The Prince says that after this you became more irritable and bad tempered. You showed an increasing and absolutely baseless resentment of him. Are you aware of this?' he asked.

I didn't want the child. But how can I say that to this stranger? I didn't want to endure yet another childbirth. It was in any case the result of a virtual rape. Philip enjoys that sort of brutal lovemaking. Particularly because, with me, there always comes a point when I can no longer resist. That flatters his male egotism colossally. Although he knows what deep feelings of loathing and disgust it produces in me always to be the loser in this unequal struggle. That child, conceived by me in revulsion and hate and spawned by him in savage triumph, was a child I simply did not want. It could never have been as children should be. I did everything I could to get rid of it. And when I succeeded in procuring the miscarriage, Philip in his blind fury would have liked dearly to kill me. And that he now calls 'an absolutely baseless resentment of him'!

'I asked whether you were aware of this feeling,' repeated the doctor.

'No,' I answered.

'Is it not true, then, that you feel resentment against your husband?'

'Certainly it's true. But I should prefer not to explain it.'

'It would be very valuable for your case if you could give convincing reasons for this completely unnatural attitude.'

He wasn't going to let me off the hook. Playing for time, I asked, 'What is unnatural about it?'

'There is a very deep-seated ethical and moral sense in the human mind that makes a woman love, honour and obey her husband.'

What this poker-faced doctor was preaching now seemed to me pure cynicism. If the King of the Belgians and the Duke of Saxe-Coburg-Gotha made up their minds to marry the King's daughter off to the Duke's son, I can't see that that's any guarantee that the King's daughter will love her husband if he is unworthy of it. And Philip *is* unworthy! Should I tell Dr Hartl that? Probably it would simply confirm his suspicions that I lack that ethical and moral sense which he thinks is so deep-seated in the human mind.

He seemed not to expect an answer from me, for he now went on: 'Was Your Royal Highness much disturbed by the death of the Crown Prince Rudolf?'

Danger! Thin ice! I answered: 'I should have thought the entire nation was deeply disturbed by that tragedy.'

'Of course,' he agreed. 'Your husband remembers you being subject to violent outbursts of weeping, far beyond the normal reactions of a mourner, and that after the death of the Crown Prince he thought you became increasingly eccentric.'

Here for once Philip was right. The outbursts of weeping did indeed happen, and Rudolf's death *had* affected me 'far beyond the normal reactions of a mourner' as Dr Hartl had just put it. But Hartl didn't know what my relations with Rudolf had been, and he isn't going to find out. It's true that I changed after his death. Philip had been quite right to believe that. Although Rudolf and I had grown far apart, he still had a very calming influence on me. Even if I spoke to him more rarely, it still did me good. After his death I was aware of a real loss.

'That's all nonsense,' I said casually. 'It's just part of this fantastic case-history that Philip and his doctor have cooked up out of a little truth and a lot of imagination, to have me locked away.'

When Dr Hartl looked like taking this up and asking further questions, I asked him to leave. I was tired, I said.

I can imagine his reproachful face if I were to tell him now how dirty my marriage was, and how clean in comparison that adulterous relationship.

When Marie arrived at the coffee-house on the Schottenring, half an hour early, Ozegovich was already waiting for her. Dear Artur was deeply shocked to hear what has happened to me. 'That Coburg creature deserves to have his neck broken!' he shouted, so excitedly and loudly that Marie had to beg him to control himself.

After she had told him about the abduction from Zagreb, the journey, and finally our arrival at the clinic, he could only sit there, shaking his head and saying over and over again, 'The poor Princess! Oh, the poor Princess!'

Marie said he was within an ace of bursting into tears.

Then she asked him to tell his own news.

When Geza and I travelled to Zagreb, Ozegovich was at Lobor, waiting for our return. To his astonishment, the day after we had left Geza's mother arrived there, to an enthusiastic welcome from Baron Fiedler. She asked Artur to leave Lobor at once, and refused to give him any information about where we were. Naturally, this worried him a great deal.

He travelled to his parents' house at Brežice, hoping to have news of us there. When several days had passed without any word, he took a train for Zagreb.

At the hotel they told him Count Mattachich had not returned since leaving the hotel on the first morning. A few hours later I had left, with three men. That was all they knew.

Myself, I think they knew a great deal more, but were careful not to say so.

Ozegovich left the army under something of a cloud. So he could not simply walk into the barracks and ask for Geza. But he knew from the old days of a café on the Jelacic Square where officers go to play billiards in the evening. When he inquired there for Geza, he was greeted with total silence. Then someone laughed aloud and said, 'If you want Mattachich you'd better try the Riviera. He's living it up in a castle somewhere there!' (I've no doubt that there were a few dirty cracks at my expense too, but Ozegovich is too much of a gentleman to repeat them.) Despite the behaviour of his former comrades, Artur had the clear impression that they knew something about Geza all right but were not going to talk.

An hour later he happened to meet his old batman Petar, now a general's valet at Corps HQ. After some fencing, and once he had promised to keep it to himself, Artur learnt that Geza was under arrest. His arrest had been kept strictly secret, but someone recognized him by chance as he was being led across the parade ground. His position in my household has made him a sort of celebrity in the Corps, and the news soon got round.

There was nothing Artur could do but return to Brežice. There Marie Fugger's telegram reached him, and he set out at once for Vienna.

Ozegovich has promised to do everything he can to get in touch with Geza. Because Geza must know, quickly, that I immediately admitted everything to Bachrach, and that no power can prevent my telling everyone again and again that I forged Stephanie's signature. Geza must tell the truth without hesitation, just as I have.

Ozegovich is on the way back to Zagreb. Once Geza has my message—and I believe Artur will manage to get it to him somehow—I shall be much happier.

The wardress, Berta Schnelzer, tells me my daughter Princess Dora is engaged to Ernst Günther of Schleswig-Holstein. This she tells me not as a representative of my family, which would be ludicrous enough, but because she read it in a paper and thought it might interest me!

I felt a humiliation so sharp it was like a physical pain. But I told the wardress casually that she was wrong; it didn't interest me at all!

Here I sit at Döbling—not half an hour by cab from the

Hofburg, the Coburg Palace, Stephanie, Dora, Leopold, even Philip—and I am forgotten and ignored by everyone. Not that I miss Stephanie particularly; but how can this sister with whom I was on such friendly terms see me locked up in an asylum and not lift a finger? She makes no effort to help me, see me, even send me her sympathy; a letter, even a flower, would be enough.

Then I had a daughter, in Nice, who loved me. Perhaps that was my mistake: perhaps though I loved her the feeling was never reciprocated. Remembering her cold, blue, doll-like eyes at that last conversation we had in her bedroom, I could almost believe it. The fact remains that Dora had been with me all her life. Until a few weeks ago. Until Ernst Günther and Philip snatched her away from me by a dirty little conspiracy. Have I no place in her heart? Do they just need to say, 'Now, you must forget all about your mother,' for her to do it like the obedient and well-bred child she is?

I could accept their not obtaining my permission for the engagement. (Though I told Bertha Schnelzer I had given it long ago—otherwise the humiliation would have been intolerable.) But they should at least have told me. For God's sake, I am still alive!

Today the Examining Magistrate, Dr Joseph Wach, appeared here to question me on behalf of the Public Prosecutor's Office.

His visit had not been announced in advance, and caused considerable upheaval. The matron brought him to me, and had already taken a seat herself when Dr Wach told her he wished to speak with me alone.

She left us with obvious reluctance.

This was the opportunity I had waited for so long. I told the magistrate everything, from the beginning, as I had made up my mind I would.

I had often before been in the position of having to sign bills of exchange, I told him, but Philip had always paid them. Then one day he suddenly refused to pay them any more; and people promptly refused to advance me the funds I urgently needed to cover my expenses on the strength of a paper signed only by myself. They insisted on my sister's signing as well. Because I had personal reasons for not wanting to ask her this little favour, I wrote her name myself, without really thinking what I was doing.

Dr Wach listened to me in silence, making little notes now and again.

I was very pleased with my statement. I had succeeded in not mentioning Geza's name at all. But then the magistrate asked me whether I handled all my financial affairs personally. That must surely be very unusual in my circles?

I had to admit that my secretary handled them for me, but under my supervision.

'What is your secretary's name?'

'Geza, Count Mattachich.' Now I found pleasure simply in speaking the name aloud. 'Geza, Count Mattachich,' I said again.

'And who were the creditors?'

'A Viennese bank. I can't immediately recall the name. But my lawyer, Dr Barber, acted as intermediary; he will be able to give you more exact details.'

'On what terms were you advanced this money?'

'I'm afraid I really don't know.'

'To whom was it payable?'

'To me, of course.'

He wanted to know whether I had actually received the money myself.

I had to say no. The payments were made to Geza, so that he could settle the most urgent debts.

Suddenly the magistrate said, 'We'd better both put our cards on the table, or we shall never get anywhere.' He revealed to me that Geza von Mattachich was under suspicion of having forged my signature and Princess Stephanie's on a bill for 750,000 guilders, received the money himself and kept it for his own use.

I protested, 'But I've just told you——'

'I know, Your Royal Highness, I know,' he assured me, 'but it is conceivable that—on grounds which I needn't go into—you are trying to protect Lieutenant von Mattachich and take the blame on yourself.'

'If Lieutenant von Mattachich was guilty I shouldn't lift my little finger to help him,' I said very slowly and clearly. 'I hope you understand me, as I have understood you.'

'Yes, Your Royal Highness,' he said; and it sounded sincere.

Suddenly I remembered something which I had almost completely forgotten. Something important! I told him at once. Barber had wired me at Nice asking me to confirm by telegram to Ritter von Kleeborn, the Public Prosecutor (I even remembered his name!), that Stephanie's signature was genuine. And I had done so. The telegram from Nice, signed with my full name, must still be in the Public Prosecutor's office.

'Quite right, Your Royal Highness,' he confirmed. 'But there again, it could be said that Count Mattachich sent the telegram behind your back and merely signed it with your name.'

'Mattachich knew and still knows nothing of that telegram,' I said calmly, and I felt that he believed me. 'I told him nothing. I even have witnesses. Ask my lady-in-waiting, Countess Fugger. She was in the coach with me when I stopped at the post office.'

'Did the Countess go inside with you?'

'No, I forbade it. But the clerk behind the counter is bound to remember me—I didn't do things very well. I'd never been in a post office or sent a telegram before.'

'Now, Your Royal Highness, I must ask you to answer me one question with complete frankness. When did Count Mattachich discover that you had forged the signature? You can't have concealed it from him for long.'

I told him the truth. I told him, too, how shocked Geza had been when he found out. How he had feared the worst, and moved heaven and earth—in vain, unfortunately—to meet the bill and so obviate the danger threatening me.

When the magistrate had gone, I called Countess Fugger in.

I told her in detail everything that had happened, and we were both very happy.

Rumours, rumours!

Rumours are going round, so fantastic, so indescribable that I still don't dare to believe them. People have been much nicer to me lately. The watchdog smiled, Olga was quite friendly, even the food has been better and has arrived at meal-times.

Marie and I both noticed it, and Marie decided to investigate the causes. She held long conversations with Bertha Schnelzer, and found the watchdog more human and approachable than she had at first seemed. About a week ago Marie gave her a little present from me. I have no money now, of course, but I gave her a pretty little handbag covered in tiny coloured glass beads, and that turned out to be exactly the right thing.

Bertha Schnelzer is a big, heavy woman who looks as if nothing could touch a chord of feeling in her; but now tears came to her eyes. 'The Princess is the victim of a terrible injustice,' she whispered. 'Everyone here knows it.'

And so the ice was broken.

Yesterday she took the decisive step. She beckoned Marie into a corner where they were unobserved, and told her excitedly that she had heard Professor Obersteiner absolutely refused to be responsible for keeping me locked up here any longer, as I was simply not ill. Apparently he said as much at lunch with Professor Sommer and Dr Hartl: Sommer agreed enthusiastically, and Hartl said nothing. The warder who waits on the doctors at table heard it with his own ears and passed the news on later. My Cerberus thinks that they're bound to let me go soon.

I did Professor Obersteiner an injustice. Although I realized that he knew from the beginning what was going on here, I didn't appreciate that he has much too much integrity to lend himself to this conspiracy for long. That was why he wanted to distract me, why he allowed me to have the piano and the painting things. He wanted to help me through the difficult days.

Professor Sommer was on my side from the start. I can still hear him saying it: 'Normal, perfectly normal!'

As for Dr Hartl, I'm not so sure. But what can a simple doctor do against two professors? Or even against one professor with the international reputation of Professor Obersteiner?

What will be the first thing I do when I get out of here? There can only be one answer to that: get the first train to Zagreb!

No. I must make no plans, must not begin to believe, must not become optimistic. I will not allow it.

But I disobey my own rules. In my secret heart I am already in Zagreb, and freeing Geza from his prison!

* * *

G

29 June 1898   The month of June is nearly over. It's four weeks today since I was locked in here, and nothing has happened. It's as if Karapancsa has forgotten me.

I lie awake at night, wondering over and over whether there's a single person alive who still thinks about me. Or whether I might lie here for ever without anyone giving a damn. I often feel that's all too likely.

Once in the middle of the night I couldn't stand it any longer; I seized the iron knocker and hammered on the door with it like a madman. My neighbours on either side swore and shouted, 'Shut up, for God's sake!' It was music to my ears.

The guard came and asked what was the matter. I couldn't answer. What could I have said? Angrily, the man went away again. But I was content. The light of his dark lantern had lit up the cell for a moment; that was all I asked. I had won a victory over night, desolation, agonizing silence.

I lay on my cot and went straight to sleep.

I've talked to Captain Sekulic. There is no fixed time within which a case must be heard. If Karapancsa feels like it he can let me fester here for months. If he thinks he'll soften me up that way he'd better think again.

Sekulic told me more or less bluntly that I had drawn the toughest Interrogating Officer of the lot. I believe him. But it's not the luck of the draw, as he thinks. Nothing is left to chance here; everything runs according to a subtle, cunning, criminal plan.

I am not forgotten! Not forgotten! What a wonderful day!
Wonderful, yet sad too. But I must try to get my thoughts in some sort of order.

This morning Gunner Trmcik brought me my breakfast. It seemed to me that he was behaving rather oddly, and handling the cutlery even more fussily than usual. He kept going to the cell door and peering out into the corridor. After he had convinced himself for the umpteenth time that the coast was clear, he came up close to me and thrust a letter into my hand.

'Chap who used to be Lieutenant Ozegovich's batman gave me this,' he muttered. 'Wants me to take an answer back as soon as possible.'

I could have flung my arms round Trmcik on the spot, ugly though the poor chap is (and may he forgive me for saying as much).

When I was alone again I stood with my back to the door, so that no one could see me through the spy-hole, and read the letter. It was from my loyal friend Artur.

It's absolutely impossible for me even to begin to describe my feelings as I read that letter. As if someone had thrown a bucket of boiling water and one of iced water over my head at the same time.

Poor Louise! My poor Louise! In an asylum!

She in an asylum, I in a prison. First round to Mr Coburg. You have to hand it to him, he's cleared things up nicely. His way of solving problems would have been a credit to Cesare Borgia.

And I spared this swine's life! Instead of shooting him down like a mad dog. Which in fact is what he is. But how could I tell, looking at the fat old man who stood there staring at me with his frightened red face? I should have killed him. Whatever had happened later, it would have been better.

I couldn't read any further. My mind was wandering hopelessly. I had only read the first half, where Artur told me what they had done to Louise. I simply couldn't take it in; my thoughts were always straying. To the duel. Philip stood there, staring. I aimed; fired; hit him. And fired again, and hit him again, and again. He fell to the ground. Dead. Dead!

Gradually I managed to get a grip on myself, and read on.

Louise asks Artur to tell me (and it seems to be her main preoccupation) that she has freely and frankly admitted several times that she wrote both signatures herself, without my knowledge. Behind my back. That I had nothing to do with the affair. And so I should tell the whole truth, frankly and without prevarication. Then they will have to release me straight away. If, she says, I am not free already by the time her message has made its difficult and slow way to me.

Finally, Artur writes, he is at my disposal at all times to act as a courier between Louise and me.

I can't stop thinking about Philip's reasons for having his wife put in an asylum. Because I agree with Louise that only he could have arranged it. Since no man (especially one as nobly born as Philip) can feel his prestige or self-respect really benefits from being married to a lunatic, he must have some specific aim in view. Something much more important than hurt vanity, public scandal and all the other unpleasant things that go with it.

I'm torturing my brain over it, but getting nowhere.

Yesterday I wrote a letter.
Trmcik passed it on straight away to this fellow Petar, Artur's ex-batman. He whispered as much to me this morning. Petar met Artur in the evening, and Artur will make his way to Vienna as fast as he can.

In a few days Louise will know exactly what my official and final statement here is going to be. That's the most important thing now.

I have appealed to her urgently to change her own statement to tally with mine. If only we can tell the same story, we shall be a good deal better off. She should excuse herself by pleading a quite understandable desire to keep her sister out of the scandal.

It was generous of Louise, but also short-sighted and wrong (my exact words), to endanger herself with that precipitate confession. No one expected or wanted her to admit to forging Stephanie's signature, myself least of all. She has only one duty: to do all she can to save her own skin.

* * *

L

It's been raining incessantly for a week. I stare out through the bars of my window at the grey clouds, hanging so low in the sky that they seem to touch the treetops.

Purkersdorf is only an hour further away than Döbling from the Hofburg. Yet it seems to me as if it were at the other side of the world. Here for the first time I feel truly abandoned. Time passes, but nothing else happens.

I never had an answer from Geza. Even Ozegovich is missing, and I shall hardly be able to hear from him now, since Marie has had to leave me.

I don't know whether Geza was sentenced, or whether he is a free man. Sometimes I ask Fräulein von Gebauer, my new lady-in-waiting, but she claims to know no more than I. I can't stand Fräulein von Gebauer. I don't trust her.

I miss Marie Fugger badly, and have no idea even of where she is. In a matter of days—no, hours—they took her away from me.

From the moment that we learnt what was going to happen, we were never left alone together for an instant. Bachrach and that legal doctor of his that he brought to Zagreb with him crouched like a couple of bluebottles on the wall, listening. We couldn't even whisper together. Olga packed my things, Marie kissed my hand, and I haven't seen her since.

Obersteiner was no match for Philip; Philip is stronger than any of us.

Before Professor Obersteiner could set me free, they brought me here, to Purkersdorf. Here no one takes any notice of me. There is not even a Dr Hartl to talk to. I am not examined, questioned; just ignored. A closed chapter.

My only souvenirs of Obersteiner are the piano and the easel. But I don't play and I don't paint. I just gaze out of the window all day long. Or simply stay in bed. At night I can't sleep: I hear screams coming from somewhere that freeze my blood in my veins. I am seized by terror, and by sympathy for these unseen companions in suffering.

Olga is still with me. Olga, the Bohemian peasant-girl. A familiar face at least. And she's a decent girl.

Dora is married. Even that just happened. She took no notice of me. Nor did Ernst Günther, of course. I wonder if someone asked her at the wedding, 'Where is your mother?' I can see her cold, child's eyes as she answers: 'Oh, but hadn't you heard? She's in a madhouse.'

* * *

G

28 August Since the beginning of the month they've been interrogating me every two or three days.

The whole of July, nothing happened. I waited. For Karapancsa, and for an answer from Louise. Nothing. They were the most wretched weeks of my life.

Whenever I heard Trmcik's steps in the corridor (you get to know everyone's footsteps here after a bit) I was in a frenzy. If he stopped outside my cell door I could hardly wait for him to open it. My hopes were dashed every time. Ozegovich has disappeared. I've heard nothing of him since Trmcik's friend Petar gave him my letter to Louise.

When I was at last sent for to appear before the Interrogator, it was like a release.

On our first meeting Captain Karapancsa behaved as if we had spoken together only yesterday. Not a word to suggest that two months had elapsed. And not a word about the abrupt ending of that earlier meeting.

When he had asked me to sit down, he inquired in businesslike but not unfriendly fashion whether I had anything to say.

I said no.

'So you insist that you did not write those signatures?'

'I insist, sir.'

Karapancsa took the record from Lieutenant Joost and read: 'In reply to the question who in his own opinion had signed the bill, Mattachich answered: "Princess Louise and Princess Stephanie of course. No one else. Any other story is pure fantasy."' He looked up at me. 'Do you remember?'

'Of course, sir.'

He handed the record back to Joost, and said, apparently casually, 'In the meantime the Viennese Provincial Court has submitted its report. The Examining Magistrate responsible, a Dr Wach, charges you with forgery and fraud. He appends a mass of documents to substantiate the charges.' He leafed through a folder. 'There is one document here I should like to tell you about at once. This is a solemn declaration by Count Choloniewsky, Steward to Her Imperial Highness Princess Stephanie. It asserts that the Princess insists most strongly that she had nothing whatever to do with this matter of the bill. Do you maintain that a respected senior official of the Viennese court would be capable of making a false declaration?'

'I don't know this gentleman, so I am hardly in a position to say what he would or would not do,' I answered.

'Very carefully put,' said the Captain, with ill-concealed resentment. 'For me, one thing is clear: Princess Stephanie, through her Steward, has made a clear and unambiguous statement on the matter. We can definitely assume, once and for all, that the signature in question is not that of Her Imperial Highness.' He looked at me. 'So how do you reconcile that with your statement at the first hearing, which I have just read out to you?'

So he's trying another frontal assault, I thought. Now we'll have to see whether my defences are good enough.

'I've been thinking things over,' I said calmly. 'I've had time enough.'

'With what result?'

'The signature of the Princess of Coburg is genuine. If you would hear in evidence what Her Royal Highness has to say about that there would be no more discussion on the subject.' I paused. 'May I ask whether the court has troubled to take a statement from the Princess?'

'You must accept that I ask the questions here,' said Karapancsa, annoyed.

Without taking any notice of that, I went on, 'So far as the second signature is concerned, I repeat, with emphasis, that I had as little to do with that as with the other. If Her Imperial Highness insists that it is a forgery, I can see only two possible explanations.'

'Which are?'

'Either Her Imperial Highness *did* sign it herself, and now that the scandal's broken she wants to follow her advisers' counsel and get out of the affair——'

'Do you realize what you're saying?' interrupted Karapancsa, furiously. 'That's practically lèse-majesté!'

'I am simply attempting to demolish the charges against myself, sir. To the best of my knowledge, the law gives me that right.'

'Continue.'

'Either the Princess—acting, I repeat, on advice—wants to disavow the signature now, a signature which only her warm feelings for her sister would have induced her to give at all——'

'Come to the point!'

'Or Princess Louise's letter enclosing the bill was never handed to the addressee, and someone else in Her Imperial Highness's household forged her signature without her knowledge.'

There was a silence. I could imagine what was going on in the minds of the men facing me.

'Why would anyone do that? Can you explain that, Mattachich?' said the Interrogating Officer finally.

The expected explosion had not come after all.

'For the same reason that Dr Bachrach offered me 100,000 guilders three months ago. For the same reason that he denounced me to this court when I refused his bribe: to separate Princess Louise and myself! And when the contemptible plot misfired, they reached for a weapon with which they thought they could render me permanently harmless. You must admit, sir, that they're well on the way to succeeding.'

'And who are *they*?' asked Karapancsa.

'My mortal enemy. Princess Louise's husband,' I answered promptly.

This was the plan of defence on which I had decided. I could stick to it without involving Louise in any way. I had explained it to her in detail in my letter, and urged her to retract any earlier statements and from now on to pursue exactly the same line of argument as myself.

Karapancsa waited until Lieutenant Joost had stopped writing. Then he said: 'I should really stick you on bread and water for slandering a Field Marshal, Mattachich. But that would only hold up the proceedings further. I want to get this affair over and done with, and so I'll let you off this time. But I warn you, don't regard this leniency as weakness. That could lead to unfortunate misunderstandings. Right?'

'Very good, sir.'

And so began the questioning that was to last throughout August.

It was clear that we had both decided to avoid further clashes. Although each of us knew what he could expect from the other, our relations grew more relaxed at each session. We had no rapport; not the slightest mutual understanding. But this very remoteness, cold and unchanging, in some strange way created a matter-of-fact atmosphere between us that we both realized was advantageous and worth preserving.

The first stage was a probing examination of my early life. From birth. I was amazed at the number of juvenile follies of mine, real and imaginary, that he had collected. Even so, the discussions proved very unproductive. After that the Interrogating Officer's curiosity switched to my first meeting with Louise, and the months that followed. Even here, as it appeared from the questions, he was well informed enough. Philip (or Bachrach) had done a first-class job. The later hearings concentrated principally on what financial resources Louise had available after her flight from Vienna, how the affair of the bill had been able to take place without my knowledge, and what I knew that could throw any light on it. My income as Louise's secretary featured largely in these discussions.

Karapancsa stubbornly refused, despite all my explanations and contradictions, to accept even a theoretical possibility that anyone but myself could have been the forger. (And of *both* signatures—I was supposed to have taken the money behind Louise's back to swell my own coffers.) And so we plunged deeper and deeper into the mass of significant detail. I caught myself out all too often trying to sway the Interrogating Officer with common-sense arguments, although I had realized long before that truth did not interest him in the slightest.

Thanks to Louise's letter, I knew that I could still rely on her completely. And in the meantime she must have had my own letter. So I could proceed on the assumption that she would have retracted her earlier confession, and that from now on our accounts would tally on all significant points. That made a great difference.

Whenever I could, I urged that I should be allowed to meet her, either in Zagreb or in Vienna. Naturally I had to pursue this argument without giving the least grounds for suspicion that I knew where she was, or the circumstances under which she was being held.

Any half-way conscientious man would have agreed at once to a meeting with the chief witness. No—he would have arranged it of his own accord long before. Not so Karapancsa. On the contrary, he informed me one day that he refused any meeting between accused and witnesses in military cases. On principle. As a result of his previous experience. What experience, exactly, he did not reveal.

From my study of the 'criminal statute' I know that he is free to conduct the inquiry exactly as he chooses. And so I could forget any hopes I had allowed myself to have that he would consent to a meeting with Louise.

Nevertheless, I continued to insist that Louise's statement would provide clear proof of my innocence. I noticed that he tried hard to avoid this topic. But that only made me cling to it more determinedly. The hearing gradually came to resemble a Graeco-Roman wrestling bout. Neither opponent had any visible advantage, but each tried to force the other to abandon his own position, in the hope of then being able to throw him.

For Karapancsa, my guilt was a matter of fact. He needed no witnesses. Especially not witnesses who might exonerate me.

While I stubbornly repeated over and over again, 'I'm sorry, sir, but probably only Princess Louise could tell you that.' Or: 'With respect, sir, you'll have to ask Her Royal Highness about that.'

When at the end of the second week of hearings I simply met every question with the answer that only Louise was in a position to give the information he wanted, Karapancsa threatened me with punishments again, and broke off the sessions.

Back in my cell, I forced myself to consider the situation sensibly, and had to admit that my tactics had failed. It was no longer any use counting on help from outside the prison.

This evening Trmcik brought me the long-awaited letter from Louise. Or so I thought. But it turned out to be a mistake. A despairing Artur told me that my letter had never reached Louise. Probably, he wrote, Philip's minions had spied on the good Countess and reported on her secret meeting with him at the coffee-house. Immediately afterwards she was taken away from Louise's side and escorted across the border. She seems to have taken refuge somewhere in Bavaria, where she comes from. But they didn't stop at that. Louise's hiding-place in the clinic at Döbling was considered no longer secure. On the very same day that the Countess was taken away, Louise herself was moved to a top secret destination. Despite trying everything he knows, Artur has been unable to find out where she is.

So the vital contact with Louise, that promised so much, has been broken again. She never had my letter. And so the attempt to co-ordinate our stories has failed.

As it grew dark in the cell, and the gathering night swallowed the last outlines of my wretched surroundings, only one certainty remained: after our latest clash, Karapancsa would 'forget' me again for a few weeks. Just as he had after our first meeting, when we crossed each other at the outset.

And so my surprise was considerable when, the next morning, Sergeant Senft arrived an hour earlier than usual. In his office he handed me over to the Sergeant of the Guard and his men.

In careful conformity to the now familiar ritual, the two of them marched me across the glacis to the court.

Captain von Karapancsa seemed particularly relaxed. Anyone who didn't know him would have thought him easy-going, almost friendly. After the Sergeant had roared out my name and been dismissed, the Captain said with an inviting gesture to the two lieutenants and myself, 'Please be seated, gentlemen.' He sounded like a croupier.

I thought of what had happened the day before, and mistrusted this peaceful atmosphere.

'Lieutenant Mattachich,' said Karapancsa, turning to me, 'it is the clear duty of an Interrogating Officer to make every effort to gather all available evidence, incriminating or otherwise, that can be relevant to the investigation and assessment of a case. Naturally this has happened and is happening in your own case, though the peculiar circumstances are not very helpful. Quite the reverse, in fact. For example it was no easy matter to take a statement from Her Royal Highness Princess Louise of Coburg, whom you have so often named as a witness. But even this has been done.'

I felt the blood rush to my head in my excitement. 'Is the Princess in Zagreb, sir?' I asked.

'No. There were imperative grounds why we could not issue that invitation.'

I was furious with myself. Could I have thought, knowing what I did, that they would let Louise travel to Zagreb?

'We asked the Examining Magistrate in Vienna, Dr Wach, to take a deposition from the Princess for the purposes of this court.' He produced a document. 'This is that deposition.' He looked more friendly than I had ever seen him.

'You had good reason to call for a statement from the Princess. She exonerates you in the most convincing way imaginable. She declares unequivocally that she herself wrote both signatures. Behind your back, Lieutenant. Without your knowledge.'

So Louise repeated to the Examining Magistrate what she had already told Bachrach. The thought flashed through my mind. Things have gone very differently to what I could have wished from her point of view, but no court could disregard this statement. That would be inconceivable.'

The Captain interrupted my train of thought. '*Both* signatures,' he repeated. 'Princess Stephanie's as well as her own.' There was a little pause; and then suddenly he was his old self again.

'How do you account for that, Lieutenant Mattachich? Can you seriously believe that a daughter of the King of the Belgians, closely related to a dozen European royal houses, would stoop to forgery?'

'I ... find it hard to imagine,' I stammered.

'You express yourself tactfully as always, Mattachich. I tell you plainly: no one would believe it. *No one!* And no court, obviously. This simply cannot be. This is ludicrous. Utterly ludicrous. If the world just turned upside down one day it couldn't be crazier than this!' He leant forward across the table. 'But do you know what *is* very easy to believe, because there are a thousand examples of it? That a woman will lie herself blue in the face to save her lover!' Then he added coolly: 'Even the daughters of kings are women, after all.'

I wondered what I should say to this—and how to say it.

The Captain showed a hint of sympathy—or was it just mockery? 'Don't waste you time worrying about it, Lieutenant. You were so determined to get the Princess's evidence. I wanted to stop you believing that we were preventing the Princess from testifying. She loves you and will say anything to help you. It's as simple as that. But even if she implicated you, it would make no difference.' He smiled with ill concealed embarrassment. 'I'm sorry to have to tell you this. The Princess is in a clinic. An institution for the insane. Dr Wach tells me that he expects her to be certified any day. That will automatically mean she has no status as a witness.'

He looked at me so coldly that I felt my skin creep despite the August heat. Then he turned to Joost. 'You may strike the Princess from the list of witnesses.'

By a brutal and cynical contrivance, Louise has been excluded from any possibility of influencing the course of the trial. They have not only locked her up, but for all official purposes they've killed her. She can say what she likes; it will be so much wasted breath. Now the train will go the way the points are set; my adversaries need no longer fear a derailment.

The Captain became more informal once more.

It turned out that he had spent some time in Vienna during July, taking statements from witnesses. Choloniewski (because Stephanie herself as a member of the Imperial Family was debarred from testifying), our former lawyer Dr Barber, the bankers Reicher and Spitzer. But above all, the distinguished Privy Councillor, Dr Bachrach. I have no doubt that Bachrach's status is less that of witness than of prosecutor; that like his master, Prince Philip, he knows no limits in what he will stoop to. Anything, if it will help to silence me and put me out of the way, like poor Louise.

One day Karapancsa produced the *corpus delicti*—that ominous bill. I looked at the two signatures, and could hardly restrain myself. My Louise had not even thought of disguising her handwriting when she wrote the treacherous words 'Princess Stephanie'. Back in Nice I was so desperate to hand over the new bill to Barber at last that I had hardly glanced at the signatures. Anyway, I had had no reason to suspect them.

Captain Karapancsa revealed to me that a handwriting expert—a man who enjoyed the confidence of the garrison court by virtue of his previous successes—had identified me as the forger of the signatures. Beyond any doubt. They had taken samples of my handwriting from Lobor, and these had been sent to the expert for analysis. The affidavit, which Lieutenant Anzi read out, closed with the pathetic sentence (I've committed it to memory): 'On the grounds and the evidence detailed above, it is certain that no other human being could have written the signatures in question on the said bill but the man Mattachich.'

The fanatical obsession apparent in this legal affidavit—a

document that should be marked by cold, factual neutrality—reminded me for a second time of the Dreyfus Case. He too had had his chances wrecked by a handwriting expert. Now I was finding out for myself how easily the trick is done.

Louise's signature, which of course would be sufficiently familiar to me, was an absolutely perfect, skilful forgery. Thus, more or less, this Herr von Uliczy in his report. Even so, he omitted any graphological proof for this statement. It had not escaped his expertly trained eye that the writing masquerading as Stephanie's signature on the bill had nothing whatever in common with the real thing. The expert solved this problem in his own fashion. In writing the forged signature, he said—and one can only marvel—I had disguised my own handwriting just enough to deceive the bankers. So the strange similarity between the two signatures (Louise's 'perfect and skilful', her sister's jotted down in my own handwriting) Herr Uliczy leaves unexplained. And no one asks him.

I pointed out all the contradictions to Karapancsa. He rejected every argument. I tried desperately to convince him that, having seen many letters from Stephanie to her sister, I knew Stephanie's signature as well as Louise's own. Why on earth would I have made such a wretched attempt at forging the one yet succeeded perfectly with the other? Surely this would have defeated the whole point of my nefarious undertaking?

Karapancsa shrugged. For him the affidavit was final.

Finally the Captain took a magnifying glass and studied the signatures. 'A careless, superficial job, Mattachich,' he said contemptuously. 'You might at least have rubbed out the pencil marks. Hopelessly careless. Here.' He handed me the glass, and the bill.

Only now could I see that parallel to both signatures in several places there were thin pencil lines. As if a preliminary sketch had been made. They were even to be seen in Stephanie's signature, which I was supposed to have written in my own hand.

I stared spellbound at the paper. It was clear that the pencil marks were not Louise's work. And equally clear what their purpose was. I felt the blood rush to my face in my anger and helpless fury.

I heard the hated voice of the Interrogating Officer. 'You're blushing, Lieutenant. That's something new. In view of this crushing evidence, perhaps you would like to make a confession?'

I bit my lip. Say nothing, I thought, or you'll make your position even worse than it is now. Although that would be almost inconceivable. It was damned hard work, but I kept my mouth shut.

From that moment I have known that Dreyfus, Jew or no Jew, sits on Devil's Island an innocent man.

In the course of the reading of the graphologist's statement it turned out quite incidentally (!) and to my boundless astonishment that the bill has meanwhile been paid.

The Interrogating Officer was at pains to play down the matter as trivial, but had to admit that punctually on 20 June the bankers had been handed the full sum of 750,000 guilders, at Philip's orders. On request, the bankers sent a statement to the Vienna Court (it was now in my folder) stating that they had been paid in full and hence had no further claim to make. For them, the affair ended for ever with the redemption of the bill.

And for me, that is the first good news for a long time.

I am no lawyer, but if the creditors have got their money (and, at their rate of usury, much more than their money) then how can there be any more talk of fraud? Now it must be *attempted* fraud, at worst. For all I know, that might make a great difference at law.

All my efforts to discuss this with Karapancsa were flatly rejected. 'I ask the questions here, Lieutenant Mattachich.' I've heard that song before.

Even so, I couldn't get the thought out of my head. That evening, chewing it over back in my cell, another idea came to me. It kept me awake half the night. In the morning I could hardly wait to face Karapancsa again.

'Sir, I should like to draw attention to a contradiction which in my opinion has become clearly apparent during the last few days.'

'A contradiction?' Karapancsa was shuffling his papers again.

'That's correct, sir.'

'By all means let's hear it,' he said, without looking up. 'But keep it short, Mattachich. We must get on.'

'As I understand it, the Prince of Coburg paid the bill punctually on the due date,' I began.

'What about it?' The Captain still didn't look up.

I had resolved to be carefully correct and polite. 'With great respect, sir, that proves that at least Princess Louise's signature is genuine.'

That brought his head up.

'There could be no more convincing proof,' I went on.

'Oh. Why is that?' It sounded both watchful and cynical at the same time.

No one moved. Three pairs of eyes were on me. The room was deathly still.

'The charge against me alleges that I forged both signatures.'

'Quite.'

'I should like to proceed for a moment,' I went on, 'on the assumption that the charge is well founded and based on fact.'

'That I can only welcome, Lieutenant.'

I refused to be aroused. 'That would mean that for my own advantage, and behind the Princess's back, I had produced a forged bill, passed it successfully, and put the money thus acquired in my own pocket for my own private use. Remember that Prince Philip of Coburg is convinced that his wife and I were carrying on an illicit relationshp; remember that he and I fought a duel for that very reason, and that since then he has left no stone unturned to separate us. How can any sane person believe that this same Prince would punctually pay a bill with which his wife has nothing to do? A bill which carries not his wife's signature but a forgery produced by his detested rival—

who, as a result, he is financing to the handsome tune of 750,000 guilders?' I paused. 'If he could do such a thing, it is he who should be in a madhouse, not his unfortunate wife!'

For the first time since we had faced each other across that table, Karapancsa held a long, whispered conversation with his aide, Lieutenant Anzi. I couldn't make out a word. Eventually he asked me, 'Is that all?'

I said it was.

Now he turned to Lieutenant Joost and said, 'Have you got that down?'

'Yes, sir,' said Joost.

'Good, let's get on,' said the Captain. He glanced at me briefly. 'In future, please confine yourself to answering the questions put to you. I shall not tolerate any more of these endless red herrings.'

And so the subject was closed.

* * *

L

Olga seemed in a rather strange mood when she brought my breakfast this morning, but I didn't pay much attention.

An hour later I happened to look out through my barred window over towards the terrace of the main building. Two warders were running up the flag, as is customary on days of national importance.

This is September. What sort of anniversary comes in September? I couldn't think of one.

I was watching the warders at their work again when I suddenly started. The flag they have just run up is hung with crêpe, and flying at half-mast.

Franz Joseph is dead, was my first thought. This is 1898, so he's sixty-eight, quite a fair age to die. And that's why Olga seemed so strange this morning. She was mourning her sovereign; my enemy.

I was still trying to establish what I felt at the Emperor's death when there was a knock at the door and Fräulein Gebauer came in. Her eyes were red from crying.

Franz Joseph is alive. But the Empress is dead. Elisabeth has been murdered in Geneva, stabbed with a dagger by a madman, or an anarchist. Fräulein Gebauer didn't know. She burst into tears again, and I was near to joining her. The futile brutality of the crime shocked me.

When I first came to Vienna from Brussels, Elisabeth was nearly forty years old: slim to the point of skinniness, very tall, very majestic and still very beautiful. I was very young then and full of zest for life; probably I caused a good deal of gossip. Since Franz Joseph is always ready to listen to anything, the Empress must have heard something as well. I felt her eyes on me at official dinners and receptions, when I was dancing, or holding court to a circle of young admirers. I never felt any censure in her eyes, only amusement and a hint of curiosity. And so I loved and admired her. Secretly I saw a sort of ally in her.

But I was too preoccupied with myself in those days to give very much thought to Elisabeth. Even so, it didn't escape me that she changed a great deal after Rudolf's death. Many people began to wonder about her sanity. She became melancholy, couldn't bear Court life any longer (convincing proof of her sanity in my eyes!), and finally brought Franz Joseph to the point of allowing her to remain away from Vienna almost permanently.

They say there were men in her life who were close to her; too close. I know that there was talk about her and Count Andrassy. Hungary can thank her affection for him for the Hungarian settlement with Austria. They used to whisper about an Englishman too—Middleton, or something like that —who must have been a brave man; and a young Greek who used to read to her.

I've no idea whether there is any more than a grain of truth in these rumours, or in others, but I hope so for her sake. But even then it probably wouldn't have been enough to make her happy. This romantic, imaginative, high-minded woman was married to a dry, insipid philistine who to her (and my) misfortune happened to be Emperor of Austria-Hungary. There was nothing she could do but throw him Katharina Schratt and make good her escape.

An escape which has now ended.

Purkersdorf Sanatorium was staging a memorial service.

The imperial councillor Dr Rudinger, the organizer of the ceremony, paid me one of his rare visits and invited me to take part. Since, as he put it, I was more or less a member of the Imperial Family, he assumed that this would be in accordance with my own dearest wishes.

I am opposed to any suggestion that comes from Dr Rudinger. So I decided to refuse but then thought better of it, and agreed.

Friday This morning the mourning ceremony took place.

Dr Rudinger led Fräulein Gebauer and myself solemnly over to the communal dining-hall in the main building.

When I came in, the assembled patients and staff rose to their feet. I have become so accustomed to loneliness that I was almost frightened.

The tables had been pushed to the side of the bare room, and the chairs arranged in rows before a dais, as in a theatre. On the dais stood an easel with a big black-draped portrait of the Empress; to either side of it was a potted palm. There were also a harmonium and a lectern.

Elisabeth was sixty when she was murdered. In the portrait she looked thirty. Her subjects only recognize her like that, for as she grew older she refused to be photographed. A little weakness for which I have considerable sympathy.

Three comfortable armchairs for us had been so arranged between dais and guests that we were displayed in profile to the spectators. Dr Rudinger had put me—and thus himself—on show, and his satisfaction at it was written all over his face, despite the sad occasion.

When I was seated in the middle chair, all the rest sat down too. The doctors and nurses sat at the front; the patients behind them.

A little man in a black suit appeared, bowed low to me, then sat at the harmonium and began to play.

I let my eyes stray over the faces of the patients; I think there must have been well over a hundred of them. Directly behind the staff, I guessed, would be the less severe cases. Many wore mourning and they looked thoroughly normal and respectable. But the farther back I looked, the more disturbed the people seemed. I met vacant stares, that showed no recognition of what was happening. Right at the back, surrounded by warders, I saw a few patients in white coats. Those are the violent ones, I thought, whose screams frighten me in the night hours. How shall I be able to sleep at all from now on, when I can imagine their faces as well, dead, agonized, blank? There are some very strong men there, in perfect physical condition. They are so strong that they have to be guarded even here. I felt terror grip me.

When the harmonium was silent again, Dr Rudinger stepped to the lectern. He bowed formally to me before he began.

At that moment I hated him with all my heart. He is a link in that chain of conspiracy that has stolen my freedom, although they all know perfectly well that I am as sane as they are. And now he was making use of me, to lend his ceremony a glow of distinction in which he himself could bask. I considered simply getting up and walking out. But the fear of committing an 'eccentric action' in view of the doctors held me back.

Meanwhile Dr Rudinger's eulogy rambled on. He spoke with a pathos that rang so false it made no impression on me at all. But the others, the patients—or at least one of them—were deeply moved. For suddenly a man began to weep somewhere back in the hall. Not like a man at all, though, but like a wounded animal, with long-drawn, chilling howls. At once other patients became restless. Dr Rudinger began to stutter and cast irritable glances at his audience. Then he gestured to the warders sitting on either side of the man. They dragged the man, now howling at the top of his voice, out of the hall. But calm was not restored. Far from it: the hall became a babel of weeping and wailing that threatened to explode at any moment. I was seized by wild and probably justified panic. Dr Rudinger broke off his speech abruptly and the harmonium-player hastened back to his seat and rushed into the National Anthem. The music seemed to calm the patients: some got to their feet, as I did too of course, and soon quavering voices were ringing out imploring God to preserve their good Emperor Franz.

As soon as the music ended Rudinger led Fräulein Gebauer and me from the hall, while the patients stood there motionless, staring at me with big frightened eyes.

On taking his leave, the Doctor apologized for the fiasco. Probably he should have prevented some of the patients from taking part, but, he said, he hadn't wanted to spoil their fun. Those were his words: 'their fun'.

Back alone in my prison, I had time to think on what Rudinger had actually said in his unexpectedly truncated speech. After he had praised Elisabeth's goodness, beneficence and beauty, he described to us (who exist outside the world and so know nothing of events) the homecoming of the dead Empress, the arrival in the mourning capital, and the funeral itself, which would take place tomorrow in the presence of every European head of state.

Every head of state? Tomorrow? Doesn't that mean that tomorrow my mother and father must be in Vienna? The Brussels Court is bound by close family ties to the Viennese one. So it is inevitable that my parents will come to the Empress's funeral.

And is it equally inevitable that they will take the opportunity to visit their 'poor sick daughter'? Yes, it is! Anything else would be inhuman.

My father may well be inhuman—I remember Cap Ferrat.

But not my mother. She will come. There can be no doubt of that.

Saturday evening The day of the funeral is naturally a crowded one: official duties, visits of condolence, receptions, and then in the afternoon the requiem mass at the Kapuzinerkirche.

I remember how it was when Rudolf died. By evening I was completely worn out. So it's no wonder my mother didn't come—one could hardly expect it. But tomorrow ...

Sunday evening I got up earlier than usual, had my hair done very carefully by Olga, and then dressed in black, as is customary after a death at the Court.

It was the longest, emptiest day of my life. No visit, no news, no message.

Today my parents must already have been on the way home to Brussels. Or perhaps my mother would be travelling alone, while my father went back to Cap Ferrat or Paris, his adopted home.

But perhaps Mama will stay on a few days with Stephanie. Perhaps she has been waiting to visit me until my grim father has left Vienna. And after all, I have done nothing wrong to my sister. Rather the reverse—this whole catastrophe only happened because Stephanie let me down.

On Wednesday Fräulein Gebauer read in the paper that after the Empress Elisabeth's funeral the Queen of the Belgians left Vienna with her daughter Stephanie, to take the waters at Spa.

* * *

G

22 September 1898 Captain von Karapancsa must have been afraid that the charges against me were too tenuous, despite all his manoeuvres. Too tenuous to present the seven judges with a cut-and-dried case, and to satisfy his superior, Philip's friend General von Bechtolsheim, with certainty. Karapancsa is an conscientious officer. He knows his duty to his superiors. So he has made some inquiries and turned up the final proof of all proofs. Today he confronted me with it.

It is a letter. A letter whose contents would convince any remaining doubters of my guilt. They have thought it necessary to shore up the false charges with false evidence, so that at the coming trial no possible hitch can occur.

The handwriting in the letter resembles Louise's. I could see that at a glance. I could also see at a glance that it is forged. It is dated 8 April this year, in Nice, and is addressed to Louise's father, the King of the Belgians. Louise (the alleged Louise) asks her father to pay the Viennese banker Reicher (!) 750,000 guilders in cash against a bill that he will present. This, she maintains, is the only way to avoid a scandal of colossal, European dimensions. She ends by saying unambiguously that in a moment of utter despair and moral weakness she added Stephanie's signature to the paper next to her own, because only against the signature of a member of the Imperial House would the bankers agree to lend her the money she so desperately needed.

After all I have learnt and had to accept within these walls, it came as no surprise when Karapancsa told me that my old friend von Uliczny (and, for safety's sake, another so-called handwriting expert as well) had identified me as the forger of the letter. Karapancsa further asserts that the letter was handed to him by the witness Reicher in person. Reicher in turn asserts that he received the letter from me, by post from Nice.

Which is, of course, a monstrous lie. But who is the liar? Reicher? Bachrach? Karapancsa?

I demanded to be brought face to face with Reicher at once. This was refused point blank. The constitution of the court gave me no right to such a meeting. What was I to do?

Where 'proof' can be fabricated, truth has no chance. That much is clear to any normally intelligent and right-thinking man. The Captain in fact is completely determined to accept blindly any forgery that comes his way, however atrocious. Though the word 'blind' is a more than cautious euphemism to describe his motives in acting as he does.

Yet I took up the unequal struggle once more with unbated energy. I denounced the letter as a vicious forgery from beginning to end. The purpose behind it, I added, was all too transparently obvious. As for the handwriting, that was the least clumsy part of the forgery, though any one who had any knowledge of Louise's writing could easily see that this was a fake. Even without being an acknowledged expert—or perhaps provided one wasn't!

I pointed out that Louise, a Belgian Princess, would naturally use French and only French in writing to her father. To prove this would be no trouble at all for the court. So it would never have occurred to me to write such a letter in German. That would have puzzled the recipient enough, before he had even seen the incredible content of the letter. I then explained in detail the relations existing between father and daughter. I told of Louise's last visit to the King in his villa at Cap Ferrat, and of the complete collapse of all the hopes she had placed in it. Leopold II would have thrown the banker out in short order if he had turned up with such a letter. Since I knew all this perfectly well, it would have been idiotic of me to have expected anything from such an unusual and, what was more, dangerous course of action. I appealed to the Captain's normal common sense. Wretched though Louise's relations with her father might be, she would never have entrusted such a delicate story to a letter, especially one that was to be forwarded by a third party. She would have gone herself, despite everything. And a highly intelligent man like the Belgian King would have become suspicious at once if a stranger had brought him such a missive.

Perhaps the most convincing proof of forgery was the date of this strange document. Here the forger had come to dangerous ground, and he had duly slipped. No doubt he had never heard that Louise and I had already left Nice for England on 3 April. In secret. On 8 April, the date on the letter, we were both in London. An inquiry addressed to His Highness the Prince of Wales would settle this at once and beyond doubt, on the highest possible authority.

As I might have expected, my argument met with a blank rejection. Karapancsa had an answer to everything. So what if I had been in London on 8 April, he jeered. No need to trouble the heir to the throne of England about that—any footman could have posted a prepared letter from me in Nice on the date in question. In similar style he rebutted every objection I raised, and forced me to ignominious defeat.

There was no more I could do but lay down my arms and await the end.

* * *

L

I cannot sleep at all now. The nights are one long torture. Jumbled thoughts haunt me, and I am in no state to drive them off. I have asked Dr Rudinger for treatment, and he has prescribed tincture of valerian.

How shall I endure it, living in this total isolation?

The worst of it is that I have no news of Geza. Yet I have admitted everything, so he must have been released long ago. Where is he? Why doesn't he make some effort to find me? Has he found another woman? A younger woman?

But I'm being unfair to him, I know. One shouldn't indulge

one's imagination like that ... but how can I help it? Again and again I tell myself: Geza is the only human being on earth who loves you. Before I knew him I lived in a world of cold egotism. Now I have no parents, no children, no husband; only Geza.

I know why my mother didn't visit me when she was in Vienna. She envies me because I have broken free from Philip, while she—who loathes my father as much as I do Philip—has remained a faithful wife. She sacrificed her youth, her beauty, her whole life on that altar. Today she is an embittered, prematurely aged woman, who resents me for escaping the fate that has overtaken her and making something better of my life. (Better? In an asylum?)

In all my life I never heard one word of tenderness from my father. Though he must know some, and use them, on his dancers and cocottes, with whom he sometimes becomes completely infatuated. He is obsessed with making money: like a Yankee businessman, a speculator, not like a King. Then his lust for power is so great that he wanted to style himself 'Emperor of the Congo'. They had a job talking him out of that. They say that unspeakable cruelties and abuses are perpetrated in the Congo with his knowledge—even on his orders. Men are lashed, tortured, murdered. Credible witnesses, missionaries and respected scientists, have described mountains of human hands, hacked off by the ruthless overseers when the natives fail to deliver their quota of latex. The population has been literally decimated since the rubber boom began: an incredible one-tenth of the natives have been murdered.

I don't believe these stories. I will not let myself believe them! But in the long sleepless nights they crowd in on my mind, and they fit well enough into the picture I now have of the King of the Belgians.

I also think a good deal about Philip. I try to be objective, to see him through eyes not clouded by my own hatred, but even then my judgement remains the same.

We were betrothed twenty-three years ago, in Brussels. I had no idea what lay before me; there was no one to tell me what happened to a virgin on her wedding night. I had never seen myself naked in a mirror, and I had only the vaguest idea of the physical differences between men and women. Of course I was very immature, but even if I had been curious enough to ask such questions there would have been no one to answer them.

On the evening of our wedding Philip came into my bedroom. He was wearing a dressing-gown. My shyness and innocence amused him at first, but then soon made him impatient. This man, a virtual stranger to me and so much older than I was, lay beside me in the bed and kissed me. My only sensation was that his beard hurt me. When he tried to push his tongue into my mouth I clenched my teeth and tried to pull away from him. He laughed, but he didn't let go.

His hands began to grope all over me. I thought that was a most improper liberty and defended myself until he lost patience altogether. With one grab he tore the beautiful nightdress I was so proud of into rags. I screamed and burst into tears. Then he threw his dressing-gown aside and stood naked before me.

The sight was so revolting, so bestial, that I wanted to vomit. I understood that something was going to happen to me now, and that I would have to endure it, however dreadful, painful and repulsive it might be. I closed my eyes and entered a living nightmare.

Philip was brutal, single-minded, and probably driven by the one thought of getting a son. This was how my father had used my mother—how countless other noble husbands had used their unloved wives.

When Philip at last left me alone I was near to taking my own life. There was blood on the sheet, and I thought I was badly injured. I was so full of loathing and revulsion for Philip that I seriously considered throwing myself from the window, simply so as not to have to see him again. But when one is sixteen years old, jumping out of windows does not come easily.

We left on our honeymoon, spent some time in the Coburg Palace in Budapest, and finally returned to Vienna.

The events of the wedding night were often repeated, and I noticed that Philip was annoyed by my coldness and indifference. He tried to arouse some reaction in me; but he didn't know how. Up to now he had only consorted with demi-mondaines and very experienced women. Innocent girls had never interested him.

In Brussels I was never allowed to drink more than a glass of wine on festive occasions. But Philip deliberately made me drunk. He taught me expressions I had never heard in my life, which produced no effect on me simply because they excited him. He gave me erotic books to read, and showed me pictures he kept hidden in a secret compartment in his library.

The pictures, the books, the heavy wine, combined to produce sensations in me that I had never felt before. But I never admitted them.

Everything I had been taught as a girl about love, fidelity, decency was utter nonsense with a man who came into my bedroom in the evenings to tell me about his afternoons with some notorious cocotte, a man who had decided that his relationship with his wife would be one of perpetual rape, which he was beginning to enjoy more and more.

But even then Philip must have suspected that I was not like my mother; not the type to endure injuries and keep my mouth shut; but that I resembled my father, and had a sense of pride that cried out for vengeance.

That was when Rudolf and I first became closer.

Everything that was so unnatural to me when I had to do it for Philip's pleasure came easily, happily and naturally with Rudolf. He was young, irresistible, charming, gentle. I needed no books, no pictures, no wine.

Those were happy years, or so I thought at the time. But they were bitter years too, as my relations with Philip grew steadily worse. He was jealous of my success, my friends, my appearance. His own adventures became more and more degenerate. Moreover he was unbelievably mean, and would have liked me to go round in sackcloth and ashes.

Today I could jump out of my window more easily than I could have done after that first night. But today my windows are barred.

XII

G

Imperial Military Prison, Möllersdorf bei Wien, January 1898
A few days before Christmas, on 21 December, the court martial —consisting of the Interrogating Officer and the seven lay judges—met to consider their verdict. A Colonel Altmann was in the chair.

Captain Karapancsa, along with the Inspecting Officer, Captain Sekulic, visited me in my cell twenty-four hours beforehand to inform me of the arrangements.

As I already knew well enough, the constitution of the court does not allow the accused to be present at these deliberations. But only now, sitting there within those bare confining walls, with every minute seeming three times its normal length, did I realize for myself just what that meant. A few hundred yards away my fate was being decided, and there was no way in which I could influence it. No way of telling my seven brother officers sitting in judgement on me—and no doubt doing their best to be fair—anything of my own interpretation of events. They would have to manage with Karapancsa's version alone. What that meant, I knew.

In all these endless days I have only once appeared before the court: on the second day, when my statement was read. It had taken up several hours.

Then the President, Colonel Altmann, asked me, 'Lieutenant Mattachich, is the statement that the court has just heard a true record of your own words?'

I got to my feet, stood at attention, and said, 'Yes, sir.'

'Thank you,' said the Colonel.

Then I had to sign the statement before the judges. And that concluded my part in the play. I had to leave the stage:

permanently. And the play was played out without the protagonist.

At dawn, as the bells of the Cathedral and St Mark's were ringing in Christmas Eve in the city, Karapancsa and Sekulic reappeared. This time to tell me that the proceedings were at an end. Only that. Not the verdict. This would be delivered to me in writing. Soon. With this Christmas present, ticking away like a time bomb, they left me.

Not until 31 December did the torment end.

The last ten days of the year were as long as the preceding 355 put together. Late in the afternoon of New Year's Eve, when it was already pitch dark, I heard Sergeant Senft's footsteps outside my door. He opened it and told me that I should be learning my fate at 6 o'clock, that is in half an hour's time. Then Trmcik came. He brushed my tunic and polished my boots till they gleamed.

Captain Sekulic arrived on parade, and he and Senft conducted me over to the court. As we stepped out into the open air, the icy cold of the dying year clutched at me. I was briefly reminded of that cold February morning eleven months ago when I had left Sacher's to go and fight Prince Philip of Coburg. Then I still dared trust to fortune. Today, things had changed. Luck could avail me nothing now: I needed a miracle.

The door to the court stood open. On one side was posted a soldier with fixed bayonet; on the other a bugler. As I walked down between my escorts the bugler sounded a call, and to its dying notes we entered the court. A dozen torches burning in iron brackets around the walls lit the room with an oppressively festive light.

Standing around the big table with its green cloth were the assembled members of the court martial, like figures in a painting. On the left of the presiding colonel was Karapancsa. On each side sat a captain, a first lieutenant and a second lieutenant from the different branches of the service. All in full dress uniform. And behind them, of course, the obligatory crucifix and portrait of the Emperor.

Sekulic announced me to the presiding colonel, who at once said, 'The Interrogating Officer will address the court.'

Karapancsa picked up the document lying before him. Aware of his own importance and success, he read out in harsh tones the following words (of which I was later given a copy):

Imperial Garrison Court, Zagreb

VERDICT

Delivered by the Court Martial acting under the instructions of Imperial General of Cavalry Anton Freiherr von Bechtolsheim, Officer Commanding XIII Corps; General Commanding, Zagreb.

Geza Count von Mattachich, born Lobor, County of Varazdin, Croatia, 31 years of age, single, Roman Catholic, suspended from duty on half pay, First Lieutenant in the Imperial 13th Uhlans (Count Paar's), stands convicted by the burden of the evidence that he did on or about 20 March 1898 in the town of Nice write upon a bill for 750,000 guilders the signatures of Her Royal and Imperial Highness the Most Noble Archduchess Stephanie, relict of Rudolf, Crown Prince of Austria, and of Her Royal Highness the Most Noble Princess Louise of Saxe-Coburg and Gotha, and that he did thereby deceive the issuing Bank, and through production of a letter referring to the said bill with the forged signature of Her Royal Highness Princess Louise of Saxe-Coburg-Gotha did cause payment of 750,000 guilders to be made against the said bill and with this deception did injure the said bankers.

Wherefore the said First Lieutenant Geza Count von Mattachich is sentenced under paragraphs 508, 97, 92, 32 and 47 of the Military Justice Act to six years' imprisonment for the crime of obtaining money by false pretences, together with loss of his title and privileges, reduction to the ranks, the said imprisonment to include fasting on the 15th and hard labour on the 25th calendar days of each months and solitary confinement for the entire first and seventh months of each year.

Zagreb, 24 December 1898

G. BRENNER, 2nd Lieutenant   S. JOSEF, 2nd Lieutenant
A. EDUARDI, 1st Lieutenant   R. GETZ, 1st Lieutenant
OTHO FREIHERR VON GOTTESHEIM, Captain
EMIL MADZARAC, Captain
ROBERT ALTMANN, Colonel Presiding
J. VON KARAPANCSA, Captain, Interrogating Officer

By long-standing tradition, the door was left open the whole time. This is supposed to symbolize the general publication of the verdict and sentence.

A second bugle call now announced the end of the proceedings.

And so I 'stood convicted by the burden of the evidence' and had injured the bankers—or rather the usurers—(who received their money punctually on the due date) 'by false pretences'. That was really an impressive triumph for Philip and his clique, one which almost commanded one's respect.

Thinking about it, as I was led back across the parade ground in the first snow of the evening, back to the prison block, I had to laugh aloud. Sekulic looked at me anxiously. He probably thought my mind was going.

In my cell an oil-lamp was burning. That was unusual.

On my cot I saw a grey-green prison uniform of some coarse, cheap material, a pair of clumsy shoes, something brown that seemed to be a cloak, and a cap of the same material.

Seeing them there took my breath away for an instant. An instant in which I saw for the first time the naked reality of the change that the recent scene in the court—which in its rigid ceremony was itself rather unreal—had suddenly brought to my existence. In spite of everything, I had entered that court as 1st Lieutenant Geza Count von Mattachich. A man who no longer existed.

I was frozen.

Suddenly in the half-light I saw my own reflection (though in those surroundings there were certainly no mirrors anywhere). I saw myself in full dress uniform on 18 August—the Emperor's birthday—ten years ago, being handed my Lieutenant's commission in glorious 'Emperor's weather'. I recognized everything quite clearly: my old commanding officer, my comrades standing round me, even the high collar on the brand-new tunic, which constricted and annoyed me so much that the tailor had to alter it later. I heard the regimental band playing the Rákóczy March. With mingled astonishment and disbelief I looked at the young officer's face—my face—radiant with unconcealed happiness and pride.

Suddenly Sekulic's voice behind me said, 'Get changed, Mattachich.' It startled me.

Sekulic and Senft stepped out into the corridor, while I, trembling with emotion, exchanged my uniform for the prison clothes.

Scarcely had I finished when a captain, a stranger to me, appeared in the doorway. He exchanged a few words with Sekulic in a whisper, then said to me, 'Get ready to leave. You will be removed from Zagreb in one hour.'

'May I ask where to, sir?'

'You'll find out soon enough,' was the harsh reply.

Outside the door of the prison block a civilian cab was waiting. Sekulic was waiting too; he wished me luck. He whispered to me in Croatian that he had never seen a prisoner transferred so fast. Usually it would take three or four weeks.

I got into the cab, where the captain and a lieutenant were already sitting. I was told to sit between them.

The horses moved off. Through the window, I watched the gaunt walls, behind which I had spent nearly eight months, vanishing in the heavy snow. I found it hard to keep calm.

If anyone had told me what lay ahead on that day when Franz, the Town Major, had brought me to the door of the prison block, I would have said he was mad. Now I knew that my time here had been a rest cure compared with what I should have to face from now on.

A coach had been provided for us on the evening train—behind the guard's van, well away from the other passengers.

My escort—now increased to five by the addition of a sergeant and two privates—seated itself in a second class compartment. I had to sit between the two soldiers, facing the officers, so that they could keep an eye on me. The guards (even on a long journey it was usual to have no more than three) were all armed to the teeth. The officers carried revolvers, the other ranks rifles and bayonets. All were from the 53rd Infantry Regiment, stationed in Zagreb.

The train was going to Vienna—that much could no longer be concealed once we arrived at the platform. Now the Captain condescended to inform me that I was being taken to Möllersdorf. I had suspected as much. This little town south from the capital boasts the worst and most notorious military prison in the Empire. The only possible place for a serious criminal like myself.

The train steamed through the last hours of the year. It was crossing an area that I knew well. But of course I could see little of it in the snow-filled night, with only an occasional pale gleam of light passing in the darkness.

No one spoke. The monotonous click of the wheels, the regular jolting of the coach, relaxed my nerves and calmed me. I thought of Louise. I tried to imagine where and how she would be passing this night.

When I was awakened by the squeal of the brakes and the slowing down of the train, I could see the outline of a station. A few voices called out cheerfully, 'Happy New Year. Good luck for the New Year!'

We were in Kanizca,* a Hungarian junction south of Lake Balaton. From here the Vienna line runs straight as a die into

* Now Nagykanizsa (Trans).

the north, through Szombathely and Sopron, where it leaves Hungary and connects with the South Austrian line.

After a short halt the train moved on. I went back to sleep. Each time I woke I saw a different pair of eyes fixed on me. My guards were sleeping watch and watch about; I was never unattended for a second.

Time passed quickly now, much more quickly than during the last few days. It was getting light. Ice had formed thick patterns on the window, cutting out all but a thin strip of sky. It has stopped snowing.

The compartment came slowly to life. The officers looked more and more frequently at their watches. Then my guards got their things together. The train slowed, and finally stopped.

We got out, and I saw that we were at Gumpoldskirchen. In the *Heuriger* taverns of this Lower Austrian wine town, known and loved far and wide for its white wine, Ferdl and I had drunk away many hilarious nights in charming (or more or less charming) company. And not very far, in the Helenental, I know a marvellous lodging house with an accommodating landlady who will open her doors at any time of the day or night and never ask to see a marriage certificate.

The express train was not scheduled to stop at Gumpoldskirchen: that was a favour to me.

Yesterday evening, on the dark station at Zagreb, everything had been done with the utmost discretion; but here there could be no question of that. Not only were all the passengers sticking their heads out of the windows to see what the unplanned stop was about; but also a couple of hundred people had turned up—including many women—despite the early hour and the cold New Year's morning to see what they could see of me. Obviously the papers had reported my conviction, and advertised my visit to Gumpoldskirchen.

The village station platform was open on all sides. It was like a fair in the Prater; a dozen policemen had to hold back the crowd as I was marched into the station building.

'That's him,' I heard.

'Don't look too good, do he?' said someone else.

'Don't be stupid. No one looks good in them clothes, do they?'

In the station-master's office my escort's duties came to an end. Like some parcel, I was handed over in exchange for a written receipt to Provost Sergeant Skarit and another sergeant from the Möllersdorf prison.

The first thing Sergeant Skarit asked me was whether I could afford a taxi. If so, we could travel to the prison in comfort. Otherwise we'd have to walk, which considering the crowd waiting outside promised to be an unusual pleasure. I naturally agreed to bear the cost of a cab, to Skarit's visible relief. Probably none of his previous customers had had this sort of reception.

A few minutes later our cab was edging its way through the gaping crowd. Once we had left them behind us, we trotted gently downhill into Möllersdorf.

Soon the high walls of the prison appeared. Someone must have seen us coming, for the heavy iron doors swung open as if of their own accord. We had arrived.

Arrived at the most depressing, horrible, infinitely bleak place on earth.

* * *

L

Geza has been sentenced to six years in prison. Fräulein Gebauer has just brought me the news.

Again and again I have told the truth, admitting that I forged Stephanie's signature; but my assertions have achieved nothing. Because I am, of course, mad.

Justice is a scandal. It has nothing whatever to do with right and equity.

'Isn't it terrible, Your Royal Highness?' asked the Gebauer woman, watching me closely. 'This ungrateful man has forged your signature. And when we all know how kind you were to him!'

By 'kind', of course, she meant something very different; but I refused to be provoked. I greeted the news with feigned indifference, and only hoped I could keep calm while she was in the room with me.

And now I'm still calm. The blow has numbed me. I can't think. Why think, anyway? I can only accept, with all the hatred of helplessness. I curse Philip, but my curses won't hurt him. He holds the strings, and when he jerks them we dance. Geza is in prison for six years, and I am in a madhouse ... for how long? Only Philip knows the answer to that.

* * *

G

Late January, 1899   I've been in Möllersdorf a month now, and I've got used to it to some extent. Man is a creature of habit. He acclimatizes damned quickly to the good things in life, and fortunately to the bad things too. Perhaps to say that he gets used to them is going too far. But he learns to endure.

My prison cell, which I share with a sixty-year-old former military official, a very agreeable man, is on the ground floor and rather damp. It measures two and a half paces by six. The main furniture consists of two wooden cots, each with a straw mattress and a straw pillow. There is even a coarse, much-patched sheet, which it appears is changed once a month. And a heavy woollen blanket. We each have a tiny table, a chair and a stool for the basin and ewer. Once again the barred window is so high that there can be no question of seeing outside. But unlike Zagreb, this place does allow light. Above the heavy iron door, just below the ceiling, is an opening leading through to the corridor. Just big enough to take an oil lamp. It is left burning all night. The guards do their rounds every hour on the hour, and can take a look at the prisoners at any time through the inevitable peephole.

The customs and rules in a military prison are soon learnt,

the instinct for self-preservation sees to that. The latter in any case are only concerned with what prisoners may not do, on pain of severe punishment.

Prisoners here are divided into first- and second-class. We can be told apart at a glance by the different caps we wear. Second-class prisoners are former privates, first-class being officers or officials with commissioned rank. The underlying class principle that controls the Austro-Hungarian Empire is followed so strictly even in prison that members of the two categories are totally separated, and virtually never come into contact with one another. The 'twos', as they're known, are put to work in the various prison workshops, and may also be hired out to work in Möllersdorf. Whereas we first-class prisoners are allowed to work, if at all, only at garrison duties and administrative chores. And then only if we volunteer to work of our own free will.

A day in prison without anything to occupy one goes very slowly. And a man who faces six times 365 such days can hardly imagine that his torment will ever end. Variety is rare. Reveille by alarm bell in the morning, at five a.m. in summer, six in winter. Half an hour's exercise in the courtyard every morning and afternoon. And the rest of the time in the eternal half-light of the mouldering cell. Only the rattle of the warders' keys and the heavy pacing of the guard beyond the double-locked door. Nothing more. Whether you like it or not, you find yourself lapsing into dreary, semi-conscious brooding. Sometimes the reality of this existence suddenly breaks through to your consciousness, and often leads to a state of unspeakably horrible excitement, which can easily break out into wild frenzy. But apart from your cell-mates, no one takes any notice. And they take as little as possible: they like to pursue their own sluggish thoughts undisturbed.

For breakfast there is brown gruel. For lunch, three times a week, there is broth with beef and potatoes—four ounces of meat on Sundays, three ounces on Tuesdays and Thursdays. On Wednesdays and Fridays we get lentils or beans; on Saturday dumplings with onion sauce. The daily bread ration is issued in the mornings too; if one is careful one can eat in the evening as well. Otherwise no more food is provided. There is plenty of water, and every second day a kind of tea. I've yet to decide exactly what this is.

It would be difficult to starve on that diet. But looking at the emaciated faces of my fellow-sufferers, I can see what a toll it takes of one's strength in the long run.

The whole prison complex is enclosed by two enormously high walls. Within the inner wall are the prison and punishment cells, the kitchen and canteen, and the infirmary. In the outer ring, between the two walls, are the workshops where the twos work, a small chapel, the administration block and the staff quarters. A prisoner must be escorted to enter the outer ring where the main door—heavily guarded in any case—is all that stands between him and freedom.

The buildings are, with few exceptions, as old as the hills and suitably decrepit. The chapel and staff quarters look just about tolerable. The whole thing used to be one of Maria Theresa's hunting-lodges. They say that in the second-class cell block you can still see the remains of paintings on the ceilings; and the ground-floor officers' cells used to be the stables.

Soon after my arrival at Möllersdorf I spent a few days in the infirmary. I had a sudden violent fever, and naturally thought my malaria had struck again. Fortunately it turned out to be nothing more than a brief but extremely acute dose of influenza. Probably a souvenir of my journey through the bitter cold of New Year's Eve.

In my ward there were three other beds, one of which was empty. In another there was a former captain, sentenced to seven years for spying for the Russians. He had just had a septic boil on his backside lanced; after three years of monotonous imprisonment this was a major event in his life, and he couldn't stop talking about it, in great detail. The other bed was occupied by an ex-lieutenant, a young, rather delicate-looking lad in his early twenties. He had been in Möllersdorf no longer than I, though what had brought him there he wouldn't say. He said in fact very little. His name was Windegg, and he already had one suicide attempt behind him: he had broken a spoon, sharpened the jagged edge on a cell wall, and tried to slash his wrists with it. This enterprise, as might be expected, brought him no more than a sharp reprimand from the Commandant and a bed in the infirmary. He would get severe punishment when he returned to the prison block, probably bread and water and a dark cell.

After two days the captain was discharged. Windegg and I didn't say anything, but it was clear that neither of us was sorry to see him go; and now that life there promised to be more congenial I was determined to get every possible advantage, however slight, out of my stay in the prison infirmary.

Here the lights were turned out at 9 p.m. After lights out, Windegg and I now began to talk for the first time, undisturbed by the captain and his boil. I learnt that he had been sentenced to two years for having a homosexual relationship with one of his subordinates. A lance-corporal in his company, whom he had had occasion to reprimand severely on a service matter, accused him, and swore before the court martial that Windegg had used his superior rank to force him into unnatural practices. Windegg told me that the whole thing was a lie from start to finish, but that the man's perjury had wrecked him anyway. He regarded his life as ruined and completely pointless. I only heard his side of the case, but from what he told me on that dark, memorable night (and from my own experience of courts martial) I was inclined to believe him. I tried to give the young man some courage, and told him in outline the story of my own case. After an hour or so we wished each other good night.

I dropped off quickly, and slept through to reveille. It was still pitch dark in the cell. I said something to Windegg, but got no reply. I said it again, louder. Still no answer. I got up and crossed to his bed, to rouse him, but the bed was empty. Then a ray of light from outside filtered through the barred window, and against it I recognized the silhouette of a human body. It was Windegg. While I slept he had quietly hanged himself with his sheet from the window bars.

I lifted the poor fellow down from the noose, laid him carefully on the bed, and pressed my ear closely to his cold breast. Nothing. This time he had succeeded. For him, the question of guilt or innocence had been settled for ever.

I don't know why I didn't call the guard at once. At any rate I sat there by his body until the sergeant opened the door and his lamp lit up the room.

'What's going on here?' he demanded when he saw me sitting on the other man's bed.

'Windegg's killed himself, Sergeant,' I said.

'What, again?' With this illogical observation he came nearer and shone his lamp in the dead man's face. He bent over him and pulled his eyelids up. 'Idiot!' he shouted then. 'Bloody idiot! It would be me he has to drop in it! It would be me. I ought to push his bloody teeth in, the dirty little pansy!' Then he ran to the door and called the guard.

I spent the whole day being interrogated: first by the doctor, then by the officer of the day, and eventually by the Commandant himself. It was as much as I could do to defend myself against the suspicion of having abetted the suicide. That night I slept alone in the room in the infirmary. I felt wretched. I couldn't stop thinking of Windegg; and the more I thought the more I understood why he had ended it.

Next day I was discharged from the infirmary. I breathed a sigh of relief when I had been led back to the first-class cell block and was once more sitting opposite my peaceable cellmate. Advantages it may have, but I've had my belly full of the infirmary.

It was one of Maria Theresa's laws that sent me here, and it's one of Maria Theresa's houses I'm in now: I'm beginning to hate the woman. Anyway, even that 'criminal statute' of hers gives any man sentenced by court martial the right, subject to certain conditions, to appeal against his sentence: first to the

Higher Court of Military Justice; as a last resort to the Supreme Military Court. Through the officer of the day I have already given notice in writing to the Commandant, a Colonel von Dravodol (who, by the way, seems a perfectly decent sort of man), that I wish to appeal whatever the conditions may be. The Commandant's permission is needed as a matter of form. As soon as it arrives (and it can't decently be refused) I'll get to work. Prisoners who can write are expected to lodge their appeals in their own handwriting. Once we get to that stage I'll have plenty to do, and the time will pass much better.

* * *

L

Dr Rudinger has been here again. But only as the representative of the Court Marshal's Office, that fountain of all things evil, to announce to me the impending visit of Professor Freiherr von Krafft-Ebing. The Baron is charged with preparing a report on me for the Medical Faculty of Vienna University. In this task he will naturally draw on the existing report by Bachrach's friend, but would like to meet me personally first.

I didn't know there *was* an existing report, but I don't care. Even this coming visit doesn't arouse my interest.

In Döbling I did all I could to convince every doctor of the injustice that was being done to me. With Krafft-Ebing I shan't even bother. I am completely at the mercy of Philip and his plans. In any case, what good would freedom be to me without Geza?

In the total wretchedness that fills my mind there is one single, tiny gleam of light, though I must admit to being rather ashamed of it. I need have no fear that Geza, locked up in a military prison, is sleeping with another woman.

XIII

Extract from the Faculty Report of 13 May 1899 on the mental condition of Her Royal Highness Princess Louise of Saxe-Coburg-Gotha, née Princess Louise of the Belgians

In reply to the request received from His Imperial and Apostolic Majesty's Marshal on 26 April 1899, Z.597, to furnish a second opinion on the court doctor's report on the mental health of Princess Louise of Coburg, because of the difficulty and importance of the case, the Faculty of Medicine has the honour to state its conclusion that the report in question is drawn up according to the rules of psychiatric science, meticulously correct throughout in its procedures and incontestably accurate in its conclusions. But in view of the importance of the case the Faculty felt itself obliged to reconsider all the circumstances from the beginning.... For this purpose the Faculty availed itself of the original medical report and of certain documents and statements made available by the Court Marshal's Office ... current observations of Her Royal Highness's lady-in-waiting (Frl. von Gebauer) relating to the Princess's behaviour and what she has said in Purkersdorf Sanatorium, and the results of an investigation by Professor Krafft-Ebing on behalf of the Faculty ...

The Princess has no understanding of the fact that she has ruined her marriage and lapsed into social and moral decadence ...

Her reasons for her insuperable revulsion for her husband and her demands for a divorce are so slight, trivial and ridiculous that in themselves they suggest a degree of mental infirmity.

Despite occasional fits of rage, the Princess is incapable of deeper, morally motivated emotional states ...

Doctors and attendants were struck by the trivial and superficial reactions the Princess showed when she was brought to the institution; and by the ease with which she adapted to completely strange and uncertain circumstances on her transfer from Döbling to Purkersdorf ...

Even when she heard of what she would call the unjust treatment of Mattachich she showed no deep or enduring reaction.

A healthy person, or even a sick person who claims to be sane, if deprived of his liberty may be expected to react violently: i.e. with appeals to every legal quarter, attempts at escape, turbulent emotional conditions and probably suicide attempts.

The noble patient toys with such ideas from time to time, but in reality she is calm, docile, eats and sleeps normally, and shows only the most superficial variations in her physical well being.

The clearest indication of the noble patient's mental inadequacy, however, is that during her year-long confinement she has taken no interest in any useful or normal occupation, and yet apparently experiences no boredom. Although at her own request she was provided with a piano and painting materials, she uses them rarely or not at all; although she spends more than 100 guilders a month on reading matter she never does more than leaf through two or three pages. She spends many hours lying in bed, fritters away time on her appearance, displays the classic tendency of the insane to cut at clothes and furnishings, often ruining new and expensive material ...

From the preceding medically observed facts one must irresistibly conclude that Her Royal Highness Princess Louise of Saxe-Coburg-Gotha is the victim of a mental infirmity, in that her mental functions and in particular the higher spiritual capabilities such as common sense, willpower and moral judgement show a marked deterioration ...

This 'mental breakdown' in the sense of paragraph 21 of the Austrian statute may in the circumstances be medically expressed as imbecility. This imbecility, affecting both intellectual and moral abilities, has developed slowly and, to a layman, imperceptibly; a personality already disposed to nervous disorders and further impaired neurotically by a severe attack of typhus in 1876 was finally damaged more seriously by violent concussion sustained in 1882. The Princess's highly experienced personal physician detected 'an increasing irritability and a more and more pronounced mental and emotional change' beginning from that date....

This 'pronounced mental and emotional change', in an adverse sense, explains why an originally harmonious marriage degenerated into something very different, why an irritable and vehement disposition led to emotional outbursts and conflicts, why a weakened moral sense came to see marriage as a burden and ultimately as a prison, circumstances which led to a taste for outdoor diversions such as travel, sport, etc. All these circumstances led to further brain damage ...

The illness was further exacerbated to its present level by the influence of Mattachich, who managed to ensnare the Princess and ultimately to dominate her completely by flattery. He encouraged her predilections for aimless travel, extravagance, sport, etc., and developed in her a taste for overindulgence in alcohol.

And so it eventually came about that the unfortunate patient fell completely under the spell of a worthless man, followed all his suggestions blindly, forgot her high rank and her dignity as wife and mother, and lived openly with this adventurer until her husband was able to free her from her degraded surroundings, hardship and financial disaster and moral and social decadence.

If the Princess were not ill the year she has spent in confinement already would certainly hve been time enough for her to recognize the undignified position to which she had fallen.... She would have turned her face in shame from a man who has committed serious crimes against the law of the land and has been punished for so doing; she would have rejected this man who abused his intellectual superiority to

273

degrade her as wife, mother and princess in the eyes of the whole world.

Yet the opposite of all this has in fact occurred: the Princess's anger is directed at the Prince her husband, the man who has saved her....

Significant proof of the impaired judgement and moral confusion from which the Princess suffers may be seen in her opinion of Mattachich. For her, he was and is a noble, distinguished gentleman, a man who has been sentenced to shameful imprisonment entirely because of the Prince's rancour towards him.... She cannot understand facts, proof, logic, but maintains stubbornly that Mattachich was her knight, her protector, and that the time in Croatia—the period of her complete degradation—was the happiest time of her life.

She hates her husband, denigrates him and her noble family ... hates her son because he stands by his father. In place of respect for her parents, gratitude to her husband, love for her children, awareness and desire to protect her own dignity, the normal attributes of a healthy person, there is only gross egotism: that ignores the patient's own duties, disregards the rights of others, and dominates utterly all she thinks and feels....

Just as she misinterprets the significance of past events, and misjudges her own present situation, so the Princess is vague as to the probable course of her future life. She regards herself as blameless and perfectly normal, her confinement as a colossal injustice, an act of vengeance by her husband ... but takes no serious thought for what lies ahead of her, being superficial and trivial in her opinions and attitudes and a totally passive character, incapable of independent decisions or actions. Even her earlier relations with Mattachich are not (at any rate not now) marked by any animated feeling. This passivity, weakness of will and extreme docility mean that the continued care and treatment of the noble patient by a conscientious and well-intentioned staff should present no difficulties, and eventually make it possible for the unhappy Princess to be allowed considerable freedom in the course of time.

The opinion of the Medical Faculty therefore is that:

Her Royal Highness Princess Louise of Saxe-Coburg-Gotha, née Princess Louise of the Belgians, has for several years suffered from imbecility induced by brain damage with pronounced deterioration of the intellectual and moral functions. The noble patient is incapable of managing her own affairs, and has no clear understanding of the meaning, importance or consequences of her action. She therefore suffers from mental illness in the sense of paragraph 21 of the statute and should receive the protection of the law.

Vienna, 13 May 1899

A. VOGL for the Deacon
DR R. FREIHERR VON KRAFFT-EBING, P.C., Professor in the University of Upper Austria

XIV

L

I have left Austria; I am now in the Kingdom of Saxony. At Lindenhof Sanatorium, not far from Dresden. Superficially, my living conditions have improved. I am even allowed to go into the town sometimes, under guard, to visit a café. As at Döbling, I still live in a separate building away from the main block; Fräulein Gebauer and Olga are still with me. So are the piano and the easel. I am allowed to go for walks, and occasionally for little excursions, always under the supervision of Fräulein Gebauer, of course. In contrast to Dr Rudinger at Purkersdorf, the head of this institution, Dr Pierson, takes a kindly interest in me.

This improvement in my circumstances means in reality my death sentence. Or at any rate life imprisonment. Geza is to be envied: in six years he will be free. But I never shall.

Philip has achieved all he wanted. The Faculty's verdict was delivered long ago. I haven't been shown the report, but I know its conclusions: I am an imbecile. I also know why I have been brought here: Geza is serving his sentence at Möllersdorf, barely fifteen miles from Vienna and Purkersdorf. Such proximity strikes Philip as dangerous. Since he couldn't have Geza moved, I had to be sent away. For that Philip needed an ostensible reason: hence the Faculty report. Probably it says there that a change of locality was advisable, and that in time I shall be allowed more freedom. Here in Saxony, of course, freedom is perfectly safe.

As a result of the report my previous status as a ward was changed to one of definite certification. Dr von Feistmantel has been nominated as my guardian. Or, as he would put it, he is to become 'a second father to the poor little girl who has lost her own father'.

Release is now out of the question for ever, since I am certified insane. That is the peak of Philip's triumph. While I sit gazing through my barred window, he can pocket the inheritance that will one day come to me from my father, with no fear that I may simply run off and leave him.

In a lengthy letter to Brussels I begged my parents desperately for help. I had to express myself carefully, as all my letters are read before being sent. I never received an answer.

I can't fight any more. I can no longer keep a grip on myself. What would be the point? It is only useless waste of effort. If I let myself go completely, perhaps I may one day enjoy the blessing of real—or rather induced—insanity.

I long incessantly for Geza. That is my deepest and last secret. No one must see or know how much I miss him. In this respect only, I still control myself.

All the people around me, from Dr Pierson down to Fräulein von Gebauer, seem to me contemptible because they are just pawns in Philip's game. But I don't show my feelings. I am polite to them, never tell them what I really think of them.

How long shall I have to live? I am forty-one years old, and according to Professor Sommer I am in good health. When Philip is dead they may perhaps let me go. But then I shall be an old woman. Whereas Geza, when he comes out of prison in six years' time, will still be a young man.

The amenities at Lindenhof include a mirror, something I didn't have in Döbling or Purkersdorf. The window-panes in which I could see my reflection there were kind: the mirror is cruel.

* * *

G

December   The first part of the year flew past before I'd
noticed it.

Day after day, week after week, I worked on my appeal: planning it, formulating the words, writing them down. I would fill page after page, and throw it all away and start again from scratch. I finished with a full-length book. I read it through again, making little revisions and improvements here and there.

At last it was finished. Accompanied by the Provost Sergeant and the Inspecting Officer, I took my sheaf of papers and presented them to the Commandant. He promised to forward it at once to the Higher Court of Military Justice, through the usual channels.

Summer and autumn came and went; I waited.

The longer I waited, the slower time passed. Outside winter came. One day the first snow fell.

A little later I was handed the following document:

> At the request of the prisoner the Imperial Higher Court of Military Justice has reopened the investigation, and finds:
>
> (1) The essential nature of the crime is subject to the corrections or limitations that the prisoner forged only the signature of Her Imperial Highness Princess Stephanie on the bill in question, and that he did *not* defraud the bankers of 750,000 guilders, but *attempted* to defraud them.
>
> (2) In view of the scale of the attempted fraud and the number of criminal acts committed, the sentence is not to be revised.
>
> (3) Paragraph 32 of the Military Punishment Act does not apply.
>
> (4) Otherwise the verdict is considered proper.
>
> *Vienna, 5 December 1899*
>
> *Imperial Higher Court of Military Justice*
> RATZENHOFER, Lt-General
> SCHALLER, Colonel, Interrogating Officer

XV

L

Today, 22 March 1900, Stephanie is marrying Count Elemer Lonyay, her 'Bosnian roadmender'. The marriage is to take place not furtively in some village church, as one might expect with such a misalliance, but in Miramar Castle—with the complete approval and blessing of His Apostolic Majesty, and in the presence of many distinguished guests.

My sister, with her tearful hypocritical timidity, has achieved all she wanted. As expected of her, she has given rise to no hint of scandal, but just waited like a good, obedient little girl. And Franz Joseph has rewarded her with his generous agreement.

Nothing the Emperor does is ever entirely altruistic; and now he has got rid of Stephanie. She will be leaving Vienna and living at Oroszvar Castle in Hungary, so I see in the Dresden papers. There never was much love lost between Stephanie and the court; now they'll both be happy.

Stephanie won't think much of living isolated in the country. For me that would be no hardship. Sour grapes! How infinitely I long to exchange Lindenhof Asylum for Oroszvar Castle! I am very envious of Stephanie.

30 March   Stephanie may have Franz Joseph's blessing, but from what I've just read she hasn't got her father's.

She announced that she hoped to visit Brussels on her honeymoon, to introduce her new husband to the King and Queen of the Belgians. But word came from Brussels that neither she nor the Count could expect to be received there.

That, to me, is the absolute limit of arrogance. What *does* the King want of Stephanie? Has she to spend her whole life playing a part, acting the sorrowing wife of an unloved husband? Or was she supposed to wait on the offchance of making another 'suitable' marriage, never mind whether or not she loved the man in question? Such conditions have brought enough unhappiness to us all, God knows. But our father wouldn't care about that. Not for a second does he consider Stephanie's happiness: he can only see that she is marrying beneath her. He is behaving as fanatically as if she were the head of the ancient House of Habsburg.

I can imagine how Franz Joseph must be laughing. To him, we Coburgs and Belgians are still parvenus. In the old days in Vienna that often used to annoy me, but today I could almost agree with him.

* * *

G

2 July 1900 Of course I shan't accept the Higher Court's verdict as the last word. Today I have appealed to the last court of appeal, the Supreme Military Court. Now it's a question of patience, waiting and hoping again.

Life here is as wretched as ever. My cell-mate completed his sentence: he was released three months ago. Since then I have been alone.

I shall soon put in a request for some sort of work to keep me busy.

* * *

L

Today I was shocked out of lethargy by some bad news in the papers. A report from the Belgian resort of Spa says that my mother is very ill, and there are grave fears for her life.

I felt tears start to my eyes.

I don't know why the news shook me so badly. In recent years I've felt no great affection for my mother. I was deeply hurt by her coldness, the way in which she cut herself off from me and left me to my fate. But suddenly I was filled with fear of losing her; and with burning sympathy.

What has life given her? Nothing. Less than nothing. I can only wish and hope that the consolations of religion will help her now to turn her face from the terrible realization that the fates have withheld from her all her due share of happiness.

I sent for Dr Pierson, and asked him whether I could be allowed to travel to Spa, to see my mother once more before she died.

The doctor said that he had nothing against the idea, provided that I was attended by a doctor, my lady-in-waiting and a maid. He was prepared to put his assistant, Dr Mauss, at my disposal for the journey. But first, of course, he would have to ask the Court Marshal's Office in Vienna, which would probably get in touch with Brussels, or direct with Spa.

I asked him to proceed at once with all the necessary arrangements, and stressed that I needed only a sleeper, not a special train.

In my mind I constantly see the picture of the beautiful mother I knew as a child. That is not what I can expect to see now. I am very frightened at the thought of seeing her again after so long. The appearance of the dying old woman will quench much of the bitterness that so often rises in me. So my desire to go to her is, to that extent, a selfish one.

When I imagine that tomorrow, or the day after, I may be travelling on a train, I become quite dizzy. How shall I behave after all these years. Very clumsily? Will people be able to tell that I am a lunatic out on parole?

I really must not be afraid of meeting Papa: he certainly won't hurry to mother's sick-bed. Mama has been living in Spa for years already, ostensibly for her health. I don't know whether the King banished her there, or whether she went there voluntarily to get away from him.

Perhaps Dora will come to Belgium to, to see her grandmother once more. Her brother Leopold should be there too. And Stephanie, of course.

I'm beginning to be almost afraid of the journey. I shan't sleep a wink tonight, I'm so excited.

Friday There was nothing to be afraid of; I can sleep easily. I shall not be going to Spa.

Vienna raised no objection; yet even today, on the edge of the grave, my mother refuses to see me. She remains implacable and cold to the end.

When Dr Pierson came to tell me of her refusal, I noticed that it shocked him as much as it did me. He tried to dress it up in kind words, and said he was sure that everyone wanted to spare me the arduous journey.

After he had left, I could cry at last.

So I shall never see my mother again, and can remember her as I knew her, beautiful and unapproachable. I must resign myself, linger on here in the twilight, and wait for the news of her death.

* * *

G

For nine months I have been working in the kitchen offices, which also involves supervision of the canteen. I keep the 'daily expenses and income' ledger.

The official for whom I work is a bone-idle pig. My first job was to bring some sort of order to his sty. Since then, I'm the best thing that ever happened to him. He does virtually nothing, disappears for hours at a time, and lets God and von Mattachich run the shop.

I get on very well with the kitchen sergeant and his staff. I do what I can to help them, and in return they sometimes let me have a helping of plum tart. Or a slice of apfelstrudel. It may not be exactly Sacher's, but it makes a welcome change.

The canteen is run by a Frau Stöger. A young, attractive girl. Dark, plump. What's more she's a countrywoman of mine. We can talk without everyone being able to listen in. Her husband works in the law courts.

Although they give us lots of starch in our diet here, to suppress certain natural instincts, it doesn't seem to work when one looks at Frau Stöger. Not with me, anyway. We're often alone together, if our books don't balance. Unless I'm much mistaken there might be something doing there.

I've got Frau Stöger eating out of my hand. Her christian name is Marie. She knows who I am, of course, and enjoys flirting with a celebrity like me. Whenever she gets the chance she questions me blatantly in her impudent, self-assured way. The other day I was standing at my desk bringing the books up to date. She comes in. 'Where's Lindinger, then?' she says. That's the Quartermaster-Sergeant, my boss. 'How should I know? No idea,' I say, and carry on writing. Then she comes close up behind me and pretends to be reading over my shoulder. She presses up close to me and shoves a knee between my legs. She uses a simple, fresh perfume, which helps to get me excited. A moment later I think I really am going mad, because her hand starts sliding round my hip to where my excitement is most obvious. Just as I think my heart is going to stop altogether the little bitch lets go, takes a few steps back, giggles at my stupid expression, and says laughing, 'Don't be frightened—I just wanted to see whether you could only do it with princesses. But you're all right, thank God.'

I had to keep a rigid control on myself; I never remember anything so difficult. But I can't take any risks. Well, not many risks, anyway. Under no circumstances will I let myself lose this lovely job. That would be simply moronic. The people here wouldn't take kindly to a *Fledermaus*-type prison.

* * *

Marie is fantastic. A real devil!

Last week my appeal was finally rejected by the Supreme Military Court. 'For want of the necessary conditions as set out in the Military Punishment Act', as they put it.

I was naturally pretty down in the mouth for a few days, and looked it. Marie spotted at once that something was up with me. So I told her about it. She listened to the whole story, and then said I should tell it to the Vienna *Arbeiter-Zeitung*. The Socialists are bound to take an interest in this sort of dirt, she says. They are very hot on that sort of thing. When I asked how she thought I would get permission to go and talk to a subversive newspaper, she just laughed. She would go! In person. She would enjoy it. I could rely on her completely, she said, and she would manage everything perfectly, so long as I could give her the necessary written information. To get it out of the prison would be no problem!

XVI

From the Vienna Arbeiter-Zeitung, *16 and 21 January 1902*

Mattachich's appeal contains an uncommonly thorough and perceptive explanation of all the grounds for suspicion against him. He names witnesses, quotes several exonerating documents, and completely fulfils all the conditions which the law requires before a closed case can be reopened.

It is impossible to give here a summary of this manuscript. It is a thick book. We must therefore content ourselves with saying that Mattachich has not merely weakened the grounds for suspicion against him; he has demolished them totally. His detailed account shows the convicted lieutenant to be a man of unusual energy and great powers of reasoning. That he was able to find the strength to compile this document in prison, without legal aid and without sight of any of the written evidence, shows him to be a man of no ordinary gifts.

The first court found Mattachich guilty of forging both signatures: which meant in effect that he had produced and passed a false and worthless bill, had deceived the paying agents with the false signatures, and had defrauded them of the sum specified. But now the second court has found that Princess Louise's signature was *genuine,* and that the fraud therefore rested on the forged signature of Princess Stephanie.

The court of first instance proceeded from the assumption that both signatures were false. From this assumption they concluded that it was Mattachich who had forged the signatures to obtain money—and that he *had* so obtained money. But the demolition of the assumption makes nonsense of the conclusions. For if the Princess's signature was genuine Mattachich could not have been hoping to work a swindle for his own purposes, therefore he did *not* produce a forged bill for the purposes of obtaining money. The same reasons that prove he did not forge one of the signatures prove equally that he did not forge the other!

The fact that the second verdict fundamentally changed the nature of the crime committed is in itself a completely convincing argument against the verdict. If the higher court can still confirm the verdict and uphold the sentence, it must be obvious to anyone that the case cries out for a fresh investigation, and that the reopening of the case is imperative in the name of justice.

Question asked in the Imperial Parliament by the Socialist Deputy Daszynski, 8 February 1902

I should like to draw to the attention of the Minister of Defence, who represents the Minister for War, an affair which took place some years ago within the Austrian military jurisdiction, and which offers a perfect example of so-called 'court justice' at its best.

I refer to the case of Lieutenant Mattachich. The lieutenant had the misfortune to win the love of a royal Princess, the love of Princess Louise of Coburg, the daughter of the King of the Belgians. This circumstance has ruined his career and flung him into the abyss—the military prison at Möllersdorf where he has already languished for four years of his six-year sentence.

It is no desire for sensation that has prompted me to lay the case of Lieutenant Mattachich before this house, and to protest his innocence here. The Social Democrats are not in the habit of representing or defending ladies of royal blood. (*Hear, hear.*) You may be sure that we intervene in the affairs of the aristocracy only with the greatest reluctance. We should be quite happy to leave the aristocracy to lie in its own dirt.
VICE-PRESIDENT KAISER (*ringing his bell*): I must ask the

speaker to moderate the tone of his remarks. I call him to order for the expression he has just used.

DEPUTY SCHUHMEIER: Does that mean that there is no dirt involved?

DEPUTY DASZYNSKI: We are not here to stir up scandal. I repeat, it is not the desire for sensation that impels me to proceed with this matter. I have today drawn to the attention of the Minister of Defence the articles published last January in the *Arbeiter-Zeitung*. The facts as set out there, and the consequences of those facts, form a cast-iron argument for the innocence of the convicted officer Lieutenant Mattachich.

During the investigation and the trial the Viennese press was for the most part under the corrupting influence of the Coburg family. (*Hear, hear.*) The same press that has for years taken the French Captain under its wing, the same press that has given so much publicity to its arguments in favour of Captain Dreyfus's innocence, this press has cravenly trampled the unfortunate lieutenant into the mire. He has been smeared by the powerful Coburg clique, although he is innocent—I repeat, he is *innocent*.

And so I offer the case of Mattachich to this house, as an example. Not in the hope of being lionized by the press as the defender of injured innocence; but because Mattachich's case is a direct consequence of an evil system; an inevitable result of the erroneous, antiquated and outdated Austrian military law.

Gentlemen. The lieutenant has, as I have said, won the favour of Princess Louise of Coburg. Her husband, who of course is something of a colleague of our respected Minister of Defence, and far be it from me to emulate the Minister in his choice of friends (*laughter*), Prince Philip of Coburg, then, has taken part in a number of exceedingly unattractive conspiracies. I shall not stir up any scandal here. I respect a man's right to a private life, even if the man is Prince Philip of Coburg. But, gentlemen, have we really reached the stage where the Supreme Commander can step in and say to this Prince: Either you fight a duel or you resign your commission? One may well imagine that from that point on the wealthy Prince was not well disposed towards Mattachich.

And now something happened which is only possible under military law. A bill for 750,000 guilders was issued, and this bill bore the signatures of two royal sisters, Princess Louise of Coburg and Princess Stephanie of Austria. This bill was issued in March 1898, and of course honoured. The question at issue, gentlemen, is whether that bill was forged, and whether fraud actually took place. The bill fell due on 20 June 1898. On that day it was paid, punctually and in full. Why? Because Prince Coburg knew that his wife's signature, at least, was genuine. Otherwise it is inconceivable that the Prince, a remarkably avaricious man—it runs in his family (*loud laughter*) —should have honoured a forged bill.

At that time, Mattachich was with Princess Louise in Zagreb. Suddenly, early in May 1898, a Viennese lawyer, Dr Bachrach, turned up there and made a statement to the military authorities in which he ascribed the forgery to Lieutenant Mattachich.

DEPUTY DR OFNER: Is that Dr Bachrach the Privy Councillor?

DASZYNSKI: That is correct. Mattachich and Princess Louise were promptly arrested. This was done at the instigation and through the agency of Dr Bachrach, who claimed—untruthfully, I believe—that he had an authority from the Emperor, as a result of which the arrests were made.

Gentlemen! Should lawyers be permitted to run round Austria-Hungary waving imperial licences to persecute and destroy innocent men? Until it is proved to me, I will not believe that Bachrach really had the Emperor's authority, or that Mattachich's arrest was founded on such authority.

But, gentlemen, the question remains: in whose interest was Dr Bachrach acting? It is clear that he could only have been acting for Prince Philip of Coburg, because it was at his urging that the Princess was confined to a sanatorium. There as a result of Bachrach's efforts she was declared insane, and Bachrach openly takes the credit for this. After the bill was honoured on 20 June, in the presence of a reliable witness, he was heard to say, 'Now we'll have the Princess declared insane.'

Well, is such a thing possible? Does it not sound more like some medieval nightmare?

And what happened next? Dr Bachrach had not one but two interviews with the Interrogating Officer. He hypnotized him. He passed on the Court's request that Mattachich should be found guilty. And, gentlemen, at the very same time the Vienna Public Prosecutor, Ritter von Kleeborn, was summoned to the Court Marshal. We know today that from that point on the pursuit of the real forger has been completely hushed up. And then we come to the verdict of the court of first instance, in which the judges calmly declare without any apparent pangs of conscience that: (*reads the written verdict of the first court*).

Below that verdict, all the names of the judges are recorded for posterity. Mattachich then appealed to the Higher Court and asked for the case to be reopened, but nearly a year passed —time means nothing in the army, and once a man is under lock and key these things can take years—I repeat, nearly a year passed before his appeal received this answer: (*reads the verdict of the second court*).

Without any new findings, without re-examining the handwriting experts who had previously stated beyond doubt that Mattachich forged *both* signatures, without admitting a single new item of evidence, the Higher Court nevertheless conceded that he had forged only *one* of the signatures on that bill.

This pronouncement by the Higher Court is of conclusive significance in the light of the whole case. For, gentlemen, if the Higher Court had simply rejected the appeal out of hand, then we might well still believe today that Mattachich had forged both signatures. But if Mattachich has not in fact defrauded anyone; if the usurers received all their money including their massive interest of several hundred thousand guilders on the due date; if not one kreutzer of this money had found its way into Mattachich's own pocket (as the judges freely admit is the case); if all these things are so, we may ask: what interest could Mattachich have had in taking a perfectly good bill with the Princess's signature and improving it with a second, false signature? Just for amusement, perhaps?

Gentlemen, I have demonstrated that the second verdict puts the whole case in a very different light. Now Mattachich finally appealed to the Supreme Court, and the Supreme Court upheld the second verdict and ruled that the application to reopen the case should be finally rejected. Yet more and more grounds have accrued to suggest that the Lieutenant is in fact innocent. For example, a forged letter was adduced in evidence; a letter in German addressed to the King of the Belgians, Leopold II. This letter has been shown by the evidence to be a palpable fabrication; and the same goes for many other so-called 'proofs'.

I admit that I am in no position to give all the facts here. But I have at my disposal an impressive array not of conjectures but of reliable testimony and irrefutable proof, the burden of which is that an innocent man has languished for four years at Möllersdorf. He had to be removed. The vengeance of a noble husband had to be gratified. And for that reason Austria has permitted a flagrant breach of military law.

Yes, gentlemen, in the interests of such rich and powerful men many things happen in this state which should not happen, and which *could* not happen if this state were a constitutional one. (*Hear, hear.*) Now, gentlemen, I put it to you: who is guilty? Who shall take the blame for the imprisonment of Lieutenant Mattachich to satisfy the whim of one rich man? The officers, perhaps? No, I can tell you that the officers are not responsible; they could never have brought in such a verdict if they had had the opportunity to hear the witnesses and the accused; if Mattachich had been allowed to put his questions to the witnesses; if the press had been allowed to report the case, if the extraordinarily capable and talented officer had been allowed free speech in an open court. Even if he could have had the services of a lawyer! But it is not difficult to get a man sentenced by an Interrogating Officer and seven lay judges, and then to have him thrown into prison.

But if we have reached the stage where such matters can openly be discussed in this parliament, then I ask the Minister of Defence: what next? As a man of honour, as a man whose long career has left him with a clear and calm conscience, can he take responsibility for Mattachich's torment and suffering upon his own head? I ask him: can he remain silent, or will he speak? And if perhaps he is not in a position to form an opinion today, I suggest that he should not hesitate to seek out the whole truth of this affair.

Gentlemen, I do not want to bring the Emperor's name into this, but I tell you, if I were a monarchist I should long ago have gone to the Emperor and brought this whole dirty business to his attention. In Vienna, certainly, the whole thing was ruthlessly suppressed in the press. But I have here a whole pile of foreign newspapers and, mark this, all these foreign newspapers come to a strange conclusion. A very interesting conclusion, moreover, though of course quite untrue (*laughter*). I shall quote a very short but typical example. A French newspaper—it doesn't matter which—draws this conclusion from the story (*reads*): 'C'est une idylle, qui se termine en tragédie—comme tout ce que touche la main fatale des Habsbourgs.' I will translate: 'It is an idyll which ends in tragedy—like everything that the fatal hand of the Habsburgs touches.'

Gentlemen, it is *not* the fatal hand of the Habsburgs but rather that of the Coburgs and the Bachrachs (*laughter*), and why should the Habsburgs play whipping-boy for the Coburgs and Bachrachs? And so I say again, if I were an Austrian monarchist, I should be the first person to insist on an immediate reopening of the Mattachich case.

I repeat: I believe firmly that Mattachich is innocent, and in this belief I am confident that, as things stand, I have the support of every decent person in this country!

XVII

G

Floridsdorf, near Vienna. Early September 1902 Thanks to the tireless efforts of Marie Stöger, with her combination of subtle female cunning and amazing masculine determination, my case has rapidly received wide publicity since the beginning of this year.

As Marie prophesied, it was the *Arbeiter-Zeitung*, the central organ of the Social Democrats in Austria, that set the ball rolling. After that the matter was officially raised by the socialist deputies in Parliament. The resulting succession of parliamentary debates lasted until the summer recess, and promised to continue to occupy the house with unabated vehemence (for the other side had of course found some spokesmen in the meantime) when Parliament reconvened in the autumn. Now at last the entire Austrian press, from right to left, had also taken up the case, and analysis and comment on every conceivable aspect began to appear.

The first article in the *Arbeiter-Zeitung* appeared on 16 January, on the front page of the morning edition. The entire issue was promptly confiscated by the censor. Undeterred the paper immediately produced a second edition, in which the lines complained of were omitted. Even the censored version exploded on Vienna like a bombshell.

My brave friend Marie not only smuggled the papers I gave her out of the prison; she smuggled the newspaper articles back in. My feelings on reading them are indescribable. I have spent almost four years behind prison walls. I had fought what seemed to me a hopeless struggle for my good name and my honour. I had done my utmost in both appeals to have the miscarriage of justice quashed. And I had suffered defeat after defeat. Now, suddenly, I knew that everything was going to change. That, apart from Marie Stöger, to whom I owed so much, there were people beyond those walls who had the means and methods available to publicize the wrong done to me not only within the borders of Austria but far beyond. This would, it *must*, produce results. The end now could only be freedom and rehabilitation. There was no other possibility.

But I was well aware that I could expect some last despairing blows from my enemies before they were ready to surrender. They came more quickly than I expected.

Everyone, not only my opponents, must know that the information used by the *Arbeiter-Zeitung* and by the deputy Daszynski could only come from me. But how was it possible that a prisoner isolated behind the walls of an Imperial military prison could communicate with the outside world? That he could contrive to slip not just a little note but apparently a whole manuscript through the double and triple security net?

The Ministry of War ordered no less a person than Field Marshal Pavek to solve this problem. He appeared at Möllersdorf with an Interrogating Officer, a Colonel Killian. For a week the two men searched, interrogated, threatened; they intimidated everyone who had to appear before their tribunal. But without the hoped-for success. I had given all my papers to Marie in good time, including my diary, which until now had never left my possession. On arrival at Möllersdorf I had hidden it in one of my boots, and had succeeded in bringing it past all the security controls.

Under the eyes of the General and the Colonel my cell was laboriously searched; the straw mattress was shaken out and carefully examined. Every stone of the walls was checked, to see if there might perhaps be a hollow one concealing a secret compartment. In vain. All the prison staff were subjected to a stringent interrogation, from the most junior private up to the Commandant himself. Also in vain. Possible informers were encouraged, promised promotion and financial reward. But all, all in vain. The burning question remained unanswered.

Marie was interrogated too. She was under grave suspicion. But no one could produce proof of her guilt. Nevertheless her job at the canteen was taken from her, and she was ordered not to set foot in the prison again.

The second victim was no less than the Commandant, Colonel von Dravodol. He was simply relieved of his command one day and put on the retired list.

That left me.

I had strenuously denied having anything to do with the events outside the prison. Since for lack of proof there was nothing they could do to me, they charged me with insubordinate behaviour towards the committee of inquiry. I won't say I had always been particularly polite, but the punishment was naturally out of proportion. It was nothing less than an act of vengeance, an admission of impotent fury.

One of the first official acts of the new Commandant, Major Franz Schonett, a man who made up in vigour for what he lacked in intelligence, was to inform me of the Inquiry's little keepsake for me: 'Fifteen days' darkness, to include three days' starvation!'

And so in the end I came to know the meaning of the punishment with which Captain Karapancsa had once threatened me at Zagreb.

Imagine a hole three and a half paces long and a bare two paces wide. A wooden cot with a few handfuls of loose straw. A water container and a foul-smelling bucket. No window. No ray of light ever penetrates this subterranean dungeon.

This kind of darkness, accentuated by the rough accommodation, hunger, total solitude and the terrible air in that unimaginably close space takes a dreadful toll of both mind and body and, as I know now from first hand, is rightly feared by every prisoner. It is not uncommon for second-class prisoners to be kept in irons during their punishment. I can imagine what additional torture that must be. That the warders in the punishment block are hand-picked torturers and sadists goes without saying.

At first you think you won't be able to stand the darkness.

You try all sorts of tricks to provide some way of measuring time, each more idiotic than the one before. When you realize the futility of these efforts, and your despair reaches its low point, you gradually become aware that there is something even worse than the eternal darkness and the loss of all sense of time: the silence. The dead silence. For the first time, as this new oppression threatens to stifle you and the sweat starts on your forehead, you realize what the word 'silence' means. Not the slightest whisper of sound penetrates that timeless dark. The guard comes round only once in twenty-four hours. You listen to their footsteps as if they were the most wonderful music in the world, but they die away and you are flung back into the void. Your own helpless protests and cries rebound from invisible walls. And when the echo has gone the silence is, if possible, even more terrible than before.

If Karapancsa had subjected me to this he might have broken me. But now not even this torture could upset my equilibrium permanently. I endured the days as one endures something unreal, as if everything was being described to me in the pages of a novel, very realistically but fiction for all that.

I never doubted that, whatever horrors this 'novel' might yet hold, I should soon finish it, and lay it aside for ever.

On 7 June the War Minister, Freiherr von Krieghammer, the superior of the Minister of Defence, felt himself obliged to try in person to stem the tide of questions and public appeals on my behalf.

He declared in Parliament: 'The legal proceedings against the former Lieutenant Geza Count Mattachich were *of course* conducted without any pressure being brought to bear from any outside source whatever, *in the normal manner*. The questions raised in support of the opposite viewpoint contained no new information which might give rise to suspicions of a miscarriage of justice and so justify reopening the case.

'The violations of the law referred to in certain publications did not in fact take place, and there is therefore no reason to institute an inquiry into this. The objections and pleas adduced by these publications are based entirely on one-sided information taken from the prisoner himself, without any regard to the very important grounds for suspicion produced by the prosecution.

'Finally, the occasional criticism of the appeal courts' findings rests on an incorrect interpretation of the relevant provisions of the Statute of Military Justice.'

These fighting words from the gentleman with the fighting name* and head of the Imperial War Ministry represented the last desperate attempt of the 'clique' to swing matters once more in their favour. But the die was now irrevocably cast. The new course the affair had taken had been endowed with an impetus and force that no one could now hope to resist.

At about 4 in the afternoon of 26 August Captain Navratil appeared and informed me that, by decree of his Apostolic Majesty the Emperor Franz Joseph I, I had been pardoned, and would be set at liberty the following day, 27 August 1902. Then he shook hands with me, wished me luck, and explained apologetically that for reasons of general security and discipline my cell would have to remain locked in the usual way until the following morning. Then he left me alone. I heard the sergeant of the guard turn the key in the lock and shoot the bolts.

On my first night in Möllersdorf I had slept well. The long journey from Zagreb and the agonizing week before had exhausted me to the point of unconsciousness. On my last night at Möllersdorf, the last after more than four and a quarter years in prison, sleep would not come. My joy at my coming freedom, great though it was, was clouded by deep disappointment and shame that my release would not be the result of rehabilitation, but an act of mercy. Through the prison gate tomorrow would walk not Count Mattachich, Lieutenant of Uhlans, but the released felon Geza Mattachich who had had two years of his sentence remitted.

I could form only the vaguest picture of the life that awaited

* *Krieghammer*, literally 'war hammer' (Trans).

me beyond the walls under these circumstances. As things stood, my next campaign would have to begin at once. The pardon alone was pointless if it did not lead to complete rehabilitation.

I had never stopped thinking of Louise. Yet the passing of time had made her seem strangely distant. Sometimes I had difficulty in remembering her face. Sometimes I thought I had forgotten how her voice sounded. Where is she? What sort of life is she living? How must she look today? What do I mean to her now?

And then there was this other woman. Marie Stöger. I owed her my freedom. That she is mad about me was perfectly clear to me. And come to that she's a damned attractive bit of woman, and wouldn't have to try very hard to force me into her bed.

All that was running through my head that night. And a lot more besides.

I could hear the sentries walking up and down in the corridor, and was aware of them opening the peephole to look in at me. At last the footsteps of the last outside patrol faded away below my cell window. Dawn was breaking.

I could see that it would be a flawless blue high-summer day.

Outside the prison gate stood a closed cab. To my surprise the driver came up to me and told me that I was expected.

I got in ... and found myself sitting next to Marie.

On the journey to the station I learnt that she had rented a small furnished room for me in Floridsdorf, a suburb of Vienna on the east bank on the Danube.

Two hours later—the clock on Floridsdorf town hall, which I can see from my window, showed twelve o'clock, and the siren at the near-by railway station was just announcing the lunch break—Marie and I were lying in my comfortable bed enjoying a little celebration.

Marie has an excitingly white skin, and the figure of a

young girl, firm and well proportioned.

When after some considerable time we came up for air, I looked at myself in a mirror for the first time for a very long time. I asked Marie whether I wasn't too thin for her taste.

'Soon change that,' she laughed. 'Main thing is that everything else is in working order. That's what matters. And I reckoned that would be all right from the beginning.'

'You've never told me anything about your husband,' I said, crawling back between the sheets.

'Nothing to tell. Nothing at all. I'll leave him.'

'For me?'

'I don't want to see him again,' she said, without answering my question. 'He'll have to see how he copes on his own. I'll slip away during the next few days.'

* * *

L

Every morning I read the *Dresdener Zeitung*. Or rather I just stare at the letters, and don't bother to make out sentences or even single words. After all these years of total isolation events in the world outside interest me little. I study the obituaries, flick through the announcements, and just barely glance at the Court Page.

As I was turning over the pages today, bored as ever, while Fräulein Gebauer sat by my bed with her crocheting, I noticed that one article had been carefully cut out of the paper.

'Have you read the paper yet, Fräulein von Gebauer?' I asked.

'Yes, Your Royal Highness,' she answered, without looking up from her work.

'Then please tell me what's missing here.' I pointed to the hole in the page.

The woman blushed deeply red. 'I don't know, Your Royal Highness,' she stammered. 'I wondered myself what it might have been.' She is a very bad liar.

'Please go to Dr Pierson and fetch me an uncensored copy,' I ordered.

'Very good, Your Royal Highness.' She stood up obediently, laid down her crochet, disappeared, and didn't return all morning.

She probably counted on my forgetting the whole thing quickly. There she was wrong. When she reappeared in the afternoon at about the time we usually go out, looking as if butter wouldn't melt in her mouth, I immediately asked for the paper.

'You'll never believe this, Your Royal Highness,' she began, blushing again already, 'but the same article is missing in every copy. I've tried, but no one can tell me what it was about.'

This excuse, probably the work of Dr Pierson, was so stupid that I thought it beneath my dignity to pursue it.

But that was not the last strange event of the day. For Fräulein Gebauer now informed me that one of the horses had gone lame, and so we couldn't go out. That was a surprise. Both the horses were trotting quite happily yesterday. Still, such things can happen.

I suggested that we should go for a walk. The doctor attached great importance to my getting some fresh air every day. But Fräulein Gebauer explained that Dr Pierson said a walk in the prevailing temperature would be too tiring for me. When I told her that I wasn't afraid of a little effort, she said that those were the doctor's orders and we must follow them.

Still no excursions and no walks. No reason given, no tim limit fixed.

What can it mean?

Again and again I have tried to get some reason out of Fräulein Gebauer. But she maintains firmly that she knows nothing.

Today Dr Pierson visited me, for the first time since the

newspaper incident and the beginning of my house arrest. The Court Marshal's Office in Vienna has asked an international commission of famous psychiatrists to prepare a new report on me, he tells me.

When Dr Rudinger had come to me at Purkersdorf to tell me of Krafft-Ebing's visit, I thought I could treat it with total indifference, because I knew that the result was a foregone conclusion even before he had seen me. Even so my long conversations with him awakened a faint hope in me, so that the disappointment at the end was the more bitter.

I didn't want to go through that again. In any case the doctors' very direct questions always worried and upset me. I tried to explain this to Dr Pierson.

The doctor has a disarmingly blunt and at the same time paternal manner which he adopts if he wants to persuade me to do something. He assured me that this time the procedure would be quite short and painless. The medical authorities would certainly bother me very little, he added, as he had been instructed to make all previous reports and observations available for them.

That infuriated me. If the doctors were to base their findings on old reports, I pointed out, it was inconceivable that they should reach a different conclusion to their colleagues. I asked Dr Pierson to spare me this new torment.

'Unfortunately, Your Royal Highness, we are unable to disregard our instructions from Vienna,' said Pierson, and I thought there was a hint of compassion in his eyes. 'We shall just have to endure them bravely as best we can.' In any case, he said, and he meant it kindly, it would be a nice change from my monotonous life here to be able to chat to such respected scientists as a Professor Wagner von Jauregg.

The proceedings were certainly short and painless. Dr Pierson had been right about that.

Professor Jolly arrived from Berlin, where he ran the city's biggest clinic for nervous disorders; the private medical officer

Dr Weber, Director of the Royal Saxon Institute at Sonnenstein, had a shorter journey, from Pirna. Dr Mélis, the personal physician to my uncle, the Count of Flanders, came from Brussels; and the great authority Professor Julius Wagner Ritter von Jauregg from Vienna. All had to return very soon to their places of work.

Each of these gentlemen was given the earlier reports to read; each had one meeting with me, at which he asked questions which I had often answered before, which only showed me how prejudiced these medical men are.

The conversation with Dr Mélis was particularly painful for me, as he concentrated on my childhood in Belgium and so awoke memories of happier times. He brought me greetings from my uncle, and also from my aunt, whom I had positively adored as a child. I was tormented by the thought of what Dr Mélis would say about me at home (suddenly Brussels was 'home'), and the awareness of my inability to influence his report in any way preyed on me more and more.

Wagner von Jauregg was my last visitor. I had the impression that he came reluctantly to perform an unpleasant duty. My case did not interest him, and he showed it.

'Please tell me something, Professor,' I said to him. 'What has really brought you here? What has happened in Vienna for Prince Philip suddenly to lay out the vast sum of money that a report from such medical celebrities must be costing him?'

He looked at me in surprise, and for the first time with some attention. 'I don't know, Your Royal Highness,' he said. 'I was approached not by your husband but by the Court Marshal's Office.'

The old song. Not Philip, but the Court Marshal's Office. It would be pointless to explain to the professor that the Court Marshal's Office only concerns itself with me at the instigation of Prince Philip of Coburg. Resignedly, I answered his questions briefly and uninformatively.

For the first time I was officially informed of the result of an examination. Dr Pierson gave me the so-called 'definitive report', and I quote it word for word.

> On the strength of the documents shown to us [no wonder!] and of our personal observations [it took them half a day to decide my future!] we have reached the following conclusions.
> 1) The condition of imbecility diagnosed in H.R.H. Princess Louise of Saxe-Coburg-Gotha continues unabated, and renders her still incapable of managing her own affairs.
> 2) The Princess's continued confinement in the closed clinic is, in view of this condition and in the noble patient's own interests [in my interests!], absolutely necessary.
> 3) We are satisfied that Dr Pierson's institution offers all the facilities necessary to provide the most appropriate and considerate treatment possible.

Then follow the names—Jolly, Wagner von Jauregg, Mélis and Weber—in that order, complete with their numerous titles, dignities and offices.

The performance is over. The spark of hope, which glowed a little despite everything, is extinguished, and life here goes on. Even excursions are permitted again from now on. I may not be recovered, but at least the horse's leg is better.

XVIII

G

This is a wretched, miserable life I'm leading, and there is only one way to change it. To change it completely. At a stroke. Today I know that for a fact, at last. I've been thinking it over long enough.

The first days after my release were one relentless whirlpool of activity. One journalist after another—before one had shut the door the next would be pushing through it. They came from all over Europe. As if Floridsdorf had suddenly become the centre of the world. As well as the press I had politicians of every colour and God knows what else in the way of sightseers. They all wanted to hear the story in detail, and preferably starting from my birth.

Even so, these encounters had plenty of variety, and often produced invitations. Depending on the rank and finances of my guests, they might invite me to anything from a beer in the 'Senator'—the cellar under the Town Hall over the road—to a mighty dinner at Sacher's. The waiters there remembered me; they greeted me as if I was some prima donna, and always kept me the best table.

Before I'd been out a week Marie turned up on the doorstep with a couple of cases, and moved in with me. I didn't mind. Since then she's been keeping house, and we hop into bed whenever we feel like it. There *is* only one bed—very practical. She's eight years younger than me, and swears that apart from her husband she's never had anything to do with a man before. If that's true she's got the greatest natural talent I've ever met.

Months went by, and the sensation I'd caused began to cool off. Life became quieter. The newspapers had had their scandal; I had become uninteresting to them. Their readers want something new. The politicians too have got all they can out of the case: I've been pardoned, and I ought to be satisfied with that, is the message I hear more and more now. The struggle to regain my honour attracts no supporters; I fight alone.

Money's in damned short supply. To be frank, I'm broke as I've never been broke before in my life. No one will advance me a groschen. Marie brought some money with her, but it's gone. It was supposed to pay for her divorce, too. Unless a miracle happens we're soon going to find ourselves with no food and no heating. Never mind the rent.

I've even thought of working. But what as?

Marie goes on at me about opening a tobacconist's shop. Or a stall in the Prater. Under her name, if necessary. We had our first row over that. Never mind names, I said; was she out of her mind? I might just as well let her go on the streets.

And now I know where my salvation lies: I need Louise! I must get her out of the madhouse. She's now in an institution in Saxony. Somehow I'll have to bring it off, though I've no idea how. But one thing I am sure of: only with her can I be what I once was.

I could kick myself for being so long realizing the obvious. It's Marie's fault. I know that without her I should still be in Möllersdorf; but she's dragged me down into this depressing, petty-bourgeois existence. Floridsdorf, for God's sake! I've never been in such a wretched slum in my life. That's how it started, and it's getting worse.

I will fetch Louise out of that place! She will proclaim my innocence to the world, and together we shall fight for what is right. She for the money owed to her; I for my name and my honour.

I am resolved to think of nothing, day and night, except how to rescue Louise. How shall I set about it? It must work, and at the first attempt too. If anything goes wrong it's all up with me. In everything I plan, everything I try, I must never forget that.

Marie, of course, must know nothing. One day—not too far

distant, I hope—she'll find out. That's time enough.

* * *

L

Our daily excursions bore me more and more. Fräulein Gebauer and I have nothing to say to each other, so I sit beside her in silence and gaze vaguely in front of me.

The route the coachman usually takes leads through a pretty little copse. The country round here is rolling, but the road has been levelled, and is below the level of the wood itself.

There was a bicycle there today. It was leaning against the slope at the side of the road, so that it half blocked the way. That struck me as odd. The coachman slowed to drive round it. A few yards farther on a man was standing on the embankment. He stared at me, never taking his eyes off me, as if he was trying to hypnotize me.

I had a terrible shock: it looked like Geza. But Geza lies in Möllersdorf Prison, so he can't be standing by the side of a road in Saxony. Even so I felt the blood rush to my head for a second.

The man was already out of sight behind us.

I turned round once. Then he suddenly raised a hand and waved, with a gesture that was incredibly familiar.

Confused, I turned round again. I must have looked very pale, as Fräulein Gebauer asked me if I was feeling ill.

I shook my head and said nothing.

Did I really see Geza? Or has he a double? The question began to torment me as I sat once more behind my barred windows. Had I taken some stranger for Geza, someone who happened to look like him, simply because I can't forget him? Am I starting to see ghosts in broad daylight? Is my long-standing 'madness' becoming reality at last?

The question began to prey on my mind; I couldn't forget it.

But then I remembered the puzzling events of recent months, for which I had never found an explanation: the visit of the foreign doctors, the ban on leaving the grounds, the missing article in the paper. Did all these events have something in common ... something to do with Geza?

Was Geza free? Could that have been what was in the article I was never allowed to read? Free? But he still has years to serve. So he must have been pardoned. Which is extremely improbable. Has he escaped then? I could certainly believe that of him.

And the longer I thought it over, the more sure I became: I had seen no double, but Geza, the real, living Geza! Geza!

And then another thought frightened me. How had I looked?

I rushed to the mirror; I became aware of several strands of grey in my hair, and a lot of new wrinkles here and there.

Quickly I called Olga, and ordered her to wash my hair at once. My hair is so curly and thick that this is always a torture, and recently I've been saving myself the discomfort from time to time. But today I sat there patiently, trying to suppress my excitement and waiting till my hair was completely dry. Then we tried out several different styles, until we found one that hid the grey.

Tuesday I spent the whole morning on my appearance. I really didn't want to lie down after lunch, in case I disturbed my hair; I lay down very carefully and never moved.

Time passed infinitely slowly.

Would Geza be there again? I couldn't stop worrying. What would I do? What would I say? I could hardly wait for the coach to drive up.

I ordered the driver to take the same route as yesterday.

As we rolled through the gates, leaning well back in the open carriage, Fräulein Gebauer gave me a sidelong glance.

'Your Royal Highness has changed,' she said eventually.

'I don't think so. What do you mean?'

'I've been wondering about it since yesterday, but I can't put my finger on anything,' she answered, and I could hear the puzzlement in her voice.

I opened my parasol, one that Geza used to find especially pretty, kept a longing eye open for him, and forgot Fräulein Gebauer.

He never came.

I asked the driver to go through the copse twice, but in vain. I didn't dare make him go past the vital spot a third time in case someone thought it suspicious.

Back at the sanatorium I felt deep disappointment. I ate nothing and went straight to bed.

The lady-in-waiting warned Dr Pierson, who came in to ask how I was.

'A slight headache, that's all. Nothing to worry about,' I told him.

He looked at me searchingly. Probably Fräulein Gebauer had told him I had been behaving oddly.

I felt no desire for a conversation; I shut my eyes and lay there motionless until he went away.

Had it all been my imagination? Or had I changed so much that Geza didn't want to see me again? Am I not 'his Louise' any more?

I forced myself to go to the mirror.

Geza was right. I am a different Louise now.

I spent a sleepless night.

Wednesday   It rained all day without stopping. I can't go out: that would be unthinkable. I stand here at the window, staring out at the downpour and dying of anxiety.

Thursday   This morning it was still raining. After lunch I lay down and fell fast asleep.

When Olga woke me, the sun had come out from behind the clouds.

I took time to get myself ready.

The driver took the same route without my having to tell him.

We were still some way away when I saw him.

As we reached him, I told the driver to stop, and climbed quickly out of the carriage before Fräulein Gebauer could realize what was happening.

I went to him. He kissed my hand. We both had tears in our eyes.

And then Fräulein Gebauer was standing beside me. As if it was the most natural thing in the world, I introduced them. 'Count Mattachich ... Fräulein Gebauer, my lady-in-waiting.'

Geza flushed as I used the title that is no longer his to use. We were both hard put to it to conceal our excitement.

'How are you?' I said. I might as well have asked him about the weather.

'Thank you, Your Royal Highness,' he said, a little hesitantly. 'I am glad to see you looking so well.'

'So you're ... free?'

'Yes, Your Royal Highness,' he said softly, and smiled, guessing my thoughts. 'Don't worry,' he said, in answer to the question I had not dared ask. 'Pardoned.'

'Thank God.' And I smiled too.

Fräulein Gebauer was whispering. 'It's late, Your Royal Highness,' she pressed me.

'Just another moment,' I said.

She seemed to agree, but having won my moment I had no idea what to do with it.

'We shall meet again,' said Geza, with a confidence that made me prick my ears up.

'Yes. When?'

Now Fräulein Gebauer had grabbed my arm, and I was afraid that she would call the driver to help her.

'Leave me alone. I'm coming,' I said, and gave Geza my

hand again. I was sorry I was wearing gloves; I wanted to feel the touch of his skin.

'Don't forget what I just said,' I heard him say, then Fräulein Gebauer hurried me to the carriage.

'Back to the sanatorium! Quickly!' she shouted at the driver.

On the drive back she said nothing at all.

Dr Pierson reproached me bitterly. He found it most regretable that after so many years in the sanatorium I had still not rediscovered the dignity that one must demand of a Princess of the Blood Royal; that at the sight of the man to whom I owed all my misfortunes I had not hesitated to speak to him, even to give him my hand. He had hoped, he said, that I had at last been cured of this indecent infatuation. But now he was forced to recognize that in all those years my attitude to Mr Mattachich had remained unaltered.

I had long lost the habit of contradicting my doctors. Now it would have been better to be silent again; but I could not. I informed Pierson that Count Mattachich (I used his old title deliberately) was the only person in the world who had always stood by me loyally, who was devoted to me, and whom I could trust absolutely. He had spent many years in prison for a crime of which I, not he, had been guilty. (Although *I* don't call it a crime at all!) Should I not speak to a man who had endured that for me? Should I not take his hand in mine?

Pierson evaded me. He was in no mood for argument. He was very sorry, he said on his way to the door, but he would have to inform Vienna of what had occurred. It went without saying, of course, that I should not be able to leave my room in future.

I have been demoted: from patient to prisoner. For two weeks I have been sitting here, locked in my room. No one visits me, no one talks to me, Fräulein Gebauer is staying out of sight, even Olga is under orders to sulk. She brings me my meals in silence, then disappears again.

Dr Pierson thinks this is a punishment, but it is not. The true punishment is that I was able to speak with Geza for one brief moment before he disappeared again for ever.

I almost regret having seen him at all. Previously, when I thought of him, I saw him in his cell at Möllersdorf. That was terrible, unjust; but at least my thoughts could find him there. Now I don't know where he is. How often did he stand in the copse, waiting? When did he abandon hope, and leave? And where did he go? How will he live? What friends has he? Instead of harsh fact, there are only questions. And one tiny consolation, to which I cling like a child. 'We shall meet again!' he said, and he said it as if he *knew*.

Against all probability, I must try to believe in that.

* * *

G

Coswig, near Dresden, May 1904 Louise's appearance shocked me deeply. Not because of her health, I mean. On the contrary, physically—and mentally too, of course—she seems completely normal. But she has aged far beyond her years.

That it gave me such delight, not so very long ago, to sleep with her is hardly credible now. A strange pair we shall make!

Poor Geza.

I met her twice. The first time we just saw each other; the second we were able to talk for a moment. That was the first step in a cunning, detailed plan of campaign, and the first important step on a long, hard road. But now the intricate machinery is in motion. I lack neither help nor money. The end is only a matter of time. I have no more doubts: I am going to succeed.

The preparations took longer than I expected. And sometimes it looked as thought I should have to give up, because I was making no progress or because the wretched money was running out.

In those bad times my new friend, Josef Weitzer, proved to be my sheet anchor. I owe him much that money can never repay. Not to mention the 30,000 crowns he has already advanced me over the last few months. Weitzer is a simple man, a man of the people, who by his standards has made a success of his life. That his heart is in the right place he has shown well enough. From my first day at Floridsdorf he was never far away—he is, in fact, the landlord of the 'Senator' cellar. When I looked out of my window I could practically see straight into his bar, and into his till.

When I was being visited every five minutes just after my release, I was often over there with some of my well-wishers. He serves good cold beer, and his wines are excellent. His wife is a good cook, too. Sometimes it happened that he used to come and sit at our table, always asking first if he was interrupting us. He bought the occasional round, listened eagerly, and soon knew my story better than I did myself.

He was the first person I ever told of my plan to rescue Louise. His enthusiasm was immediate and violent—he not only promised to say nothing to Marie or his own wife, but undertook to give me any financial and active help he could. I couldn't hurt the good man's feelings, and accepted his offer. Today I can say that he has kept his word: he was and is the foundation stone of the whole enterprise.

A happy fate sent me my second confederate: a French nobleman, a very lively man both in spirit and (because of his profession) in fact. Henri de Nousanne is his name: out of sheer enthusiasm and for his own pleasure he is a journalist. He writes for the Paris paper *Le Journal*, in which his family has financial interests.

In the autumn after my release de Nousanne was in London. The Russian revolutionary Trotsky had just escaped from his Siberian exile and fled to London, where he met his accomplice Lenin. De Nousanne had met both men, and written long articles discussing their insane ideas. He's a bit mad himself in many ways. But I can overlook that, because his youthful enthusiasm is very valuable to me. Anyway, he is convinced that we haven't heard the last of the two Russian revolutionaries. He swears that they could be a very great danger to the Tsar and to the whole system of government in Russia. Sheer madness, obviously. But for personal reasons I've been careful not to tell him too forcefully what I think.

Young de Nousanne just happened to hear of me last spring, and (typically) decided to come and see me at once.

He was very much moved by the condition in which he found me, and asked straight away whether he could help, and if so how. He would be only too happy if I could use his services. I seized the chance that had so unexpectedly occurred, and told the young Frenchman of my plan. He appreciated that considerable sums of money would be needed to bring it off, and made me a fascinating offer. He offered me money; hard cash, and he didn't want it back. All I had to do was give him a written undertaking to publish the whole story of Louise's release, once it had been safely accomplished, in the form of an interview with him in *Le Journal*. And Louise herself was not to make any statement to any other paper. I agreed, of course. And so de Nousanne, or his paper, put at my disposal all the money I would need to carry the thing off. We agreed on a certain figure for my previous expenses, plus a monthly salary of 4,000 francs for a maximum of one year— that is, 48,000 francs.

The fourth member of our group is a Prussian. Which makes us a genuine international conspiracy. Daszynski introduced the man from the north to me when he was spending a few days in Vienna some months ago. We got on well together from the start. His name is Albert Südekum, and he's a journalist like de Nousanne, a socialist deputy like Daszynski— though not in Austria, but at the German parliament in Berlin. Before his election Südekum was an editor in Leipzig and Dresden. He still has excellent and reliable contacts from those days in the Kingdom of Saxony, and I can rely on them for absolutely any kind of help I need. Which means a great deal; particularly as, since I've been here, I've been able to see for myself how dazzlingly well those contacts operate.

My first step was to get the most detailed possible on-the-spot knowledge of my coming zone of operations. And so I spent four weeks slinking round this damned district like a thief, until I found out all there was to know. The difficulties we shall encounter here on the day are considerable, but not insuperable.

Before I left with my information to plan the next stages with my friends, I had to give Louise a sign. To let her know that I am free, and that I care what happens to her. After toying with all sorts of possible and impossible ideas, I realized that there was only one way to be sure of achieving the purpose I had in mind. I had observed, of course, that Louise made regular excursions from the sanatorium; I must risk meeting her personally during one of these and explaining more or less unambiguously what was afoot. This, I knew, would obviously put not only Lindenhof but probably Vienna on its guard. But there was no other way. My plan is that now the meeting with Louise has actually taken place I must turn my back on Saxony for a few months, and let the grass grow over things. My enemies must believe that I had no more serious intent than to see Louise just once more, after all that has happened.

Tomorrow morning I leave for Berlin, to tell Südekum how things are going.

* * *

L

Bad Elster, Hotel Wettinger Hof   I've been taking the cure for four weeks now in Bad Elster, a village in Saxony.

After more than five years in the madhouse, this place is like Biarritz, Nice, Ostende, San Sebastian and the Isle of Wight rolled into one. The place is very popular with honest citizens, clerks and workers, and their equally honest wives.

I'm the first real, live Princess ever to come here. So I cause a great sensation. Especially as in my case the Princess is mad, and goes around complete with retinue and guards.

The retinue consists of the inevitable Fräulein Gebauer and my Olga, who has gradually become a friend to me. The guards are commanded by Dr Mauss, Dr Pierson's assistant and representative. Dr Pierson, and the bath supervisor Herr von Alberti, command an army of police, warders and spies, some in uniform, some in plain clothes. When I stroll down to the pump-room with Mauss and Fräulein Gebauer each day, to take my regular glass of the disgustingly salt water, I have two men walking in front of me and two behind. When I go to the bathhouse to take a mud-bath, four men stand guard at the door. When we eat in the hotel dining-room, all the doors are watched.

The mounting of the guard is so exaggerated that the other visitors must think me either a public danger or a subject for deep compassion, depending of course on whether they think me an imbecile or perfectly normal.

Anyway, I am certainly the chief attraction of this bourgeois little spa town. As soon as I walk into the Kurpark with all my hangers-on everyone is rooted to the spot; they stop talking and gawp after me with their mouths hanging open.

I have Dr Pierson to thank for this unexpected holiday: after my meeting with Geza and my subsequent house arrest he was unhappy to see me becoming more and more wretched. He contacted Vienna, and was told that he could arrange for me to take the waters somewhere where I could be closely watched all the time. The choice of spa was obvious: the wife of the hotelier here was first married to Dr Pierson's brother, then after he died she married the owner of the Wettinger Hof, a Herr Bretholz.

As for the hotel, suffice it to say that it is the best available; which says very little for Bad Elster.

Even so I am making considerable progress; even this closely guarded freedom is enormously refreshing. I make supervised visits to the concert hall, the theatre, and any other entertainments the spa authorities see fit to provide. It may not be very much; but it is much, much more than I have had for a very long time.

This evening Fräulein Gebauer, Dr Mauss and I dined in the hotel as usual. We were served by a young waiter, who paid noticeable attention to me. Thank God, neither of my companions noticed it. The waiter stood behind them, and fixed anxious, wide eyes unwinkingly on me. Then he walked round the table, and passed so close to me that he brushed against me and my napkin fell to the floor. He stammered, 'A thousand pardons, Your Royal Highness. I will bring you another one at once.'

A few moments later he handed me a new damask napkin. As I unfolded it, I felt a letter hidden in it.

The waiter was standing behind my companions again and watching me excitedly.

I do not know where I found the self-control; but without batting an eyelid I slipped the envelope quietly into a pocket of my dress, without breaking off my calm conversation with Dr Mauss. I saw the waiter, relieved, slip away.

As soon as I decently could I pleaded a headache, and retired to my room, followed by Dr Mauss and Fräulein Gebauer. Dr Mauss wanted to give me a sedative, Fräulein Gebauer wanted to sit with me, but I insisted on being alone. They locked me in and promised to come back and see me in a little while.

I took the letter from my pocket. The envelope bore no address. I tore it open and unfolded the letter. My heart hammered as if it would burst when I saw Geza's familiar hand.

'My darling,' he wrote. 'Everything is ready for your escape. Don't worry, it'll work. Theo, the young waiter, is one of us. He admires you. He will keep you informed. But first I must know that you are willing. Tomorrow morning at ten o'clock, come out onto your balcony, holding a white handkerchief in your right hand. Then I shall know you agree. We shall never have a chance like this again. Remember that, and be brave.

And above all, remember that I love you. G.'

I don't know whether Geza suspects what he has let himself in for, or how well guarded I am. But I have no way of warning him. I can only do what he asks, and I shall do it, blindly.

From a quarter to ten until a quarter to eleven I stood on the balcony. Never in my life had I been so punctual, or so patient.

Fräulein Gebauer, who was reading the newspaper inside the room, wanted to know what ever I found so fascinating about the view—why I couldn't tear myself away from it.

I looked out across the little square to the streets that converged in it, the villas and gardens that lined them. Somewhere, invisible to me and yet so close, Geza was watching me. I was very excited, and at the same time happier than I had been for many years.

If Fräulein Gebauer was a better judge of character she would certainly have been suspicious.

Saturday No news of Geza; my time here is almost over. Next Friday we shall be leaving. Does Geza know that? Is he hurrying accordingly? Could something have gone wrong? Could someone have traced him and arrested him? Questions chasing each other through my anxious, sleepless mind.

Now it is I who stare questioningly at the young waiter during dinner. When he is out of sight of my companions, Theo shrugs his shoulders helplessly. So he too knows nothing.

Sunday If it doesn't work now, I shall spend the rest of my life behind the walls of an asylum. The thought is dreadful beyond words.

Today Dr Mauss said, 'Your Royal Highness was practically recovered. But there seems to have been a little relapse during the last few days. Am I right?'

Absolutely right.

Perhaps the mud baths were too tiring for me, he suggested. Perhaps I should give them up.

I tried to persuade him that our stay was too short, and it would be better to extend it, but he said that was out of the question. I should be grateful to Dr Pierson for getting Vienna to agree to the four-week visit I'd already had.

Monday I excused myself again with a recurrence of my headache; Olga undressed me and locked me in my room. Then I read the letter that Theo slipped me today.

Geza has thought of everything. With foresight and cunning he has prepared for any eventuality. He has watched the hotel closely, checked on the guards, allowed for every possible source of danger. Like a general on the eve of the battle.

It will be Wednesday night.

Theo will unlock my door. Geza has taken a wax impression of the key, and had a duplicate made. (I hope it works!) I am to take the absolute minimum with me; not more than Theo and I can carry, but of course bringing all my jewels and money. (In fact I have no money to bring.) I must carry my shoes in my hand and walk in stockinged feet, as the boards in the corridors creak horribly. The guard in the room opposite has been bribed; I have nothing to fear from him. All entrances to the hotel are locked and guarded, so Theo will take me down from the first floor to the ground-floor room of an Austrian friend, a Joseph Weitzer from Floridsdorf. If I wanted to get a sight of Herr Weitzer in advance, he would be sitting alone at a small table near the door in the dining-room, and wearing a pink carnation in his button-hole. Weitzer's room is at the back of the hotel; with his help I shall climb through his window, and straight into Geza's arms.

Tuesday Joseph Weitzer is fat with a huge appetite, and already looks so excited that I don't know whether he will survive the night's exertions.

When he noticed that I was watching him he fixed his eyes on his plate, trying to be inconspicuous. But he kept nodding his head, to answer my unspoken question, and fingered the pink carnation in his button-hole to be sure I should not overlook it.

Even Theo is affected. His normally pink and healthy face was pale, and he dropped a plate during dinner, which made everybody jump.

I hope my nerves are better.

Wednesday night I am sitting in my room, dressed and ready.

In less than an hour Theo will come and let me out. Beside me is a little case with my jewellery and essentials; a bundle of clothes is lying on the chair. I am wearing a coat and a hat with a veil, and my heart is thumping violently.

I know that I am taking an enormous step; walking into danger, and abandoning the doubtful safety of the sanatorium for total uncertainty.

If this escape succeeds—and it *must* succeed—if Geza can rescue me from this twilight world, I shall be in his debt for ever.

XIX

Articles in the Neue Freie Presse, *Vienna, 1-6 September 1904*

Vienna, 1 September 1904 At present there is still no word as to the whereabouts of Princess Louise of Coburg, kidnapped from Bad Elster two nights ago. The theory is still that she and her abductor left Bad Elster by motor car and have fled to Switzerland or France. So far all attempts to trace the Princess have proved unsuccessful.

The kidnapper is Geza Mattachich; of that there has never been any doubt.

The Princess is believed to be dressed in her normal outdoor clothes. She took nothing with her except a small handbag containing her remaining jewellery. This is believed to be of relatively little value, probably no more than 5,000 crowns.

Dresden, 1 September 1904 Inquiries into the escape are being pursued with frantic energy in Bad Elster. The authorities are also involved, as the case is being treated as one of kidnapping. After the Princess's family and Dr Pierson had been informed by telegram, the first orders for the pursuit were given. The trail led to Bavaria, but it is suspected that this clue was deliberately left by the abductors who must have reckoned with an immediate and energetic hue and cry. Agents have been sent out in all directions from Bad Elster, and the number of reported sightings of the motor car used for the escape is growing all the time.

Dr Pierson is expected in Bad Elster later today. Meanwhile Fräulein von Gebauer, who is reported to be in a very disturbed state, and Dr Mauss have returned to Lindenhof Sanatorium.

Vienna, 2 September 1904 Prince Philip was spending

yesterday at his castle at Ebenthal, Lower Austria, on his return from a trip abroad when a message arrived from Dr Bachrach containing brief details of the escape. The news caused the Prince very great shock. During the day more messages arrived with further news. The Prince decided to leave for Vienna, to hold discussions as to the next steps. He is expected to arrive here some time tomorrow. Dr Bachrach and the Princess's guardian, Dr von Feistmantel, were informed from Bad Elster.

Brussels, 2 September 1904   The details of the abduction of Princess Louise have caused a major sensation here. This makes it the more remarkable to read in the official newspaper *Étoile Belge* that on Thursday evening the Royal Palace, the palace of the Count of Flanders and the Foreign Ministry were all unable to confirm that the escape had in fact taken place.

Vienna, 2 September   The following information was received by interested persons in Vienna today. The trail left by the refugees, which led to Hof in Bavaria, has been followed further. Reliable reports suggest that it might lead to Switzerland. It is known that the Princess and her party left Hof yesterday morning for Munich, where they arrived in the afternoon. They left again by the next train for the Lake of Constance. In the evening they reached Lindau, but did not stay there long. Where they went from there is as yet unknown. But the party is known to be in Switzerland, and it seems likely that they travelled from Lindau to Zürich.

Paris   King Leopold of the Belgians has arrived in Paris. He neither knows nor cares where his daughter is. He certainly has not seen her, and has no intention of doing so.

Vienna   We learn that discussion took place this morning

between the representatives of Prince Philip of Coburg and of the Court Marshal's Office, Princess Louise's guardian, and other interested parties. As a result of these discussions it would appear that steps are being taken to institute criminal proceedings against the Princess's abductor, Geza Mattachich.

Bad Elster (Interview with Supervisor Alberti): 'On Wednesday evening I accompanied the Princess to the theatre. She was in very good form, and promised to return on Thursday, the day before her intended departure, to attend the benefit performance for the great local favourite Hanna Proft, the actress. I showed her to her carriage. The Princess had supper with her lady-in-waiting, Frl. Gebauer, and her physician, Dr Mauss. At about midnight the maid left the Princess in bed in her room. The balcony door was locked, as was the door into the corridor. The curtains were closed and secured with pins, as the Princess sleeps late in the mornings. Everything was still in place in the morning, when the escape was discovered. The chambermaid informed the Doctor and me, as well as the lady-in-waiting and the hotelier, Herr Bretholz. The latter at once suspected the visitor named Joseph Weitzer, who claimed to come from Floridsdorf and occupied a room on the ground floor; he has in fact disappeared.

'Unless the Princess sends me a postcard,' Herr von Alberti went on, 'I shall have no idea where she is. She took her jewel-case and contents with her. She has a set of diamond studs the size of hazel nuts, worth about 80,000 crowns each, pearl necklaces, brooches and the valuable rosary given to her by Pope Leo.'

Brussels, 3 September The Brussels newspapers, irrespective of political allegiance, have all taken up the story of Princess Louise's escape from Bad Elster with great enthusiasm. In court circles, where the surprise was naturally an unpleasant one, a certain scepticism is evident.

Berne, 3 September Commenting on recent press reports that Princess Louise of Coburg was staying in Zurich, or in the Burghölzli clinic (formerly run by the psychiatrist Dr Forel), the Swiss news agency has announced that following extensive inquiries it can be stated with almost complete certainty that Princess Louise is not in Zürich.

Bad Elster, 3 September 1904 The Princess left a farewell note for her maid. The note is written on blue vellum, in pencil. It begins DEAR OLGA and contains the following significant lines: *I am free. God has heard my prayers. Farewell.* Finally the Princess thanks her maid for her services.

Vienna, 5 September It is now known that Prince Philip of Coburg has applied to the Court Marshal's Office for assistance, in accordance with the terms of the Hague Convention of 1896 which we quoted recently. After investigating the facts of the case the Court Marshal's Office has decided that the Hague Convention is applicable, and has officially ordered that Princess Louise must be returned to her husband. According to the Convention, as soon as the Princess's whereabouts are discovered the Court Marshal will apply to the government of the foreign country concerned for extradition, and this government will return the Princess to her husband, by force if necessary.

Brussels, 5 September The Brussels Committee of the Belgian League for Human Rights has petitioned the Swiss Government not to hand over Princess Louise of Belgium to her husband's representatives, unless a commission of psychiatrists appointed by the Swiss Government itself has first confirmed that the refugee Princess really is mad.

Albert Südekum, the Social Democrat member of the German

Parliament who helped to effect Princess Louise's escape, has made the following statement to the Paris newspaper *Humanité*:

'Princess Louise of Coburg is at present in a place of complete safety. After her escape from Bad Elster she travelled via Hof to Berlin, where from Wednesday to Saturday she stayed "in the house of a Social Democrat deputy".

'She stayed in fact with me. I promised Mattachich long ago that in the event of a happy outcome to his plan, he should count on the hospitality of my home. The assertions of some German and Austrian legal experts that the Princess could not be arrested in Germany are irrelevant: certainly she could not be charged with any offence, but the most transparent innocence is not always proof against brute force. The Princess has already discovered this for herself, when without any legal proceedings she was taken from her bed in Zagreb and confined in an asylum. It is true that the Emperor Wilhelm has decreed that one should not meddle in such affairs, but at a time when acts of crude violence are being perpetrated against the Russian exiles, such decrees become meaningless.

'During her stay in my house I often had the opportunity of a long conversation with the Princess. I may therefore permit myself to pronounce on her condition. She is an extraordinarily lively and interesting woman, and in my opinion she is in complete possession of all her mental faculties. Certainly she has the weaknesses one would expect from her background and upbringing. She is much too much the princess to be able to be like other people. But if that alone were grounds to commit a person to an asylum, then in twenty-four hours every palace in Europe and elsewhere might as well be converted into a madhouse.'

XX

Bougival   Never in my life have I been so unbelievably happy.

I sit here at the open balcony door, writing at a pretty little table, and I look out over a wild, wonderfully overgrown country garden with fruit trees, vegetable beds and hundreds of bright flowers. It is all peaceful and beautiful.

After the excitement of the last few days I have had a really good sleep at last, and tomorrow we shall be moving from Bougival, where M. de Nousanne has lent us his country house for a few days, and going to Paris.

Downstairs in the salon Geza is giving him the promised interview for his paper; the two of them have been at work on it for hours already.

Today I can laugh at the memory of how I followed Theo the waiter in my stockinged feet, creeping through the corridors and down the stairs of the Wettiger Hof hotel in Bad Elster, but then I was in deadly earnest. With every step I became more vividly aware of the terrible danger Geza was running for my sake. If we had been caught, I should simply have been taken back to the sanatorium as if nothing had happened. He on the other hand was risking the freedom he had won so bravely.

Outside Herr Weitzer's door I was ready to turn round and go back. But Theo had already vanished; the door was open. A hand reached out to me in the darkness and drew me into the room. I could discern nothing but the dim outline of the window.

A voice whispered, 'Please put your shoes on, Your Royal Highness.'

I slipped them on.

At once my unseen accomplice led me over to the window. 'Hurry, hurry, Your Royal Highness,' he whispered. I sat on the sill and swung my legs over. Already I felt Geza's arms reach up to take me and lower me gently to the ground. Now Weitzer passed my scanty luggage out through the window then climbed out himself.

We followed a narrow path between the gardens until we reached a street where an old carriage was waiting. When I got in I saw a woman sitting there, and quickly sat down next to her. Geza and Weitzer sat opposite us.

As soon as the carriage moved off, Geza introduced my neighbour.

'This is Frau Marie Stöger,' he said. 'She will wait upon you and keep you company.'

I was overwhelmed. Although Geza must have had so many other things to think about, he had thought of engaging a female companion for me. I pressed his hand gratefully.

'I'm very happy that your escape has succeeded, Your Royal Highness,' said Frau Stöger. There was nothing servile or subservient about her voice; rather was it self-assured. That pleased me too.

Geza had prepared a route on the map which would bring us to Hof without need to use the busy main highways on which they would be searching for us very soon. But the driver missed a turning in the darkness, with the result that we missed our train to Berlin, which left Hof at 4.45 a.m. There was no other train for hours. We had to try and remain as invisible as possible until then. On the driver's advice we drove to a little hotel; there was only a single room free there, so Frau Stöger and I shared that while Geza, Weitzer and the driver stayed down in the hall.

It was soon daylight, and I was able to see my new servant as well as merely hearing her. Her face is interesting without being beautiful; she has dark hair, dark eyes above prominent, slavic cheekbones, a wide mouth and that pleasant, soft, assured voice.

I asked her to undress me. This request threw her into

confusion: I could see that she had never been a maid before. I lay down on the bed for a few hours, without being able to sleep however, while Frau Stöger sat in a chair by the window. This time we reached the station in good time. The driver shook my hand vigorously; he received a lavish tip from Geza, and promised not to return to Bad Elster before the following night so that we could get a good start in the meantime.

In Berlin Herr Südekum fetched us from the station and took us to his home, in Düsseldorferstrasse out in Wilmersdorf, a quiet, little-developed district at the edge of the city. There we were very well looked after until it was time for us to move on again. From the beginning we had decided to make for Paris; only in a republic would we feel safe from deportation. In this assumption we were supported by Herr Südekum, a Social Democrat deputy in the German Parliament and an intelligent, humorous man.

'You are the first socialist I have ever met,' I told him.

He answered laughing, 'Take a good look, Your Royal Highness. No horns, no tail, no cloven hoof. Not even a red handkerchief!'

Herr Weitzer, who had spent the night in a Berlin hotel, came out to Wilmersdorf in the morning to say goodbye to us. I thanked him with all my heart for his self-less assistance.

Only now did I discover that the original plan had been to take me away from the sanatorium at Lindenhof. But right in the middle of the final preparations I had left, all unsuspecting, for Bad Elster. Which, in the long run, had been an advantage.

We discussed with our hosts, who wanted to come on to Paris with us, how we should manage the journey. The shortest route, through Belgium, we ruled out from the start. I should be too easily recognized there.

Herr Südekum offered to drive us to Metz in his motor car. We knew we would have to reckon with an extradition order from Vienna, and leaving German soil would be the most hazardous part of the journey. Sudekum thought we should not try to slip out of Germany secretly 'through the back door', as he put it, but simply go to Metz and take the

Paris train. Geza agreed, and the suggestion was adopted. Most of the papers reported us already out of the country, which suited our plans very well.

After four days' rest in Berlin we set off. The chauffeur was told that I was a distant relative of his master's. A cape, goggles and veil rendered me almost entirely unrecognizable. We avoided the major towns and spent the nights in remote country inns. Südekum's cheerfulness and sense of humour turned the adventure into almost a pleasure trip. And so we came unmolested to Metz.

As a precaution, we boarded the train in two separate parties. Geza travelled with Marie Stöger and Frau Südekum, while I took a compartment with Herr Südekum.

I must admit that I was now very nervous. When the ticket-collector came round I was shivering. Südekum pushed a note into his hand, and the man wished him and his 'lady wife' a pleasant journey. When he had gone we both had to laugh. 'I wonder, said Südekum, 'whether he thought I was Prince Philip or you were one of my party members.'

After we had crossed the French frontier without arousing the slightest suspicion, we all celebrated the successful escape with a glass of champagne in the buffet car.

The Südekums stayed on in Paris while Geza and I, with Frau Stöger, were met at the station by M. de Nousanne and driven direct to Bougival.

Yesterday the Südekums came out to see us, and we said our goodbyes after an excellent dinner. Today they are returning to Berlin.

* * *

G

Paris, late September. Grand Hotel. Rooms 21-4 For the third time here I am in the same rooms, in what for me is easily the best hotel in the French capital.

I feel really at home here; I enjoy the respectful courtesy I receive from everyone from the manager down to the junior page-boy. The series in the *Journal*—eventually there were four articles, each running to several columns and some starting on the front page—has, without any exaggeration, made me overnight one of the popular celebrities of Paris. De Nousanne and his paper have recovered their costs all right. So have I.

But the press sensation didn't end there. Up to now we had been literally in hiding down at Bougival. Now that we are officially in Paris there is a constant cloud of reporters buzzing about us. We can hardly move without running into them and their endless questions. I cheerfully admit that I enjoy all this very much.

When I first occupied these rooms seven years ago, I threw myself into all the excitement and variety of cosmopolitan Paris with the naïve enthusiasm of a country bumpkin out on the town. A country bumpkin whose beautiful, rich princess had literally fallen into his arms overnight! A year later, on our return from London, I could already foresee the sad ending of the fairy tale. Anyone who can begin to understand how catastrophic the crash was when it came will understand too the kind of feeling—no, the intoxication—which races through me in Paris today.

Louise is living in the Hotel Westminster again, as she did in those memorable spring days back in '98. I noticed that she was feeling to some extent as I do. A feeling which in her case manifests itself in a hitherto unsuspected orgy of shopping. And after what I've lived through, when I say 'unsuspected' it means at lot!

Thanks to de Nousanne, who has proved really generous to us recently, we are well provided for money. In any case, since the publication of the interview the trades-people here are falling over each to extend credit facilities to the famous daughter of Leopold II and her entourage. No wonder: with the massive boom in rubber and copper over the last few years the value of the Belgian Congo (and therefore of Louise's expected inheritance) has increased tenfold. What our creditors in Nice had to put up with has been completely forgotten, and no one can blame me if in the present situation I prefer not to remind people about it.

The excellent Marie, who gets prettier every day, is also living at the Westminster; she has adapted marvellously to our new way of life and joins in everything. In no time at all she has become a perfect Parisienne. None of the elegant gentlemen who eye her so lustfully in the Opéra or the luxury restaurants would suspect that only a few months ago she was running the canteen in an Austrian military prison. I can hardly believe it myself when I look at her today.

To be honest, I too am hard at it, fitting myself out according to my new status. I have never had nearly so much pleasure from hunting down a waistcoat to match a suit, or the spats to match a new pair of shoes.

But the most important thing, the *only* important thing, is to get Louise examined by the best psychiatrists we can lay our hands on. With the help of Henri de Nousanne I have already taken steps to arrange this. The doctors must show the world the scandalous crime Philip of Coburg and the Viennese Court perpetrated against Louise.

Once that is done, I can think about taking up my own case again. Though I really don't know, with the way things are now, whether all the bother will be worth while. The whole world still addresses me as 'Count', or even 'Your Excellency'. So for practical purposes the degradation of Zagreb has already been reversed.

What more do I want anyway?

* * *

L

Stephanie is in Paris!

As soon as she heard that I was free she hurried straight here from London, instead of travelling directly to Bohemia where her daughter by Rudolf, now married to Prince Windischgrätz, is expecting their first child. The Count and Countess Lonyay are staying at the Hotel Bristol. Soon after her arrival Stephanie sent me an unusually friendly letter, asking whether I would meet her.

I sent her a superb bouquet of flowers, and a note saying that I would call on her at four o'clock this afternoon.

We rushed into each other's arms, half laughing and half crying. Lonyay greeted me with a beaming smile. He has grown a little older and a lot more dignified since Abbazia.

Stephanie at once raised the subject of my alleged insanity. She swore that she had really believed in my illness, because Philip's description of it had been all too convincing.

I had to tell everything, omitting not the slightest detail.

The tears poured down her cheeks as I spoke of the terrible years in the asylum. She was deeply shocked, and raged against Philip, as well as against Franz Joseph who had sanctioned the whole thing.

She marched to her writing table, scribbled a few line on a sheet of paper, and handed it to me. It read: H.R.H. PRINCE PHILIP OF COBURG, *Seilerstätte, Vienna*. Have just seen my sister again. Louise is no more mad than you are. Am deeply angered by your unjust treatment of a poor, innocent woman. Will do all I can to restore the honour you have taken from her. PRINCESS STEPHANIE.

She called a footman and asked him to send the message at once.

She assured me too that she would write to Franz Joseph this evening and ask him for an audience. She will go and report to the Emperor even before she goes to see Erszi in Bohemia. She is convinced that he has never heard the full story. So, she says, it is imperative not to keep it from him a minute longer.

Outwardly, Stephanie is unchanged. The years have had little effect on her. But she has gained amazingly in self-assurance. The old Stephanie would never have telegraphed to Philip, never have gone to see the Emperor. I know, of course, that this hectic burst of activity is supposed to make up for all she has left undone in the past few years. Even so, I am touched and grateful.

When we entered the hotel foyer together, a crowd of journalists were waiting. Stephanie told them how happy she was to see her sister again in such good health, and stressed the great injustice that had been done me. Tomorrow it will be in all the papers.

The three of us dined at Maxim's. When I got back to my hotel I was a little tipsy and very happy.

Today I had a letter from Stephanie enclosing a note from the Emperor that was waiting for her when she and Count Lonyay arrived at the Imperial Hotel in Vienna.

Vienna, 28 September 1904

DEAR STEPHANIE

In answer to your letter, I must inform you that I shall not see you.

Your interview with your sister after her scandalous flight to Paris; your emphatic support of her after all that has happened (proof: your extraordinary letter to Prince Philip of Coburg); the shameless press campaign which has been started as a result—all these things make it impossible for me to receive you.

I am resolved to have no contact whatever with the whole sad affair, which thank God is nothing to do with me, and can only hope that with the help of the lawyers on both sides everything will be brought quietly to a suitable conclusion.

There is one further urgent request I should like to make of you: that you do not visit Erszi now, as your present excited state would certainly have a bad effect on her health in view of her pregnancy.

Hoping that you will comply with my request, with my best wishes   FRANZ JOSEPH

Poor Stephanie! For the first time in her life she wanted to stand up for a cause, and already she has run up against the same old patronizing tutelage under which she suffered so long.

My sister says not a word about whether she will obey the Emperor and not go to her daughter. She does not even express any anger at the suggestion.

I am afraid that the brave new Stephanie was only an illusion, or rather a fleeting apparition, summoned up by genuine compassion for me but already banished again to the shadows of the past.

* * *

G

Victory! Victory right down the line!

After an exceptionally thorough session of observation and examination which lasted for months (and which Louise endured with really miraculous patience) the report of the French medical commission has been published today. The three major authorities in the country, experienced doctors and professors all, Doctors Magnan, Dubuisson and Granier, have cast their vote. It refutes point by point everything that has been said by so-called experts about Louise's mental health, and leaves a depressing picture of the honesty or technical competence of the doctors who have previously studied the case. All of them (and there were plenty) can decide for themselves which of the two charges they would prefer to admit.

The last section of the main part of the Paris report is entitled *Clinical Analysis of the Facts* and culminates in these sentences: 'In her present condition Her Royal Highness reveals not the slightest sign of illness. Whether one analyses her mental capabilities in the strict sense or her moral capabilities one may look in vain for any sign of madness or impaired awareness.'

Now the report must be sent through diplomatic channels—

via the French Ministries of Justice and Foreign Affairs—to the Austrian Embassy here, thence to be forwarded to those officially responsible for her, the Austrian Court Marshal's Office in Vienna.

To formulate the official appeal against certification we need the help of a good lawyer. Henri de Nousanne has recommended Raymond Poincaré. He is a member of the Senate, has several times served as a minister, and has the very best contacts with every conceivable official and semi-official court, in France and out of it; Louise will be sending for M. Poincaré during the next few days and asking him to take up her case.

* * *

L

Yesterday I received a touching letter from Olga.

She is in Dresden, and asks me to take her back into my service. After my escape the Court Marshal's Office at once accused her of negligence, dismissed her from Bad Elster, and did not even give her the money for her fare home to Vienna. She assures me of her devoted respect, asks me to forgive her for having spied on me at first under the doctors' orders, and explains that it became clearer and clearer to her how bitterly wrongly I was being treated. She expresses her joy at my successful escape in really sincere terms.

I asked Geza to send for Olga at once. He looked at me in astonishment and asked whether I was dissatisfied with Frau Stöger.

I answered that of course I would keep Frau Stöger on, but only as a companion. Olga had become a first-class hairdresser and really good maid under my supervision, whereas Frau Stöger took such duties rather lightly.

I didn't tell him that I don't like having Marie Stöger too close to me. I dislike being dressed and undressed by her: she always looks at me rather scornfully while she does it. Olga on the other hand performs her duties in a matter-of-fact and efficient way, and I don't need to worry about what may be going on in her mind.

Geza promised to send her the fare at once.

* * *

G

16 January   Louise has been free of her 'guardians' for a long time now; and yesterday her marriage was at last ended, after some unbelievably tough horse-trading between the lawyers of the two sides in the court of Gotha. (In the absence of the two principals, of course.)

Prince Philip and his loyal lackey Bachrach vied with each other to throw every conceivable obstacle into the road. Every lie, every deceitful pretext was dictated by a clear strategy: to prevent the divorce at any price. But we were no less determined to force it through. Philip (with the unstinting support of his children and his son-in-law the Duke of Schleswig-Holstein) was trying to keep his hands on the Belgian inheritance. Which was precisely what we intended to prevent.

If it was in essentials a battle between lawyers, still Louise and I had to be constantly available for consultations, checking of facts and filling in of details. Those were hectic and exciting months for us, swinging from hope to fear depending on how the battle was going at any given time. The opposition kept one hypocritical finger pointing firmly at Rome and the inviolable sanctity of the marriage sacraments. But our lawyers found out one day that Philip, as the scion of a ruling German house, could be dealt with under Coburg civil law. This was completely legal, rendered the divorce laws of Catholic Austria entirely superfluous, and deprived the Pope of any say in the matter.

Since the grounds were adequate to convince any child, we applied energetically for this kind of divorce. At the same time we took care that the papers were kept informed. In Vienna it was said that Philip had thrown a fit, and stayed in his palace all day refusing to see anyone. Only after the Emperor had been told of the latest development and ordered him to bring the affair to an end as soon as possible could Philip be induced to take the necessary steps.

From then on events moved out of the dazzling limelight of the Vienna stage. The last chapter was written in the cloistered calm of the little German town of Gotha.

By this time the decision was only a formality. After our lawyers' brilliant attack had broken through the enemy lines, Louise couldn't wait to finish the thing. She could think of nothing but the longed-for divorce, and showed herself much too ready to compromise over the financial terms. For the first time since we had met my suggestions and warnings were ignored. The result shows it. Louise receives from Philip a lump-sum payment of 200,000 guilders, plus an annual allowance of 42,000. In exchange she renounces all her Coburg rights and titles, and will in future style herself Princess Louise of Belgium. The Brussels Court will allocate its once-and-future princess extra pin-money to the tune of 35,000 guilders per annum. Which makes in all 77,000 guilders (or 154,000 crowns, which sounds better but comes to the same thing).

A newspaper here, reporting the divorce this morning, pronounced: 'The Princess will therefore have no need to worry about money in the future.' An assertion which I definitely take leave to doubt.

Otherwise, a load has certainly been lifted from our minds. Even if the big money that we originally hoped to get from the divorce unfortunately hasn't turned up. But her father will not live for ever. He's over seventy, a fair age, and they say he's not in the best of health nowadays. No wonder, the way he lives. When the time comes Louise will get a fortune, and needn't hand any of it over to Philip of Coburg. That's some consolation for a missed opportunity.

If I'm not much mistaken, a new life lies before us. I think one can call it that without exaggerating. It contains many question marks. But I'm not going to worry about them as I used to. I simply don't want to. I am instead firmly determined

335

to enjoy what there is to enjoy, and otherwise to take things as they come. Though that's not to say I'm not damned curious to know where we go from here.

Tonight there's a big celebration to start things going. We've reserved the back room at Maxim's, and all our old friends will be there, along with many new ones.

We've given Paris something to talk about again: the divorce celebrations at Maxim's. It's already being talked about as the event of the season, though the season has only just started. Louise is almost as pleased about that as she is about ending her marriage at last. Not without reason, I must admit, because *tout Paris* accepted the invitation to celebrate her return to high society. Or at least, almost *tout*.

The Bourbon and Bonapartist nobilities were as well represented as the cream of Republican France. The normally icy relations between the various factions seemed to have thawed for a night in honour of the hostess as the warring camps put dynastic and political strife behind them. The plutocracy took its place alongside the real aristocracy, successfully striving to prove that its womenfolk had diamond necklaces fit to set beside any duchess's tiara. A few refusals which hurt Louise deeply at first (especially those from the Count of Paris and the Baron de Rothschild) were soon forgotten, and as the champagne flowed more and more freely the atmosphere improved all the time. Even so, I think many of them were there out of mere curiosity. Whether they will throng to answer Louise's future invitations seems to me more than a little doubtful.

When I asked the young Baroness Montlong for a dance she ostentatiously turned her lovely head away from me. I was immediately aware of the gesture and of what it meant. Apparently quite unmoved, I wandered past her to a vase of flowers, broke off a carnation and stuck it in my buttonhole. I had kept my temper and my face and shown nothing, but my self-control had been put to a damned hard test. I spent a few minutes listening to a conversation between Poincaré and the

Belgian military attaché. Our lawyer was riding his favourite hobby-horse—the armed conflict with Germany which he regarded as inevitable and imminent.

If it does come to that, Austria will probably be involved. A nice mess that'll be. The thought of having to enlist as a common soldier did my temper no good at all.

I looked around for Louise. And it occurred to me that our guests—man or woman, young or old—were all as alike at bottom as peas in a pod. They were all dreadfully rich, dreadfully self-confident, and horribly sure that those privileges would be theirs unto death. An enviably fantasy!

Then I spotted Louise. She was dancing with Vallencourt, the heir to France's biggest coal-mine. He is much younger than I am, a millionaire who can do what he likes and ignore what he doesn't like. I'm nearly forty, a cashiered officer, a pardoned criminal without a heller of his own money in his pocket who has to resort to all kinds of tricks to survive. It suddenly struck me that none of these splendid people would condescend to exchange a word with me but for the ageing woman over there on the arm of the universally adored Vallencourt.

What could they all think of me? What did they all think of me, with their irrepressible gaiety and their impeccable good manners? I should have liked to ask them while they were all there, drinking Louise's champagne and eating her caviare. But what would have been the use? I knew the answer already. To hope for anything else was a foolish illusion. Baroness Montlong had already shown me that.

I must confess that I had more to drink than was good for me. Not that I was drunk: at least I kept up appearances perfectly until the end. Only when all the guests had left (we had to stay that long) did I call for a last glass of champagne, shout 'Good luck!', drain the glass at a draught and, still shouting 'Good luck', throw the glass at the wall, where it shattered into splinters.

Louise and Marie both confirm this episode. Myself, I haven't the slightest recollection of it. The evening is long past, and my mind is a blank.

Budapest, 22 March 1919.   Count Michael Karolyi to the Hungarian People

Until now, we have governed in obedience to the will of the people and with the support of the Hungarian proletariat. But now we must accept that force of circumstances demands a change of policy. Not only are we threatened by anarchy and the collapse of the national economy, but in our foreign affairs too the position is critical in the extreme. The Paris Peace Conference has decided to subject the major part of Hungary to military occupation. The ceasefire line is from now on to be regarded as the national frontier. This obviously reflects an intention to make Hungary a concentration area and theatre of operations against the Red Army fighting on the Rumanian border. But the territory stolen from us is to be given to the Rumanians and Czechs, who are to defeat the Russian army.

As provisional President of the Hungarian People's Republic I call on the workers of the world to lend their support against these measures. The Government and I myself have resigned; power now lies with the people.

MICHAEL, COUNT KAROLYI

Budapest, 23 March 1919.   Broadcast by the Hungarian Soviet Government to Lenin

The workers of Hungary, who yesterday night assumed control of the country, greet you as leader of the workers of the world. We express our revolutionary solidarity with you, and offer our greetings to all the revolutionary workers of Russia. The Council of People's Commissars has appointed Bela Kun as

Commissar for Foreign Affairs. The Hungarian Soviet Government requests a defensive alliance with the Russian Soviet Government.

Broadcast from Moscow, 23 March 1919

This is Lenin speaking. My sincerest greetings to the People's Government of the Hungarian Soviet Republic. And particularly to Comrade Bela Kun. I have just read your message to the Congress of the Communist Party of Bolshevik Russia. It was received with boundless enthusiasm. A communist salute and handclasp from:

LENIN

XXII

L

Budapest, 11 May 1919 Tomorrow morning I am to be taken out to the parade ground, put up against a wall and shot. So the sailor said, and Berlinger nodded. He is the gaoler. An old official.

How absurd, that I should die such a dramatic death. But in the end it will be all the same to me.

My cell is darker, damper and more miserable than any Geza ever had. If only I knew whether he is still alive.

I'm at Budapest station, ran the postcard I got from him three years ago. *Our transport's just leaving for the Russian Front. That's all I know. I'll send more news as soon as I can. Don't forget me. And love me. Yours for all my life*, GEZA.

I can still read the postmark clearly—*Budapest, 2 June 1916, 8.30 a.m.*

Soon after that the Russians broke through in force near Luzk and took 200,000 Austria-Hungarian prisoners. Geza among them. At least, so I fervently believe, though I have never heard from him again.

That postcard is all I have—that and the little black oilcloth notebook with his diary. Marie Stöger found it when she was packing Geza's things, after they hauled him into the army at a moment's notice and sent him off somewhere. It was all so rushed that he couldn't even say goodbye.

It was wretched luck that we happened to be in Munich the day war broke out. Just passing through. Suddenly we were completely stuck. I was classified as a hostile alien and my papers confiscated. And Geza had to report to the Austro-Hungarian Consulate that same week.

I wonder whether it will be soldiers or sailors that shoot me?

Since Geza went away I leaf through his diary every day. I understand nothing but my own name, which crops up again and again amid all the Croatian words. But I know what the words mean though I can't read them: that Geza loves me, that I'm his whole life, that I mean everything to him. Everything!

Olga and I lived for a few weeks in a dreadful garret in the university quarter of Munich. It was a hard winter, and we had nothing to eat but turnips. Marie said that there was a Croatian student living in the next room—the pale young man whose arm had been amputated. He passed me sometimes when I was sitting on the chair on the third-floor landing to rest and get my breath back. He would translate Geza's notes for us, Olga says. But I refused. I already *know* what they say.

My feet hurt, and there's a pain in my back too. Not long now.

It took me two whole weeks to travel from Munich to Budapest. I couldn't risk going through Austria, so I travelled by Prague, Brno and Bratislava. In ancient railway carriages; sometimes in goods wagons. We stood whole days and nights in sidings, giving priority to endless transport trains taking prisoners of war home.

The whole time I was consumed with impatience. I *had* to be in Budapest when the prisoners arrived from Russia. Count Karolyi, the new President of Hungary, would surely help me to find Geza. I knew him well from earlier days.

But while I was penned up with a crowd of strangers and working my way across Bohemia, Karolyi resigned, the Soviet Republic was proclaimed, and Bela Kun came to power.

I had only one small bag with me, so light that I could carry it myself. It held Geza's notebook, his postcard, my own Morocco leather diary that I have so long neglected, a piece of soap, a towel (property of a boarding-house in Schwabing that I had to leave when I could no longer pay the rent), a toothbrush, comb, nightdress and a bottle of perfume. The bottle has long been empty, but it still smells wonderful. And of course Olga's passport. She practically forced it on me, although

I got my own Belgian papers back from the police immediately after the war. Olga says in revolutionary times one must travel as a bourgeois, not as a princess.

I think I'd prefer a military firing-squad. Their aim would be better. But it's bound to be sailors.

Geza had hardly gone out of the door when Marie Stöger said that her old uncle's son had been killed and he needed her help. Should I have said that I was an old woman and also needed her help? I didn't say it. I was hurt, for like a fool I had imagined that after all those years she had some affection for me. Also I was embarrassed because I owed her so much money. Like us all, she had counted on my father's will. After his death it came out that he had left the Congo to the Belgian nation and had contrived all sorts of swindles to cheat us sisters out of the rest of his fortune. When the war started there was no more news from Belgium. My allowance from Philip was long spent. What could I do to pay Marie Stöger? I myself had nothing.

I won't let them blindfold me. Uncle Maximilian didn't let them blindfold *him* when they shot him out in Mexico.

At the station in Budapest I simply didn't know what to do. Never in my life had I felt so lost. There were red flags hanging everywhere; crowds of workers and soldiers thronged the streets. The shops were closed, the hotels barricaded. I stood there helplessly clutching my suitcase and realized for the first time the insanity of this adventure, of which Olga had so earnestly warned me. After Karolyi's fight there was no one to whom I could turn.

I was very tired and very hungry. Without thinking, almost like a sleepwalker, I made for the only place in Budapest that has ever been any sort of home to me: the Coburg Palace.

All the windows had been smashed; long red banners trailed from the balcony. The palace was occupied by sailors. I should have turned round, but I walked blindly on to disaster.

As soon as I stepped into the familiar hall I felt I was mistress of the house; I was angry at the devastation I saw. Too exhausted and overwrought to control myself, I behaved high-handedly and arrogantly. Despite this—or perhaps even because of it—I almost managed to overawe the insolent young men. But then their leader came along and asked to see my papers.

I gave him Olga's passport.

He studied it suspiciously.

Then someone shouted, 'Hey, that's the Princess!' One of our old gardeners rushed up to me and kissed my hand.

Now the sailors saw me as a proven spy who had slunk into Hungary on forged papers, an agent of the aristocracy, a betrayer of the cause of proletarian revolution, as they call it.

They wanted to shoot me on the spot.

I didn't argue or defend myself, I simply said nothing. That infuriated them. They decided to take me across to the Hadik Barracks, to wring the secret of my mission out of me before they shot me.

With red flags flying and half a dozen sailors in the car and on the running-boards we drove right across the city and over the Elisabeth Bridge to the barracks.

Geza used to love cars. He was absolutely mad about them. On this journey I closed my eyes. I tried to pretend he was sitting beside me, going for a spin through the Bois de Boulogne.

At first they put me in the main prison, but after only half an hour Berlinger took me out and led me to a cell. There I stayed, alone. For a whole week.

Berlinger treats me well. He calls me 'Your Royal Highness'; once he even brought me a bar of chocolate. It came from Gerbeaud, he says. Gerbeaud! The best chocolate in the world. In a world which no longer exists.

Today I was taken for trial. I expected to be brought before a judge, but it was only sailors again.

Berlinger says that it's fashionable to be a sailor during revolutions. There are more of them running around now than there ever were in the whole Austrian navy.

I answered no questions and kept my mouth tight shut. Even when they told me that the death sentence would be carried out tomorrow morning. By a firing squad.

Since then I have been getting used to the idea of dying, and I find it quite bearable. If I had admitted why I came to Budapest perhaps they would have believed me and let me go. But that was precisely what I didn't want. Freedom has no more enchantment for me. I see no reason to go on living. Tomorrow—or today as it is now—I shall be relieved of the necessity to take a decision which would probably have been too much for me. For that I could even be thankful.

I leaf through Geza's little black book and my own notebook to pass the time. When Berlinger comes to fetch me I shall give him both books and tell him to burn them.

I shall never know now whether Geza is alive or not. But what good would it do? We did many things wrong. But we loved each other. That pays for everything. That is all that matters.

Out there on the parade ground I shall still be thinking of him. When the sailors take aim at me, I shall call out his name, as loudly and as often as they will let me, and I shall be nearer to him than I have ever been.

Epilogue

Louise was not executed, but—apparently on the personal intervention of Bela Kun—released without any explanation. She found refuge at her sister Stephanie's castle at Oroszvar in Hungary. Louise had to promise Stephanie never to see Geza Mattachich again, if by chance he was still alive.

A year later Mattachich was released from imprisonment in Russia. In autumn 1923, when he was dying, he asked for Louise, and she hastened to Paris to see him. He died there in her arms on 1 October. Louise, who had broken her agreement with Stephanie, could not return to Oroszvar. Completely alone and penniless she made her way to Wiesbaden—why Wiesbaden no one knows. Five months to the day after Mattachich's death Wolff's telegraphic bureau reported that Princess Louise of Belgium had died of heart failure in Wiesbaden.

At Wiesbaden Registry Office the editor of these notes confirmed that the Princess had lived there, in a little boarding house run by a Frau Holzmann and her daughter.

The daughter is still alive today, in an old people's home. The old lady well recalls her former lodger. She remembers her as an eccentric old woman who wrote endless letters but rarely received any. She was not popular in the boarding-house: her endless tales of her royal lineage and the massive fortune to which she was entitled bored the other residents. To the Holzmanns these tales were nothing but pathetic excuses, for the Princess was always behind with the rent.

One morning the servant girl who was taking her breakfast in came running out of the room screaming. Louise lay dead on the floor beside her bed.

The *Wiener Neue Freie Presse* reported on 5 March 1924: 'Princess Louise of Belgium was buried at 2 p.m. today in the South Cemetery at Wiesbaden. The body lies in an oak coffin enclosing a second coffin of zinc lined with satin. The cortège was followed by some thirty people, most of them members of Wiesbaden's Belgian colony. The Princess's daughter, the Grand Duchess Theodora of Schleswig-Holstein, was the only member of her family in the procession. Philip of Coburg, the long-divorced former husband of the Princess, died in 1921; and her son Leopold was murdered in 1916 by his lover, a woman from the Viennese demi-monde. Next to the Grand Duchess Dora walked a court official from Brussels as the representative of the King of the Belgians. It was noticed that the cortège included a detachment of the Belgian Army of Occupation, consisting of three officers and several other ranks, carrying a wreath with the Belgian colours. The ceremony went off very smoothly, and lasted barely fifteen minutes. The simple grave, paid for by the Grand Duchess, is marked by a plain cross. No one would suspect that here is the last resting-place of a woman who was once the glittering focus of Vienna high society at its zenith.'